CHOKING SAM

삼 절식시킴

a novel
by
William DeNisi

First Printing

ISBN 10: 0-9771075-1-5

ISBN 13: 978-0-9771075-1-3

Published by Lakeside Communications Publishing

www.lakesidecommunicationspublishing.com

Los Angeles

Printed in the United States of America

For Lynne

Chapter 1
Fountain Valley, California

Morning's first light cast an amber glow over the perfectly arranged rows of rooftops. Shoes in hand, Milt Johnson opened the front door of his home on Redwood Circle and padded softly outside. He did this, as was his custom, each morning of his life. A considerate man, his movements were quiet and measured, so as not to awaken Pearl, his wife, of forty-eight years.

In 1963, Milt and Pearl had brought their young family to the brand new community of Fountain Valley. Carved from Southern California farmlands, Fountain Valley was a developer's dream. Touted as a planned community, it was affordable, orderly, with great schools and practically no crime. In short, it was the perfect place to live and raise a family.

Back then, Milt worked as an engineer for one of the aerospace conglomerates that seemed to employ about half of Southern California's exploding population. Now-a-days, Milt and Pearl lived their quiet life of retirement, alone.

Milt was still in good health, owing largely to his daily fitness regimen of walking, which he performed with religious regularity and always in the early morning. As the mood struck him, he would walk five or six miles each day.

Pearl, on the other hand, was not similarly blessed. Like most that had made it into their seventies, she had been managing a long and growing list of old age infirmities. These days, she was content to simply stay at home.

Easing the door closed, he sat on the porch and slipped his feet into the battered old Nikes. As he tied the laces, he marveled at how comfortable they were, like old friends. *Why*, he thought, *did they insist on calling them running shoes? Old farts like me hardly ever run.*

Laced up tight, he started out down the street and turned to the right on Carnation. Usually, he would walk the few blocks out of his tract and then stroll over to the abandoned airfield in the middle of

Mile Square Park. Daily, he would head for the three old runways that formed a near perfect concrete triangle.

He knew the terrain well. Like his old Nike shoes, Mile Square had that back-of-the-hand familiarity. He believed that most folks that came to the park had no idea what an important flight-training center the place had once been. Through several wars, hundreds, maybe even thousands, of pilots had honed their take-off and landing skills in the middle of what had been bean and strawberry fields.

Milt was a busy and proud man for his senior years. He kept the family home in perfect order. His pristine yard was always tidy and well-manicured. The brilliant yellow and white paint of the near half century old home sparkled. The Johnson home was the standard by which all of the neighbors measured the appearance of their homes.

When not working around the homestead, Milt volunteered. He worked at his church and the community hospital. He also volunteered at the small city police department one day of each week.

The Senior Volunteer Program was a huge success for the small city police force. Shortly after the program started, a local paper ran a buried article with a couple of pictures. On a slow news day, CNN caught wind of the story and sent out a camera crew. After several news cycles of international television coverage, the Orange County town of Fountain Valley had become famous.

Senior volunteers never did anything that actually required law enforcement. And, they absolutely never did anything that would put them in harm's way. At least that was the way it was supposed to work. Like the others, Milt Johnson was proud to be a part, proud to serve.

As he rounded the corner onto Carnation, a flash of movement caught his eye. Ahead, something scurried around a front yard bush. He adjusted his glasses in the early light. Whatever it was, it was gone.

He was having a quiet dialogue with himself about senior hallucinations when… He saw it, again. It was a child!

A toddler, a little boy, perhaps, two years old, darted around a shrub and stopped. As Milt came closer, the child cautiously peered out. A knot of wild black hair capped curious dark eyes that looked out from a tiny oval face. He was dressed in a blue flannel sleeper, the kind with covered feet.

"What the heck...?" Milt picked up his pace and approached the boy, all the while looking around to see if there was anyone else. He saw no one. The street was dead quiet.

He stopped in front of the lad. Mindful of frightening him, he knelt on one knee and spoke softly to the boy at eye level. "Hi there, little man." The child and the senior regarded each other.

Milt noticed that the feet of the sleeper suit were stained with something dark. There was a smear of rust red across the right side of the child's face and neck. Milt ventured a tentative touch to his hands and face. He didn't feel cold. The early morning air was about fifty-five degrees. So, he guessed that the child hadn't been outside for very long.

Recognition clicked. Milt realized that the smear on the lad's face looked like dried blood. Quickly, he checked over the tiny body. There were no injuries. The little boy appeared to be fine.

"I'll bet your Mommy and Daddy don't know that you're outside - going for a morning walk." He gingerly picked up the lad, forcing a smile and trying to be as unthreatening as possible.

He looked around, trying to figure out what to do. His first thought was to try knocking on some doors, to see where the little tyke belonged. He thought briefly about walking back to his place and calling the police.

Two doors away, a motorized garage opener whirred, and a door yawned its way open. A man emerged. He walked out onto the driveway and picked up the morning paper. Unfolding it, he looked over the front page.

Still holding the boy, Milt headed towards the man. "Say there, friend! Excuse me."

The man with the paper looked up and smiled. "Good morning." He said, with a little shake of his paper.

As Milt got closer, the man's smile faded. Curiosity took its place. "Well, hi there!" He said in that tone of feigned sincerity that many adults use when speaking to a child. "Whaddya got there?" When the fellow noticed the red smear across the boy's cheek, he added. "Is he hurt?"

"No - I think he's okay – I just found him wandering around back there." Milt pointed behind him. "Do you know him, know where he belongs?"

The man tucked the paper under his arm and angled his head as if to better look at the child's face. "No – don't think I do - know him, that is. Say, is that blood on his face?"

From the open garage behind them, a woman approached. She clutched at the front of her pale blue robe. "Charlie - what's going on? You're going to be late for..." Her comment faded as she became aware of the child in Milt's arms. "What's this?"

Milt explained that he'd found the little tyke wandering. The woman listened, squinted and pointed her arm northwest. "You know... I think he might belong over there." She was pointing towards a home on the corner of Spruce and Carnation. "There's a family of - Orientals - that moved in there - about six months ago."

Milt took another good look at the boy's face. Some how it had not registered before, but she was right. The boy definitely had Asian features. He brushed a shock of straight black hair away from the lad's brow. "Is that your home over there? Huh, is it? Is that where you belong, little fellah?"

The child was silent. He eyed Milt intently and blew a soft stream of saliva bubbles through rosebud lips.

The woman continued. "Yes, I think I'd check there first. That's probably where he belongs."

Charlie folded his newspaper and handed it to his wife. He asked her. "Do you know their names – the family?"

Embarrassed, she shook her head. "No - really don't. I've just – a few times - seen a man and woman and a couple of small ones, about like him."

Milt said, "Well, I guess I'll head over that way..."

Impulsively, Charlie said, "I'll go with you."

The two men started off toward the corner house. Milt shifted the child over to his left hip and extended his right hand towards Charlie. "I'm Milt Johnson, by the way. I just live a few blocks over - on Redwood."

The man gripped his hand briefly. "Sorry - I'm Charlie Mayer... Thought you looked familiar. I've seen you, walking by here, before."

"Yeah, I'm a walker – nearly every morning about this time".

The trio approached the house on the corner of Spruce. They stopped on the sidewalk directly in front of the large, two story. Milt's discerning eye noting that the exterior could use a little freshening, and the grass and shrubs were a touch overgrown.

Three sets of eyes locked on the front door. It stood ajar. A line of small red foot prints emerged from the opening and followed the line of the walkway. The prints were exactly the size of the boy's tiny feet. The trail of impressions was darkest near the door and faded to lighter shades as they traveled away from the house.

Milt re-examined the child's feet – and then looked back at the line of small footprints. "I think we found your home, little man." His tone was somber.

Charlie paled at the sight of the open door and the realization of what could be behind it. He spoke in halting tones. "I... I don't like the look of this. Maybe we should call the police..."

Milt thought about it. *Charlie is right. This whole thing looks suspicious as hell.* In his head, curiosity was wrestling with logic. Curiosity was winning. Milt made a quick decision. Abruptly, he handed the child to Charlie and started towards the open door. "I'm just going to knock on the door - you know – to see if I can get anyone's attention."

Milt stood at the doorway. He pressed the button and heard the loud chime from within. He rapped his knuckles on the doorframe and called out. "Hello! Is anybody home?" He listened and heard nothing. He called out again and waited. There was no response.

Standing in the doorway, he could plainly see the trail of small bloody footprints going back inside the house. The tiny foot impressions criss-crossed back and forth, suggesting that the child had been wandering through the mess for some time.

The common sense side of Milt's mind told him to back off and call the cops. He knew, from the little that he'd seen, that there was something bad, something seriously wrong inside this home.

He looked down at the wheat colored carpet. The small bloody footprints stood out in stark contrast.

Milt felt a tingling sensation as the hair on the back of his neck stood at attention. Everything about this place screamed danger! The illogical, the curious side of his mind was reeling. There was a thrill, an almost prurient excitement, at play. This was a feeling that old Milt hadn't tasted in some time. And truthfully, he relished it.

It wasn't like watching something on TV... This wasn't like reading a book. This - was real! He lingered at the door and continued his mental juggling.

From the relative safety of the sidewalk, Charlie called out. "Milt - I really think we should just back off. Let's call the police!"

Milt's response was no response. He simply stood there, feet numb and rooted in the open doorway. He continued to study the interior, at least what little he could see. His response to Charlie's plea was to raise a hand, and offer a quick silent wave.

Finally, his feet recovered. With curiosity still battling reason, he cautiously stepped inside.

Doing his best not to step on any part of the bloody prints, he moved forward. A few feet into the entryway, he paused to get his bearings. There was a staircase directly ahead.   Next to that, an archway opened into a living room. Off to his right was a kitchen and dining area, and to his left there was a dim hallway. It was from the hallway that the trail of bloody footprints came. The trail stretched off towards the back of the home, the dark part. Keeping his feet on the carpet edges, he moved tentatively down the hall.

Milt's pulse was pounding in his neck. Reason surfaced and told him that he had no business here, nor did he have any rational idea as to what he was doing. On one hand, social convention suggested that he was an intruder, of sorts, that he really didn't belong here, that he should really have knocked more, or at least called out for someone, a few more yoo-hoos, perhaps.

He pressed forward, bolstered by the part of his mind that had always yearned for a taste of excitement. *Face it*, he thought. *Policemen and firemen get to do all the exciting things.* By comparison, Milt's life had been pretty calm. One might even call it dull! Okay, a professional lifetime of developing airplane parts had been challenging. Raising a family was no small task and being a good father and neighbor counted for something, right?

Thoughts tumbled over and over as he moved further down the hallway. Dim light faded to blackness. Not even a fragment of light peeked through the closed doors that lined his pathway. His mind continued to churn. He was being a good neighbor now, wasn't he? That's really what he was doing here, wasn't it? Or was he just playing cop? He paused, willing his eyes to further adjust in the dank stillness.

There was this strange odor. He'd noticed it right off when he stepped inside. He couldn't quite identify it. It wasn't a dirty smell. He was thinking that it might be an odd cooking odor, or... His left foot squished - into something wet.

He realized he was directly in front of a door. He reckoned that it led to one of the bedrooms. It was slightly ajar, off the latch about a half inch, but not really open. Tentatively, he started to push the door. He froze as his fingertips stopped short of the handle. Thinking about it, he moved his hand up high near the top edge and pressed the door gently.

He knew about contamination of evidence, like fingerprints. Milt read a lot. He knew about this stuff. The door opened.

The first thing to hit his senses was the smell. Much stronger here, it was a complex, almost putrid smell, like nothing he'd ever experienced. It hung in the room, stifling, almost smothering, like a wet blanket.

As the door swung wide, he surveyed the interior. Dim light diffused around closed mini-blinds. The light was barely enough to make out shapes. A few feet in front of him there was a bed, against the far wall a mirror and dresser. On the left was a doorway leading somewhere, maybe to a bathroom.

He panned his vision from left to right. Then, he looked down. On the floor, right in front of him, there was a form. Mottled blotches of dark and light made it difficult for him to discern exactly what it was. For a fleeting instant, he imagined that it might be some kind of animal. His still roving eyes stopped on a light switch! His hand went to it. He stopped again, not wanting to touch it. Fumbling in pockets he withdrew a ring of keys. Using one as a tool, he flicked the switch lever up. Bright light flooded the room.

The grisly scene hit Milt's consciousness like a solid punch to the gut! He gasped and took an involuntary step backward. At first his foot stuck, then it squished into something, like stepping on a wet sponge.

He yelled. It was mostly an unconscious act; it was really more like a long wail! When that sound dissipated, he continued to make repetitive moaning sounds as his darting eyes took in the horrific sight before him. He clamped a hand over his mouth.

Sprawled on the floor was the body of a child! No, it was a woman - a very small woman? He couldn't be certain. The head was smashed, split open like a broken watermelon! The filmed over eyes stared out, locked, upon the unseen horrors that ended her life. The arms and legs were splayed in positions so completely unnatural, Milt was certain that her bones had to be shattered. And there was blood, dark red blood, everywhere.

He felt dizzy, white spots floated in his vision. He squeezed his eyes shut tight and sagged against the doorjamb. He bent over, with hands on knees and tried to control his breathing. When he reopened his eyes, he was looking down at his feet - feet that were standing in a thick pool of congealed blood.

Milt felt bile rise into the back of his throat. There was so much blood. The carpet was saturated, and still, the gore floated thickly above it. Blood, hair and glistening grey brain tissue was splattered over everything, the bed, the walls, even the ceiling.

He gagged. Desperately, Milt willed himself not to vomit. Turning away, his shoes suctioned through the mud-like gore as he ran back down the hallway.

Chapter 2
Kunashir Island

By any standards she was a small vessel. Eighty-eight feet from bow to stern, with a double deck cabin and wheelhouse positioned amidships. She had the look of a Spanish built trawler. Her aft bore the characteristic down sloped deck and square motorized gantry with swinging davits to handle the fishing gear. A single scoop of her gigantic nets could bring in tons of gleaming fish. Her steel hull was painted an intense, lime green. Occasional splotches of red-brown rust forced their way up through the layers of paint and streamed away towards the shiny black water in which she was moored. The pocked surface of the cabin walls and deck fittings attested to forty years of thick white enamel. On each side of her bow, the boat's name was proudly emblazoned in white and red letters. The writing proclaimed, in both Japanese and English, "Mitsui Maru".

Hiroshi Takehashi moved about the small wheel house in short economical steps. Captain and owner, Hiroshi had fished the waters of the northern islands of Japan nearly all of his sixty-four years. Born to a family of fisherman, he had gone to sea at the tender age of nine and never considered doing anything else.

He poured steaming tea into his favorite mug. He called it "lucky blue cup", a slight misnomer since the cup was actually white, or had been white many years before. Just beneath the rim there was a wide color band of light blue glazed into the ceramic. The cup, like Hiroshi, was vintage, battered and bore all the scars of many years of faithful service. In an act repeated thousands of times, he drew the steaming cup to his mouth and carefully savored the first sip of the day.

He put the kettle back on the little stove and switched off the propane burner. Turning, Hiroshi stepped through the narrow starboard door and stood at the rail. He surveyed the glass-like calm of the harbor waters. He squinted at the pale glow, barely visible on the eastern horizon, the first hint of new morning sun. He turned his weathered face to the north and gazed over the rooftops of the sleeping village. Scattered lights twinkled a silent greeting through clear night air.

Standing just ahead of the wheel house, he ran his gaze in an arc across the night sky. He sniffed at the air and took another pull from his steaming cup. With the practiced eye of an old fisherman, he examined the twilight sky of morning.

He faced east and studied the changing horizon. The first rays of dawn peeked. At his back, black night stubbornly clung to twinkling starlight. In front, the heavens changed color with every click of the boat's old brass clock. Erratic strokes of gray came first. Moments later, the pastels obediently followed.

Reluctantly, the night sky yielded, swapping its indigo for light blue. Broad splashes of color magically appeared, as if they had been cast from the brush of a frustrated painter.

Horizontal swatches of charcoal slashed across the skyline. In seconds, the bottom edge of each burst into flame. Blazing tones of red, pink and blood orange momentarily illuminated the morning sky.

As quickly as the colors came, they faded, erased by the white hot fire of the climbing yellow sun.

A tear misted in the corner of Hiroshi's eye. Despite a lifetime of ocean sunrises, the majesty of the morning sky never failed to touch his soul. He bowed his head and quietly uttered, *"The rising sun, once again, asserts his divine presence – Hii."*

The Mitsui Maru lay at anchor in a small cove on the west side of Kunashir Island. Part of the Kuril Island chain, it was first in the string of islands that run north from Japan into the territories of Russia. A few miles across the channel, to the southwest lay Hokkaido, the northernmost of the main Japanese islands.

While Kunashir was actually the property of the Russian Federation, in this part of the world, people didn't seem to care much about who claimed to own whatever scrap of land that stuck up, here and there, out of the sea. On these desolate northern islands, survival was everyone's most important concern.

Like the people who lived there, life on the Northern Islands was tough. Harsh and unforgiving, winter was nearly ten months of snow, ice and unrelenting wind. The warm season, with days that seldom rose above ten degrees Celsius, lasted a mere two months, at best.

His dawn ritual complete, Hiroshi pronounced this day to be *a good fishing day*. Turning to re-enter the wheel house, he caught a glimpse of something, a flash across the northern sky. It was a streak, a brilliant blue-white line of light, moving at incredible speed! It flew low across the skyline and disappeared into the west. He barely had time to blink, when the light reappeared. This time it streaked from west to east. Then – unbelievably - it just stopped!

In the fraction of a second that it took Hiroshi's mind to form the question, the light halted. It simply hung, suspended, a motionless pulsing blue-white orb, dangling in the early morning sky.

Above the sleepy village, the glowing ball of light eerily floated, and did so without a sound, in apparent violation of all known laws of physics.

He stared in fascination, as the light just hung in space, slowly pulsing, like a miniature lighthouse. Mesmerized, he stood, feet locked to the deck, excitement rippling through him.

No stranger to weird sights, Hiroshi was, after all, a seaman of the northern waters. He had seen about everything. But, never, never before, had he ever seen anything quite like this.

His eyes flicked a quick glance toward the wheel house. He thought briefly about his old 35 mm. camera. Silently, he swore, shook his head, and wished he'd bought film for the old Konica. His gaze shifted back to the still stationary orb.

Suddenly, it moved again. Like a bullet, the light shot straight up! Then it danced in zig-zag fashion, back and forth and finally it slashed away to the west and winked out.

Hiroshi was stunned! He stood at the rail, trying to process what he had just witnessed, when it began. The Mitsui Maru rocked on its moorings. Seized by growing tremors, the boat jerked and pitched, wildly! Lucky blue cup slipped from his fingers and smashed, showering shards across the heaving deck.

He gripped the handrail. Horrified, he stood mute, and witnessed the cataclysm unfold around him.

First, there was the sound. It started as a low guttural roar; coming out of nowhere, and then, it was everywhere. Louder and louder it grew, until it shrieked and howled with such intensity, he thought his eardrums would burst! Hiroshi doubled over as earsplitting pain seared through his head.

Recovering slightly, he lifted his face and stared out at the still sleeping village. Less that a quarter mile distant, he could see structures begin to tremble, then shake, then disintegrate with the violent intensity of a killer earthquake!

Like enormous black asphalt snakes, roadways leapt up and down and writhed over and over in great waves. Bicycles, cars, even trucks, were tossed like toys. Waves of pain thudded through his head. He squinted, forcing his eyes to focus.

He cried out as he watched row after row of neat little homes and shops crumble before his eyes. Relentless waves of oscillation, pummeled the tiny village, reducing it to rock, gravel and dust.

Through the growing haze, he could make out people running. He could hear their screams! He watched, horrified, as people that he knew and loved were buried by the liquefied rubble that poured across the village.

The horrific destruction continued minute after minute. It was as if a giant invisible hand had descended from the heavens and rained blow after blow until the homes and shops were obliterated.

Mercifully, after what seemed an eternity, the shaking eased, faded, and then finally stopped. Boats in the anchorage continued to bounce in the unsettled water.

Minutes passed. Hiroshi, on his knees, arms still locked to the railing, looked out over the expanse of destruction. The devastation before him was unfathomable.

The little village that, only moments before, had been safely sleeping, cradled by the gentle slopes of the island mountains, was gone. The slopes were gone, as well, cleaved away, and like molten lava, had oozed down, burying everything in its path.

Hiroshi's mind could not believe the images his eyes conveyed. Like most Japanese northern islanders, he had lived through his share of earthquakes. But this… This was unlike anything before! This was unimaginable.

He hauled himself back into the wheel house and grabbed the radio microphone from its cradle. He took a moment to collect his wits, then pressed the transmit button. Despite his best efforts, his first utterance over the airwaves sounded hysterical. He paused and willed himself back together. He re-transmitted his Mayday signal.

He was so tightly focused on the radio that he missed the moment the waves came. The first swells were small and simply rocked the trawler on her moorings. The big one was a giant that curiously flowed away from the island. The rogue wave carried a chunk of pier, a boxcar size construction of wood and steel, which the quake had ripped away from its pilings.

The slice of pier, like a gigantic surf board, washed along, riding the crest of the giant wave. Moving like a grotesque torpedo, it headed directly for the starboard side of the Mitsui Maru.

As Hiroshi screamed into his radio, the deadly missile struck. The wheel house was obliterated. The steel hull of the sturdy trawler was ripped in half. The forward section rolled and flooded in seconds. The stern piece swamped, and was instantly sucked to the bottom.

In less time that it took to pour a cup of tea, Hiroshi Takehashi, was forever entombed into the cold dark sea.

Chapter 3
Santa Ana, California

The voices of the CNN news readers chattered on. The television monitor bracketed to the wall in the Orange County Sheriff's office briefing room flickered with continuous images of death and destruction. The pictures were of smashed buildings, piles of rubble, emergency service vehicles and workers hustling about. Interspersed throughout were the requisite pictures of broken bodies, wailing women and children.

"…one of the worse earthquakes to hit Japan since…"

"…preliminary estimates indicate that the temblor may be a seven point nine on the Richter…"

It was Tuesday morning, and the large wall clock showed a few minutes past eight. The conference room was filling rapidly. Most carried coffee and notebooks. Stacks of papers, flyers, bolos and copies of reports advertising the latest and greatest of various crimes were being passed around.

"…centered near Hokkaido, which is the most northern of the Japanese islands…"

"…reports of casualties are streaming in…"

A pink bakery box containing a fresh load of delectable sugar laden belly bombs drew the attention of more than a few of the attendees of this daily morning ritual.

"…thankful that the epicenter of the quake appears to have hit one of the least populated…"

"Okay people! Let us all settle down and commence with the morning's festivities!" Intoned Lieutenant Harold Blair. "Would somebody please mute that damn TV?" The pitch of his voice clearly signified that his statement was really more along the lines of an order. CNN fell silent just as a musical ad for feminine hygiene products danced its way across the grisly scenes being reported from Asia.

"Come on folks; let's get this over with. Lord knows we've got enough dead bodies and other problems right here in Orange County to keep us all plenty busy." Blair moved his bulky form behind the head table, laden with papers, clipboards and the other debris that was necessary to conduct the morning briefing session of the O. C. Sheriff's Investigation Squad. The collected group represented some of the best and brightest cops in the business. As investigators, or detectives, as Hollywood calls them, it was their job to follow up on the myriad of rapes, robberies and homicides that happened inside the Sheriff's considerable jurisdiction. Their task was to investigate these cases to conclusion, and when able, build prosecutable cases. The object was to take the offenders out of society, in some cases, permanently.

Orange County is one of the crown jewels of Southern California real estate. Nestled just south of Los Angeles, the county is comprised of thirty-four small cities and numerous unincorporated areas which spread out over nearly eight hundred square miles. Home to some three million people, O.C. boasts of world class beaches, mountains, lakes, big money, pricey real estate, great schools and a fifty billion dollar annual economy. It is a tourism magnet, a great place to raise a family, and home to some of the most successful businesses in the world. To paraphrase a quote from another famous detective, in the minds of many, O.C. is the place and the stuff that dreams are made of.

The room settled to near quiet and Blair began to hit the crime highlights from around the county over the last twenty four hours.

"Another drive by shooting in Santa Ana last night, right around the corner on Fifth Street." He said referring to the location of the Sheriff's main administration building. "Obviously a gang thing, two kids, one fourteen and another fifteen year old - both Hispanic boys - were hit. Both are gonna make it. Santa Ana's got this one. There's nothing really in it for us."

Blair continued, recapping the various crime events of interest. Standing at the back of the room, a tall man listened. He leaned his athletic, six foot plus frame against the wall, and sipped at a steaming cup of dark coffee. He absently brushed dark red hair from his forehead. Shifting his weight to the other leg, he continued to follow, intently absorbing the details. His pale blue eyes that looked out over the morning scene bore an odd, haunted look.

His name, at least the name that he was known by here, was Michael Sullivan. Most simply called him Mike. Known to be an exceptional investigator, Sullivan had come to the Sheriff's office a scant few years before. The official file showed a job transfer, of sorts. The personnel dossier declared that Sullivan had been a Special

Agent of the Federal Bureau of Investigation. His record included all of the standard stuff, even a little fluff, such as letters of commendation, past performance evaluations and other such minutia that one would find collected in an official government file. The most significant piece of information about Sullivan's file was that the entire thing was a fabrication. Sullivan's co-workers didn't have a clue. The personal legend that had been constructed for Michael Sullivan was so well crafted, it would pass virtually any test.

In point of fact, only one person within the Sheriff's office knew the true story of Sullivan's background, and then only the parts of the story that he absolutely had to know. That person was Bradley Hamilton, the elected Sheriff of Orange County, elder statesman in California political scene and the undisputed boss cop in the County of Orange.

Hamilton was a legend in his own right. A powerful and intensely prominent figure in California politics, Hamilton had been elected to the office and then overwhelmingly re-elected for four consecutive terms. Depending on your position and political orientation, Hamilton was revered, hated, respected or feared – or all of the above. The one fact that everyone agreed upon was that Hamilton's shop, the Orange County Sheriff's Department, was considered to be one of the absolute finest law enforcement outfits in the world!

A few years earlier, Hamilton had been asked, personally, by the President of the United States for a favor. He was asked to take in a man, give him a job and – oh, by the way – ask no questions. Political capital and favors aside, Hamilton had done as his President had asked, and he had not regretted the decision for a moment. Sullivan turned out to be one of the best cops he'd ever had the pleasure to know. In the few short years of his tenure, Sullivan had excelled. In case after case he had demonstrated that he had an uncanny nose for police work. Sullivan had been responsible for clearing some of their most difficult cases. One of those cases involved a fanatical Arab terrorist bomb building group that had been operating right in the heart of Orange County! Sullivan's methods weren't always by the book, but he was effective.

Blair's voice droned on. "Last night in Fountain Valley – if you haven't heard already - there was a particularly nasty double homicide – an Asian couple."

A few folks perked up and offered a bit more attention. "Looks like it might have started as a home invasion. Both victims were killed by blunt force trauma to the head and knife wounds. The victims were husband and wife. There were two little ones in the home when it happened. Apparently, the kids are okay, but they are way too little to help out. Fountain Valley, of course, has the lead on this one. We've just been asked to assist with CSI - and whatever else we can do to back them up."

A tall soft spoken man with brown hair and round silver framed glasses in the middle row of seats raised a hand. "Lieutenant."

Blair looked up, "Yes, Mr. Greer?"

"Isn't this - like - the third one of these - in as many weeks – head bashings, I mean?"

Blair blinked, "Fourth – actually, if you count the Fullerton case – the older guy found in his home, about a month back. What was his name?"

One of the ladies in the back spoke up. "Jung, I think."

Greer leaned forward a bit as if to make his point. "Westminster had the husband and wife, both killed by blunt force trauma to the head, in their home... then Irvine had one, sort of similar... another couple - both victims were Asians, both were killed by head bashing, again in their homes... And now Fountain Valley's got one! Is it just me or does anyone see a pattern here?"

Someone else added, "Wasn't there a gunshot wound on the guy – I'm talking - the Irvine case, here – wasn't he shot in the head and the woman was BFT?"

Blair nodded and jotted some notes. "Tell you what... Greer, since you seem to have a handle on this, go ahead and get with the 'Dicks' from Westminster, Irvine and Fountain Valley and see if any of these match up. Might as well toss in the Fullerton case, too!"

"What are these - all Viets – squabbling over who owns a strip mall? Jeez, these friggin' gooks!" The irritating nasally voice came from North, their resident smartass, and bigot.

Blair's eyebrows arched and his gaze burned into the man. His voice got cold. "No – Fountain Valley's victims are Korean... and I'll thank you to leave your personal bias outside!"

North shrank back a bit. "Well - at least - they're just killing off each other..."

Greer interrupted, trying to put the conversation back on a meaningful track. "Westminster's case was Korean victims, too.

Anybody know what Irvine's was?" He looked around the room at shaking heads.

Blair nodded. "Okay. Greer, follow up on that. You might have an angle…" As an afterthought, he added, "And the Fullerton case – the victim's name – Jung – what's that, Chinese?"

From the back of the room Sullivan shifted his shoulders on the wall and answered the question. "No, LT". He used the investigator's affectionate, but respectful nickname for Lieutenant Blair. "The name Jung is also Korean!"

Chapter 4
Santa Ana

Detective Sergeant Mike Sullivan leaned back in the chair in his cubicle and rubbed his eyes. He glanced at his watch. It was Friday and almost quitting time. *Time to get the hell out of here.* He thought to himself. For Sullivan, it had been an interesting week. Although he'd worked pieces of several cases, the main one, for him at least, had involved a serial rapist. He'd just wrapped it up.

It turned out that the suspect in a series of sexual assaults had been a mousy little man who, for the past six months had worked as an insurance clerk in a large Santa Ana medical clinic, just for women. Most of his co-workers had assumed that the little pervert was gay. His affected behavior was actually an elaborate cover. He had been choosing his victims from the large patient base of the medical practice.

He would pick out young attractive women that he knew to be single and lived alone. Patient files contained a wealth of information. He'd stalk them, and then, at the opportune time, always at night, he would force his way into their homes, wielding a knife and wearing a black leather head mask, and not much else.

The suspect's victim count had hit an even dozen before the connecting piece of information finally became apparent. Sullivan and his associates had identified the suspect, staked and followed him, as he went about the process of targeting victim thirteen. The most fortunate thing was that they'd nailed the guy before he'd killed anyone. Score one for the good guys.

Now, Sullivan actually had two whole days off – together! He was just starting to think about the weekend when his desk phone lit up. He grabbed it. "Mike Sullivan!" He announced into the handset.

"Hola, Mikey – Que Pasa?" The caller was his friend and pal of the past few years, Charlie Gomez. Gomez was an interesting character in his own right. In his late thirties, he was a Harvard educated attorney, good looking and filthy rich. Heir to a vast shipping conglomerate fortune, Charlie was a Vice President at Gomez Transport International or GTI as the firm was known, worldwide.

Gomez and Sullivan went back together – way back. Truth be known, Other than Hamilton, Gomez was the only other soul that knew most of the true story about Sullivan – or at least about the person that came to be known as Michael Sullivan.

"Hey, Charlie, where've you been?

"I am, at the moment, calling you from the cabin – wondering if I could entice you to break away from all your super sleuth duties - to come out here and visit with me and the family - and talk over a little business prospect – one that might involve some DSRV diving for me and you!"

"No shit!" Sullivan knew that GTI had been dabbling in marine salvage operations in various parts of the world. Deep Submersible Remote Viewing vehicles were underwater subs, some were robots, and some were manned. All were used to explore depths that men could not dive with conventional equipment. "Okay! You've peaked my interest, what else you got?"

"No, no, Senor. Not over the telly. This one is confidential, absolutely so secret that it can only be uttered face to face and then only whispered!"

Gomez and Sullivan had been diving buddies for years. Most of their underwater excursions had been in the coastal waters off Southern California and the Channel Islands.

Mike was more than just interested. He was ready for a trip, especially a diving trip! "You know, pal – you're calling at just the right time – I'm getting ready to take my first few days off in…" He thought about it for a moment. "Hell, I don't even know – maybe three or four weeks. I'm in – definitely in!"

"Great, now how fast can you get out of that office of yours and get down to the airport?"

"Just watch me. Whaddaya have for me – one of those slick corporate jets to whisk me out to the 'cabin'?"

Their talk about the "cabin" was a bit of an inside joke. The cabin was actually a compound, of sorts, consisting of rambling ranch style structures. The main house alone amounted to over ten thousand square feet. The cabin was a luxurious vacation home for the Gomez family and friends. Actually, the place was more like a five star resort. Nestled in the foothills of the Rocky Mountains, just east of Durango, Colorado, the "cabin" was, in truth, a several hundred acre working ranch, complete with cattle and horses. For generations, the sprawling ranch, known simply as the "cabin" had been the official family retreat, the scene of many happy gatherings of which Sullivan, as an adopted son of sorts, had the pleasure of enjoying, many times over.

Gomez responded with mock sympathy. "Sorry, Bud. This time you're gonna have to tough it out. Can you make do with an American flight? If you get your butt in gear we can have you here in about..." There was a pause and some rustling. "Three hours, give or take".

"Charlie... You mean... I actually have to fly – commercial – like - common people?"

"Unfortunately, yes – just this one time – try traveling like a normal person. I understand it can be a very liberating experience." Gomez chortled to suppress his laughter.

"Okay. I'll suffer through it. So it's American out of John Wayne?"

"That's it. They're holding a ticket for you - under your real name."

"Under my..."

"Sullivan. Michael Sullivan – that's the real name I'm talking about."

There was a pause in the conversation, an odd silent spot.

Gomez continued. "Geez, don't have a cow! This is Charlie, you know... I'm not about to disclose any state secrets here."

"Okay. So I guess I'll see you in a few..."

"Whoa, Mike. Say, what about that beautiful tall lady friend of yours? You want to bring Audrey along? You know, we just barely have the room here. But, I'm sure we could fit her in – somewhere."

"Yeah." Sullivan laughed. "Probably in your bedroom!" Sullivan teased his friend, who possessed a global reputation as an A list eligible bachelor or a super-rich playboy, depending on which publication one read.

"Amigo, I'm shocked. How could you ever suggest such a thing? After all, she is your woman! Do you think I have no honor?"

"Charlie, this is Mike on the phone! I'm the one who knows all about your honor!"

"Right, sorry... Anyway, I'm intimidated by women who have an IQ over one eighty and have initials after their name." Gomez was referring to Dr. Audrey Bushnell, a physicist with the U.S. Atomic Energy Commission. Audrey had met Sullivan and Gomez a couple of years earlier, in a harrowing set of circumstances involving fanatical Arab terrorists plotting to use nuclear explosive devices on the west coast. That episode had nearly cost the lives of both Gomez and Bushnell, and had, in fact, tragically ended the lives of hundreds of people in Central California. Sullivan had been quite taken with Audrey and the two had been pursuing a long distance, on and off, love affair since that time.

"Actually, at the moment, Audrey is in Russia!"

"No kidding! I'm surprised you didn't go with her - just to show her around."

Sullivan let that one fall flat, choosing not to respond. Finally Gomez picked the thread back up. "That girl does get around doesn't she? So, what's she doing this time?"

"Yeah, she does – get around, I mean." Sullivan replied, closing his eyes and conjuring up thoughts of the long auburn hair, piercing blue eyes and gorgeous... "This time she went to a Russian nuclear laboratory, something called Chelyabinsk-70, in Snezhinsk, about 900 miles southeast of Moscow."

"And there she is doing, exactly what for international relations?"

"Its all part of the nuclear stockpile stewardship program. You know, we, that is, our government, is spending a bundle trying to keep the former Soviets from hemorrhaging their nuclear inventory and their technical people to every little third world demagogue that's got some cash!"

"Oh, yeah."

"So we send our people over there for a while, then, they send theirs over here to places like Los Alamos, Scandia and some of our other labs, probably with a trip to Disneyland thrown in."

"Funny, isn't it?"

"What's that?"

"How the world has changed. It's like there's no more secrets anymore. At least not about nukes and stuff like that!"

"I don't know that I'd agree totally with that one..." Sullivan's voice trailed.

삼 질식시킴

The 767 lifted and climbed away from the shimmering tarmac of John Wayne International Airport. The hot Santa Ana winds of that September day caused the air traffic pattern at the Orange County airport to be reversed. Instead of the normal pattern of taking off towards the ocean, the sleek craft rose to the east through the unusually warm air. The aircraft pitched up, assuming a radical angle of attack. This was partially due to the cowboy attitude of the young first officer at the controls, but mostly it had to do with the fact that takeoffs directed to the northeast did not require the ridiculous reduction of engine throttles that supposedly reduced jet noise to the residents of the prestigious Back Bay area of the City of Newport Beach. At 1500 feet the young pilot floored it and banked the aircraft to the right, heading for a quick stop at Phoenix and then on to the much smaller regional airport at Durango, Colorado.

Sullivan spread his large frame over seat 3-B. The first class seat spacing enabled him to relax and travel in some degree of comfort. Next door, seat 3-A was vacant and the broad shouldered Sullivan used the aisle seat to grab just a smidgen more of spread out room. He fiddled with the new fangled control panel on the armrest of the seat trying his best to make the seatback recline. The footrest extended and retracted, the overhead light went on and off, but the seatback stayed rigid. He was just about to softly utter an expletive when the attractive and very attentive forty-something stewardess appeared to refill his wineglass with Chardonnay.

"Let me help you, sir." The offer came with a warm smile and a definite twinkle. With an upraised hand, she reached across his lap, the backs of her long perfectly manicured fingers lightly brushing the material of his slacks. With an exaggerated push, she depressed the seatback release key. "It's this one, right here." The seatback silently slid rearward.

"Thank you..." He read from the gold nameplate that rode atop her well shaped breast - "Leilani - and the name's Mike." He flashed an equally warm smile. "Never could get used to a pretty lady calling me, sir!"

The stew radiated another perfect smile upon him. "We're just here to make you comfortable, Mr. Sullivan. Anything - else I can do for you right now?"

Mike swore that the word 'anything' was punctuated with a very subtle drop of the right eyelid. This was not a whole wink, not a big leering kind of wink, but rather just a gentle, fractional dropping of one eyelid. The move was subtle, her message was unmistakable.

"Actually, I'm all set - and thanks again." He said as he watched her gracefully turn and move on to the other first class travelers.

He eased back in his chair and gazed out the window into the nothingness below. Taking another sip of the excellent wine, he played different thoughts through his head. Another one of the best kept secrets of California, he thought with a grin. Some of the best wines were being made in Southern California! This one came from the town of Temecula, just on the other side of the coastal mountain range from Orange County. Mike held the small glass of perfect amber liquid up to the light and gently swirled the contents, examining its clarity and cling. His quick mental trip to Temecula took him to thoughts about another old friend of his, another cop, this one retired now. He recalled that the fellow lived in the mountains out that way. They hadn't talked in some time; he resolved to call his old friend when he got back from this little jaunt.

His reverie was broken by Leilani, the stew, gently touching his shoulder. He looked up as she knelt down next to his seat. "I'm sorry to bother you..." She said in a soft and confidential voice. "But, we just took a call for you over the radio. It's apparently quite important." The look in her eye and the emphasis on the word "important" was interesting. Mike bet that this sort of thing did not happen everyday. She continued. "The Captain asked me to give this to you." She handed him a small folded piece of white paper. He opened it and read the handwritten line. It said, "Doug McClure – 202-456-1414".

Leilani pointed to the Sky phone in the seatback cradle. "Do you know how to use that?"

Mike nodded. "Yes, I do – and thanks!"

The stewardess radiated yet another perfect smile and gracefully disappeared. Sullivan shook his head as he wondered what the hell this was about. He pulled the handset from its cradle and slipped a credit card into the reader. He punched in the numbers. There was a slight delay, two rings, then an answer. A very professional female voice announced. "Good evening – this is the White House. How may I direct your call?"

Sullivan was momentarily taken aback. While he recognized that the area code was D.C., he'd just assumed that his friend, Special Agent Doug McClure of the F.B.I., a man that he hadn't seen in months, would be at his own office in the Hoover Headquarters Building. He recovered quickly and said, "Doug McClure, please – Mike Sullivan returning his call". He added the last bit as an afterthought.

The crisp feminine voice replied. "I'll connect you, sir."

After another pregnant pause and some electronic sounds McClure's voice boomed out of the tiny handset speaker. "Mike, is that you?"

"Yeah - Doug, Hi!"

"Sorry to interrupt your little vacation, but..."

"Wait a minute. How'd you know I was on a plane – and this plane to boot?"

"Uh, well, I needed to talk to you and called around and heard you might be going somewhere for the weekend and..."

"Don't bullshit me, Doug! Have you got a tail on me?" Anger flared in Sullivan and his voice rose.

"No! Of course not! I just had some people call around – and we found an outbound plane with a Michael Sullivan on the manifest - you're not the only hotshot detective around – you know!"

Sullivan went from boil to low simmer. "Alright! Sorry. So, just what is so damn important that you have to spend taxpayer's precious dollars to find me on my first days off in – hell - I don't even know how long?" Before McClure could formulate his answer, he added. "And how come I'm talking to you at the White House? I thought you got that Homeland Defense posting after our - you know - last deal!"

"Actually, you're not – talking to me at the White House – that is."

"I'm not?"

"No, you're not."

"Okay, I give up. Where am I talking to you – at?"

"Mike, I'm talking to you from Air Force One."

Chapter 5
Durango, Colorado

The American flight touched down at the Durango – La Plata Airport. The small but modern facility was an amazing leap from the wagon rutted roads that originally provided access to the frontier mining town.

Following the Civil War, the population of the sleepy little mountain burg virtually exploded with people looking for riches. Miners, real, imagined and wanna-bees, their families and the usual assortment of hangers-on came in droves. The railroad crews that blasted through the canyons and passes could not lay down track fast enough to carry the precious ore and service the burgeoning population. Little towns of the region sprouted like weeds to support and leech off of those seeking the gold, silver and later, lead and copper from the mineral rich southwest Rockies.

Overnight, places that had been nothing more than wide spots in the road became real honest-to-God boom towns. They had names like Ouray, Silverton, Telluride and Grand Junction. Life and commerce flourished. They set up stores for hardware and supplies, saloons and dancehalls; they even built schools and churches.

Most of the mining camps turned towns exist today in one form or another. However, their main industry in modern times is tourism. Annually, hundreds of thousands of people pass through the southwest portals into the Rocky Mountains.

Sullivan and fellow passengers exited via a drive-up stairway directly to the tarmac. He followed the queue moving toward the small terminal building. He had just spotted Charlie Gomez, waving from the other side of the chain link fence. He was dressed casually in a pair of Levis and a long sleeved patterned shirt.

Charlie had just caught Mike's attention when a large man dressed in a severe grey business suit, stopped Sullivan's walking progress by stepping directly in front of him.

"Excuse me, sir. Are you Detective Sergeant Michael Sullivan?" The man's hands were both empty. The left was partially raised, in open-palm fashion, as if in half salutation, half order to halt.

The right hand hung half bent, not too loose, ready for action, but not immediately threatening.

Mike made the stranger instantly. He had close cropped brown hair. He wore glasses with light sensitive lenses, the kind that adjust light to dark with changes in the light level. At the moment they were dark brown, but not so masking that Mike couldn't make out the seriousness of the eyes. He wore a miniature flesh colored earphone in his right ear. From the earpiece, a coil of wire ran down his neck and disappeared into the collar of his freshly laundered white shirt. His tie sported a perfect Windsor knot. Like the suit, the fabric of the tie was a pattern of nondescript muted colors. On his left coat lapel there was a small gold, silver and blue enameled pin.

Sullivan knew the pin. It was like a coded badge, a special password that was changed daily and had significance only to a small group of people, very serious, very capable people. The man wore a carefully tailored, medium priced suit that failed to camouflage the tell-tale bulge of the large frame firearm that he carried on his right side. His black shoes were actually soft boots, laced well above the ankles, boots that were suitable for running and…

"And you are?" Sullivan's voice interrupted his mental analysis of the government man. "Special Agent…?" He let the question hang in the air.

"Moore, Sir. Mr. McClure sent me to escort you to…"

Charlie Gomez had been watching the interaction between the obvious Federal man and his deplaning friend. Gomez approached the two men in full view of Sullivan but within the blind spot of the other man. Following his in-flight call with McClure, Sullivan hadn't been able to reach Charlie to tell him he would be delayed – for just how long, he wasn't certain.

"What's up, Mike? Problem?" Gomez asked as he closed with the pair.

Government man turned his head just enough to evaluate Gomez. Before he could speak, Sullivan answered.

"No, everything's fine. This is Special Agent Moore. Moore, meet Mr. Gomez – my associate."

Moore nodded at Charlie stating his acknowledgement with a flat, "Mr. Gomez." He didn't offer a handshake. Neither did Charlie. Moore turned back to Sullivan. "Sir, I was told you would be alone. We have a helicopter waiting to transport us to…"

Mike stopped him with a grin. "It's okay, Moore. Just whistle up McClure on that radio of yours and tell him that Mike brought Charlie along for the ride." Sullivan shot a quick wink at Gomez.

The Agent nodded and stepped aside. He spoke into his sleeve. After a moment of serious back and forth conversation, he stepped back over to the two men. Charlie stood by, bouncing up and down on the balls of his feet, grinning from ear to ear.

"Sir, Special Agent McClure has instructed me to bring both of you. Now, would you and Mr. Gomez follow me - this way - please?"

They walked briskly, the Agent directing them to the east, away from the main terminal building.

"I just knew he would." Gomez quietly mouthed to Sullivan as they followed their escort at a brisk pace.

Sullivan just nodded his response.

"So, where're we going?" Charlie added with a grin.

Mike shrugged his shoulders. "Shortly after I boarded the plane, Doug McClure found me – sky phone - and he wants to meet – about what – I have no idea."

The trio walked about three hundred feet around the side of one of the terminal buildings. Once they turned the corner, they saw that they were heading for a sleek blue and white Bell Jet Ranger. The Pilot sat in the right seat, headset in place, rotors still but engine turning at idle. The three men climbed aboard and belted in. When Sullivan had his noise canceling headset in place, he flicked the panel switch to intercom. He said, "Charlie, you on?"

Gomez nodded affirmative.

"Moore, can you copy me?" Sullivan asked.

The Special Agent turned and nodded. His voice sounded tinny as the whine of the rotors increased. "Yes, sir, Mr. Sullivan, I can hear you, just fine."

"Can you tell us where it is we're going – uh - to meet McClure?"

Moore blinked. "Yes, Sir – I'm sorry, I thought you knew – we're going over to NORAD. It's only about a twenty minute hop from here."

The pitch of the helicopter engines increased and they lifted off. The pilot banked the craft and skimming treetops and low buildings climbed steadily into the east.

Chapter 6
Tustin, California

It was a familiar dream, a variation of a theme that often shook him from a fitful night. He was a child again and back at Our Lady of Lourdes Elementary School. He and his classmates were about nine or ten. They sat primly, attired in their school uniforms, he in the tan shirt and dark brown corduroy pants. They sat at the old style wood and metal desks attached to wooden tracks and arranged in rows, like obedient little parked trains, spaced evenly across the train yard of the classroom.

The teacher moved briskly back and forth across the front of the room. She waved a long wooden pointer stick, alternately directing it, at words written in chalk lettering on the board, and then at the students. As she paced and lectured to the class, she would tuck the pointer under an arm, much like a military officer with a swagger stick, and continue the march towards higher education.

The pointer stick was about three feet long and made of sturdy but flexible wood, like birch or ash. A metal eye for hanging it on a nail next to the chalk board had been fitted to one end. The other end had a black rubber tip shaped like an armor piercing bullet.

Of all the symbols of the Roman Church and Catholic school, to an impressionable ten year old, the pointer stick was surely one of the most potent. A nun with a good wrist could snap out the deliverance of corporal punishment before one could pronounce the phrase, venial sin.

Her name was Sister Mary Louise. She had an angelic round face that squeezed out from the stiffly starched white headpiece that covered every bit of her countenance from an inch above the eyes to an inch below the chin. This was a garment that would have made a Muslim Mullah proud.

The ominous black dress and veil she wore was the severe ankle length habit of the Sisters of the Presentation. Around her waist was wrapped a two inch wide black leather belt, of which an end piece draped down her right side nearly three feet. The dangling end piece of the belt was a formidable weapon, and when wielded by an accomplished master, it could be silent and deadly accurate. Like the pointer, the belt was a symbol of religious power, a symbol known and feared by generations of children that had tasted the sting of the lash for their behavioral transgressions.

Like many of the nuns, Sister Mary Louise was of an age that was indeterminate by the likes of nine and ten year olds. She had large liquid brown eyes that curiously reflected both a twinkle of mirth and a depth of sadness at the same time. He knew that those eyes were capable of boring into his very soul. He knew, beyond a shadow of a doubt, that Sister Mary Louise could read minds. How else could she know exactly when to call on him in class – to answer that question – the one that she knew he did not have the proper answer.

He kept his head down, watching only the moving black hemline broken by the peeking toes of Sister's black Victorian, ankle length shoes. He knew it. He could feel it. She was getting ready to do it again. He tried to blot out all thoughts of his presence in class by retracing the initials in the worn wooden desktop. He forced the grey lead of the yellow pencil into the scarred lines that formed, "TG"! He kept his eyes down, so maybe she wouldn't see him. He sensed her approach. He could feel her presence – hear her voice. She was calling him – over and over. "Tim Greer, Timmy Greer!" Then her voice changed. Now, it was a bell – a tinny, irritating bell. It was ringing incessantly, over and over.

Detective Tim Greer forced his mind up from the sticky mud of deep sleep. He groped for the telephone and tried to focus on the green iridescent letters of the clock radio atop the nightstand. Through the blur, he could barely make out the numbers. It read 3:21 AM. Fumbling the receiver off the cradle, he pulled it to his face and scratched out a nearly inaudible, "Hullo…" His throat was so dry his first attempt at speech sounded like the croak of a hoarse bullfrog. He pulled himself upright and put on his glasses. The act of which forced him into a higher plane of wakefulness.

Tim's wife stirred next to him. She pulled the pillow over her head, uttering a muffled, "God – Tim, who's calling at this hour?"

Greer was sitting on the edge of the bed, scratching and yawning as he spoke softly into the phone. "Uh-huh – yeah – I'm the guy." He listened to the man on the other end of the phone. "Uh-huh. How many bodies?" The person he spoke with was the duty man at the Sheriff's department, the guy who made most the middle of the night calls to roust out Detectives and the CSI teams that were needed for the latest nocturnal editions of human carnage.

He covered the mouth piece and twisted back towards his pillow covered wife. "It's just work, Honey. Go back to sleep."

She tightened the pillow over her head and just groaned. Greer uncovered and went back to his conversation. "Okay – yeah – tell them I'll be there as fast as I can."

삼 질식시킴

Exactly twenty eight minutes later he was in his car, with cell phone pressed to ear, driving west on the twenty-two freeway through Garden Grove. Greer said. "I'm just trying to get a handle on this series of murders – we've got four, maybe five now, including this one – all Korean victims…"

His conversation was with Detective Marty Blayloch from Garden Grove Police Department. Like many of the Orange County police agencies, they were too small to warrant full time people to work homicides. The people who picked up those cases were usually seasoned investigators that handled varied case loads, usually grouping murders with other crimes against persons, such as rapes, assaults and sometimes robberies. Blayloch was a youngster who, though not exactly new to police work, was bright enough to welcome any help he could muster. He gave Greer directions to the crime scene.

Minutes later Greer's Honda pulled off at the Magnolia Street off ramp. He went north to Lampson and doubled back to Gilbert, then went north a few more blocks. He had gone so far; he thought he'd missed it. That's when he spotted the street sign for Royal Palm and braked. He made a tight left and then a couple more quick turns. As he drove, he sized up the neighborhood. The area was mixed, big houses and little ones, most looked to be fifty plus years old. Several were ranch style, a few were cottages. The trees lining the streets were huge. There was none of that regimented symmetry to the homes that was so prevalent in most of Orange County.

In the next instant, he realized he didn't need to watch the street numbers any longer. The crime scene loomed in front of him, lit up under the night sky like a Hollywood movie set. Two white vans were parked in the street. Atop each were giant multi-headed halogen lights that bathed the large front yard of one of the homes with an eerie blue white iridescence. Sparkles of light danced from the shiny surface of the yellow crime scene tape that surrounded the yard. Uniformed and plainclothes people milled about.

He pulled his car to the curb and shut off the engine. A uniformed officer approached. Greer took in the scene and popped open the car door while digging for his credentials. He spotted a half naked form, possibly that of a woman, draped across the front walkway, her arms and legs akimbo in a manner only possible in death.

As Greer started to talk to the uniform, another guy, a young one, with a full head of sandy colored hair, ducked under the yellow tape and made straight for Greer. He wore a dark pullover, levis with a waist holstered Sig P 220 and a Garden Grove P.D. silver and gold shield clipped to his belt. He was stripping a latex glove from his right hand as he spoke to both Greer and the patrol officer. "I'll take care of this guy." He clapped the uniformed man on the shoulder and turned to Greer. "You must be Tim! Hi." He stuck out his ungloved hand. "I'm Marty. Thanks for coming down so quick."

Chapter 7
Cheyenne, AFB

Sullivan and Gomez knew about NORAD. The North American Air Defense Command was a relic of the cold war. Originally organized by U.S. and Canada to provide early warning of a Soviet penetration of airspace by missile or aircraft, the Air Force operation had been handed an entirely new mission after the brutal attacks of September 11. Today, the focus of the highly skilled men and women that make up NORAD has changed. They now use their ground-based radar, airborne radar, satellites, fighter aircraft, and intelligence capabilities to enforce absolute control of the skies over the United States and Canada.

NORAD headquarters is located on the grounds of the Cheyenne Air Force Base. As predicted, after twenty-two minutes of flight time, the helicopter eased down from its low cruising altitude and settled on a pad located on the western edge of Cheyenne AFB. A grey sedan, driven by yet another earphone wearing government man, was waiting for them. Without ceremony, they were loaded in and the car sped off, weaving between an assortment of military aircraft and large tan buildings. After a few minutes of driving, the car came to a halt near a complex of buildings. There was a glut of cars and several clusters of people milling around.

Charlie Gomez spotted the distinctive aircraft first. The Boeing 747-2G4B looked as magnificent as it was gigantic. The enormous blue and white aircraft loomed above everything else that surrounded it on the tarmac. Charlie thought the enormous aircraft looked like a giant Gulliver tethered to an ant-like army of Lilliputian workers that surrounded it. The aircraft gleamed in the distinctive blue, white and gold. Emblazoned on the sides was the seal of office instantly recognized anywhere in the world. Beneath the Stars and Stripes, she bore the tail number VC-25A.

From their rear seat vantage point, Charlie punched Mike in the shoulder and blurted out, "Jeez – Mike – is that, is that...?" A look of awe captured his face.

"Yep," Sullivan said casually. He looked over at his open-mouthed friend. "That's it. You're looking at Air Force One!"

The car came to a halt. Doug McClure stood waiting. He waved at their approach, but his ever serious face hung grimly. A moment later they were out of the car.

Charlie commented, "Old' Doug doesn't smile much, does he?"

The greetings were perfunctory. McClure led the way to the giant staircase that ended at an open doorway into the huge fuselage. They ascended.

Minutes later the men entered a compartment that looked like a cross between a sports bar and a conference room. Gomez, no stranger to amenities offered by immense wealth, was wide-eyed at the airship's interior. The layout and furnishings were nothing short of spectacular. The few clues that suggested they were actually aboard an aircraft, such as chairs with seat belts, oval aircraft windows, and a slight curve to the outer walls, were lost to the functional elegance that made up the private airborne office of the leader of the free world.

McClure closed the door and motioned for Sullivan and Gomez to take seats around the highly polished burl wood table.

"Nice office, Doug!" Charlie quipped as he held up one side of the seat belt. "Will we need these?"

McClure looked momentarily puzzled, and then glanced at his wristwatch. "No... Actually, we're on the ground here for a few more hours. The President had a meeting and..."

Sullivan's impatience was brimming over. He interrupted. "Doug, how's about telling us what's going on here."

"Absolutely! By the way, Mike, I want to apologize for dragging you over here – like this... And Charlie, I'm glad you're here, as well. I've actually been trying to get in touch with both of you."

Sullivan glanced at Gomez with a look of curiosity.

McClure continued, "Your names came up on this, uh, case. I've been leaving messages around - might have known that you two were up to something, together." He finished with a clumsy grin.

Charlie chimed in. "What's the deal, Doug? Why Air Force One? You get a promotion we didn't hear about?"

"Actually, I..." The door to the conference room opened about six inches. A hand and arm encased in a plaid western shirt sleeve, with the cuff rolled up, protruded through the opening. The voice, with the distinctive mid-western twang, made some concluding remarks to persons unseen. Momentarily, the arm was followed in by the whole person. In that instant, each of the seated men came to their feet.

The man who entered the room was, if nothing else, one of the easiest people in the world to recognize. After all, he was, arguably, one of the most photographed. Fit and trim, sporting a thick head of white hair, the long sleeve western shirt, blue jeans and well worn pair of low heeled boots, the Vice President of the United States looked every inch the embodiment of his middle American heritage.

"Hi there, fellas! Sorry to keep you waiting!" The current administration had changed many things in the manner of work relationships and pecking order of its key members. Gone were the days of the Vice President of the United States languishing around with make-work and do-nothing responsibilities. The wartime footing of the nation in the wake of the 9/11 and other attacks on U.S. soil had changed, some believed forever, the way business was being conducted. It was common knowledge that this Vice President was a powerful member of the insider club, and was second only to the main man in all affairs of foreign policy and national security.

He approached Gomez first. With his right he pumped Charlie's hand and with his left he gripped his shoulder. Cool blue eyes conveyed intelligence and a sense of personal connection that was this man's hallmark trait. He had a knack for instantly making whoever was in his presence feel like they were, at that moment, the most important person on earth and that they were old friends, as well. His natural charisma was impressive, to say the least. "You must be Charles Gomez." His comment came out more like a statement of fact than a greeting. "You know, Charlie – may I call you Charlie? - I met your father once. Hell of a man! – and I know all about your part in that terrorist thing last year – I personally want to thank you, both of you..." He looked over Gomez and held Sullivan's eyes for an instant. "Gentlemen, for your personal sacrifice and hard work in defense of our country."

Gomez mumbled some words of response and the Vice President then turned to Sullivan. "And, of course - Michael Sullivan!" The Vice President was grinning from ear to ear. "I want you to know that I'm honored to finally meet up with you. Your fine reputation precedes you, Sir! It very well precedes you!" He shook hands and clapped shoulders again, although with a bit of upward English owing to the size of Sullivan.

"Mr. Vice President." Sullivan responded respectfully with a slight bow of his head.

"Sit, please sit, gentlemen, sit." He took a chair for himself and the other three settled back down. "Douglas here, been taking good care of you guys?" He flashed a smile and a look towards McClure.

McClure answered, "We've just arrived, Sir. I haven't had a chance to even begin, as yet."

"Okay, then… I suppose we should get started." Almost as an afterthought, he slapped the table. "Where are my manners? You folks have been traveling. Let me offer you some refreshments – perhaps something to eat?"

Both men politely declined.

"Well, at least, have something to drink?" He glanced at his watch. "Hell, I don't even know what time it is." He turned and spoke towards the cabin door. "Henry!"

Instantly, the door opened and a young airman with distinct Hispanic features stuck his head through the door. "Yes, Mr. Vice President?"

"Henry, could you bring us some of those Mexican beers the President hoards so dearly?" The airman withdrew with a nod and a toothy grin. Less than a minute later, the door reopened and Henry placed ice cold bottles of Dos Equis Reserva Especial beer in front of Sullivan, Gomez and McClure. Each colorfully labeled brown bottle was accompanied by a chilled mug perched atop a coaster bearing the seal of the President of the United States. Without mention, the Vice President received a bottle of sparkling water in lieu of the beer. McClure nervously poured a bit into his glass.

"Please forgive me for not imbibing." The Vice President offered. "Doctor's orders and all – ever since my last little heart hiccup." He raised his bottle in a silent toast. Sullivan and Gomez returned the little salute and ignoring the mugs, took healthy pulls right out of the sweating cold bottles.

The Vice President's expressions reflected the myriad of issues at hand. His face went quickly from grin to frown. "Okay, well, let's get down to it." He nodded and pointed to McClure who opened a folder in front of him. The manila folder had a wide red band on the front and rear covers. Above the band was stamped "CODEWORD

MATERIAL" in broad black letters. Beneath the band were the letters "CHOSN".

A nervous McClure was just about to form some introductory words, when the Vice President held up a hand. "Doug, how's about I paint the broad picture and you can fill in all the little details these folks need?"

McClure cleared his throat and said, "Of course, Mr. Vice President." He then clammed up and the Vice President continued.

The VP swiveled in his chair so that his full gaze and attention was on the visitors. "Gentlemen, once again, your government requires your assistance."

Charlie sat up in his chair and nodded silently.

"It seems that someone lost something – something very important, something very dangerous - over in the Sea of Japan. Problem is, the damn thing's in waters that are claimed both by our good friends of the Russian Federation and our not such good friends from the Democratic Peoples Republic of Korea, otherwise known as North Korea!" He let the statement hang in the air like a bad smell. "Problem is – that we need to get this thing before anybody else does – there is more than one nation that wants to salvage this – uh - thing."

McClure punched at some recessed buttons in the table. A computer image filed a bulkhead with a multicolored map of the area. The Vice President eased out of his chair and approached the map. He placed his finger on a spot of water a few inches from the northeast shore of North Korea and about the same distance due south of the Russian territory of Khrebet Sikhotelin. "It's somewhere, right about here." He tapped on the LCD screen as if to emphasize the point, momentarily blurring its image. "I'm told the dang thing is in a few thousand feet of water." He eased back into his chair and paused.

Sullivan spoke up. "Mr. Vice President, I'm not certain what it is that you..."

The Vice President, who had been intently watching Gomez, blinked and turned his gaze to Sullivan. "I'm sorry Mike. I think you misunderstand." He flicked his eyes briefly to McClure, then back to Sullivan. "This entire operation – the reason we are meeting – well, is really more in Mr. Gomez's department." The Vice President returned the full focus of his attention to Gomez. "Charlie, once again, your government finds itself in some what of a pickle. As you know, we've come to Gomez Transport International before to handle - how shall I say - special contractor missions. Well, this is another one of those..."

He momentarily searched for the right words. "…delicate situations where a certain level of deniability is required."

Charlie was quietly somber. The Vice President continued. "GTI has always managed to come through for us. Well, this is another one of those occasions.

Charlie just nodded. Sullivan's eyes darted from the Vice President, to Gomez, then McClure, then to the display map. He held his mouth in a tight line and said nothing.

The Vice President continued. "By all rights we should just go on in there with the Navy and cordon off the area and run our own salvage operation. Problem is, we'd be stepping on too many political toes, way too many. Hell, we'd probably start another major shooting war." He paused as if to let the idea settle. "Charlie, we know that GTI already has some Deep Submersible operations going on right now in the general area…" He trailed off looking at McClure.

McClure glanced at some paperwork in front of him and said, "Oshima?"

Charlie nodded. "Ŏ Shima Island." He corrected the pronunciation. "It's a little bit of land just off the southwest tip of Hokkaido." Charlie seized the moment to insert the obvious question. "Mr. Vice President, just what is that you are - I mean that we are - looking for?"

The Vice President rubbed a hand on his blue jean clad leg. His eyes went to McClure and then back to Gomez. "That's just it. We don't actually know!"

Chapter 8
Garden Grove, California

Blayloch and Greer crossed the street and approached the recording officer, a slight blond woman, who was diligently noting the entry and exit times of everyone working the crime scene. Blayloch gave the recording officer Greer's bona fides. As they ducked under the yellow barrier tape, he offered Greer a set of latex gloves and steered him via a somewhat circuitous route to the body that lay crumpled on the front walkway. Carefully they stepped between the numbered plastic evidence markers, several of which surrounded the body. Blayloch began a running narrative. "The first calls came in about 1:45 AM. It came in as a four-fifteen, a family fight call, sounds of people shouting – hysterical yelling and crying – that sort of thing."

She lay sprawled in a prone position. The right side of her face was pressed into the grass. Her head was leaning back at an unnatural angle to her torso. At first glance, the head seem to be partially detached. Her dark eyes, with their characteristic oriental symmetry were fixed open, staring into a lifeless infinity. The left arm was folded unnaturally under the torso, left hand protruding from under the body at the right hip. Her right arm was splayed out and twisted, rotated forward so that the hand rested palm upward. Twelve inches from the right hand lay a handgun. Greer recognized it to be a Colt revolver, .38 caliber, blue steel, a two inch. He thought it was probably a Cobra model.

Blayloch continued talking. "So by the time the first black and whites get here, we've now got 'shots fired' calls – we get a total of six calls, all from the neighbors." He paused a moment, looking around. "It must have been quite a ruckus."

No stranger to homicides, Greer momentarily struggled with that emotional part of his mind that he knew he had to turn off, at least for the next few hours. *You know how to do this. She's not a human being any longer. This body is just a lifeless shell. Tighten up! Do your job. Help these guys figure out who did this horrible...*

Mindful of where he was placing his feet, he squatted next to the woman's body. She was attired in a short sleeve cotton nightdress with a tiny pink and blue flower design, probably about knee length, although he couldn't tell for certain. The nightie was bunched up around her hips. He saw white cotton panties and blood. A great deal of blood had pooled under the body, indicating some major wound, not immediately visible from Greer's perspective. The right forearm bore several cuts, slash marks. The idea of defense wounds bloomed in his thoughts. She probably raised her arms up- trying to ward of the blows of her attacker.

Blayloch continued his narrative. "First officers on the scene find her down – right here – she's still moving a bit, but obviously bleeding out and close to death." He took a breath. "The front door – there - was standing wide open. The patrol officers go in – and find another body. That one's an Asian man. He's dead – lying just inside the front door - on the living room floor. By the time the officers cleared the house and secured the scene, this poor thing was completely gone. Medics arrived and, being the heads up boys that they are, they pronounced both of them right in place and we didn't have to move them at all." Blayloch's head bobbed up and down. Greer knew he was seeking approval for the officers handling of the scene.

"Okay…" Greer muttered noncommittally.

He studied the woman's face. It had the roundness and flat presentation so common to many Koreans. She's just a kid, probably not more than eighteen or so, and pretty. At least she used to be pretty, in life. He could feel that chill of sadness creeping up inside him. He forced it back down.

Blayloch continued on like someone had punched the play button. "The guy inside sustained multiple stab wounds to the chest and the big one – if I've got it right – is a deep neck slash on the right anterior neck – major bleed out – a real mess."

He paused for a moment and sucked in a breath. "My guess is – when we get around to turning her over – we're probably going to find the same thing on her."

"Any ID on the victims? Greer asked.

"Yeah. The family name is Sung – father and daughter, we think."

"Anybody else at home?"

"No. We just found these two – neighbors tell us they're the only two that live here." Blayloch dropped to a position of sitting on his haunches alongside the victim's head. "We didn't find anything else in the house, no other people, no pets – nothing."

"Anything on the gun, yet?"

"Interesting – that item." Blayloch scooted over so he was right over the pistol. "Couple of theories – One, it belonged to the bad guy and maybe he dropped it. Two, it belongs to the victims and maybe they were attempting to defend…"

"You said you had some shots fired?"

"Yes. Two or three shots, depending on which neighbor you talk to." Blayloch put his face right down to the weapon. Only inches away he examined it closely with a small penlight. He sniffed at it and continued to talk while he twisted and turned trying to view the gun from all angles. "Can't exactly tell until we can pick it up. CSI techs have already done their crime scene stills in film and digital. As soon as they do video we'll bag it, and then, we'll be able to learn more."

Greer nodded again.

"We've got a couple of things going already." Blayloch smiled. "We can't get the serial number until we pick it up and open the cylinder. This model's got the serial number stamped on the inside. I've got ATF standing by to give us a history on the piece."

"Yeah, they're good at that." Greer added, mostly for encouragement and conversation filler. "Any gun shot residue?"

"Yes, that's in progress. My guess, the female victim fired the gun. We've done a gun shot residue swab on both victims' hands. The preliminary, the field test GSR kit, came up positive on the female's right hand. And, the gun smells like it's been recently fired. It'll be a few hours before we can get a laboratory positive." As an afterthought Blayloch added, "Nothing from the male victim's hands?"

Just then another detective approached. "Marty."

Blayloch looked up. "You should look at this." The other investigator hooked a thumb over his shoulder. "I think we've got some egress blood spatters."

The trio walked about thirty feet across the front lawn. At the edge of the concrete sidewalk, a technician was on his knees operating a portable ultra-violet light. As the tech moved the violet hued light across the grass, and over to the walkway, a series of dark splash marks jumped out at them. The marks ranged from a quarter to half inch in diameter, and looked like blood droplets flashing their fluorescent road signs in the unnatural light.

The tech with the UV light started talking, excitedly, the minute they walked up. "I don't have the exact starting point yet, but the line of splatters comes generally away from the female victim and heads across the grass, on to the sidewalk and trails off to the south."

Both Greer and Blayloch examined the line of droplets. They were classic fresh blood spatters from a moving object or person. The direction of travel was evident from the orientation of the fine droplets that broke away from the circle or oval of each gob of blood.

Blayloch was on his knees, sighting a line from the victim across the lawn and sidewalk heading away from the scene to the south. With a grin he said to no one in particular. "What do you wanna bet this blood didn't come from either of our victims?"

Greer nodded and raised his eyebrows. "Maybe a third victim?"

"Or, maybe a wounded suspect." Blayloch stood and brushed off his knees. "Ready to see the inside?"

Greer nodded and the two men moved towards the open front door of the house.

Chapter 9
Cheyenne, AFB

The Vice President leaned in on Gomez and studied him intently. "Before we go any further, I need to impress upon both of you, just how delicate – and how highly classified - this situation really is."

Gomez glanced at Sullivan and responded. "Mr. Vice President, I think we…"

"Listen." He spoke over Gomez with a semi-apologetic wave of the hand. "I know I don't need to lecture you two on all the crap that's going on in the world today. We're up to our butts in the Middle East, with no end in sight, I might add. We're dealing with a sluggish world economy, a good portion of our international 'friends' hate our American guts. We are absolutely hemorrhaging with over spending and trade deficits and…" He spun his chair around to gesture at the LCD map display. "This little fat clown that's running the DPRK, at the moment, cannot even feed his people, yet he's running all over the world collecting every scrap of nuclear and missile technology that anyone will trade, sell or give to him."

He turned back to the others. "We know that he's presently got at least three or four small nukes. And we believe that he's sitting on enough yellowcake to cook up a sufficient amount of plutonium to make another half dozen. The Iranians sold him a crappy reworked old Soviet mid-range missile system – so now he's got a half-assed delivery system. We know he's got one of the largest standing ground armies in the entire world – and that his army is extremely well fed, trained and fueled."

The Vice President took a breath and drummed his fingers on the table. "For that we can mostly thank the previous resident of the White House, who's administration stuck their collective heads in the sand, sent this jerk money, food and fuel ostensibly to buy off his insatiable desire for all things nuclear."

The Vice President paused and sipped at his water. His audience sat quiet and waited. "And now, we believe 'the dear leader'…" The reference was to the national nickname personally chosen by and forced upon the population by the North Korean dictator. "We believe that the little maniac has gotten his hands on a weapon of unimaginable power, a weapon that could make nuclear power seem laughable."

Sullivan broke in. "Sir, I don't understand. What kind of weapon is more...?"

"More than nuclear?" The Vice President finished the question. "Do you recall some discussion in the news recently about some large atmospheric explosions happening in North Korea?"

Sullivan nodded. "Yes, there was some initial belief that they were small nuclear detonations - but I guess that was later discounted – no radiation or something."

"More like the stories were played down - more like the skillful application of disinformation. I think that's the current term for lying to the press. What they were, or at least what we believe, are disruptions in the earth's crust, earthquakes, only tightly focused earthquakes, ones that are capable of releasing considerably more energy than conventional nuclear bombs."

Sullivan and Gomez sat, quietly listening.

The Vice President leaned over and rubbed his palms together. "Okay, here's the deal. First, I've got to know that you gentlemen are definitely on board with this project. Second, before we can talk further, that is, in more detail, I have to clear you guys for codeword access." He paused for a moment and folded his hands in front of him. "Do you understand the implications of all this?"

Sullivan was looking a bit strained. Gomez jumped in. "Mr. Vice President, of course, GTI is available, always, to work with the government. Say the word and we can and will immediately re-task and re-position our marine operations in the Sea of Japan."

The Vice President nodded. "Good, and thank you. I knew we could count on you."

McClure pushed some papers toward the Vice President, who scanned them quickly and passed one each to Sullivan and Gomez. Sullivan read his over and looked up with curiosity etched on his face. It was the standard National Security Secrecy document that ensured if one were to divulge any classified information, that they would forfeit everything dear, including life, liberty, all personal possessions, family fortunes and that, further, even their descendants would forever be trashed. Both men scribbled out signatures and pushed the papers back across the table. The Vice President countersigned the documents and handed them to McClure.

Busy work completed, the Vice President began anew. "Now, remember the nine plus earthquake in east Asia some time back?"

Mike sat up. "Yes, of course, the Sumatra thing. That was the worst natural catastrophe in some thousand years or so. Loss of life and devastation occurred on a biblical scale – it triggered an enormous Tsunami wave that hit three or four continents."

Gomez nodded and added. "Over two hundred thousand people died!"

"Actually, the exact toll will never be known. Some knowledgeable estimates bring it closer to three hundred thousand!" The Vice President clarified.

"I don't get it. Earthquakes, tsunamis, floods – we're talking natural events here – forces of nature. How do those events connect to the Koreans?" Sullivan asked.

"The Vice President sat back in his chair. He pushed his glasses up onto his forehead and rubbed his eyes. Re-adjusting his specs, he looked at Sullivan and Gomez. "This is the fun part." He began. "This is the part where I talk, you listen and after a while…" He paused for effect and watched their faces intently. "You'll probably begin to think that your second to the Commander-in-Chief actually has a screw loose."

Sullivan shot a look at McClure. All were quiet and waited for the Vice President to continue.

"You may recall that in 1947 a flying craft was reported to have crashed, in New Mexico, just outside of a place called Roswell…"

Chapter 10
Durango, Colorado

Hours had passed. Sullivan and Gomez were seated on leather sofas in the enormous living room of the "cabin". Yellow-orange licks of flame crackled through dry fir logs inside the massive stone fireplace that was the centerpiece of the magnificent room. Hand hewed posts rose twenty feet to support an intricate network of beams that formed the log framework of the lodge, the main building of the ranch complex.

The two sat opposite one another, nursing full stomachs. Sullivan was flaked out, completely sated, feet up and eyes at half mast. The firelight cast flickering shadows on the walls behind him. He held a crystal snifter goblet at eye level. The amber liquid swirled and danced through a prism of colors refracting through the leaden glass. "Good dinner." He said matter-of-factly. "No, actually it was a great dinner!" He corrected himself.

Gomez, similarly indisposed from the fine food and liquor, laughed in response. "I'll be sure to tell Cookie you said so."

"Hell, I'll tell her myself at breakfast." Mike said as he twisted his watch around to where he could read it. "Which is – what - a couple of hours from now?"

"Close. We should probably get some sleep."

Mike set his glass down. "You knew all about this, didn't you?" His tone was accusatory.

"No. Not all about it. Just about some of it. Charlie kicked his right foot up on to the ottoman. "Anyway, I got dialed into the deal, only a couple of hours ahead of you."

"And McClure's call to me in the plane… You set me up, you bastard. Didn't you?"

"Harsh words, my friend." Charlie grinned and leaned over gesturing to the tray of after-dinner liquors. "More brandy?"

Sullivan shook his head. Charlie continued. "They wanted me - or more accurately - they wanted GTI's marine salvage team. And, you know, I have to go along to supervise…"

"Of course you do."

"So, if I have to go - then you have to go."

"Thanks."

"You're welcome. After all, you're the one that's always getting me into these fun deals; I just thought it was about my time to reciprocate."

"Thanks a bunch."

"You're welcome."

The fire consumed a moment of silence between them. The flame popped loudly and knifed through an upright log. When it broke off, sparking chunks fell on to the stone hearth making a little shower of orange fire across the hearth. Charlie set his glass down, got up and grabbed a small brass shovel. He coaxed the hot coals back into the firebox. He returned to the sofa where they both sat basking in the silence.

Finally, Sullivan spoke. "So, what's your take on the UFO story?"

"You mean, do I think the VP has slipped a gasket?" He didn't wait for an answer. Rather he slipped into his lawyer oratory voice. "If that man is nuts, well then, I guess there are quite a few booby hatch candidates within our government."

"You have to admit, that was quite a story!"

Charlie reflected a moment. "Granted. However, it's not exactly a new story. After all, for longer than you and I have been alive, people have been talking about UFO visits, crashes, strange little people. Hell, there's an entire culture, a belief system that supports and feeds these stories."

"Yeah, well, I don't know about you, but this is the first time I've ever had a sitting Vice President of the United States tell me that we really did get a craft and extra-terrestrial bodies at Roswell - and that there was and still is a major cover up - and that some of the best minds in the world have been working for over fifty years to reverse engineer their systems - without much success." He leaned over for the bottle. "Maybe I do need some more of that brandy."

"Help yourself." Charlie continued. "Sightings of flying saucers, discs or whatever, have been so prevalent and spread out all over the world, well, it's not a great leap of logic to acknowledge that some place other than Roswell, New Mexico, may have had an unscheduled landing."

"I always thought that the Roswell weather balloon story smacked of paranoid government." Mike interjected.

"Case in point..." Charlie went on. "The Cheorwon UFO sighting in the spring of 1951, right in the middle of the Iron Triangle combat zone of the Korean War, was apparently well documented. An entire U.S. Infantry company watched this giant craft hovering around a battlefield for some forty minutes. Some of the G.I.s even shot at it, later telling of hearing their M1 rounds clink off the craft's hull. Then apparently, in what might have been retaliation, the craft hovered over them, and bathed the group in some kind of light before it sped off. Later, a lot of men got sick - sick enough to be evacuated. They all had dysentery and some kind of weird blood disorder. There were other reports as well, including one of a UFO crash deep inside North Korea."

"So in a nutshell, our government thinks that the DPRK had a UFO crash in the fifties – that they were able to recover the craft on the QT and, like us, have been working on making technology from that craft work – and that they have now fashioned something from that alien technology that they are using like a weapon to make earthquakes and tidal waves?"

"Yep. And the aircraft that was tracked going down in that corner of the Sea of Japan might have that device onboard. And we want to get it before they do."

Mike eased back, and let his mind sift through the complexity of what they had learned earlier that day. North Korea was a tiny backward nation, forged out of the political infighting between the U.S. and U.S.S.R. at the close of World War II. Currently the country was run by the second generation of a brutal family dictatorship that was hopelessly locked in an impossible time warp of failed pseudo-communism.

The current leader of the country had managed, probably with the help of his communist sponsor nations to the north, to develop a fledgling nuclear capability, and a crude missile system. This was the very same guy who let his people freeze and starve in order to keep his gigantic military tuned up for the foretold coming invasion from America. The guy, who was at best a little strange, and quite well may be mentally ill, may now have stumbled upon some kind of doomsday weapon gleaned from the alien technology of a crashed UFO.

The United States, the policeman of the world, was rightly concerned about the North Korean problem; but at the moment, Uncle Sam was fairly well stretched out dealing with the Middle East and some half dozen other world hot spots. Sullivan did agree with the

Vice President's assessment. It wasn't exactly the best time for the USA to bully the North Koreans. On the other hand, doing nothing was clearly not prudent.

"So, just what is it that your GTI team is going to do?" Sullivan asked. "You guys gonna just cruise over there, drop anchor and go get this thing, what with the Russians and the North Korean Navy patrolling around the area?" Sullivan thought about it for a moment. "Do the North Koreans even have a Navy?"

Charlie laughed. "They have something. Don't you remember the great North Korean victory at sea over Commander Lloyd Bucher's little un-armed radio ship?"

Sullivan nodded. "Yes. It was the Pueblo. They kept those guys for, what, six, seven months?"

"More like a year or so, I think."

Another long pause punctuated by big yawns all around stalled their conversation. Sullivan picked up the thread. "So what we really know is…" It was more of a statement than a question. "What we think is… That our North Korean friends flew some kind of a small jet – probably an old MIG that they got from the Russians – and that they had their secret doomsday thing on board and were probably testing it, again…"

"Yeah, that's it." Charlie rolled out a colored National Geographic Society map between them. He poked at a spot in North Korea. "The aircraft was tracked by National Reconnaissance Office satellite imaging and Japan Defense Forces Radar. They think it took off from somewhere deep in the north, up around the China border - around here."

Mike leaned over the map. "Hyesan – isn't that where the North Koreans are known to have some of their nuclear research facilities."

"Yep, and its right on the China border. Then the plane goes northeast over Russian territory." Charlie turned the map reading off the names by the firelight. "Vladivostok and Nakhodka and some other little coastal towns. Then, it goes across the Sea of Japan, skirting just to the north of Hokkaido and then it just disappears."

Sullivan studied Charlie's finger tracings over the map. Charlie continued. "Then, minutes later the thing reappears, westbound; but now, its moving deeper across central Hokkaido and goes back out over the Sea of Japan."

"Any idea how high the plane was?"

"They don't know for certain, but think most of the time they were tracking it around twenty to thirty thousand feet."

"No transponder?"

Charlie just looked at Mike.

"Sorry, silly question."

"Okay, so, the key points of information are...   When the aircraft disappeared – this time frame coincides perfectly with the Kunashir Island earthquake and tidal wave that happened just about here." He had his finger on the west end of the island just off the east coast of Hokkaido.

"I remember hearing about that quake on the news, just a few days ago." Sullivan said.

"Right. Now, on the return leg, the aircraft is tracking very erratically – its like, he can't keep it in a straight line – its doing a zigzag pattern, but sort of random like, no rhyme or reason to it. Then, when he gets to this spot of water..."

"The shared offshore waters between the DPRK and the Russian Federation." Sullivan added.

"Exactly. Right here, the plane disappears again. This time their pretty certain it went right into the drink. Some local intelligence sources on the ground reported the aircraft making a hard water landing and some search and rescue activity in this area."

Sullivan picked up the map and angled it to be better illuminated by the firelight. "Hard water landing - eh?"

"It's - sort of a euphemism. You know, as opposed to a soft water landing."

"Charlie, you crack me up!" Sullivan put the map down. "So even if the GTI guys can get in there, what's to say they won't be hassled by the North Koreans or the Russians or even the Sea Scouts?"

Charlie was grinning again. He sat back and folded his hands behind his head. "Do you remember the story of Howard Hughes, the CIA, and a ship called the Glomar Explorer?"

Mike sat back and closed his eyes for a silent moment. He began to speak. "I remember a little about that. It happened in the early seventies, I think. Wasn't that a CIA plan to recover a Soviet missile submarine that went missing?"

"Correct! The sub sank in the Pacific, not too far away from Hawaii. It was believed to be sitting in about 17,000 feet of water - too deep for any conventional diving operation - back in those days."

"So the CIA cooked up this plan whereby a special salvage vessel was built – the Glomar Explorer. Howard Hughes owned the company that built the ship."

"Also correct. The cover story was that this specially fitted ship - it had a series of cable operated claws amidships - was going to be used to mine mineral deposits from the ocean floor – mostly BS – but a good story."

"So what happened? GTI buy the ship?" Sullivan asked, kidding.

"Actually, yes, we did."

Sullivan sat up. "Really? That's what you've got working in the Sea of Japan?"

"Yep. GTI moved into marine salvage operations about six years ago. We acquired this small Oregon company, one that was making cutting edge deep water submersibles, both manned and robotic. These guys had some great ideas and engineering concepts, but they were eating the putty out of the windows."

Sullivan's face contorted with curiosity.

"They were just under funded." Charlie clarified. "The acquisition took care of all that, and now United Marine Submersibles is a strategic member of the GTI corporate family."

"And the Glomar Explorer?"

"Well, it was used for the one mission in 1974, which was partially successful – they managed to recover a portion of the Russian sub – then the ship was mothballed for years to the US Navy reserve fleet. We cut a deal with the Navy. We got a long term sweetheart lease on the Glomar. We paid for the refit and upgrades giving it all the latest bells and whistles, which included mating it with some of the most sophisticated submersible products of UMS."

Sullivan was wide awake now. "Charlie, you dog. You never mentioned…"

"I - was really supposed to keep the yap shut on this one. You see, the deal is, we have this on-going thing with the Navy."

"Oh, there's more?"

"A little more. Part of the deal is that we got some help forming a crew, a special well-qualified crew. The Navy arranged to have some special ops members, including some real interesting and qualified guys go into an early retirement program." Charlie grinned at that one.

"And now they're on the GTI payroll…"

"Serving as the Captain and select crew members on the GTI salvage and exploration ship, Glomar Explorer." Charlie finished the sentence for his friend. "The deal is that we handle certain events or jobs where the government requires, ahh..."

"A degree of planned deniability?"

"Exactly!"

"So basically, GTI is running a contractor spook shop for the CIA and the Navy."

"Umm, more or less."

"And you were going to tell me about this – when?"

"Whenever we decided to go diving – maybe in a submersible – maybe in the Sea of Japan."

Sullivan grinned and just shook his head

.

Chapter 11
Santa Ana, California

Greer pushed his blue key card against the reader at the side entrance to the Orange County Sheriff's Flower Street Headquarters. Being a Saturday, there would only be a skeleton crew of folks around the office, and probably no one in the Detective Bureau. The reader flashed its LED display from red to green. The electric door latch clicked and the steel clad door opened. He adjusted his glasses and, as was his habit, smiled and waved to the CCTV camera that stood sentinel at the door.

Somewhere in the bowels of the county building a computer recorded the information that Senior Investigator Timothy Greer had entered the building at 10:36 AM, Saturday, September 10th. Rather than wait for the one elevator that was operating on the weekend schedule, he vaulted the four flights of stairs, taking several steps at a clip. He marveled at his Starbucks enhanced energy level, especially considering that he had spent most of the previous night at the Garden Grove double murder scene.

He shouldered open the door to the Detective Bureau and was surprised to see Mollie sitting at her desk, phone cradled in the crook of her left shoulder, simultaneously talking and typing furiously at her computer keyboard. The work title of the fifty-something multi-talented woman was Investigations Bureau Secretary, but it was common knowledge that she was more akin to a top non-com in a military outfit. At least that's how she approached the job. Mollie was the consummate, special assistant, drill sergeant, surrogate mother and all-around-office-manager to the men and women that populated the bureau.

Greer walked by her heading for his cubicle. Not wanting to incur her wrath, he mouthed a respectful but silent hello and waved as he passed by.

Mollie reached out and grabbed his coattail, effectively halting his forward motion. "Wait – Tim – Here!" She handed him a pink fan of message slips.

He took them from her outstretched hand, mouthed another silent thank you and continued on toward his desk. He plopped down in the chair and read the message papers. One was from Blayloch. It had a little scribble that said the Colt Cobra did belong to the Sungs, but the title was clouded. It also said, "More on EM." He wondered who EM was.

The other two messages were from Dr. Mikami, who was one of the lead pathologists that worked in the Coroner's Division next door. Both slips had the boxes checked that indicated "Call back." The second one, timed some forty minutes after the first, had a written message "Call back ASAP! RE Sung"

Like many counties throughout California, the Coroner's duties were incorporated into the Sheriff's office. In Orange County the elected office was actually that of the Sheriff-Coroner.

There had never been, in the history of the office, a Sheriff that was an actual coroner, in the qualified sense. It was one of those little quirky things that just happened and people seem to put up with it into infinity. In most counties, real coroners were actually qualified physicians who directed a healthy staff of talented folks. In Orange County, Dr. Mikami was one of their best.

Just as Greer started to dial the number, Mollie poked her head over the cubicle wall. "Want some coffee – its fresh – just made a pot?" She pointed towards the coffee room.

"Yeah, thanks, I would. Say, what are you doing here on a Saturday?"

"Why Timothy, I'm here taking care of you, of course. I heard you pulled a double murder last night - in Garden Grove."

"What... Do they - call you at home – to tell you these things, Mollie?"

She pushed a finger into the center frame of her glasses and rolled her eyes. "Hardly, I come in sometimes on the weekends, just to get caught up. Blair owes me, so now and then, he feeds me a little over time. It comes in handy; I'm saving up for another cruise, you know."

Greer just nodded.

"Make your calls, I'll break my long-standing rule against feminine subservience and bring you a cup."

She started off towards the coffee room. Greer said to her wake, "Thanks, Mollie."

Her voice fading as she got further away, "No need to thank me. Consider it an act of mercy... Your eyes - they look like they're bleeding – Oh, by the way – 'More on EM'?"

"Yeah," Greer replied.

"It means E-Mail – more on email." Her voice trailed off as she went around the corner.

Greer dialed the phone thinking, *that damn woman is psychic*.

삼 질식시킴

A few minutes later the side door to the Detective Bureau slammed and Sullivan moved through at a quick step. He too, paused at Mollie's desk. "Hi Mollie. I'm surprised to see you down here on a weekend?"

"And, a good morning to you, Sergeant Sullivan." She said with feigned Irish lilt in her voice. "If you must know, I'm working overtime for Internal Affairs – today we're following you around." Mollie spit out this entire passage with a straight face, never once lagging from her furious typing speed on the computer.

Sullivan rolled his eyes and grunted. "Oh, good – more trouble – just what I really need." He moved off towards his desk.

"Greer's in – if you want to see him. At least he was a minute ago."

Sullivan stopped mid stride. "What's Tim doing in?"

"Garden Grove had a double one-eighty-seven last night - more Koreans. You know, Greer's been working to see if he can connect the dots on the Asian killings around the county. At least, I think that's what he's doing."

"He do any good?"

"I don't know. I was bringing him some coffee just a few minutes ago, I went into the coffee room, came back out and he was gone." She shrugged her shoulders.

"You were – let me get this straight – you, Mollie, were bringing Tim Greer - coffee?" Mike's look was incredulous.

She shrugged her shoulders again and her face colored to a bright shade of red. She went on, deftly changing the subject. "He might have just gone next door to see Mikami. He'd gotten two messages from the Doc – sounded like his pants were on fire."

Sullivan turned and continued on to his desk. He gestured dramatically with arms outstretched. "My God, what has this world -

and in particular this Sheriff's Department - come to? I mean Mollie, of all people, the Mollie, the one that strikes fear in the hearts of all detectives..." He played it heavy. "Mollie, actually bringing coffee to the likes of Tim Greer. Woman, we're going to have to send you out for a psych!" He tossed this last bit over his shoulder as he sat down at his desk.

Chapter 12
Santa Ana, California

There was no answer at Mikami's extension. Greer grabbed his notebook and headed for the exit door to the stairwell. Since the early 1980's, the Coroner's office, which housed the County's central morgue and toxicology lab, was located just west of the Sheriff's Administration and Main Jail Buildings.

Greer hit the ground floor landing and popped out into the brilliant late morning sunshine. In less than a minute he crossed the landscaped grounds between the buildings. Approaching the locked front door, he held his electronic key card to the reader. Once again, the light turned green, the door clicked open. Steeling himself, Detective Tim Greer sucked in a breath and stepped over the threshold. *Here I go - from the world of the living to that of the dead.*

Although new to the Sheriff's Investigation Bureau, Greer was an experienced cop. He had a demonstrated nose for ferreting out the salient facts. Not exactly an old salt, he had, nonetheless worked his fair share of brutal crimes. But, murder was the crime that one never quite got used to. Homicide investigators dealt with this emotional conflict in a variety of ways. Humor, though unprofessional and guardedly kept away from the public, was the most common psychological defense mechanism employed. Some homicide investigators demeanor while working particularly gruesome crime scenes was downright bizarre. Many homicide investigators, especially the old timers, viewed the expression of any emotion or feelings for the victims as a clear sign of personal weakness.

Greer had his own take on this dilemma. He viewed himself as the victim's last, best advocate, the one person who might exact some small measure of justice for the horrible treatment suffered by the victims, at the hands of their killers.

Greer hated death. He abhorred murder and anything that compelled him to spend time around dead bodies. To Tim Greer, each case that he worked became personal. Besides hating the killer for the crime he had committed, Greer would eventually focus his revenge upon the guilty party. It was pay-back for subjecting Greer to the aftermath of the killer's evil deeds. Each case quickly became a deadly game of Tim versus the bad guy. And Greer, was determined to win.

He found the pathologist in one of the dictation rooms talking into a grey plastic microphone. Mikami raised a hand, part in greeting and part a command to stand by. The wiry pathologist finished dictated his last thoughts and clicked off.

The Doctor, nearly twice the age of Greer, had a formidable reputation in forensic pathology. Greer had worked a few cases with the man and had developed considerable respect for his knowledge and capabilities. To Greer, each case with Mikami was like a semester length course in the science of death, condensed to a few hours.

Conversely, Mikami respected the talented younger man, but did little to communicate that fact. If anything his comportment towards most cops was less than collegial. "Ah, Mr. Greer – just passing through or did you finally find time to read my messages?"

"Hi Doc!" Yeah, sorry - just got in and I couldn't get anything but your voicemail, so I thought I'd stroll on over on the chance that I might catch you."

All business, Mikami, got up and pushed by Greer as he came out of the small room. "Walk with me." He commanded. "I posted the Sungs – father and daughter, apparently – this morning. I found something – kind of peculiar. I thought it might interest you." They walked toward the back of the building. The direction, Greer knew all too well, was toward the autopsy room.

Greer swallowed and followed meekly. He briefly considered a protest, but, knew it was futile. "Is this something - you can't just tell me – you really have to show me?"

Mikami rolled his eyes. "Come on, its better that you see it for yourself."

They pushed through twin stainless steel doors. The air pressure in the meat cutting rooms caused the rubber seals on the doors to make an air sucking sound as they opened and closed behind the men. Passing into the Examination Room, the temperature dropped a good ten degrees. The lower temperature and the slight negative air pressure in the room were ineffective efforts at stench control. The all-too-familiar smell of dead human flesh hit Greer in the gut like a sixteen pound sledge hammer.

They worked their way past two rows of post mortem examination tables. Two of the stainless steel tables were occupied with bodies encased in opaque, heavy gauge, clear plastic. In neither case was the plastic sufficient camouflage to hide the gore within. Greer's stomach lurched.

Mikami observed Greer's obvious distress. Ignoring it, he launched into a running commentary. "These two are from a traffic accident – a head-on – happened last night down on the I-5 freeway, in San Juan Capistrano. I'm going to post them right after lunch." He added with a hint of mirth in his eyes as they continued walking through.

Greer felt the bile rise in his throat. He said nothing more and obediently followed the doctor. Turning the corner, they reached the storage unit and row upon row of stainless refrigeration doors. Mikami mumbled a few words to the attendant in the room. The man consulted a clip board full of papers and said, "They're in L-2 and M-2".

They found the appropriately numbered doors situated side by side at the middle level of three tiers of body storage. Mikami unlatched the chrome handle on M-2 first. He opened it wide, sliding the steel tray out about three feet. The body was encased in a black plastic zippered bag. They stood over the form on opposite sides of what Greer assumed would be the head.

Mikami placed his hands on the edge of the table and began his preamble. "This is the elder Sung. Of the father and daughter victims… from what I'm told."

Greer nodded, "Yeah. He is So-Rhe Sung, the father… and the daughter is Keiko Sung."

"Okay." Mikami continued. "Mr. Sung, here, was stabbed multiple times in the chest, arms and back by a thin bladed knife. The weapon - it's got a blade dimension of about one half inch by six inches – kind of like a filet knife, maybe a fish filet or similar blade. I think we counted 37 significant wounds. He probably got hit in the chest the first few times. Then, he threw his arms up to defend himself, like this." Mikami raised his arms in front of him and turned to the side as if he were cowering from an attack. "Then he got hit several times in the forearms and underside of his right arm as he turned away to the left…" Mikami, in his demonstration was now turned about 180 degrees to the left, head down, arms raised and starting to bend at the back and knees. "The assailant continues to stab repeatedly on the upper back of the right side, puncturing the right lung, severing bronchial tubes and finally - one of the fatal wounds – the rear stab into the back of the heart."

Greer watched in silence and simply nodded.

Mikami continued. The most serious wound, the one that clearly was the immediate cause of death was a slice across the front of the neck. It's a classic – almost ear to ear throat cut – severing the carotids, windpipe and nearly everything else. He bled out..." He added, "Quickly."

Mikami put his hand on the zipper and paused. "You ready for this? It's kind of gross – but I have to show you..." The statement was a little out of character for the doctor, who generally ignored any emotional response of the minions to his post-mortem endeavors.

Greer nodded breathing through his mouth. "Yeah, about as ready as I'm ever gonna to be."

Mikami slid the zipper down and folded the plastic away from the body. The remains of So-Rhe Sung looked pale, old and withered. Greer knew the man was a mere 64 years old. But, the cadaver that lay before him might as well have been an ancient Egyptian mummy. Greer knew from experience that death often dramatically and unkindly changed a person's appearance. When the spark of life left the host, the only thing left was a carcass, a lifeless hulk, and it never was quite as sanitary as depicted on TV and the movies.

Greer steeled his mind and followed Mikami's narration of the examination of the wounds and the story they told. "As you can see, the head is nearly detached from the body. The knife blade stopped at the cervical vertebrae – but the assailant was strong – very strong to be able to do this in – what really looks like one slicing motion."

The cool and skilled investigator's side of Greer's mind took over and he keenly followed the pathologist's narration of the wound sequence, his re-creation of the direction of movements as well as the general discussion of all the minutia of evidence. In his mind's eye, he was able to visualize the final seconds of So-Rhe Sung's life, as he struggled vainly to ward off his attacker.

"And this is the interesting thing that I want you to see." From a pocket of his lab coat, Mikami produced a pair of latex gloves and pulled them on. He angled the victim's head towards Greer. The lifeless jaw hung agape. Mikami fingers applied still more disrespect as he forced the mouth open even further. "Look at this!" He pointed to the inside surface of the lower front teeth. There was a fine gauge wire, it looked like stainless steel. The wire was perfectly formed over the lingual surface of the lower incisor teeth. The two ends of the wire terminated on either lower canine tooth, the terminating ends lost within a dot of some kind of adhesive. Mikami's face beamed. His grin was the look of one who just found the winning ticket to the Super-Lotto.

Greer didn't quite get the importance of the find. "Just what is it that we're looking at?"

"Well, that's it. We don't know… exactly. We see things like this often. They are… retainers, orthodontic retainers, you know?"

"You mean - braces?"

"Yes – orthodontic braces. Often, they are installed as permanent retainers - when they finish straightening a person's teeth. The formed wire holds everything together – helps to keep the teeth in their proper positions."

Greer nodded, "Okay, but I still don't get the significance."

"Neither did I – other that the fact that this guy is a little old for braces. Until…" Mikami stepped away, towards the attendant's desk. In a moment he returned with a hand held gray plastic electronic device, about the size of a large TV remote control. He flicked a button and the device beeped. A green alpha-numeric display panel illuminated. "When I was finishing up with Mr. Sung, we had an Officer from the Animal Control unit come in. She was helping us identify some possible canine bite marks on a victim from another case. Well, she walked by Sung on the table and her reader…" He tapped the device he held. "It went off."

Greer was perplexed. His face showed it.

Mikami continued. "So, she takes this out and starts waving around scanning for the source."

"Source?"

"The source of whatever was causing her identification scanner to go off. This was it! Right here – in Mr. Sung's mouth – this dental appliance – it is, apparently, a passive electronic device, activated by RF – that's radio waves – and it triggered her identification scanner, the type they use to read pet ID micro chips that people have installed in their dogs and cats."

"Okay… So, I'm still not quite getting it. So, what's it – the reader – say?"

"Well, here." Mikami passed the reader over Sung's lifeless head and the little machine beeped and the display lit up. He angled the readout so Greer could see it. It had a string of letters, numbers and other unintelligible characters. Tim took the device from Mikami's hand and tried it himself. Each time the device passed within a few inches of the head, the reader beeped and the greenish display refreshed itself. Each time the reader display was identical. Greer flipped open his notebook and wrote down the display information, exactly as it appeared.

Mikami watched over his shoulder. "That's odd."

"What's odd, Doc?"

The numbers, I think they're different than they were when I first saw them in the exam room."

"How so?"

"We can check, I wrote them into my notes. They're in the dictation room." He started to remove his gloves. "That's about the story with Poppa Sung... You want to see the girl?"

Greer's mind was saying, no thank you. But his voice said, "Sure." They closed up M-2 and moved over to L-2.

Mikami quickly went through the wound narrative on the daughter. She also had been stabbed repeatedly and her throat had been slashed, mostly on the right anterior side of the neck. Mikami theorized that the same weapon had been used. Cause of death was most certainly loss of blood, most likely from the neck wound. Other than that, the condition of the daughter's body was not remarkable. They closed the refrigerated door and left the storage area.

Greer asked. "Any ideas on the dental appliance?"

Mikami slapped his forehead. "Christ. I almost forgot to tell you – This may possibly the most important part..."

He had Greer's attention. "Which is?"

"I've seen the same kind of dental appliance or retainer before – recently." Mikami stopped talking and just looked away, in his odd, I-know, you-don't-know manner.

Finally Greer broke the silence. "Okay, Doc. What's it gonna take to get you to tell me? Drugs – torture – buy you lunch...?"

Mikami blinked back to the present. "Oh, sorry... two other recent homicides – few days ago – the Fountain Valley case – husband and wife? The husband had one of those things. And the other was – let me think – maybe two, three weeks back, Fullerton case – another sixty, or so, year old Asian man – he had one too. I'm pretty sure."

"Pretty sure – of what?"

'They were all identical. They were just like this one – cemented in place with a sort of dark colored adhesive compound. All three cases had the same looking retainer appliances on the bottom lingual front teeth. All three had the same dark colored adhesive for anchoring. Curious."

"Okay Doc – why is it curious?"

"Well, for one, we don't use dark colored adhesive in the States. Everything today is white, or the off-white shades of tooth enamel color..." Mikami appeared to drift away momentarily in thought. He returned. "Second thing, all were men, and all were Asian men. In fact, if memory serves me, all were Korean men!"

They ended up back in the dictation area. There was a bit more discussion between the men. Greer took more notes. Finally finished, Tim headed for the door and Mikami returned to his dictation room. Just as Greer approached the exit, Mikami popped his head out and said, "Greer - one more thing."

Tim turned, hand on the door.

Mikami said. "The Jung woman, the daughter – her first name is Keiko."

"Yeah."

"Just a thought... might not be anything, but Keiko - that's not a Korean name. Sung is, but Keiko – that's Japanese."

Chapter 13
Santa Ana, California

Sullivan required a short visit to his office to clear up a few items before he and Gomez flew off to Japan. After their meeting in Colorado, Sullivan phoned, Lieutenant Blair, telling him that he needed some vacation time. Blair gave him the okay.

Mike jumped on an early morning flight. Landing at John Wayne Airport, he went straight to his office. In the couple of hours that he had been in, he'd made some phone calls, dictated a few memos, reports and generally had cleaned up his desk to the point where he could take off with a fairly clear conscience.

He was just about to pack it in when Greer loomed over his desk. "Hey, Mike. Gotta minute? I'd like to bounce something off of you."

It took Greer nearly twenty minutes to bring Sullivan up to speed on the details of the Asian murders. Sullivan followed in attentive silence. In his short tenure with the Orange County Sheriff's office, Sullivan had developed quite a reputation. Time after time, he'd demonstrated an uncanny ability to see through the haze, to conjure up information, facts, and make something workable out of the glut of information that clogged many serious cases. Approaching legendary status within their small community, Sullivan was clearly their ace.

A certain aura of mystery flowed around Sullivan. People knew that he had worked for the FBI before coming to the Sheriff's office. A few of his coworkers suspected that there might be more to the man's story, but no one knew that the Sullivan legend was just that, a legend.

Greer admired Sullivan. He often wished he could divine just what quality it was that set the big man apart from the other, mere mortal investigators they worked with.

Sullivan listened to Greer's story. From time to time, he glanced at the wall clock. He knew that Gomez would be waiting for him at the Executive Hangers at John Wayne. Since they would be flying a GTI corporate jet to Japan, he didn't exactly have to worry about missing his flight. He wanted to give Greer as much time as he needed. Finally, Greer was winding down. He concluded with the information about the dental appliance. Sullivan had a short series of questions that he'd mentally filed away.

"Crime Lab going to handle the dental device?" Mike asked.

"Yes, Mikami's taking it out – as carefully – as he can. Actually, he's got a reserve deputy, a Mike Burke – this guy's a regular orthodontist – he's coming in to remove it, properly. Then I'll take it and book it myself to the Crime Lab." Greer pushed up his glasses and rubbed his eyes. Returning to his notes he said. "I'm also getting the lingual dental device from the Fountain Valley male victim. His body is still at the funeral home. The Fullerton victim was cremated and I'm still trying to find out what happened in the Irvine case."

Sullivan sat back. "What else connects these crimes?

"Well, they are all Koreans. None of the male victims had been in the country very long, three to four years, tops. They all had alien registration ID with their personal effects. At least two of them had Permanent Resident cards. But, curiously, Immigration. doesn't have anything on any of the victims from the Fountain Valley, Fullerton or the Garden Grove cases in their automated files.

Sullivan guffawed a bit at that. "That's not real surprising. Those guys aren't exactly known for their bureaucratic proficiency."

"So I've heard. Comforting, isn't it – I mean with what's going on in world and all. Anyway, I've got an I.N.S. investigator chasing down the records for me. We'll probably have more on that in a day or two."

"Our Crime Lab – we got somebody who's good with electronics?"

"Hope so. If not, I guess we'll find out."

Sullivan furrowed his brow. "If there's a problem with that, I know a guy – an outside guy – that can help us."

"Good. Anything else you can think of that I'm missing here?"

For about a minute, Sullivan mentally drifted through the details. Finally he spoke. "Tim, I think you're on the right track. There is, clearly, way more here than meets the eye, as I'm sure you've already figured out."

Greer nodded.

"These killings smack of hits, almost like – we're-going-to-teach-you-a-lesson - kind of hits. Keep digging and I bet you will find a more significant connection between these people."

Greer nodded again.

Sullivan took a pen and scribbled on a piece of paper the name "Kim" and a telephone number. "Go talk to this guy. He and his wife own a little grocery store right here in town. They're major conduits of information within the Korean community. Tell them, right off, I sent you. In fact, on second thought, I'll call ahead for you, just to grease the skids."

Greer took the paper and nodded again.

Sullivan took the slip back from Greer. He wrote another name and number on it. "Here's another second thought. Skip the crime lab. Take the dental things directly to this guy. Call him, he'll tell you where to meet – don't be alarmed if he's a little strange – or if he wants to meet someplace like you're doing a dope deal. He's good – really good. In fact, he just might be about the best for this type of thing."

Greer eyes examined the paper, then came back up to meet Sullivan's gaze. "Stretch?"

"Yeah, that's his name. Oh, and don't even think about running the phone number. It'll probably come back 'not in file' or registered to somebody in Alaska or Minnesota." Sullivan chuckled knowingly.

"Also, follow up on the extra blood spatters at the Garden Grove scene. Work on the lab guys to DNA the samples right off and start eliminating all the known possibles. You know, the victims, some cop that cut his finger at the scene, the paper boy. You know the drill."

Greer's pen raced over the page of his notebook.

Sullivan concluded with a grin. "If you're really lucky, maybe your female victim plugged the guy with her pistol - and he'll show up somewhere."

"Yeah." Greer smiled. "With a matchable slug in him." He added, " That's about as likely as the suspect dropping his wallet at the scene with his driver's license in it."

"Stranger things have happened." Sullivan stood up. "And Tim, one more thing…"

"Yeah?"

"Go get some sleep. You really look like crap."

It was high noon when Sullivan drove his classic Mustang convertible through the security gate of the General Aviation side of John Wayne Airport. His Sheriff's credentials got him an immediate wave through.

GTI leased several hangers on the south side. He drove a short distance and stopped by the open doors at the end of a metal building. A red and white Leer Jet 45, a compact, twin engine corporate model sat on the pavement, fuselage door standing open. Gomez was walking the exterior of the craft running his hands over the control surfaces and eyeballing everything his pilot's eye could see. This was the pre-flight inspection. For a pilot the caliber of Charlie Gomez, a pre-flight was a near-religious experience. Sullivan pulled up as Charlie was examining the tail and elevators.

Charlie waved and pointed for Mike to park inside the hanger. Sullivan knew the drill. He often flew with Gomez. He pulled his Mustang inside the hanger and parked it next to Charlie's old Explorer. He grabbed his duffel bag and walked out dropping it to the pavement. He then put his weight into sliding the large metal doors of the hanger into a closed position. Finally, he secured the doors with a heavy brass combination lock. Finishing these tasks, he grabbed his duffel and climbed aboard the airplane where Charlie now occupied the left seat and was working through a pre-flight check list.

Sullivan stowed his bag, closed and locked the fuselage door, then he worked at the task of shoe-horning his considerable frame into the cramped right side seat. First he moved the seat to the extreme rear position. Then, he opened the six-way belt to its maximum limits.

"They really don't make these things for big guys, do they?" Sullivan commented as he buckled in.

"I guess they expect all pilots to weigh one-fifty and be five foot, six!" The last few words of Charlie's response had the electronic tinny sound of the intercom as Mike slipped the headphones over his ears. Charlie exchanged a few words with ground control. Minutes later the sleek little craft angled onto runway one nine right and assumed the next-to-go position. Moments later, the sleek aircraft screamed down the runway and leapt into the mid-day sunlight.

They cruised straight out into the middle of the Catalina Island Channel before Charlie made a turn to the north. Sullivan watched in awe as Gomez made the task of flying this complicated machine appear to be little more than driving a car on a Sunday afternoon. Sullivan was also a skilled pilot with considerable time in a variety of aircraft. But he bowed to the superior skills of Gomez, a natural, who by virtue of position, opportunity and wealth had developed the skills to expertly pilot nearly anything that had wings or rotors.

Once they were well into the flight, Sullivan spoke up. "So – how come we didn't rate a driver this time?"

Gomez gave a toothy grin in reply. "Well, Senor – I was just - barely walking by – and I thought – ese, I'd really like to drive that airplane!"

Sullivan laughed. "You really do a very bad cholo, you know?"

"Yeah – well, sorry. Actually, I thought it would be nice to get some seat time in the Leer – for both of us."

"It's okay by me. You know I love these things..." He looked around and gripped the yoke. "You gotta manual or something that goes with this?"

It was Charlie's turn to laugh. "No. But I have some lunch! You hungry?"

"Always! Whaddya got?"

"Ready to take the plane?" Charlie said as he slid his seat back on the rails.

"Whoa – wait a sec. Lemme at least get my bearings here." Sullivan quickly surveyed the instruments. "What's our first destination?"

"ANC – Anchorage International - Alaska, that is. We gas up there – then I thought we might push it all the way to Sapporo, on the Island of Hokkaido. The airport there is KJCO – also known as Sapporo-Okadama. Ever been there?" Charlie flashed him a look.

"No – well, I've been in and out of Japan a few times, but never on Hokkaido. You?"

"Only once. This will be my second visit. Weather's similar to Seattle this time of year."

Charlie continued to unbuckle. "Ready to take it?"

"Yeah, I've got the airplane."

Gomez got up out of his seat and headed aft. "Your airplane." He said as he moved back to the main cabin.

Sullivan was doing some quick calculations. He called out over his shoulder. "Hey, aren't we cutting it kind of close – for both legs – have you checked the fuel/distance thing?"

Charlie re-appeared. He held two white sacks with golden arches on the sides and two pint size bottles of chilled water. "Big Macs – I just needed a minute to nuke them." He handed one sack to his partner and slid back into his seat. He set his sack aside for the moment and re-buckled in. "You are, as usual, uncannily dead on with your fuel/distance calculations. However, what you don't know is that since you last flew with me, in this beauty, we had some auxiliary tanks installed. We now have a range of 3400 nautical miles – and we're not really fully loaded. So with any luck…"

"And maybe a tail wind." Sullivan added through a mouthful of hamburger.

"Exactly, we should make it. I'm figuring" – he consulted his flight computer – "about six hours on the first leg and a tad more for the Hokkaido jump."

Chapter 14
O Shima Island, Japan

Crossing longitude 180° added the extra day to further insult and muddle the body clock, already reeling from the long trip from California to Japan. On, what should have been, the following morning, the rising sun of Japan was on their backs as their chartered Mitsubishi helicopter made the hop from Sapporo to the southern edge of tiny O Shima Island. They landed at a small strip that had been carved out of the hillside, just above the terraced seaport town of Aonae. As if to underscore their distain for the place, the helicopter pilots flew off as soon as their two passengers had walked clear of the rotors. Mike and Charlie carried their duffles and ambled toward some buildings.

"You sure there are people on this island?" Mike asked.

Gomez shot him a look. "Absolutely, several thousand people and about ten times as many monkeys."

"So, if there's no scheduled air service, it must be fun to get here by boat."

"Ferry service – that's what they got - long, tiring, not-too-elegant-ferry service." Their feet crunched on the gravel path.

"I wonder if we can scare up something to eat around these parts." Sullivan grabbed a look at his watch. "I don't know whether it should be dinner or breakfast." He looked around. "It doesn't much look like folks get up very early around here."

Before they had boarded the chartered helicopter, Charlie spoke via satellite phone with Norris Marshall, Captain of the GTI vessel, Glomar Explorer. The ship, along with the marine salvage crew, and their submersibles, was anchored a few miles southwest of the island. "Captain Marshall said he'd send a boat for us at first light. They might be down there now – waiting for us." Charlie gestured toward the sleepy little harbor that lay shimmering below in the early morning light.

They started down the slope. They passed rows of rice paddies, then some small cottages and eventually the path turned to stone paved streets. The continued their walk, passing more homes and closed shops. Not a soul stirred.

"At least it's all downhill." Sullivan's voice echoed the clomping timbre of his downhill stride.

Twenty minutes later, they arrived at the harbor. It was small, roughly a quarter mile across. It formed a half moon shaped bay that opened out to the south. From the ring of land around the bay, a few fingers of rickety docks poked tentatively into the water. The piers were weathered grey and cobbled together, with no rhyme or reason to their layout. A few fishing boats lay at their moorings.

Sullivan dropped his duffel and sat down on a piling. "Guess we wait a while."

"Not for long – look."

At the end of one of the wharfs, a white Boston Whaler bobbed. A khaki clad crewman stood on the dock holding the bow line and looking their way. Another man stood at the pilot station of the boat. Gomez waved an arm overhead. Both crewmen returned the salute.

"That looks like our ride," Charlie said. They slung their bags and headed for the boat.

The short trip out was uneventful. For the latitude and time of year, the sea was quite calm. What little swell there was came up from the south at long intervals, a condition that made for an easy ride. The trim little open deck Whaler cut through the blue water like a powered knife. Its turbo-injected Mercruiser engine hummed a throaty tone and the stern split a clean white wake that trailed for a hundred yards.

Sullivan stretched out near the bow and tilted his face into the morning rays.

The little boat motored for fifteen or so minutes when Charlie walked forward and slid down next to Sullivan. He pointed. "Turn around and behold the other wonder of Mister Howard Hughes."

Sullivan, not realizing they had closed so quickly with the ship, angled around for a look. His first impression was one of surprise. The Glomar Explorer was huge – the size of a small aircraft carrier – nearly 700 feet overall. It had three enormous derricks amidships and several lesser gimbaled davits. The ship's hull was painted in a series of black and brilliant orange bands – the colors of the GTI Corporation. All structures and rigging above the main deck were painted in a brilliant white. Projecting from the stern, there was a small helipad with an MD 500 helicopter neatly tied down. The helicopter also sported the black and orange colors of the GTI Corporation.

"She's not much to see from the outside, but inside, she's a gem." Charlie announced with obvious pride.

"You were going to tell me about this right? At least one day?"

"Hey… You of all people know all about classified crap. Now that you've been cleared – well, I can tell you anything and not worry about going to Leavenworth!"

Sullivan was marveling at the looming ship. He thought that she looked like a cross between a freighter and a factory. "So, tell me about the Glomar."

With a grin and child-like eagerness, he started in. "Okay. She was built with an enormous open "Moon Pool" amidships. Parked inside her and completely hidden from view is this specialized and highly classified experimental submarine. They call it 'Huey'."

Sullivan's eyes widened a bit at that piece of information. Charlie continued. "As submarines go, Huey is quite small, about two hundred feet from stem to stern. But she is the absolute latest item in cutting edge submarine technology. She's powered by – get this - a system of super-quiet, and very secret, steerable hydro-jet thrusters. No conventional screws! She's super stealthy and fast, able to cruise submerged, virtually undetected, at speeds exceeding forty knots. Her motive power comes from hydrogen fuel cells that produce only clean water and oxygen as waste by-products. Both elements are recovered and reused."

"How long can she stay down?" Sullivan asked.

"Another big secret – since she can be refueled and re-aired from sea water – theoretically the answer is indefinite. We really don't know. I guess it becomes a function of how much food and supplies she can carry.

"How does she mask her presence, especially since – you told me she carries the submersibles on her back?"

"Another new development… The hull is created from titanium and spun polymers. The submersibles fit into special compartments that blend into the stealth designed hull. For anything conventional to even see her, let alone track her, they half to be closer than about 500 meters. At distances beyond that range, she is literally invisible. Another feature is that her pressure hull is constructed similar to a DSRV. She can dive to depths that are unheard of for even the best nuclear powered sub."

Sullivan whistled softly as the Whaler drew alongside the ship. A pair of motorized davit cables were dropped and connected to their launch. Motors whined and in moments the small craft was plucked from the sea and secured to a stand. Sullivan and Gomez stepped onto the Deck of the Glomar Explorer.

The ship's First Officer, a slender fellow, by the name of Dubord stood by to greet them. "Welcome aboard, gentlemen!" He extended a hand to Charlie first. "Mr. Gomez... Nice to see you again, Sir."

Charlie introduced Sullivan. "Mr. William Dubord - the ship's First Officer."

"If you will follow me, we'll get you gentlemen settled in." Dubord led the way, through passageways and stairwells ultimately bringing them to small side by side crew cabins – sparse but like everything on the ship, efficient.

"Captain Marshall sends his compliments and requests you meet him in his private mess whenever you are ready." He was being polite, but the inference was clear. Meet the Captain, now! "Also, you may notice" – they could plainly hear the clanking of the anchor chain being hauled up and the pitch of the massive diesel engines changing indicating an increase in RPMs – "that we will be underway immediately."

Gomez answered. "Thank you... and I expect we are ready to meet the Captain, now." Turning to Sullivan he said. "I think we might find some of that breakfast you were looking for." He clapped Sullivan on the shoulder as they again followed Dubord through the labyrinth of the ship's passageways.

"Thank God for food," declared Sullivan.

Chapter 15
Newport Beach, California

Greer thought he may have the wrong place. When he telephoned the man called "Stretch", there was an immediate recognition and willingness to cooperate. Sullivan had obviously spoken with him. Tim understood the man had an office or shop in the area, but for some reason, the guy called "Stretch" didn't want to meet there. Instead, Stretch instructed to meet him at a donut shop, next to the Aquatic Center dive shop on Pacific Coast Highway, right where Superior Avenue turned into Balboa Blvd. as the roadway went out onto the peninsula.

Greer was early. He went into the shop and ordered a coffee. It was fresh brewed and stored on the counter in those big black vacuum pump jugs. The coffee smelled great. He was attended to by a young Asian woman who politely waited while he inspected the colorful array of pastry and donuts, trying to decide if he would continue the fight against larger love handles or simply surrender to the great taste of a fresh glazed puffed with raspberry jelly.

He was saved from the critical decision when a yellow Porsche Targa slid into the parking space directly in front of the shop's door. Greer casually watched as the driver extracted his six foot plus frame from the tiny car and ambled in to the shop. Greer mentally jotted the license plate number from the Porsche's front bumper to his mind's notebook. The man coming through the doorway was at least six foot, five. He was dressed in Levis, old blue Nikes and a Hard Rock Café Tee. He had the squared off face of midwestern ancestry, a shock of brown hair that was gel styled in the popular bed-head look. The glasses were the topper. He sported a pair of metal rimed glasses that looked like they had been made from the bottom of two coke bottles. The man spoke. "Mr. Greer…?"

삼 질 식 시 킴

They sat in a booth in the rear of the shop. No one was near. On the table were coffees, donut fragments, crumpled napkins and two clear plastic bags, each neatly stenciled with the word "Evidence". The bags contained the freshly removed dental appliances from the victim's mouths. Greer had finished his story, and Stretch was staring at the bagged devices like they had the black plague.

"So… Stretch – think you can you help us out here?" Greer asked with more than a hint of skepticism in his voice.

Stretch handled the devices through the plastic bags, turning them over and examining them through his gigantic lenses. He muttered. "Uh huh."

"You know, this is highly irregular. Giving these things to you might…" He pondered for a moment. "Actually, no might. It will, screw up what we call the chain of evidence. Hell, I don't even know your name or where you'd be taking them… I'm only doing this because Sullivan…"

Stretch plucked off his glasses and regarded the Detective. Greer looked back into a set of cool blue eyes that registered way off the IQ, and patience meters.

"Mr. Greer, ah, Tim… May I call you -Tim?"

Greer nodded.

"I'm sitting here spending time with you - talking to you - only because Sullivan asked me to." He paused for a beat. "The way I get it, he wants me to examine these things and figure out what they are – or what they do. He obviously doesn't have faith in the people you were going to take them. So… here's the deal. Can the lecture and make a decision right now. Either you give them to me – no questions asked - or I walk – now!" Stretch concluded with a polite smile and placed his hands flat on the table as if he was about to stand.

Greer blinked. He realized that he was about to royally piss this guy off. He quickly weighed what he knew. His first impression was that this "Stretch" guy was most certainly an eccentric and probably a flake. It was that versus Sullivan's insistence on using him. He quickly made his choice. "Sorry Stretch. It's just that I've been up now" – he glanced at his watch – "pushing thirty hours. I'm getting a little thin on everything. Please consider these items yours – for now, at least. How do you wish to proceed?

"Okay… Wait here." Stretch walked out to his car, popped the forward bonnet and retrieved a small metal case. Returning, he placed the case on the table and clicked it open. Sliding back into the seat his eyes connected with Greer. He said. "This is a RF tight enclosure. It dampens radio waves - from going in or out." He picked up the devices and placed them inside. Then he closed and latched the case.

Greer swallowed hard, visualizing that he was watching his precious evidence slip away.

"Here's what we'll do. For now, you run your paperwork like the items are booked into your locked desk drawer, a temporary evidence locker or whatever you've got. I'll go right to work on these and I'll call you when I've got something."

Greer nodded. "Do you have any idea when you might be getting back to me?"

"Not really..." He offered a quick handshake. "But it was nice to meet you." Stretch slid out of the booth and stood. Scooping up the case, he said. "Call you as soon as I can." He ambled out the door.

Chapter 16
Sea of Japan

They were seated around a circular table in the Captain's ready room, just off the bridge. After a seaman's breakfast of scrambled eggs, sausage, bacon and buckwheat flapjacks slathered in butter and maple syrup, the men were relaxing over mugs of steaming hot coffee. Present were the Captain, Norris Marshall, First Officer Bill Dubord and two other men, who had been introduced as the principal members of the GTI Submersible Team, Phil Sells and Ken McMillan. Sullivan made them all for regular Navy – the last two were probably SEALS or ex-SEALS. At least they both had the look, intelligent, tough and wiry with that little glint of crazy in their eyes.

Similar to the crewmen that had retrieved them from the dock, everyone at the table was dressed in tan utilities, each with an embroidered black name patch over the right pocket. There was no visible indication of rank. It didn't appear that element was necessary. Everyone knew the pecking order and conducted themselves accordingly. The Captain was addressed as Captain or Captain Marshall. Everyone else was addressed as Mister, followed by their surname.

Marshall was an interesting and formidable figure. He looked as if he should be commanding a battle cruiser. Compact, barrel-chested, sporting a head of buzz cut salt and pepper hair, he looked like he ate nails for breakfast and smiled only on select holidays. Sullivan liked him, right off.

The Captain spoke. "If you Gentlemen don't mind, we'd like to get right down to business."

As if on queue, Mr. Sells got up and ushered out the last steward. He spoke to someone outside the door, then re-entered, closed and bolted the cabin door behind him. There were two small windows to the cabin, he shuttered both, then returned to the table.

Moving the remaining cups and spoons out of the way, Dubord laid out charts covering the area of the Sea of Japan from the Korean Peninsula to the Japanese Island chain.

Captain Marshall started right in. His leading remarks were introductory, about his crew members. "Let me begin by explaining who we are and what our jobs are. Mr. Dubord, here, is our First Officer. His job is to be the mission commander. He also skippers our sub, Huey. Mr. Sells is the Submersible Unit Commander. He and his people pilot our experimental submersibles, both manned and robotic. We call them Dewey and Louie. Mr. McMillan is our, uh" – he appeared to grope for the correct word - "tactical manager. McMillan and his team member are responsible for contingencies, which in this case, includes other folks that may be hostile towards our intent to salvage and…" He again appeared to cogitate for the correct phrase – "ensuring that whatever it is that we're going after doesn't harm us before we can neutralize and secure it."

Neither Gomez nor Sullivan spoke. They just listened to the Captain's remarks and nodded.

Turning to Gomez, the Captain continued. "By the way, Mr. Gomez, if you don't already know, just like you and Mr. Sullivan here, everyone at this table has been cleared for full access to information about this project – codeword Chosn and any other label that may get attached to it. Understood?"

"Absolutely," said Charlie. "And we will be happy to share with you any information we may have picked up that you may not already have."

The Captain continued. "Gentlemen, before we get started, I feel the need to explain some ground rules." While his remarks were obvious overhead statements intended for guests and crewmembers alike, it was plain that the next subject was being aired to ward off potential chain-of-command problems. "As you all know, Mr. Gomez, here, is a Vice President and principal executive of our Company, GTI. He and his associate – ah - Mr. Sullivan, are here to observe - as we undertake this delicate mission." He flashed a glance towards Charlie and Mike. "As such, they will be doing just that – observing." Operational control of the mission will be ours, just as it always is." The Captain nodded to Gomez.

Gomez, following the Captain, took his cue. "That's absolutely correct. Mr. Sullivan and I appreciate the opportunity to tag along – but I would like to reiterate that we are not in the chain of command. This is your mission and full operational control is with you-all." There were grunts and nods around the table.

Marshall picked it up. "That being said, lets talk about what we know, what we don't know and what we think we can do."

The Captain and his top managers had been thoroughly briefed via scrambled text messages and secure Com-Satellite links. They had conversations with the Office of Naval Operations at the Pentagon and briefings from the main intelligence agencies. The obvious fingerprints of Presidential authority were all over the project, insofar as much of the intelligence community was actually cooperating. They had, no doubt, been ordered to share everything with this select team with virtually no restrictions.

Captain Norris explained that the National Reconnaissance Office was down-linking continuous real time satellite images of marine traffic in the target area. The CIA had a few, precious few, assets on the ground in the seaport towns of the DPRK and the Russian Territories that flanked the area. Any information coming from those sources was promised as fast as possible.

Overall, it appeared that all US intelligence agencies were cooperating with this special contractor job. Sullivan listened, but inwardly was less enthusiastic. He knew all about inter-agency cooperation. He quietly and skeptically listened and absorbed everything he could.

The group spent the next couple of hours going over all the available information about the North Korean flight, its track, and direction of travel, the location where the craft came down, seafloor imagery, depth and seafloor contours of their likely search area.

Gomez told the ship's company of their meeting with the Vice-President and McClure. Both Sullivan and Gomez shared what little information they had.

Their plan was simple, but bold. The target area was about two hundred miles due west of O Shima Island. The Glomar Explorer would steam at a leisurely pace to a point about halfway across the Sea of Japan. There, it would stop. The ship would drop its deep water anchors, in that area about 15,000 feet. It would then appear to commence marine bottom survey operations and test samples for oil and other recoverable minerals – just another routine marine survey expedition. Notifications had already been issued to all surrounding countries, shipping companies and other interested parties in the form of a marine activities advisory that the Glomar Explorer would be working at this location for at least a week.

What would actually happen was this. Dubord took over the narration of the recovery plan. "Once the Glomar is secure on station, we take Huey and dive deep." He used a pair of silver compass pointers and angled a path along the chart. "We follow the contours of the seafloor - along this way - that enables us to stay at maximum depth. When we get to the target area..." He placed an overlay contour chart on the table, one with higher resolution of the area. "We will run, depending on if there is anybody around, magnetometer sweeps if we have to be quiet, or side scan sonar if we decide we can make a little noise."

"Is anybody around there now?" Sullivan asked.

"Yes, but it only appears to be a couple of small craft, maybe trawler or patrol size. A few days ago, when this event happened, both the Russians and North Koreans immediately brought ships into the area."

"What happened? They just go home?" Gomez asked.

McMillan jumped in. "Our radio intercepts of their discussions were interesting. Basically, the Koreans were first on scene. Then the Russians did over-flights and later their patrol boats showed up. The Koreans were telling the Russians they had lost an aircraft and it was in their territorial waters - and no thanks on the offer of assistance for rescue operations. The Russians countered with, no, it's our territorial waters and if your plane was military - they, the Russians - have to ensure their safety by neutralizing any potential armaments. It went on like this for a day or so, the Koreans kept changing their story – first it was a military craft – then it was civilian. Their last story was that the flight was an un-manned drone and that it was doing atmospheric sampling and went out of control – hence, no live bodies on board, no need for Russian search and rescue – please to go home". McMillan mimicked the Asian brutalization of English idiom.

Captain Marshall picked it up. "Truth is neither the North Koreans or the Russians have any assets in this area that are capable of salvage ops at this depth. Our job is to get in and out before they can get over here with equipment that can work these depths."

Up to this point their discussions had centered on logistics, speed and stealth. Their task was to get in to the area, find the craft, grab what they could and get back out to the Glomar – all without being detected.

Dubord finally asked the question that was on everyone's mind. "Do you gentlemen know what it is – that we're looking for?"

Gomez leaned back in his chair, he checked Sullivan, and then looked at the faces of each of the men around the table. All eyes were on him. Charlie cleared his throat and appeared to select his words carefully. "We have received essentially the same information that you have. And quite frankly, we're both more than a little skeptical." Charlie glanced to see Sullivan nod and continued. "We are both experienced pilots and have a firm belief in wings with air under them – but – there are people in our government, smart people, who sincerely believe that we may be looking for a craft that flies around on magnetic power – magnetic power that is taken directly from the gravity field around the earth." The group was stock-still silent. Not even a breath could be heard.

Dubord broke the silence. "This magnetic field theory – it's been around forever, it's like the alchemy of energy science. Engineers – and I might add that several of us on staff here are engineers – have chased the dream of using magnetic lines of flux as a power source. But this is mostly the stuff of science fiction. It's always proven to be impossible – it violates one of the fundamental laws of physics – that you cannot produce a level of energy from an event that will exceed the amount of energy you put in - or consume."

Mr. Sells raised a finger. Sullivan had been watching this quiet man. He had the appearance of a consummate military professional. He wore rimless glasses that gave him an owlish, almost professorial look at times. Recognition played over his face. He said. "If, the North Koreans have done it – that is, harnessed the power of the planet's gravity field – we can stop worrying about their tinkering around with nuclear materials. They've got something now that is virtually more powerful than anything else on earth... Hell, they may have tapped the very energy source of the earth."

Chapter 17
January 1952 - Yellow Sea

The twenty-five foot swells rumbled under the bow of the 34,000 ton aircraft carrier, CV-9, the U.S.S. Essex. The huge ship churned through the darkening late afternoon waters. The brass pointer of bridge to engine room telegraph was set at "Ahead One-Half". She made a steady twelve knots. Captain W.F. Peck gave the order, "Helmsman, bring her into the wind."

The helmsman spun the wheel. Presently he answered. "Aye Sir, we're into the wind at three-two-zero."

"Very good, hold your speed steady." Captain Peck turned to the OD, the Officer of the Deck. "Ready the ship for flight operations."

Claxons rang throughout the vessel, and the ship's crew, some 3400 souls, prepared for another night of action.

The Essex was on what would be its final tour of combat operations in the Korean War. Already a seasoned combat veteran, the Essex had seen severe action in the pacific theatre throughout WWII. She was well known and feared in places with names such as Wake Island, the Gilberts, Tarawa, Kwajalein, Luzon and the Marshall Islands.

For this, her third deployment within the Korean "police action" theatre, she was outfitted with a squadron of Fighter-Attack Aircraft, the venerable F4U Corsair. The Essex also had a complement of AD-2's, the navy's single engine dump truck of an aircraft, commonly called "Spads". Each Spad was capable of carrying a whopping 8000 pound bomb load to the combat zones of the north. The Essex had another surprise for the North Korean air forces. She was the first aircraft carrier to carry and launch the new F2H Banshee twinjet fighters on combat missions.

It was common knowledge among Navy fliers that since the introduction of the twin jet Banshees some months earlier, the Russian made MIG 17's and 19's, which had dominated the skies of North Korea with their superior speed and maneuverability, had taken to running away from the more powerful Banshees.

In full flight gear, the pilots assembled in the Pilot's Ready Room and poured over the floor to ceiling maps that depicted the tortured movements of Blue vs. Red over the Korean Peninsula. One of the AD pilots was Lieutenant Abraham L. Griffin, age 26, from Bangor, Maine. At this briefing, "Abe Griffin and fellow AD driver, John Holter, would learn that their target would be deep into northern territory. Their mission was to drop their TNT loads on a key bridge which spanned a major tributary of the Yalu River, just north of Cha'son, almost into Communist China. The two AD's would be escorted through "MIG Alley" by two of the new F2H Banshees. It would be a long trip in and out for all four aircraft. But they expected to accomplish their mission unimpeded.

In quick succession, the planes catapulted from the flight deck and flew north, over water, toward their land insertion point, the western coastal town of Chongui. Turning to the east and flying low over the terrain, the setting sun blazed red in their rear view mirrors. The AD's led. The twin-jet Banshee escorts had a speed differential problem. They cruised much faster than the lumbering Spads. The answer to this dilemma was the "Thatch Weave" maneuver. As the Spads trucked on in a straight line toward their destination, the escorting Banshees, or Banjos, as they were affectionately referred to by their pilots, flew above the Spads in a scissoring pattern, weaving back and forth, each fighter providing a full field of 180° of cover against enemy aircraft or "bogies".

Per protocol, the pilots maintained radio silence. They had a scant 150 miles to go before they would be on their target.

Suddenly, out of the southern darkness, two North Korean MIGs appeared at their three o'clock. Yellow arcs of light from tracer bullets flashed through the sky. The right side escort Banshee dove and the left side escort climbed to engage their attackers.

Griffin felt his plane shudder as the enemy 20mm explosive shells slammed into the rear fuselage and right wing of his AD. High octane gasoline streamed away from the aircraft and ignited in a flare of red-orange flame. Griffin had been flying at one thousand feet. Now he struggled to maintain that altitude. In a matter of seconds, he knew what he had to do. He tucked his legs in tight. With his left hand he reached into a small compartment and grabbed the canopy release. He hauled back on the lever and his canopy blew away. Hurricane force winds and choking smoke enveloped him. He reached above his head. With both hands he gripped the ejection handle and with all of his strength, he pulled down. A curtain dropped over his face and Griffin, encased in the flimsy aluminum cage of the ejection seat, sailed through the air in dizzying ballistic arc. His breathing mask ripped away. He felt, at first, crushed by the G-force. Then, he was momentarily weightless. Just as he became resigned to the horrible dark smashing death that was rushing up to take him, hypoxia mercifully claimed his consciousness.

삼 질식시킴

He awoke slowly, painfully. At first he thought he was dreaming. He was cold and wet and lay chest deep in putrid water. He could hear excited voices, yelling – lots of jabbering that he couldn't understand. Then he was being pulled along, dragged by the lines and harness of his chute. White hot pain seared through his left shoulder. His legs didn't work, they flopped uselessly behind him. Now he was pulled up out of the water and laid against a muddy bank. Small soldiers in strange tan quilted uniforms crowded around. There was yelling and screaming. Several people kicked him and slammed rifle butts into his body. He tried to cover his face but his left arm didn't work. Someone held his right arm. There was a loud thunk – a blow to the head. Merciful clouds of darkness engulfed him.

삼 질식시킴

Dim light penetrated the hut from many spots. He lay on a makeshift cot. He blinked repeatedly, trying to clear his vision. Most of the blur finally receded. He looked around, taking stock of his surroundings. The cot was small, barely large enough to hold him. It was nothing more than heavy cloth, like canvas, stretched over a wooden frame. Above him the roof was thatched – some kind of dried grasses. Painfully, he turned his head to one side. He could see walls made of what looked like blocks of mud and straw. In the center of the small room, there was an old metal stove. A blackened chimney-pipe angled up towards the roof. A fire smoldered inside. He could smell the smoke, and see the occasional yellow flicker of light through the seams. He tried to lift himself up, but he was unable to move anything more than his head. He could see that the upper part of his body was wrapped tightly with a dirty tan cloth. His left arm was completely immobilized. He managed to flex the fingers of both hands, and was gratified to feel rough fabric against his fingertips.

Presently, he became aware of a horrible odor. He swiveled his head around trying to determine the source. Slowly it came to him. He was lying in his own filth, his own excrement and urine. Insects buzzed and crawled around the lower portion of his body. Abe Griffin squeezed his eyes tightly closed and prayed for death.

삼 질식시킴

It was morning. The PA system blared out the tinny, static laden sounds of the record player screeching out the marching song that he had come to hate so much. The chorus of the loyal people of the Democratic Republic of Korea sang the praises of another day in service to the Great Leader.

He awoke. It was day four hundred and twenty seven of his captivity. He knew that his count was off, but 427 was the number of days he could remember. There were more days, weeks, maybe even months he could not remember. He knew that he had been badly injured, and had been moved from place to place before his mind became clear enough to remember, and to count.

Lying there on the flimsy cot, inside his small cell, he carefully lifted himself into a sitting position. His near useless left arm hung by shredded bone and muscle that still attached it to his body. He waited a few moments for the webs of sleep to clear. He stood and shuffled the three steps to the wooden bucket.

With his right hand, he uncovered himself from the pajama-like uniform and voided his bladder. He bent to pick up the bucket, then turned and shuffled the four steps to the thick wooden door. He waited.

Presently, the loyal people's chorus concluded singing. The guard banged on the door with his truncheon. This was the daily morning signal for the prisoners to stand by their cell doors, part of the routine that he had learned so thoroughly. The door clanked open, and he stepped outside. In the dimly lit hallway, Griffin and the handful of other prisoners were a pitiful and haggard group. They were not allowed to speak to one another; they were not allowed to congregate. The rules were such that the prisoners had to maintain a distance of five meters between them at all times. Any violation of the rules meant an instant and savage beating from the sadistic guards.

As required, each of the prisoners bowed upon exiting their cell. The bow was to be made from the waist. Each prisoner's head must bow at least as low as his hips. He could hear the recitation over and over in his mind. It was a painful movement for Griffin, but less painful than blows to the kidneys and genitalia from the guard's clubs. Such was the swift and certain punishment for failure to perform.

The prisoners turned in single file and moved out slowly to the right. They trudged along in a halting gait. For Griffin it was twenty three steps to the lavatory area, which was, in reality, nothing more than an open benjo ditch and some decrepit piping with a trickle of filthy water. Griffin shuffled, maintaining his required distance. Finally, it was his turn at the facilities. He emptied his bucket. With little more than a scrap of cloth and water, he did his best to wash off some of the grime and rinse out his mouth.

Each prisoner was allowed about one minute for this daily ablution. He turned and was about to reenter the line to return to his cell. One of the guards - Griffin referred to this one as Bluto - stepped in front of him and poked him severely in the chest with the end of his club. Wincing at the pain, he stood in place and started to perform the obligatory bow. The guard stopped him with a glancing blow to his bad arm. Bluto said, "You – come!" He again prodded Griffin and pushed him out of the line toward another building.

He was taken to a windowless room; the single door slammed shut behind him. The room in which he stood was within a part of the prison he had never before seen. The walk was long, more than three hundred steps. It was common practice for prisoners to wear a gunny sack over their heads when being moved any distance. That did not happen this time. Griffin had a clear view of his transit from one side of the prison facility to the other. This side was new to him. It wasn't the torture area. It wasn't the laughable medical treatment area. Griffin decided that he must be in an administrative or office section.

The room was devoid of furnishings save for a solitary small wooden chair and table. On the table there lay folded a clean pair of prisoner uniform pajamas and a pair of thatched sandals. He didn't know what to do or expect. So, he simply stood and waited.

Time passed. He didn't know how long. But it seemed like an hour or maybe two. The door to the room finally opened and an officer walked in. He was tall for a gook, perhaps five foot ten inches or better. His uniform was impeccable. The dark brown leather was brilliantly shined. The yellow, red and gold braid shoulder boards signified the rank of Major of the North Korean Peoples Army. The man within was Asian, freshly scrubbed and shaved. Griffin recalled later thinking that he did not look like a ground soldier. Even his fingernails were clean and well manicured. The officer's freshly cut hair was dark and shone with the greasy slick of pomade. He stood off to the side and regarded Griffin with curiosity. Another soldier came in behind the major and placed a wooden chair on the floor. The guard bowed slightly and retreated, closing the door behind him.

The Major seated himself at the table. He unbuttoned his tunic and withdrew a fresh package of Camel cigarettes. He placed the cigarettes and a small white cardboard box of matches on the table. He continued to regard Griffin, who stood stock still, mute, with eyes downcast. After a moment, the Major picked up the Camels and removed the red cellophane ribbon. He deftly opened one corner of the foil package. He tapped out a single smoke and inserted it between his lips. From the match box, he removed a single stick and struck it to flame. He held it inches from the cigarette and continued to watch Griffin as the flare of the match subsided.

Finally he touched the flame to the cigarette and shook out the match. He took a deep drag and tossed the smoking match stick to the floor. He removed the cigarette from his mouth Russian-style, with thumb and first finger. He exhaled a blue cloud of smoke, then he spoke. His English was near perfect and bore the slight accent of eastern American upper class culture. "Lieutenant Abraham Griffin... you may be seated." He gestured with an open palm toward the remaining chair.

Puzzled, Griffin lowered himself into the chair. The Major pushed the cigarettes toward Griffin. With a grin, he said, "Have a smoke. In fact, have them all. They are for you."

Griffin tentatively reached with his good hand toward the package. When his hand was within an inch of the Camels, a metal tipped swagger stick appeared from nowhere and slammed down across his knuckles. He winced in pain and quickly withdrew.

The Major leaned into Griffin's face, grinning. "Perhaps – first - we should have a little talk. The Major sat back resettling himself in the chair. He continued. "My name is Pak, Major Pak. I have come, today, to take you away from this place..." The Major paused for effect – as if he waited for that pronouncement to settle in.

Griffin showed no reaction. The Major continued. "You are to change into these clean clothes. In a short while, we shall bring you some food and later – you will be taken to your new – ah - home."

Griffin said nothing. But his eyes darted about with the wariness of a caged and frightened animal.

"The war is over... but perhaps, you did not hear about that... Your pitiful American army has capitulated in the face of the superior forces of the Peoples Republics of China and North Korea." Major Pak delivered these lines enthusiastically, exuding all the pride he could muster.

Griffin was stunned. His rational side told him that Major Pak was certainly lying. But another part of him, the beaten-down part, just didn't know. It seemed like he had been in this hell hole forever.

"Although combat operations have been suspended - the matter of our struggle to re-unify Korea - it is not really over. We have merely signed a temporary armistice" – Pak drew out the syllables of the word 'temporary" with great dramatic flare – "with the imperialist Americans. Our struggle – the great struggle of the people's communist movement continues – and you - you shall be providing a great service to that struggle. In return for your service, we shall allow you to live" – the major chuckled – "and, who knows? We may even allow you to marry and have a family." Major Pak laughed aloud – like this was some great joke that only he understood.

Chapter 18
Sea of Japan

Following their meeting with the Captain and crew members, Sullivan and Gomez went back to their cabins. It had been decided that both of them could go aboard Huey during the search for the Korean aircraft. Gomez had some experience piloting the submersible, Dewey. If Dewey was deployed, he could second the pilot, Mr. Sells.

Sullivan knew that he was just along for the ride, but it was an experience he was not about to miss. Neither of them would be worth having aboard the sub if they didn't sleep off some of their accumulated jet lag. So as the Glomar Explorer churned through the northern Sea of Japan, the two slept.

Hours later, refreshed and clothed in the non-descript khakis worn by the other crew members, Dubord led Sullivan and Gomez on a tour around the Glomar Explorer. They had covered most of the ship, and had just arrived on the Moon Pool catwalk. Beneath them, fully enclosed within the bowels of the ship, lay the submarine "Huey". The sleek craft was just shy of 200 feet from nose to stern. Her futuristic dark hull was an odd dark slate color that cast no reflection from the brilliant fluorescent service lights above the pool. Two thirds of the boat's hull was under water and she was held in place by a series of vise-like clamps that tightly gripped her in eight key places.

"These docking clamps hold Huey in a rigid position so we don't break or shake anything loose when the Explorer is under way." Dubord explained.

Sullivan let out a low soft whistle. "She certainly doesn't look like any sub I've ever seen."

"And I'll bet she doesn't run like any sub you've ever seen." Dubord added with obvious pride.

"What makes her so stealthy?"

Before he answered Sullivan's question, Dubord cast a quick check-in glance to Gomez. Charlie nodded his affirmative and Dubord began to speak. "It's a combination of the same technologies that are used to make aircraft stealthy, absorptive coatings and shape. Shape has a lot, perhaps most, to do with it. Sonar reflection theory is not all that different from Radar. Although, there are some inherent differences. The flow and drag of water around the hull is a big part of it. If you are, say, dragging a big square box around under water, it is lots easier to detect than, say, if you're dragging a needle around. We use similar principles in the design. Absorptive coatings have been around for years and the technology just keeps getting better. You send just about any signal in the spectrum towards her – that includes all conventional band radars and virtually all sonar equipment in use today - and she just absorbs the energy, rather than reflect it back."

"Amazing. This paint job looks like it's practically sucking the light right out of the air?" Sullivan exclaimed.

"That's because…" Dubord continued, "In a simple, non-scientific manner of explaining it, you are just about right. The coating absorbs virtually all light wavelengths, as well. When we're under way, this ship is practically a ghost."

Sullivan said, "I am impressed."

"Here, be just a little more impressed." Gomez pointed to the seam running lengthwise down the back of the hull, just behind the sail. "The manned submersible fits into a rear compartment, right there. Those are doors that open wide, similar to those on the space shuttle."

Dubord picked it up again. "For most missions we carry one manned submersible, that's 'Dewey' and up to three of the robotic submersibles. We call those 'Louie One, Two and Three. They are stowed in a similar closed compartment up on the foredeck.

A Motorola text pager beeped at Dubord's belt. He unclipped and read the message. "Gentlemen, we are just about to arrive 'on-station'. We'd better get on board Huey. Are you ready to see the inside?"

Sullivan nodded, and they followed Commander Dubord down an open hatchway. When the last of them was aboard, a crewman secured the hatch and the gangway was removed from the submarine's hull.

They followed Dubord through tight passageways and water tight compartments until they arrived at the main control station. Sullivan thought the room looked more like the bridge from the Star Ship Enterprise than the driver's seat of a submarine. The spacious compartment was located in the forward portion of the boat, just north of the sail. It was arranged with control stations for three crewmen facing forward, one of which was the actual driver. There was no "ships wheel" or anything that remotely resembled one. Instead the ship was piloted with a joy stick that looked like it should have been on a kid's video game. Ahead of the three crewman control stations, there was a bank of large plasma display monitors, two tiers of four screens, arranged in a concave fashion. The electronic images on the screens were segmented and coordinated to give the appearance of windows to the outside. Behind the three mentioned control stations and slightly elevated for view, there was the Captain's chair, an electronic wonder in its own right.

Crewmen rushed about preparing the Huey for descent. Dubord slid into his chair and motioned for Sullivan and Gomez to take a couple of jump seats attached to a bulkhead behind him. The jump seats were like fold-out steward seats on an aircraft. "You guys better get belted in. The Explorer will drop us in a few minutes. When we first get going – sometimes the ride is a little bumpy." He immediately went back to busying himself with the pre-launch activities for the sub.

Gomez could see that Sullivan was a bit wide-eyed over the set-up. "Not bad... Eh, Amigo? You like one of these for Christmas?"

"Amazing is more like it. Those view screens... Are those actual images of the outside?"

Charlie finished belting in and looked at the forward screens. "Yes... and no. Yes, it is outside view right now..."

Mike could see what looked like a view to the forward part of the Moon Pool and part of the hull of the Glomar Explorer in the top segment. In the lower portion, it looked like water from a medium blue to dark blue in color variation.

"The can change the imagery from a series of sensors around the hull. The images come from conventional hi-res, low-lux video cameras as well as infra-red, thermal imaging and a few other viewing sensors that are – uh - developmental and..."

"Classified is the word, I think." Sullivan said with a grin.

"Yeah - that too."

Sullivan's brow furrowed. "Does she have any weapons on board?"

Durbord spun around and rejoined the conversation. "No... The rationale was that they'd invest in technology to make her stealthy and fast. Of course, just about every available space is crammed with sophisticated electronics. So, she's not designed to fight, as much as she is to sneak around undetected. The operational plans always involve having somebody around to protect her, or, to not put her directly in harm's way."

"Yeah, I know how that goes... By the way, what's the latest intel from our operational area?"

"Fresh satellite photos show two boats in the area right now – both North Korean. They think one is a Corvette, a kind of large Navy or Coast Guard patrol boat and the other is believed to be a 'fishing trawler' – you know, the kind that are crawling with antennas and towed arrays."

Sullivan nodded. "Electronic eavesdroppers. So, what are we doing – just driving right in on top of them... or underneath them, I guess."

"Actually, our good friends from the Japanese Navy have arranged a little diversion about fifty miles to the south. There's going to be a fire or something on a small boat. We're hoping that their Mayday signals will take most of the surface traffic away from our target area - at least long enough for Huey to get in and take a look-see around."

"Sounds like fun. So, how do we talk to the Glomar without tipping our hand and location?"

"More new toys from your friends at the US Government... These ships are equipped with a new and highly classified form of a digitized underwater communication system. This one sounds – to the casual listener - like whale song."

"You're kidding... It really sounds like whales talking?"

"Precisely, it sounds like whales calling to one another – and so far, no one – we believe – has tumbled to, or decoded the new system."

"Sweet."

"And the backup to that, is the antenna or surface buoy that talks via a secure satellite – that works if the sub is near the surface or even in a jam - we can release it on a tether."

Sullivan looked to Gomez. "Charlie, I had no idea you GTI guys were into all this techie stuff. You know who would really get his rocks off over this boat...?"

"Stretch!" They both said the name at the same time. Speaking of him, remind me later to tell you about a little something I sent his way just before we left – only mildly interesting – nothing like this stuff."

Huey was released from the mother ship, and she immediately started her deep descent. Sullivan felt the ship pitch forward and the cabin pressure build. His right hand went to his nose, and he pinched his nostrils to equalize his ears.

Minutes clicked into hours. The little boat cruised deeper and deeper. All conventional light was blotted out. External spotlights on the hull provided a narrow cone of illumination directly in front of them. One by one, the mosaic forward view on the video screens was replaced with streaming data or colorful virtual imagery that Sullivan did not begin to understand. The expert crew did understand, and they studied the displays intently, as if – Sullivan thought – *their very lives depended on what they were watching*.

The single center screen retained an image of the terrain they were passing. Other than the moving cone of light and the occasional strange looking deep sea creature that ventured across the field of view, that screen was blank.

Sullivan watched over Dubord's shoulder. The red numbers of the digital depth display soon clicked over to five figures. The center crewmember, Connor, the one who appeared to be doing most of the driving, called out the depth. "Crossing over ten thousand feet, Sir."

Dubord acknowledged matter of factly. "Crossing ten thousand." He glanced at the moving color display to his right. It was like a GPS depiction of the seafloor. "Level and continue two-four-seven."

"Level and two-four-seven." The pilot acknowledged.

The small sub creaked and groaned as the titanium hull fought back against the enormous outside pressure.

"Connor."

"Sir?"

"In just a moment we will hit the entrance to LP-1. Drive on in and follow it for..." Dubord consulted his display console. "About fifty miles, running more or less, due west"

"Got it, Sir. LP-1 – mouth of the canyon – dead ahead."

"Very good." Dubord wheeled his chair around to face Sullivan and Gomez. Just then, the pressure hull groaned loudly.

"Does this thing always make this much noise?" Sullivan asked wide-eyed.

Dubord smiled. "Sometimes, she makes even more noise. Don't worry, Mr. Sullivan. Huey can take a lot more than ten thousand feet."

Sullivan did some quick math in his head. "So we're at – what – some three hundred atmospheres right now."

"Very good, Mr. Sullivan." Dubord glanced at his console instruments again. "About three hundred forty atmospheres…"

"My God. That's like more than four thousand pounds per square inch of pressure!"

"Very close. Look at it this way. If the hull fails, it will be so fast, you'll never even know." He delivered that pronouncement with a toothy grin.

Sullivan looked at Gomez and swallowed hard. "That's comforting."

Dubord leaned over towards them with a small flip chart of plastic coated pages. He showed them squiggly lines on a page. "Thought maybe you'd like to know where we're going. We just entered LP-1. That's a designation for an undersea canyon, not quite as big as the Grand Canyon. It runs generally east-west. We're cruising just under the lip of it. It provides perfect cover for our approach. We'll run this path for some fifty miles or so. And, when we emerge at the other end, we'll be right in the general vicinity of our search area."

Gomez looked at his watch. "So, maybe ninety minutes or so?"

"Or less… Perhaps you should get with Mr. Sells now and saddle up on Dewey."

"Okay." Charlie unbuckled. He turned to Sullivan. "I guess I'll see you later."

Dubord answered. "Don't worry about Mr. Sullivan, here. He can help me run the boat."

Mike's rolled his eyes as Charlie headed aft. Mike settled back into his seat, feeling about as useless as teats on a boar hog.

Chapter 19
Summer 1952 - North Korea

A considerable amount of time passed. Just how much, Griffin wasn't certain. He'd long ago stopped counting the days. Since his first encounter with Major Pak, it could have been several weeks; it could have possibly been months. His situation had changed – dramatically.

In the company of Pak and a handful of soldiers, Griffin had traveled north, first by truck, then by railroad car. The rail trip was agonizingly slow, with stops every few miles. He slept a lot, floating in and out of consciousness. The jostling from the unpaved roads and old train cars was brutal on his less than poorly healed injuries. Overall, he estimated that the entire trip spanned several days.

Far away from anything that could be considered civilization, they came to a place nestled against some foothills. Later he would figure out that the hills were the edges of a small mountain range than ran from northwest to southeast. At a point where the rail line ended, the travelers were shifted to a flat bed truck, with Griffin and two guards riding in the open back. That day's journey amounted to several hard hours over rutted dirt and crushed rock roads.

Although he had no definite idea as to where they were, his internal compass and dead reckoning ability continued to work, at least a little. He figured that they had mostly been traveling north, that they might now be in the extreme northern part of the Korean Peninsula, possibly even into China.

Along the way he watched for landmarks that he hoped to identify, but he never saw anything that made sense to him. The terrain was hilly and the vegetation sparse. Where ever he was, it felt like late summer or fall. The daytime temperature was cool, the nights were downright cold. The sparse hillsides were a mottled patchwork of tans and browns sprinkled with the occasional hints of green and orange.

When they finally arrived at their destination the place turned out to be completely unlike anything Griffin had imagined. Rather than a prison stockade or walled encampment, he found he was within a small primitive settlement. Too tiny to be called a village, the place amounted to nothing more than a small cluster of huts. The surrounding area was absolute desolation for miles in every direction. Without ceremony, he was directed to and simply told to stay in one of the huts.

Compared to his previous accommodations, Griffin's hut was like a small two room mansion. The basic structure was rough but sturdy. It was wood framing that had been plastered over, inside and out, with a substance that looked like mud and straw, maybe with a little cement mixed in. He took it to be the Korean version of adobe. All of the huts were similarly built. The roofs were made of an over-layed pattern of fired clay tiles, the edges and seams having been filled with the adobe plaster. The house had a wood door, two frame casement windows with real glass and rudimentary wooden furniture. It was divided into two spaces which were, roughly, the same size.

One room was dominated by a large open hearth fireplace decently built of stone and mortar. Clean water, water that actually tasted good, came from a central well that was located nearly in the middle of the cluster of huts. Toilet facilities were in the form of outhouses positioned down slope and some distance away from the group of buildings.

Griffin marveled at the fact that people actually lived in this place. All around him were the sounds and smells of life. There was the smell of wood fire and cooking. He heard people talking and even heard occasional laughter.

For the first couple of days, he was essentially left alone. No one explained anything to him, and Griffin could not quite figure out what the program was to be. He was a prisoner, yet the place was more like a Boy Scout camp than a prison. There was no fence or bars on the windows. Even the door to his hut wasn't locked. There were a few uniformed soldiers about, but most appeared generally disinterested and he rarely saw them carry weapons.

There were also several women who appeared to belong to the facility, encampment or what ever it was. Whenever he saw one of the women, they were always attired in the modest full ankle-length native Korean dress. They eyed him curiously, but never spoke.

Each day, in the late afternoon, one of the women would bring him food. It was always the same middle-aged woman. She had a broad, flat face, tight black hair with flecks of grey and a mischievous twinkle in her dark eyes. Each day, she brought him a large covered ceramic bowl filled with steaming white rice. Occasionally there would be a piece of meat or fish with the rice. On other days, the rice would be accompanied by a small round bun of brown bread.

After many days of the food lady's visits, in his mind, Griffin named her He called her "Jane". After more time, he openly referred to her as "Jane," then "Mistress Jane." Eventually, he got to the point where each day, at food delivery time, he would engage Mistress Jane in a bit of one-sided conversation. He would bow, thank her for his food, and inquire as to her health and that of her family. All the while, "Jane listened with rapt attention. Griffin, believing that she didn't comprehend a fragment of his conversation, would nonetheless make comments about the weather, sports or other inane topics. She was always pleasant, offering smiles and attention, patiently waiting for him to finish his recitations. Each day, as Griffin concluded his thankful conversation, she would bow slightly, turn and with a wave of the hand, be off.

Within a few days of his arrival, a daily routine was established. Each morning, he walked the short distance from his hut to another building. He was told that he was attending the "Peoples Orientation School". The single room structure was arranged with tables and chairs and a chalkboard at one end. There, he would report to Major Pak or one of the others. He was required to attend this Orientation School each day for several hours. Griffin was the only pupil.

Major Pak was clearly the main figure at the "school". However there were two others that he frequently interacted with. They were a Mr. Kim and a Mr. Chang. Both were middle aged Korean men who possessed a rudimentary knowledge of English. Kim's and Chang's English was bad; so bad, it was often difficult to understand. It was, as if, the two had learned their English solely from books or, at best, from a teacher who was, clearly, not a native speaker.

Griffin was given a single book. It was the book. He was told he must keep the book with him at all times. He was to guard and care for the book and if any harm came to it, he would be severely punished. The small volume was cloth covered and hard bound. It consisted of one hundred and forty two pages which were crudely printed in fractured English. The title was "The History of the Democratic Peoples Republic of Korea As Taught By The Great Leader Kim Il Sung". The content of the book was arranged in five main sub-titles.   Those were, Old Korea, Modern Korea, Anti-Japanese Fighting, Motherland's Liberation and Korea of Juche.

Griffin was told that every day he was to read and to commit to memory portions of that book; that each following day he was to have "discussions" with his teachers, wherein, he would recite the assigned passages and discuss the content of the lesson.   All of the sessions were to be held in English.   Eventually, he was told, he would be learning the Korean language. He would be required to learn, to read, write and speak Korean fluently. It would be then, and only then he was told, that he would be able to fully comprehend the complexity of the guiding Korean philosophy of Juche.

Griffin played along. On his first overnighter with the book, he returned to his hut and read nearly the entire volume. It was written in a halting prose that sounded a good deal like Mr. Kim and Mr. Chang speaking English.   It was pure propaganda, a blatant attempt to re-write history into a justification for the modern day atrocities constantly heaped upon the Korean people. The common theme was simple; the Imperialist Americans were to be blamed for virtually everything that had ever happened including World War II and bad weather. There wasn't much in Griffin's life that gave him reason to feel gleeful, but he could not help but stifle laughter as he read many of Great Leader's passages.

Griffin adapted, but his nerves were constantly in a state of low-grade agitation, waiting for the other shoe to fall. Meanwhile, he attended his "school" sessions. Blessed with a decent mind, he found the "memorize and recite daily" commands of his captors to be ridiculously easy to achieve.   One day, just for the hell of it, he pretended to be unable to remember the day's passages. Major Pak, in a demonstration of power, had Griffin punished. Later that day, when Mistress Jane delivered his food bowl, she did so with great sadness and left immediately. Removing the cover, Griffin found that there were only a few pitiful grains of rice at the bottom of the bowl. The next day Pak warned him that future transgressions would result in "corporal punishment".

Eventually, other books in English appeared. There was never anything contemporary and seldom anything written by an American. There were a couple of Dickens stories, One by T.E. Lawrence and a couple of volumes by British authors of whom he had never heard. He was given occasional packages of cigarettes. The brands were always American, Camels, Lucky Strike or Pall Mall. Infrequently a Hershey chocolate bar would be included. Griffin theorized that these items were coming from aid packages intended for war prisoners, the bulk of which, he was quite certain, never made it to their intended recipients.

Nearly every day, Kim or Chang would have something written in English for Griffin to read and explain to them. Mostly the items were old newspaper pieces or magazine articles. Sometimes they were excerpts from personal letters. Griffin looked forward to these sessions. It was the only time he could get his hands on something current from the English speaking world. Griffin would read, then discuss and interpret. They would listen, take detailed notes, ask questions, and write more notes. So it went, day after day.

Over time, it became apparent that at least part of Griffin's real task was to polish the English language skills of Kim and Chang.

The two were interested in, for example, contemporary idiomatic expressions. Every language has contextual expressions and English is fraught with them. Almost daily, sometimes for hours, Griffin would patiently explain the concept of metaphors, similes and sports analogies that have crept into the daily lexicon of the American language.

Occasionally, Griffin would, in a small act of rebellion, ensure that at least some of his information was bogus as hell or would, at least, hopefully have Kim and Chang sounding like complete blithering idiots if and when they tried to use their new found English skills.

On his off time, and there was considerable off time, he managed to construct a calendar upon which he resumed tracking time and his activities. Being a good military man, escape was always on his mind. He was constantly evaluating his chances. By far, the largest barrier to freedom was the fact that he was in no physical condition to leave. One arm was nearly useless and one of his legs had been badly injured at the time of the bailout from his damaged bomber. The major injuries to the leg had healed but the foot twisted inward and the muscles and ligaments were plainly not right. Running was out of the question. He was capable of hobbling along for short walks, but anything of distance resulted in considerable pain. He rightfully suspected that his keepers understood his physical limitations. They obviously considered him to be virtually no escape risk at all.

What bothered Griffin most was the comment by Major Pak, on the day he'd been taken from the prison. It was Pak's statement that the war had ended, that the Americans had lost and or some kind of a truce had been signed. If any of that was true, why wasn't Griffin being repatriated. Why, then, was he not going home? Each time he tried to raise the subject with Pak or one of the others, he was told the same thing; they could not discuss that topic with him or they had no information.

Fall turned to winter. Days became short and cold. Some snow fell, though it rarely stuck for more than a few days. The huts were livable, warm, heated by smoky fires of black coal. There seemed to be an abundance of the stuff.

Nearly a year passed. One day, in the afternoon, a truck lumbered up the road, winding a dusty trail towards the settlement. Griffin was in the middle of a session with Kim and Chang, each of them equally interested in the approaching truck, craning necks, trying to get a glimpse of who was coming. When the truck was finally close enough, they could see that it was Major Pak, returning after an absence of nearly three weeks.

Griffin squinted at the distant truck. In the open rear, there was a small person. It looked like a young woman, hardly more than a child. She was dressed in prisoner pajama garb with wrists bound. She was thin and her face was framed in clumps of unkempt black hair. She had a wild eyed look, like a caged animal.

The girl was unloaded from the truck. Following a short discussion, she was led by a single soldier to Griffin's hut. Chang, sensing Griffin's curiosity, abruptly stood and announced. "School over, for today. Mr. Griffin, go home now!"

Griffin quickly stood, politely thanked both Mr. Chang and Mr. Kim, bowed as required, nearly forgot to pick up his copy of the 'DPRK Bible' and quickly left the school building. He loped along, moving as fast as his damaged legs would carry him. As Griffin arrived he stopped the soldier, a regular guard that he knew. He bowed, then asked in halting Korean. "What is this man - woman?" He quickly corrected.

The guard's answer was flat and dismissive. He said, "Friend – new friend." And he walked away.

Chapter 20
The present – Sea of Japan

The submarine's ability to see and avoid the canyon walls and jutting buttes was uncanny. Silently, the boat flowed through the dark water. Great craggy monoliths and pilasters rose from the depths and suddenly blossomed in the small sub's path. The helmsman, eyes glued to the color displays that played across the screens in front of the bridge crew, deftly steered the craft around the obstacles. Sullivan, in his jump seat, pressed his back against the bulkhead and marveled at the engineering miracle in which they rode. He thought it was similar to flying through a canyon in a hot jet helicopter. That experience had been one of the high spots of his aviation avocation thus far. Although he had no hand at the controls of this magnificent boat, this ride was rapidly becoming a close second.

"Sir, we're coming up on the end of the canyon - ETA five minutes."

"Roger that." Dubord answered crisply. "Ready the boat for stealth mode."

"Aye, Sir." The helmsman answered. A series of blue lights flashed on and off rhythmically in each compartment of the ship. Everything and everyone aboard instantly settled down to a hush whisper. The machine noise from the sleek boat amounted to a faint whooshing sound, not much more than the soft vibration of a gentle breeze blowing through the leaves of a tree.

Dubord spun his seat around and stood up. Grinning at Sullivan, he said. "This is where we really start to earn our money. You'll need to get comfortable now. Once we emerge from the canyon, we have to run silent for two, maybe three hours. Want anything – or need a head call?"

Sullivan waved thanks. "No Sir, I'm fine."

"Well, I'm going to grab some coffee, myself." He took a step towards the rear of the bridge. Then, almost as an afterthought, he turned back to the instrument console on the arm of his command chair. He punched a button. "Mr. Sells! You guys about ready, back there?"

"Aye, Captain. We are shipshape in Bristol fashion!" The muted reply was soft and tinny in the single wireless earpiece Sullivan had been given. Everyone on board wore them: the system provided un-restricted communication throughout the boat.

Dubord rolled his eyes. "That Sells – he's also our naval historian – that's his antiquarian way of telling us that Dewey is ready to swim – It means they're bolted in and ready for deployment when we open the aft doors."

Sullivan said. "On second thought maybe I will take a cup of that wonderful ship's coffee."

Dubord nodded and the hatchway behind him abruptly opened. Instead of a swinging door, the hatchway moved like the bladed iris of a giant camera lens. A crewman stepped through with two steaming white mugs.

Sullivan accepted his gratefully and sat back in his seat, to wait.

삼 질식시킴

The helmsman's voice had a serious, all business-like tone. "We are closing - three, two, one. Mark - we're in the open, Sir." His voice was whisper.

Dubord responded softly. "Do we have company?"

The crewman at the starboard control console was facing away from the Commander. He raised a hand. First he held up one finger, a moment later he raised the second. Then his voice could be heard, soft but clear over the intercom. "Two contacts, Sir – both surface. Standby." His fingers flashed over the computer console. "One is a Corvette – probable Tral class. Probably North Korean – the sound signature matches their number seven-two-eight." A moment later he added. "It's the Yang-Tou."

"Very well. And the second?"

"Not confirmed. She's noisy, twin screws, diesels – sounds like a trawler – maybe – eighty – hundred foot. Sir, both ships appear to be on a wide circular track – clockwise – the trawler is trailing the Yang-Tou by five hundred yards."

"Anything sub-surface?"

"Nothing yet, Sir."

"Okay, keep at it." Dubord spun around to Sullivan. "The second one is probably a 'fishing boat', a North Korean listening trawler." He said quietly. "She's no problem to us. The first one - the Tral - that could be dicey. That's a Russian made ship, about 200 feet long. The DPRK has five of them, two in the Tral class. It's a piece of crap. But, she's got a compliment of ASW equipment on board, two racks of depth charges and some of the older style sound seeking torpedoes."

"That's comforting." Sullivan's reply was terse.

"Not to worry, we'll give both these guys the dodge. At least - of what we can see so far – it all matches up with the latest satellite info we have – just two ships in the zone – and no surprises..." Dubord's voice trailed off.

"Do you expect we'll run into any other submarines? Sullivan asked.

Dubord allowed a faint smile. "Absolutely, we find them all the time. Everybody's got subs, at least one or two, even the North Koreans. Damn Russians and Germans sold them to just about anyone who had some cash."

Not certain of what would be an appropriate response, Mike just nodded. Finally he offered, "And they really can't see or hear us?"

"Can't see is most likely not the most accurate term. How's about we say, they generally can't see us. If we stay in stealth mode, most of these guys would have to scrape our hull to find us. Where we become vulnerable is when we open our doors to deploy the submersibles. Then, we're a tad more observable."

"And the submersibles..."

He shook his head. "Depending on what she's doing, Dewey can be fairly quiet, but she'll show up on decent sonar." He tapped on his wristwatch. "It's just about time for our Japanese friends to start the fireworks show."

They sat in deafening silence. Everyone was busy, but very quiet. It was so quiet on the boat that Sullivan began to hear soft little sounds that were normally so neutral, they would be non-existent in most situations, or at least would have blended silently into the background. There was the soft sound of men breathing, the plastic clicking of computer keys and the random chair squeak. There was, literally, no other sound on board.

Dubord ordered passive magnetometer scanning the moment they neared the crash target area. Active sonar would have been quicker, but they dared not use sonar until the surface ships left the area.

The small submarine entered the search area. Nearing the continental land mass, the seafloor steadily sloped upward. The incline of the slope became steeper, the closer they got to land. They estimated that they would find the remains in a three square mile area at depths ranging from six to seven thousand feet.

Sullivan heard the Sonar man's voice softly in his earpiece. "Sir - the Tral – her engine RPMs are coming up... She's moving out. Looks like she's heading south at one-eight-five."

"Copy, one-eight-five." With his right hand, Dubord flashed an okay sign with thumb and forefinger to Sullivan. They waited.

Minutes later, the Sonar man's voice again broke the silence. "Now the trawler is picking up speed. She's definitely broken her circular cruise pattern – she's also heading south." He turned around in his chair and grinned at Commander Dubord. "I think the Japanese just gave us a two alarm fire, Sir."

Chapter 21
Anaheim, California

The HappyLand Motor Hotel was, what some might call, moldy old. The wood and stucco two story structure of economy lodging was built just about the same time Walt Disney opened the happiest place on earth. Back then, Anaheim was mostly orange groves, pocked here and there by the occasional cluster of light colored small tract homes. With the coming of the mother of all amusement parks, a spattering of hotels, motels, hamburger joints, beer bars, souvenir hawkers and other diversional delights followed in quick time.

HappyLand Motor Hotel, the name of which intentionally had no space between the words Happy and Land, was one of the first to appear on Harbor Boulevard. Over its half century of life, and several incarnations of gaudy décor, the neon sign out front incessantly blinked its beckoning message to the masses that flocked like lemmings to the sands of Disney. Come here and stay cheap!

The well painted over complex was rated one star. It provided accommodations and respite for visitors of not-too-discerning taste. The place was perfect for those large families that were vacationing on a small budget. It was also perfect for the junkies and johns that just needed a room for a fix or a half hour quickie.

HappyLand, and a few other joints just like it, filled a niche, a social need. It was a place where one could stay awhile without attracting too much attention. The secret to this economical bliss was simple. One only needs to have the right frame of mind. One simply did not worry about what might have stained that mattress before your visit.

With key in hand, the large man approached the door to room 232. The dingy, formerly white plastic Do Not Disturb sign hung on the loose door handle. He was tall and muscular, a good six feet or more. He moved with the casual agility and easy grace of a predator cat.

Around him there was an air of confidence, more like an aura of power that flowed with him. People approaching on the street would generally avert their eyes or simply move over as he passed by. His unusual hair was thick and about the color of dark blood. His skin tone was a mid-winter pale and the eyes, the eyes were the most curious of all. The haunting eyes were downright spooky.

The man's eyes were such a dark brown color that they looked nearly black. Much like a feral animal, direct frontal lighting was required to distinguish any line at all between the pupil and iris. The shape of the eyes was a wide oval, but the position was odd. They slanted ever so slightly upward on the outer edges. It gave him, who otherwise might have looked like any other visitor from Omaha or Paducah, an almost alien look, with a slight oriental cast to his face.

The door rattled open, and he stepped through the doorway. It was about four o'clock in the morning. It would be a couple more hours before the generous California sunshine would break and once again illuminate the world of mouse for yet another day.

The room was dark, the drapes drawn tight. A sick coppery stench permeated the air. On one of the beds, there was a partially clad man. He hovered precariously between sleep and wakefulness. Startled from this twilight of, he quickly raised his upper torso and groped for the knife which had slipped from his sweaty hand. Before his fingers found the locked open blade, a white hot lightening bolt of pain fired through his body. He gasped in agony, but stifled the scream that formed in his throat. His head fell back against the pillow.

"Relax Jiro; it is I, your brother, Ichiro." The tall man spoke in hushed tones. The language was Korean. The name he used, referring to the man on the bed, was Japanese. It meant second born. The speaker's name, Ichiro, was also Japanese. It meant first born.

He closed and locked the door before putting down a brown paper sack. "I brought you some food, and even more important, medicines for your injuries."

Ichiro went to the bedside and gingerly removed the nasty looking blade from Jiro's fingers. He sat down and felt his burning face. Fever raged in his brother's body as the Staph infection, from the festering gunshot wound to the shoulder, ate its way through his body.

It had been such a simple job. All they had to do was kill an old man. The fact that the old man's daughter was present was not a big deal. As with all the other traitors, they had killed on this mission, their instructions were simple. Make a statement. Brutally kill everyone in the house. Had Jiro not been so intent on defiling the woman, he could have dispatched her without giving her the opportunity to put up a fight.

In another turn of bad fortune, Jiro's wound could have been a clean, through and through, shot. But, the round fired from the revolver wielded by Kieko Sung had been pressed to the flesh just underneath Jiro's left clavicle. The .38 caliber slug tore its way through muscle, bone, ligaments, and blood vessel. Then, it carved out a chunk of scapula as the bullet ricocheted and stopped without exiting the body.

With a contact gunshot wound, most of the chemistry expended in the process of expelling the bullet goes right into the body. The mixture of burnt and unburned gunpowder and its chemical derivatives such as barium and antimony fused with seared blood and tissue to form a Petri dish of bacteriological filth. Staphylococcus, streptococcus and a myriad of other biologicals that normally exist in the body in harmless stasis are eagerly waiting, in the wings, so to speak, to pounce and feed on their host.

Keiko Sung, clad only in her nightie, had fought bravely but in vain. Alerted by the ruckus when the intruders broke in to the home, she grabbed the pistol her father had thoughtfully provided only a few days earlier. Ichiro had taken the father and killed him quickly. It was by default that Jiro went to work on Keiko. Had it not been for his unnecessary decision to rape the woman, he might have left the premises unscathed. However, through twisted logic and his predilection for perverted male dominance, he sensed this was a perfect opportunity to torture another traitorous victim.

Like a magic trick, the woman had produced the small handgun out of nowhere. It was almost unbelievable. Ichiro and Jiro were professionals. To be certain, Jiro had done his job. He had killed her. But, how could this have happened? How could this simple peasant woman have so gravely injured one of the DPRK's finest assassins?

The fraternal twin boys, Ichiro and Jiro were the product of the union between Lieutenant Abe Griffin and the Japanese woman that had been abducted from her homeland by North Korean agents when she was only fifteen. Taken to the special prisoner settlement run by Major Pak and his associates, she was "assigned" to live with Griffin. It took many years, over seventeen years, in fact, before nature had finally taken its course. The offspring of Griffin and his common law wife, Natsuko, had been taken away by the couple's keepers when the babies were only three months old.

Prized for their Caucasian appearance and exceptionally high intelligence, the children were spirited away to a secret location. There, they were raised and expertly schooled. Immediately the brothers were enmeshed into the gauzy world of oriental philosophy, dogma and marshal arts. Rather than focusing upon any one of the major disciplines, such as Karate or Tai kwon do, they were rigidly instructed by experts in the method and spirituality of all of the fighting arts.

They were encouraged by psychological specialists to develop behavioral traits that would be considered fundamentally deviant in most civilized cultures. The communist mind molders taught the brothers to develop the callous cruelty of a sociopath toward the suffering of others. Their instruction began with the torturing and killing of small animals. Then they graduated to torturing human beings. Ultimately, they were taught to murder.

By the time the brothers had reached their mid-teens, they had both killed more times than they could remember. They actually enjoyed the act of killing. They enjoyed it as much as one might enjoy playing a casual sporting game.

As their training in the lethal arts reached its crescendo, their patrons had arranged for a continuous stream of live bodies to be available. A nearby penal colony provided most of the victims. The condemned were mostly petty criminals. Some were political prisoners. All were brought to the Brother's Training Compound, as it was called. None of the prisoners left upright.

The boys were taught to kill in virtually every conceivable manner. They became experts with knives, razors and stabbing instruments of all types. They learned to kill by snapping delicate cervical vertebrae, by garroting and common strangulation or suffocation in unlimited variations. They had mastered the art of killing fast as well as torturously slow. At an early age, they could both expertly handle firearms and later, as young adults, they learned all about using precision explosives. Hand to hand combat was mere child's play. They were strong, quick and deadly. The cannon fodder for their ambitious training included men, women and even children.

Ichiro and Jiro were thoroughly schooled in other subjects as well. They were functional in all the dialects of Korean and Japanese by early teens. When they reached young adulthood, they could speak perfect American English, mimic all the regional dialects, and even quote baseball trivia like a couple of boys that had been raised in the shadow of Wrigley Field.

The twins had been brainwashed by constant exposure to socialist doctrine. At a tender age, each could quote chapter and verse, all of the twisted political rationale and dogma that the communist world used to dominate their people. It was an ideology that fostered fear and hatred of the west, a hatred that was particularly focused towards the United States and Japan.

Ichiro and Jiro were agents of the Democratic Peoples Republic of Korea. They were the ultimate espionage products from the paranoid dictatorial system that believed they must have the perfect agents to use against their enemies. Ichiro and Jiro were those consummate agents, ones that could blend in and appear to belong inside any community within Japan or America.

Ichiro pulled the dressing away from the front of his brother's wound. He noted with satisfaction that the major bleeding had stopped. Jiro had lost a great deal of blood. For the moment, there was little he could do about that. Focusing on items that he could deal with, he unpacked his booty and laid the items across the nightstand. There were rolls of sterile gauze and tape. There was a bottle of hydrogen peroxide, a box of 6" gauze squares, a white plastic bottle that was labeled, "Keflex - Cephalexin – Capsules 500 mg."

From the pockets of his windbreaker, he withdrew several pre-loaded syringes. Each were labeled, "Morphine Sulphate Solution – 30 ml. – Controlled Substance – Schedule I". The final items were several tubes of Triple Antibiotic ointment. He added these to his growing pile. Then he rose, stripped off his jacket and went to work.

Jiro's eyes fluttered. Once again, he spoke in raspy Korean. "What... what have you brought?"

Ichiro stripped the plastic sleeve from one of the morphine syringes. He expertly popped off the needle cap, angled the number 20G needle upward and gently pushed on the plunger until a droplet formed. "Here, this will take away the pain, my brother." He slid the needle into the upper muscle of Jiro's good side and injected the clear contents. Then he shook four of the two toned green Keflex capsules from the container, and helped Jiro to swallow them with some water. He choked and coughed, but eventually got all four pills down.

Ichiro then went to work on the wounds. He stripped away the ragged, blood soaked dressings he'd made last night, when he had literally dragged his brother back to the hotel after the fiasco with the Sungs.

Jiro again stirred, the morphine was already beginning to drop its magic veil, easing the pain from his consciousness. He coughed again and again. Each time his body would convulse with the spasms of cough, he would shudder from the pain. Slowly, the cough spasms became more tolerable as the narcotic flowed through his veins.

Ichiro was cleaning the wound. He spoke softly. "The injection is morphine – and the four capsules, they are a strong antibiotic. And when I finish dressing your wounds, you must eat some of this food."

"No – I cannot eat…"

"Jiro, you must! If you do not put food into your stomach, you will vomit the antibiotics. You must force yourself!"

Jiro nodded his agreement. He lay quiet. Alternately he watched his brother work and gazed at an imaginary something that moved in the air, his pupils constricted to pinpoints.

With the crushing pain lifted, Jiro became more lucid and conversational. He asked. "Where did you get these things?"

Ichiro laughed. "I found a medical office. It is called Urgent Care Center. I broke in". He grinned in pride. "There was no alarm, if you can believe that – and I found everything we need, for now…" His voice trailed off as he receded back into his own thoughts.

His mind was flashing through all of the things he now had to do - on his own. Immediately, he knew he couldn't keep Jiro in this place. People would come around, room cleaners and such.

They still had one more target to deal with on this mission. Failure of the mission was not an option. He finished with the bandages. Jiro's wounds were bad, but they could have been much worse. His brother had a good chance of survival, but he had to quickly regain sufficient strength to sustain a move.

Their working protocol was to move every one or two days. They had already been at this place for two nights. Ichiro knew they could not stay much longer.

Conflict ranged within him. He loved his twin brother in a manner that most people could not understand. He was, however, a professional. And Jiro was now a liability to the mission. Both of them understood that if Jiro did not respond quickly, Ichiro would be forced to deal with his brother's condition in a most unpleasant manner.

Chapter 22
Sea of Japan

"Helm, take us to two thousand feet above the seafloor."

"Aye aye, Sir. Two thousand above." The helmsman replied.

Sullivan felt the pressure differential change in his ears as the boat's nose angled upward. All eyes were focused on the large red digital time display above the view screens. Sullivan, Commander Dubord and the entire bridge crew watched as twenty eight long minutes clicked by. Dubord explained that it would take at least that long for the North Korean ships to steam a sufficient distance away, a distance that would allow undetectable use of Huey's broad spectrum search capabilities.

"Carter." Dubord directed his next order to the Lead Sonar and Systems crewman.

"Yes, Sir." Carter replied.

"As soon as we get to depth, do a look-see for anything within range, both surface and below. If we're in the clear, I want a snapshot – three hundred sixty degrees."

"Roger, Skipper. Snapshot."

Dubord angled his head back toward Sullivan. In a low voice he explained. "What we're going to do - is this." He held his hands one above the other modeling his explanation. "We're going to two thousand feet above the seafloor. Once we get there, we level off and do a quick sensor scan to make certain we don't have company. If we're in the clear - and I think we're gonna be - then we use our high end sensors. We're going to do a circular scan with ground penetration."

Sullivan nodded but puzzlement showed on his face.

"Ever see the satellite mapping plots – you know – the low orbit ones that survey the planet with infrared?"

"Yeah, they show pretty good detail – rocks and stuff about a foot across."

"Exactly. Well, we can do that and one better from closer in. We've combined the IR with ground penetrating radar and magnetometer. In about two minutes, from two thousand feet above the seafloor, we can survey a circular area of roughly three square miles. Our resolution is so tight, we can practically read the fine print off a beer can."

Dutifully impressed, Sullivan let out a soft low whistle.

"We can also see below solid surface material – so we can ID objects that – say – have penetrated to a depth of ten meters or so." Dubord grinned. He was obviously proud to be able to talk about the technical marvels of his submarine. "All of this is classified, of course."

"Of course." Sullivan responded. "Goes without saying…"

The helmsman interrupted. "Coming to depth, Sir." Mike could feel the boat start to level off. "We're at sixty-two hundred feet – two thousand above the floor."

"Carter?"

The sonar man scanned his displays for a pregnant moment. "We're clear, Sir. No Company."

"Okay, gentlemen. Snapshot!"

Heads bent to displays. Fingers flew over the console keyboards and switches. There wasn't a sound other than the crew's furious activity. Sullivan watched colorful dancing patterns illuminate most of the front end display screens as thousands of gigabytes of sensor data streamed into the boat's computers.

Dubord's head bobbed and his eyes flicked from screen to screen. To Sullivan, it was just a maze of flashing colored lights. But, he knew the specialists that surrounded him were maximizing the opportunity to do their techno-thing. Frustrated, that he had nothing useful to do, he blew out a long breath in a sigh. He waited as the eternal seconds ticked by.

"Snapshot complete!" It was Carter's voice again.

Dubord barked. "Helm, get us outta here – ahead full and take her down to five hundred above!"

The boat surged forward and the nose pitched down. Dubord got out of his command chair to better watch the forward display screens. He spoke over his shoulder to Sullivan. "We just made so much noise back there – electronic noise that is – that we have to flee the scene, just in case someone may have overheard our scans."

Mike just nodded.

Dubord continued. "Now, let's go take a look at what we got."

The key players of the bridge crew huddled around a glass table that was really a horizontal display screen. Various colored maps and graphs were layered on the display. Items and layers could be enhanced and isolated depending on the settings. Carter, the lead sonar and sensor guy was talking. "Right here, the data shows a scattered debris field that's consistent with an object breaking up and sinking." He pointed to an area on the display. "Significant chunks of the material are metallic, and they're located right along here." He used the eraser end of a pencil to trace out an imaginary cone on the display.

One of the other crewmen said, "That part of the seafloor slopes at an approximate thirty degree angle. Other than the debris, it looks fairly clear. Recovery should be no problem – for the big pieces, at least."

Dubord checked the faces of each of his crew. They all nodded their agreement. "Gentlemen, it looks like we found our North Korean aircraft. Let's go get it!"

"Pick out a smooth parking spot and set her down." Dubord's direction was to the helmsman. He punched another button on his console and spoke to the submersible crew. "Mr. Sells, Mr. Gomez... Are you gentlemen ready to go for a little swim?"

"Aye, Sir. Dewey has all the data plotted and we are ready for separation." Sells' voice had assumed a disembodied treble pitch as they had disconnected their umbilical and were now speaking via the secure ship to ship trans-water link.

"Roger Dewey. We're gonna set Huey on the floor. Stand by."

There was a soft thudding sound throughout the boat as the helmsman, using the steerable vertical thrusters, expertly dropped the sub onto the sandy bottom. Dubord gave the signal to open the rear hatch. Servo motors hummed and the rear doors yawned open like a giant mouth in slow motion.

All eyes were on the central LCD viewing panel. Its current video feed was the systems monitor for Dewey. The panels left and right of the central showed alternating views outside the boat, including a clear shot of Dewey, resting beneath the open doors of the rear hatches, cocooned in her berth. On the central panel, several bar indicators were changing from amber shades to brilliant green. When all the bars were green, Dubord gave the command for separation. The submersible looked like a giant metallic spider with arms folded in tight over her bulbous body. She rose away from her mother submarine, and floated off into the eerie darkness.

Dubord keyed his mike. "Phil, don't dilly dally around... Just grab the big pieces and get back here. We really don't know how much time we've got."

Sells reply had the tinny sing-song characteristic of a sideband signal. "Roger that, Skipper. We'll be quick."

Fascinated, Sullivan watched the images on the display panels as Dewey emerged upward from its womb-like berth. In seconds the craft was clear of the sub. On the display panel currently labeled "Camera Image 2", Sullivan saw a pale flash of a face in one of Dewey's view ports as the craft passed close to the stern video pickup. He couldn't tell if it was Sells or Gomez. He watched as the awkward looking craft moved silently away into the inky blackness.

삼 질식시킴

Sells tinny voice came over the ship to ship. "Huey, we're over the debris field. I, uh, think we'll do a quick once-over before we start to pick up stuff... Uh, so far, it looks like this thing broke up pretty good... The biggest piece is only about a meter or so... Nothing really recognizable so far... Just a bunch of junk."

"Roger that, Phil." Dubord replied.

Sullivan moved closer to the Commander. "How big a piece can they recover?"

"Quite a bit, actually. The biggest item they can grab is a little better than three meters square – say, about a ten by ten foot mass. But, they can bring back quite a bit. Dewey's got a collapsible mesh carry-all – we call it the little red wagon – that deploys from the rear of the submersible. They'll use the articulating arms to pick up objects and place them in the wagon. Then, they just drag the whole mess back home."

Quiet minutes ticked off. Sells voice broke the silence on the ship to ship. "Okay, Huey. We've gotta pretty good idea of the field layout. We've shot some digital video and now we are going to commence recovery... The biggest pieces seem to be on the pointy end of the cone of debris. So, we're gonna start there."

"Roger - starting recovery."

"What the hell..." Sells normally implacable voice was tinged with excitement. "Boss, we've got something odd here..."

The men aboard Huey could hear the chatter between Gomez and Sells. "There – at just about two o'clock – it's flashing blue..."

"Bringing the stern about clockwise…"

"Okay. That's good… There it is again… kind of a bluish glow… and pulsing."

"Yeah, I see it – looks about half buried in the silt – bring the bravo arm to it."

"Huey!" It was Sells voice.

"Go ahead, Phil." Dubord replied.

"We've got an object in the debris field that's got – if you can believe this – it's emitting a blue light - kind of pulsing blue light, quite bright, actually!"

"Roger that. Whaddya think?" Dubord replied.

"Dunno, Skipper. I've never seen anything quite like it. This is way too bright to be bioluminescence… Whatever it is… It's got great batteries… maybe some of those rabbit batteries, to be still juiced up and working at this depth." His tinny voice trailed into a burp of tinny high-pitched laughter before the sound was clipped off.

Dubord chose to ignore the humor. "Dewey, what do your sensors show?"

"Non-ferrous, metallic mass… No radiation, a faint low frequency RF field… Computer projects it to be about one third buried and… It's only about one and a half by two meters overall – yeah, we can pick it up, easy."

"It's your call. Bring it home, if you can."

"Roger that… Here's another interesting tidbit. The closer we get to it, the brighter the light pulses become… We've got a camera on it now. Can you see this thing?"

All eyes were glued to the forward display. Dewey's brilliant halogen light beams penetrated the black water with gauze-like clarity. Bright metal chunks of all sizes, most with ragged edges lay scattered across the ocean floor. One of the large pieces rhythmically glowed with flashes of light. On the control room display, the light was an eerie blue leaning toward purple in color and it pulsed. It pulsed with a rhythm that was close to the rhythm of a human heartbeat.

"Skipper…" It was Carter, the Sonar man. His voice was tinged with excitement, but it was all business. "Contact at one-six-five – another sub - a probable Kilo – range thirty five hundred and closing at the angle."

"Shit." Dubord's utterance was soft and nearly unable to be heard by anyone other than Sullivan. He barked orders. "Carter, plot and confirm."

"Aye, Skipper"

"Dewey – Go quiet – Immediately! Acknowledge."

There was an infinitesimal pause. Sells tinny voice returned. Even with the mechanical distortion, the tone of his speech bled the gravity of the situation. "Dewey - parked and quiet."

"Carter – I'm waiting."

"Aye, Sir. It's definitely a Kilo, unidentified – and a noisy one – bad bearing on prop shaft, I'd guess…"

"Cut the crap, Carter. Where's she going?"

"Yes, Sir. Her course is two-four-three. I'd say she's just cruising by… south of us, at about five hundred feet depth… and if she tracks true, she'll get a little closer – say - a little less than two thousand yards."

Sullivan watched Dubord intently. His eyes begged the question, but he knew enough to keep quiet for the moment. Everyone aboard seemed to be holding their collective breaths.

Chapter 23
Newport Beach, California

Greer found the small industrial center off Superior Avenue without much trouble. Most people have difficulty imagining that a posh town like Newport Beach, a place known for hyper-expensive waterfront mansions and overindulgence in everything on a grand scale, would have anything as common as a light industrial area. But, it does. In a charming northern corner of town, abutting its neighbor, the City of Costa Mesa, one could find a smidgeon of light industrial spaces, mobile home parks and the like. It was here that Greer parked his Honda, and knocked on the blacked out windows and door of the unlabeled suite where Stretch, a scant half hour before, had urgently asked him to meet.

Greer heard the immediate response within to his knocking. Instead of the door opening, there was a flurry of keys turning and latches un-bolting. After what seemed to be an interminable time, the door was finally unlocked and pulled open a couple of feet.

The NBA sized techno-geek beckoned him to enter. "Thanks for coming right over." He said. "I've got something - I think - you'll be interested in."

From the detritus stacked in the small office space and piled against the inside of the door, and the rust breaking squall of the door hinges, it was readily apparent to Greer that people seldom used the front door. He surveyed the mess. Everywhere his gaze landed, there was a floor to ceiling collection of electronic junk. From this, his finally tuned police mind deduced that this place was either seldom used or there must be another entrance. He spoke. "Not a problem. I just didn't think I'd be hearing from you so quickly…"

Only two days had passed since Tim had handed over the suspicious devices that had been removed from the mouths of the murder victims.

"Yeah, well, normally, you wouldn't have. But, you're Mike Sullivan's bud, so…" There was an abrupt pause behind the thick glasses. It was as if Stretch's train of thought had abruptly jumped tracks. "Anyway, I did some quick preliminary checking on these things and…"

Tim could not believe the level of chaos associated with the litter and junk inside the place. He'd known some eccentrics in his time, but this one nearly took the cake. As he precariously stepped over piles of electronic detritus, and angled his way through small mountains of junk, he told himself that no one could really work in an environment like this.

Stretch led him through the maze. Their movements disturbed and misted the air with dust and pollen that most likely had accumulated in place since Neolithic time. The allergy prone Greer felt his sinuses begin to seize. There were radios, computers, large and small equipment cabinets, antennas, metal concave dishes of all sizes and many other things Greer could not identify. The place looked like a surplus warehouse, an electronic bone yard or a scene right out of a sci-fi movie.

Finally, when they had trail blazed their way to the rear of the place, Stretch stopped where a shop, of sorts, had been set up. Greer was led to a small workspace that was an amazing oasis of order, compared to the chaos of the rest of the place. There, atop a workbench, on a blue rubber pad, surrounded by a small army of electronic test and monitoring equipment were the two dental appliances.

Stretch eased down onto the single tall stool that was positioned in front of the workbench. "Mr. Greer… What you've got here is downright spooky!"

"Spooky?"

"Right. Now, one of these things had been deactivated, probably broken in the process of removal. On the other hand – the second one is working just fine – sitting there, just chirping away."

Greer stood next to the workbench, looking down at the items, his face a mask of pained confusion.

Turning to some of the adjacent equipment, Stretch clicked a couple of switches and turned up a dial. "This is the voice of the working model." He said. He cranked up a volume control and a stream of electronic white noise, really not much more than a low hissing sound filled the room.

Greer adjusted his glasses. "I don't get it."

"Have patience - you will. Here, look at this!" Stretch pointed to a green display, not unlike a small computer screen. There were criss-crossed tracings that looked like multiple cardiac monitors in an intensive care unit.

Tim looked, but the flickering display meant nothing to him.

"What - I think - we got here, is a self powered, ultra high frequency, spread spectrum, digitally encoded transponder that can be interrogated by a wide band directed RF signal resulting in a low omni-direction microburst response signal data stream that includes status intelligence and GPS coordinates."

Greer blinked. "Huh? Could you give that to me in English, please?"

"I thought I just did." Stretch frowned, his impatience with the un-initiated to electronic wizardry more than showing. "Look. This is how I think it works..." He picked up one of the devices. "Say, I want to know where you are at all times... So, I put this little do-hickey in your mouth. It's like a little radio transmitter that sends out a signal only when asked. We call that interrogation." Stretch chuckled. "That's a term you cops should be able to identify with." He fingered some controls and watched for Greer's reaction out of the corner of his eye.

Greer let the gibe slide by. He listened.

"So... when I want to know where you are and maybe some other information, I send my interrogation signal – like so..." He punched a button and the response was a burst of tones from the speaker, tones that sounded a bit like the gobbling of turkeys. An intricate pattern of dancing green lines and other unintelligible graphics instantly appeared on the display monitor. The signal lasted for a few seconds and then stopped. Stretch continued. "The transmitter's data stream has imbedded coordinates" – he pointed to the screen – "and those data reference directly to the Global Positioning System. And then, by simply interpreting the GPS coordinates, I know right where you are." Folding his arms across his chest, he rocked back on the stool, his face assuming a Cheshire cat grin.

"So... You think this is some kind of personal locator device?"

"Correct-a-mundo! At the very least, that! The data stream that this thing transmits in response to interrogation is huge. It is way larger than is necessary for simply transmitting a simple GPS location. It's like, sending a small novel, on the order of fifty to a hundred megabytes of data with each burst."

"Wow. All that is coming out of this little thing?"

"Yep. There's some great technology used in this gizmo. Any idea who made it?"

"Not a clue. I was kind of hoping maybe you could help me with that part."

Stretch glanced at the oversized electronic watch-like device that was strapped to his left wrist. He touched some buttons on the device and watched the small readout screen.

"That's quite a watch you've got there." Greer commented.

"It's a little more than a watch..." Stretch responded. "It's more like a remote control to a - a rather big computer that I use. Earlier, I recorded a few rounds of the response data and right now I'm running it through the computer, trying to decipher it. On the surface, I'd say it contains one hell of a lotta information."

"Like what, for example?"

"Like – in addition to where you are - what your body temperature is, heart rate and so on... Hell, I don't really have a clue. I'm just saying; it's a big data stream."

Greer realized his mouth was hanging open. He closed it. "I'm still amazed and way back at the GPS part. How does it work? I mean... Is it like that stolen car locator system?"

Stretch thought about that for a moment. "Yeah, it's similar, but way more sophisticated. My guess is that it works with a satellite. The satellite sends down the interrogation signal, the device responds – reports in, if you will – then the response is relayed to a ground station."

"But, what makes it work? I mean... I don't exactly see batteries hooked up to it."

"I told you, this is really pretty cool technology. This stuff is so advanced, its way beyond cutting edge. This is stuff that – well – hardly anybody has access to, even our illustrious government.

"So, where'd it come from?"

"Beats me. But it's the kinda stuff that super-geeks have wet dreams about. Whoever made these, they have a real gold mine here. I mean – just look at how the thing works... A combination of internal power, chemical power, apparently that uses the body's own fluids - saliva." Stretch reached over the devices and flicked a couple of switches. "Watch this." He pointed to a meter, then leaned over and let droplet of saliva run on to his forefinger. When he touched the saliva finger to the device, the needle on the meter pegged to the right.

Stretch's eyes were a little glazed. "Is that cool, or what? It's like a little chemical power cell... And it also uses reflective power, inductive, most likely, from the satellite interrogation signal. This thing really is amazing!"

Greer gingerly picked up one of the dental appliances. "So, this thing is on right now and it's telling somebody – when asked..."

"Interrogated."

"Yeah, interrogated... Then it reports its location?"

"Yep."

"And it's reporting right now – where we are?"

"Umm, not quite. This room is sort of insulated. The transponder's signals can't get in or out."

"Really!" Greer replied. "That must be difficult. How'd you do that?"

"Long story... Look, check your cell phone. Five bucks says it's not working."

Greer fished through his pockets and produced his phone. He looked at the display, then turned and showed it to Stretch. The display blinked "No Service".

Chapter 24
Sea of Japan

Dubord studied the control room displays. Alternately, his eyes flicked from the screens and across the control room crewmembers. Each was pursuing their assigned tasks with virtually no sound. Dubord's strained his ears. The boat, the crew, everything was incredibly quiet. The sound, or lack of it was unnerving, like a silent communion with death. They watched and listened and waited.

Finally, Dubord turned and looked at Sullivan in the jump seat. He moved his head close to Mike's and in a soft whisper he said, "This is an old Russian sub, a diesel electric boat. It could be anybody's, Russian, North Korean, hell, even the Iranians own a couple... we don't know for certain – the Russians sold these damn things to practically everyone – if I had to venture a guess – I'd bet that this one is North Korean."

Mike nodded his understanding. He whispered. "Can they see us?"

"Probably not... Not unless they get real close. But they can see and hear Dewey. She's vulnerable as long as she's out there.

"Skipper, sonar!" It was Carter's distinct voice but in hushed tones.

"Talk to me, Carter." Dubord's reply was equally soft.

"Sir, the Kilo's turning toward us... She's coming to... She's now tracking at two-six-oh."

"Nav, give us a mercator display." Dubord ordered. Instantly, one of the forward bulkhead LCD panels displayed a computer generated overhead projection map of the area. The locations of Huey, Dewey and the approaching Kilo blinked in different colors. The menacing Kilo was appropriately colored red.

"Skipper, we got enough for computer ID match on the Kilo. It's the Han-Sung... That's North Korean, known numbers to be three-five-seven."

"Okay... What do we know about her? What's she got?"

Carter's fingers flew over the keyboard. "Looks like she's an early model - an 877 basic model - not known to have the Lada refit.

She can carry..." Carter was reading from the screen. "Eighteen torpedoes with six in the tubes and twelve stored on the racks. Alternatively the torpedo tubes can deploy mines. The submarine can carry 24 mines with two in each of the six tubes and twelve on the racks. Two torpedo tubes are designed for firing remote-controlled torpedoes with a very high accuracy. All torpedo tubes and their service systems provide effective firing from periscope to operational depths. The computer-controlled torpedo system is provided with a quick-loading device. It takes only 15 seconds to prepare stand-by torpedo tubes for firing: The first salvo is fired within two minutes..."

"Enough- thanks Carter - Roger all that. How about her ears?"

"Skipper, this model came with both active and passive sonar... some models could handle a small towed array, although I don't hear the sounds of one... Again, I think this is a probable 877 basic class Kilo."

"Good. Let's just hope our DPRK friends haven't scraped up the money for any systems upgrades." Dubord again leaned over towards Sullivan and spoke in a voice barely above a whisper. "It's an older model with – hopefully – older systems. We should be okay. They're practically blind and deaf compared to us... Unless they're already on to us, or they decide to go active with their sonar we should be good..." His voice trailed.

Sullivan studied the face of the young naval Commander. He knew he was in the presence of a one-in-a-million caliber of man. For those who would deign to command a nuclear submarine, it was an exclusive club, indeed. Most candidates begin with IQs within the sheer genius range. Coupled with that would be a level of technical and engineering training that dwarfs the total education of most professionals. Added to that was the necessity to be a capable people person, adept in the fine art of managing a diverse group of highly trained professionals who constantly worked under great stress. On top of all that was stacked the fact that this particular sub was like no other. It's very existence and operation was covert and hidden within the private sector. Dubord and his crew lived a life of constant plausible deniability. The stress had to be enough to crack most men.

Mike stood close enough to Dubord that he could see the fine sheen of sweat appear over the officer's face. It was actually quite cool inside the submarine. He was betting - hoping actually - that Dubord was equally cool, inside his head.

More eternally long, life-consuming minutes ticked past.

It was Carter's voice that again broke the silence. "Han-sung is still tracking steady at two-six-zero. She's passing right over us..."

Sullivan could feel the collective sigh of relief from the control room crew and himself. All eyes watched the LCD map display. The blinking red indicator for the Kilo class submarine moved steadily away from their position.

Dubord was on the ship to ship. "Dewey – copy - the contact is leaving the area?"

Sells disembodied mechanical voice returned. "Roger that... We are parked and shut down, by the way."

"Good. Stay that way until we're certain this guy is outta here."

"Roger that... We're ready to go collecting whenever you give us the okay."

삼 질식시킴

Dubord gave it another sixteen minutes. Finally, he cleared Dewey to commence salvage ops. Inside Dewey, Gomez and Sells re-approached the debris field and using the robotic arms of their submersible, they gingerly picked up key pieces of the wreckage and stowed them into the "little red wagon". Sullivan, Dubord and the other control room crewmembers listened and watched the time display.

Seventy eight minutes later, Dubord was on the ship to ship getting a status report. He was encouraging Sells to wrap it up. He rightly figured that the ship on fire ruse would have played itself out by now, and the patrol vessels could be returning at any time.

Sells was speaking. "We've got nearly a full load now, Skipper. We're going for that one piece with the blue light right now... Then we'll be on our way back home."

"Okay... But, shake a leg."

Despite the sophistication of the sensors, video displays and the data transmitted ship to ship, what they could not see from their Control Room perspective was the totality of the scene that was playing out at the debris field. Sells had expertly used the Dewey's thrusters to position the submersible slightly down slope from the last piece. Just as before, when they neared the object, the blue pulsations grew more frequent and intense. The light emanating from the wreckage actually appeared to pulse faster and brighter the closer they came.   Sells settled the craft onto the seabed for stability and Gomez moved the large spider-like arm with the large gripping hand toward the piece of wreckage.

Charlie had practiced with the submersible's collection system previously in the Seattle factory computer simulation room.   Like flying, simulators were a less than perfect substitute for the real thing. He'd been at the collection controls throughout this entire mission. Gomez got along with mechanical things.   He was more than just getting the real hang of it.   He had it down.   Sells piloted and Gomez retrieved.   They were a good team.   Charlie eyeballed a spot on this piece of wreckage where he thought he could get good purchase.   The titanium arm angled forward from overhead.   He corrected with a bit of left slew.   His fine tuning brought the arm into a near perfect position.   His left hand operated a joy stick and the right was inserted into a virtual reality glove.   Over one hundred sensors within the glove tracked the miniscule muscle movements of his fingers and transmitted the exact commands to the robotic arm.   He gently pinched his thumb and forefinger together, commanding the mimic robot arm to grip the piece.

What happened next was like a lightening strike – and just about as devastating.   When the gripping arm made contact with the piece, an arc of blue-white fire ran up the arm and enveloped the tiny submersible.   Immediately, all onboard systems crashed, the lights blinked out and they were thrust into blackness.   The submersible began to vibrate with bone-jarring intensity.   After a few seconds, the craft was blown away from the debris field.   It was as if a giant finger had reached down and flicked away an undesirable speck of lint.

The experimental craft had considerable safety features built into its basic design.   Among those was the ability for the crew module, an elongated sphere, to be separated from the rest of the craft for a minimally controlled, buoyant emergency ascent.   This happened automatically.   Explosive bolts blew.   Interlocking pins slid away and control cables detached.   The working guts of the submersible, including the power modules, lighting, thrusters, articulating arms and all of the collected items stored in the little red wagon, quickly sank to the seafloor.   The submersible parts plowed into the ocean bottom silt, stirring up billowing dark clouds of particulate matter.

The bulbous crew module, like an amputated spider's abdomen, slowly floated away.

Chapter 25
Buena Park, California

Ichiro cruised by the house on Palomar Street. The September sun had just dropped over the horizon. For a few more minutes, there would be sufficient light to enable him to scout out the home of his remaining target. Early evening was a good time to case. People were out and about – moving. One more grey Ford Taurus, such as the rental car he drove, could easily pass by the location several times without raising so much as an eyebrow of interest.

He prided himself on being the consummate professional, and for good reason. He was at the absolute top of his game. He was smart, confident, strong and agile. His superior physical conditioning and rigorous training had turned him into an incredibly dangerous man. He was both skilled and psychologically adept at the acts of hunting and killing human beings. Despite all that, he was having difficulty with the task at hand. For the first time, while on a mission, his thoughts were clouded.

Earlier, and against his better judgment, he had left Jiro alone inside the Anaheim motel room. Ensuring that the "do not disturb" sign was hung on the door was the best he could do. Ichiro had stayed with his brother through out the entire day. Jiro had required two more of the morphine injections. It was necessary to keep him sedated – at least drowsy if not completely out. The downside was, that in his stupor, he was unable to eat. Without food, Jiro continued to weaken.

All day Ichiro guarded and cared for his brother. He planned his moves for tonight and cat-napped when he could. On two occasions, he had managed to forestall the entry of the cleaning ladies, once in the late morning and one other time, when a woman knocked on their door in the early afternoon. He believed - he hoped - that they would not be again bothered by hotel personnel until the following morning. By then, he would have to take action. He had to move Jiro or…

His train of thought abruptly braked. These thoughts were absurd and unacceptable. He was allowing these scurrilous and wandering thoughts to weaken him! He summoned his mental discipline. As the Ford slowed at a four way stop, he briefly closed his eyes and took in a deep breath. He could feel the anxieties flowing away from his consciousness. He forced his mind to clear and to focus - to focus on completing the mission and nothing else.

As he re-honed the edge of his mental blade, he recited the mantra of his homeland. It was the dogma of Korean Communism, the catechism with which he had been raised.

He believed that Americans were lazy, slothful and dumb. He believed that capitalism was innately wrong, that uneven distribution of goods and wealth bred a society of classes in which the masses were forced to live in poverty and subjugation. He despised the Americans. To him they were nothing more than cattle - unfit for anything other than slaughter.

Once again, he abruptly chastised himself for such having ridiculous thoughts. He reminded himself that the targets on this mission were not Americans. They were Korean citizens. No... They were scum that had formerly been citizens of the DPRK... They had been privileged to work for the people on the most sensitive of military projects... They had been entrusted with the greatest of his Motherland's secrets - privileged and entrusted for the greater good of the Democratic Republic...

The results of their project, the power that would rightfully flow to their comrades and their homeland would surely result in the elevation of the DPRK to a country of superpower status. Then, finally, their country could be re-united, and the vision of their Great Leader would be fulfilled. The one, country of Korea would become the greatest military and economic leader of not only Asia, but the entire world.

Ichiro's mental meandering abruptly switched to the task at hand. The former comrades that he and Jiro had been tasked to hunt down were now nothing more than vermin. They had violated their sacred trust. They had abrogated their responsibilities to their Korean brethren. The traitorous scum had taken their secrets and fled... Like thieves into the night, they had defected and found their way into the U.S. - only to be welcomed and coddled by the Americans, their sworn enemies. They had sold their precious secrets for money and personal comfort.

A sneering smile formed across Ichiro's lips. Now, he and Jiro had come to even the score. The brothers were performing their most important mission yet, in the service of the people. Here, in the very heart of America, Ichiro and Jiro were exterminating those vermin that had turned against friends and family, the family of the Korean people.

Ichiro had only this one remaining target. After tonight their mission would be complete. After tonight's task, they would make good their escape.

For the umpteenth time, he cruised past the pale yellow house with the white trim, his ferret-like eyes memorizing every detail. Like many of the Orange County neighborhoods they had visited on this mission, the homes that lined the streets were at least fifty or sixty years old. Arranged in neat little rows, the roadways had once been acres of citrus groves, yielding year after year the oranges and lemons that fueled the early economy of Southern California. After World War II, the groves had dropped to the crushing bulldozer blades of developers. The terrain had been carved into perfect rectangular blocks, each with twelve home sites, seventy five feet by one hundred feet deep. On each site was perched a small house, less than a thousand square feet of living space. With cookie-cutter precision, the tiny houses had been mass produced, each with two or three bedrooms, a kitchen, small dining and living rooms and a single bathroom.

Before they became neighborhoods, they were called G.I. housing tracts or projects. Following the war, the tiny, affordable houses were built by the thousands all over California. The demand for homes was nearly unquenchable. Returning soldiers and sailors from all over America either stayed in the Golden State or soon returned to it after their return to places like Des Moines, Cleveland, Boise and Tupelo.

Ichiro again passed by the house on Palomar. This was to be his final circuit and he completed it in a clockwise fashion, so he now viewed everything to his right. He clicked open the glove box and removed what looked like a common digital camera. He pressed the button to power on the device and the lens assembly clicked and whirred as it telescoped into position. As his car passed by he briefly held the camera at eye level and pressed the shutter button, as if he were snapping a picture. Then he brought the camera to a position where he could view the small color picture screen. A smile of satisfaction returned to his face as the radio transponder within the very body of his target acknowledged the man's presence. In Korean Ichiro said softly but aloud. "Ah, Mr. Ahn Kyong Sho is presently at home."

He noted the position of trees, shrubs and the tiny detached garage building in the rear. He took in the shared fence lines with the adjacent homes, cars parked in front of the homes, both on the street and in the driveways. The target's house was third in line from the end of the street. At the top of the block, the intersection of Palomar and the cross street, Sumner, he turned right and spotted a good place to stash his car and from there to make his approach.

He checked the time. He had several hours to kill. He pointed the rental car back towards Anaheim and the HappyLand Motor Hotel.

Chapter 26
Sea of Japan

The soft circulation of air within the sub's control room did little to soothe their concern. Everyone sat on pins and needles, sweating out whatever was going to happen next.

When the noise spike came, the crew's group reaction looked somewhat like an ungainly dance troupe. In unison, hands flew up to ears that wore the remote communications devices; the jagged squeal raked across their senses. The caustic noise sounded like giant fingernails being dragged across a chalk board. Data that had been streaming to the forward displays abruptly stopped. Most of the display screens went to black or to flickering raster.

Dubord popped his earpiece out. "What the hell was that?"

Carter was the first to respond. "Some kind of energy burst – not quite an explosion – I think."

Others began to report in.

"We've lost the telemetry from Dewey."

"Sir! The Kilo is now diving - and turning toward us. She's picked up on - whatever that was!"

Carter's voice broke in again. "Sir, best I can figure – something bad, very bad, happened with Dewey. We got the energy burst, followed by a failure of all major systems on Dewey and…" Carter swiveled in his chair to face Dubord. His voice was somber. "Then, we got a crew capsule jettison signal - and after that nothing…"

Dubord was on his feet in a flash. He moved to each of the key crew stations. At each console, he hunched over the shoulders of his crewman and read the displays for himself, confirming their interpretations of what had just happened. Finally, he stood stock still, a worried look set into his face. He stood like this for several seconds, one hand wrapped across his lower jaw, the other tucked into a back pocket. Time crawled. The crewmen watched their Captain's face, waiting for what seemed an eternity, but in reality was only a second or two. Abruptly, Dubord started barking orders. "Comm! Flash traffic to the Glomar. Give them our status."

"Aye, aye, Sir."

"Sonar – Give me constant updates on the Kilo."

"Aye, Skipper."

"Anything little noise, I mean anything at all, especially like a tube door opening or any fish sounds, tell me - right now. Got it?"

"Aye, Sir – Skipper, it looks like she's headed right toward the debris field now - at six hundred feet and descending."

"Copy that… Helm, stay slow and as quiet as you can, but take us up and over to the field – Carter!"

"Sir?"

How many layers between us and the Kilo?"

Carter studied his displays. "At least three good ones, Skipper. One's at twelve hundred, another at twenty one hundred and a fat one about thirty five hundred. His crush depth is only…"

"Rated at three hundred meters – I know – thanks."

"I wouldn't be playing any loud music or banging cans together, Skipper, but my guess is he can't hear us at all way down here."

"Very well – Move the boat – but lets stay very damn quiet - people." Heads nodded all around.

Sullivan had bounded to his feet when the energy jolt was felt. He stood directly behind Dubord, heart pounding from the adrenaline, knowing better than to open his mouth. His guts were sinking at the likely prospect of what may have just happened to Gomez and the other guy in the submersible, but he held his tongue.

Vibrations shuddered through the boat as the sub broke its mild suction contact with the sandy seafloor. The ship ascended slightly and then surged ahead. Mike felt the slight forward motion.

Some of the forward visual displays began to show data including computer imaging of their progress over the seafloor. Within moments they were over the debris field. The sophisticated sensors created ghostly green-hued images, seeing with their uncanny ability to look through the infinite blackness, even where the most brilliant lights could not penetrate.

"Anything at all on ship-to-ship from Dewey?"

The communications officer shook his head. "Nothing, Sir. Just absolute quiet."

"Okay. Keep trying."

Dubord finally turned to face Sullivan. Their eyes locked and while nothing was said, a good deal of understanding passed between them. After a moment, Sullivan started to speak. "What…"

Dubord cut him off with an upraised open hand. "Wait – Carter, have you replayed your data?"

"Yes, Sir – several times now. There's nothing new."

"Give it to me again, anyway – chapter and verse."

Carter began his recitation. He droned on and on with technical mumbo-jumbo concluding with, "then, we got the crew capsule jettison signal - and then - nothing - since then, no more data."

Sullivan could see the mind working behind Dubord's sparkling eyes. Dubord spoke again, "Time since the event?"

"Eleven minutes and counting, sir."

"Carter, give me a rate of ascent projection for the capsule."

"Aye, Sir." The crewman's fingers flew over his keyboard. Data flashed on his screens. In a moment, he began to speak. "If the design spec's hold and the emergency buoyancy compensators work – meaning the compensators weren't damaged in the event - they should reach the surface in ninety-two point four minutes from separation…"

"Okay. Plot that time and work out a layer flow…"

"Way ahead of you, Sir." A slight smile formed at the edges of Carter's mouth. "I should be able to tell you almost exactly right where and when they should pop up – just gimme a minute." Carter, fingering his keyboard furiously, went back to work.

Dubord turned to the sonar crewman. "The Kilo?"

"Sir, she's over us now – slowed to steerage speed – and she's holding about seven hundred foot depth. She's not gone active – yet."

"Very good." Dubord turned back to Sullivan. "Sorry Sullivan… What were you saying?"

Mike was trying to formulate the correct question. "How bad…"

"How bad is it?" Dubord, not one for small talk in a crisis, finished Sullivan's question. "I won't BS you, Mr. Sullivan." He took a long breath. "Right now, it's just about as bad as it can get. All indications are that our submersible was subjected to an energy burst of some type – maybe some kind of a low order explosion. We don't just know exactly. We've got that North Korean sub above us – she can't come down this far, but they could send a remote - or worse, a torpedo down to visit…" Dubord's eyes darted from screen to screen as he talked. The serious eyes flicked back to Sullivan's face. "We've got indications that Dewey separated... That means... You see, Dewey was designed so that the crew module can separate from the working platform. In the event of a catastrophic emergency, the crew cab separates and theoretically floats back up to the surface."

Sullivan nodded. "Yeah, but won't it just pop up like a rocket – I mean doesn't the capsule's buoyancy increase logarithmically with the ascent as gases expand?"

"Yes and no. Yes, insofar as your understanding of the physics – that part is correct – in an uncontrolled ascent they'd go faster and faster, to the surface and a certain death. But, the designers anticipated some events like this tried to build into her some pretty sophisticated automatic systems, including buoyancy compensation. The issue now is, have those systems been compromised. For all we know, the crew cab and our guys could have been blown to pieces..."

"Or if the pressure hull is damaged... they'd be crushed like..."

Dubord just nodded.

"Sir, more bad news." The voice was the second sonar crewman. "Surface ships inbound – two again. The same two we had before – positive ID. It's the Yang-Tou and that twin screw trawler."

"Great! More folks for the party." Dubord turned to the driver. "Helm, are we about over that field?"

"Coming up on it now, Skipper. He toggled some controls and three of the foreword screens began to show a greenish panorama display of what was ahead and directly below.

All eyes went to the forward screens.

Sullivan marveled at the display. The imagery was mostly green and yellow, but was so detailed it was like flying in a sophisticated airplane simulator. The ship literally flew over the terrain. The Sea floor unfolded below them. They cruised silently over rock piles, arroyos. Gigantic buttes and outcroppings loomed up and scrolled silently away to the bottom edge of the screens.

"Skipper, we're on the debris field - now."

Dubord stepped forward for a closer look at the screens. He spoke over his shoulder, eyes never leaving the scrolling screens. "Can you colorize the displays?"

One of the crewmen nodded and touched controls at his console. He spoke, "Won't be perfect, sir... but here you go." Instantly the collage of screens making the panorama went from greens to brilliant colors. The reds, blues, yellows and oranges were so intense the entire display looked more like a movie dreamscape than actual seafloor.

"Try to tone it down a bit." Dubord suggested.

The crewman clicked a few key strokes and the colors muted down to more believable levels.

"Okay people… Now, let's find our submersible."

"There - Skipper. There's the cone pattern of - junk. Chunks of the airplane wreckage scrolled across the screens. One of the larger pieces at the edge of the field pulsed with an eerie bluish glow.

"And there it is… Sir, I think that's the blue thing they were after."

"Roger that… and keep some distance from that thing!"

"Aye, Sir."

"Anything that looks like Dewey… or parts of her?"

"Nothing yet, sir."

"Very well. Circular search pattern."

"Aye, Sir – circular pattern." The helmsman responded.

"Skipper…" The businesslike voice was Carter's. "I've got the surfacing plot." He stood and approached the table top display. Once again using his yellow number two pencil, he tapped the glass display. Both Dubord and Sullivan moved to the table and looked down at the map display. Carter explained. "They should zig-zag a little going up, and they'll pass through several layers, but the prevailing current influence is westerly… so, they should surface somewhere right about here, give or take a quarter mile or so." The eraser tapped a spot on the display.

"Good work, Carter." Dubord actually showed a hint of smile. "Plot it and work out an ascent course for us. I want to be on station at that exact spot, say… three minutes before they surface."

"Aye, Sir." Carter turned and briskly went back to his work station."

Dubord started to move away toward his station. Sullivan stopped him by grabbing his forearm. His voice was low. "Can you pick them up? Is that what you're aiming for?"

Dubord considered the big man for a moment. He looked down at Mike's hand on his arm. Embarrassed, Sullivan released his grip. Dubord's gaze returned to Sullivan's face. Finally he spoke. "Maybe… Look, I know Gomez is your friend, but we've got a lot at stake here… and there's a lot of variables in play. If - and note I say if

- the crew module gets to the surface, and if our surfacing plot is anywhere near correct, and if they are alive and have enough steam left to exit the module - yeah, we can pick them up."

Mike nodded and stepped back. Dubord leaned in and eyed him squarely. His gaze was even and his voice low. "Understand me, Sullivan. I want these men back, too. Hell, Right now I want these guys back in good shape more than anything in the world. But you and I both know we might be just going after crushed bodies. After all, something – what, we don't have a clue - punted that submersible practically into the end zone. Then, after the crew module separated, they have to ascend six thousand feet." He paused a moment as if to collect his thoughts. "There's a good possibility that Sells and Gomez are now the consistency of peanut butter and jelly. I've got thirty-two more souls in this boat. As long as we stay down here we've got the edge. The moment we surface, we are exposed to serious jeopardy."

"Sir, we've got something here!" The helmsman's voice was tinged with excitement. "I think we found Dewey's platform!"

Everyone angled to watch the forward display consoles. Below them lay the severed work platform of the submersible Dewey. The platform consisted of four rows of elongated cylinders which contained the power modules and much of the working guts of the tiny craft. The jumble was held together by a maze of tubes, cables and intersecting rectangular contraptions. The platform was laying on what had been its starboard side. A quarter of the superstructure was buried in the silt of the sea floor. Its spider-like arms were splayed out in a death-like pose. Curiously, there appeared to be little or no damage to the unit. It almost appeared to be fully intact with the glaring exception of the missing crew module.

"It appears completely powered down, sir. There's not a hint of activity there. All of our sensors are flat."

Dubord nodded. "Carter. How far is it from the... that blue thing?"

"We are one hundred and twelve meters from that location, sir."

Dubord looked at Sullivan. "Damn... Something knocked that submersible three hundred feet in..."

"A blink?" Sullivan offered.

Dubord nodded.

"Sir! Active sonar from the Kilo!"

"Acknowledged... Carter, can we go evasive and still make the surface rendezvous?"

Carter checked the time and clicked furiously at his keyboard. "Yes, Sir. It'll be close... but, we can make it – with just about enough for your three minute margin."

Dubord made a snap decision. "Systems! Launch Louie and park him near that blue piece of wreckage."

"Aye Sir."

"Helm – the minute Louie is clear of the boat, head for Carter's rendezvous coordinates." Dubord quickly surveyed the serious faces of his crew. "Let's go get our men back!"

Chapter 27
Santa Ana, California

Greer hung up the phone and slumped back into his chair. "God Damn FBI..." He muttered aloud to no one in particular. He leaned back and tried to rub away the spreading pain behind his temples. Three days ago he'd visited the FBI field office in Santa Ana. He met with an Agent and laid out his theory about a possible connection between the Korean homicide victims. He had even included the information about the similar dental devices having been found in some of the victims. He had chosen not to describe what he had learned from Stretch about the electronic properties of the devices, at least for the time being. The Agent had been polite and attentive, and had dutifully taken copious notes along with Greer's list of victims. The Agent had promised to look into it and get back with him. Now that Agent was not available, not returning calls.

Just now as Greer plunked his phone handset back into the cradle, yet another Agent at that office had told him that his original Agent had been sent somewhere for a temporary assignment; and he didn't know anything about the Korean homicides. Greer's face went dark. He fumed.

Lieutenant Blair stuck his head over the wall of Greer's cubicle. "I can practically see the steam coming out of your ears! Lemme guess, you're trying to get some cooperation from the Fender and Body Institute."

Greer leaned back in his swivel chair. He stared blankly at his boss. Then he brought his hands down and loudly slapped open palms onto the arms of the chair. "Christ, what is it about these guys? I mean... you'd think we worked on different planets or something."

Blair tried for his most concerned expression. "Oh, Timmy... Yah know, we do inhabit different worlds..."

"Come on Lieutenant, why can't these guys be a little more forthcoming? Christ, we're all cops aren't we?"

Before Blair could formulate a response, Greer's telephone started its incessant electronic trill. Greer glanced at the Caller-ID and looked up sheepishly and said, "Sorry, I gotta take this." He reached for the receiver.

Blair waved and disappeared.

The call was from Sullivan's Korean friend, Mr. Kim, the convenience store owner and unofficial oracle within the Orange County Korean community. His message was succinct and simple. "We need to talk; come to my store."

Greer was up and out of there like someone had jabbed him in the butt with a hot poker. He paused momentarily by the sign-out board and scrawled "beeper" next to his name.

Exactly seventeen minutes later Detective Tim Greer walked through the front door of Kim's Market on Bristol Street.

Mr. Kim greeted him cordially and ceremoniously escorted him into a curtained rear room. There, in the modest living space that he shared with Mrs. Kim, Greer was asked to sit and offered tea.

Impatient to move things along, Greer had considered refusing, but immediately thought better of it and gratefully accepted the tea - black.

The dark steaming brew that Mr. Kim poured from the ornate white porcelain teapot was mouth-puckering bitter. Greer sipped at the vile brew and forced a smile, while watching Mr. Kim shovel spoon after spoon of white sugar into his own cup. Greer was certain that at any time the handle would emerge with a disintegrated spoon because the acid-like brew had dissolved it. Never-the-less, he managed to smile and sip lightly at his cup.

Mr. Kim positioned himself directly across the small table and facing Greer. Their heads were no more than a foot apart. Kim, like Greer, also wore glasses, albeit, his were many years dated and had thick heavy lenses. At the short proximity, they gave his eyes a giant-size, almost owlish look. Kim fished in his shirt pocket and removed a soft pack of Marlboro cigarettes. He shook one out and offered the smoke to Greer.

"Uh… No thank you. I - uh - don't smoke."

Kim shrugged and stuck the cork tip between his lips. From no-where, a silver Zippo appeared and ignited the smoke. The Zippo had the insignia of the 1st Calvary Division, old horseshit and gunpowder. Greer knew the distinctive emblem. His Father had served in that unit during the Korean War – the Korean conflict – as it was called.

A halo of blue grey smoke wafted around the salt and pepper head of Mr. Kim. He took a long drag and exhaled, mostly all over Greer. Tim briefly thought about discussing the dangers of second hand smoke, but vetoed that idea. Greer had rightly had figured out that Mr. Kim was sizing him up. He decided to let Kim lead the dance. He held his teacup, sat quiet and waited.

Finally, after a few more lung-wrenching drags and the appearance of great pondering, Kim began to speak. "I am talking to you about these things... because you are... " Kim appeared to be choosing his words slow and deliberate, more an act of conscious deliberation rather than unfamiliarity with English. "Because you - are an associate of Michael Sullivan." He paused on this point as if to make a point. "Michael Sullivan - is a man that I trust - and under different circumstance - I would rather..." Again, Kim considered his use of words. "I would rather be telling this information to Mister Michael Sullivan."

Kim's pause begged for a response. Greer finally spit out, "I understand - and I appreciate your candor, Mr. Kim. And I remind you that Sullivan sent me to you in the first place." He added somewhat lamely. "And right now, Sullivan's gone – he's traveling somewhere – out of the country, I think." He added even more lamely.

Mr. Kim stabbed out his smoke. "I know. That is why we – you and me – are having this little talk now." He grinned and gestured in a circle. "Now, I will tell you everything that I know – everything that I have learned about this problem."

Greer nodded.

"But, you should know that even more Korean peoples can be hurt - even killed - if this information is not handled correctly." The syllables of the word cor-rect-ly were long and exaggerated.

"I understand." Greer nodded.

"Mr. Greer, you are correct - in your assumption that there is a connection between the Korean peoples who have been killed. In each case..." Kim paused and ticked off fingers as he slowly named each of the victims. "All of them - the victims - were from - what you refer to as North Korea."

Greer nodded sensing that he was finally onto something. The obsessive side of him desperately wanted to take some notes; but the common sense side dared not to upset what he perceived was a very delicate balance at work. He continued to sit and nod and listen.

"Each of these Korean peoples came to the U.S. as immigrants seeking political asylum. Most came very quietly." He grinned. "Some came – how is it you say – with wet back?"

"You mean they were illegal immigrants"? Greer nearly bit his tongue hoping he had not stemmed Kim's flow with his question.

It was Kim's turn to nod. And he continued. "These Korean Peoples are - each is a specialist, a scientific specialist. All of them worked on projects that the North Koreans consider very - confidential."

"You mean like secret stuff – top secret things?"

"Yes – very, very secret things - military things."

Greer nodded, redoubling his efforts to keep his mouth shut.

These Korean peoples left... they escape... and come to America. Some come through Canada; others went into Japan and Mexico and then come into the U.S." He paused and sat back a bit and smiled. It was as if he was savoring this next piece of the story. "Some came" – He leaned back in to Greer - "with the assistance of your U.S. Government."

Greer pondered this for a moment. "I see." A light bulb went off in Greer's head. "Do you know what kind of assistance?"

"Yes. U.S. government gave money, houses and jobs. In some cases they helped in reuniting families - brothers, sisters and children. They also helped them with papers, identity and immigrations."

Greer sat upright as another flash bulb popped in his mind!

"The talk within the Korean Community is that these specialists were... killed... as punishment for their traitorous acts. You see, the North Korean leaders are...

"Murdering bastards?"

"The word I was thinking of was... cruel. They wish to make example... make example by hunting down and killing all who would leave the motherland of Korea – that is – North Korea. That is why – in many cases - even other peoples – innocent peoples – like wife, and children are also killed."

The pieces of the puzzle were starting to coalesce. Greer felt a surge of excitement course through him. He held it in check and listened on.

Kim withdrew a fresh smoke and re-created the blue cloud. "The word is that these peoples were working on a secret project that would give North Korea great status – they would be a super-power country – like America. They left because they did not want the crazy leaders to have this power. They – like many of the Korean peoples - want for re-unification of our country – but, do not want it to be under the iron fist of a crazy man!" To make his point, Kim balled up his right hand into a fist and slammed the table top. The tea service jittered, but survived. "So now they are to be punished." Kim sat back in his chair. "That's it!"

Greer interpreted this as a possible end point. He had a ton of questions and thought it timely to venture a few. "So, what do they say - in the community - about who might be doing these murders?

Kim held up both hands and shook his head. "Nothing – it is a question that I have asked. Everyone just believes it is gangsters – gangsters hired by the North Korean leaders."

"You mean - American gangsters?"

"Don't know. Could be - could be any gangsters - who would kill for money."

Briefly the thought that Mr. Kim might be watching too much TV flitted through Greer's mind. "Okay... Have all the scien... I mean specialists been killed – or – are there more of them?"

"Don't know."

"Okay... does anyone – that is anyone in the Korean Community - know any more about this situation?"

Kim pondered that one a moment. "Don't know... but if there are more peoples who know about situation... I am certain they would not talk - to you." That final piece of information was delivered matter-of-factly, without hint of emotion.

It was Greer's time to ponder. Finally he asked, "Is there anything, anything more – no matter – how small or insignificant you might think it may be, about this... situation..." He purposely used Kim's word. "that you could tell me today?"

Kim answered immediately. "No, Mr. Greer. I have told you everything I have learned."

Greer nodded and placed his teacup on the table. "Thank you, Mr. Kim. And thank you for the tea, as well." He rose to leave.

Kim followed him out into the store stopping just near the front door. "Mr. Greer."

Tim turned to face him.

"When Mr. Sullivan returns... Please tell him to visit me."

Greer regarded the elder Korean man and briefly wondered how much he had purposely not been told today. "I will." He answered with a wave and left.

Lieutenant Pat Black of the Buena Park Police Department sat back in his chair and ran a hand over his thinning hair. A twenty-eight year veteran of police work, he had seen and heard nearly everything, he thought. But this one had nearly – no – this one had taken the cake. He looked at his watch. It was nearly 6:30 PM. He had assumed his role as the evening shift Watch Commander a scant two and a half hours ago.

Just minutes after his shift started, the desk officer, a two-striper by the name of Barlow, had called him on the intercom. Barlow was a good street cop with lots of savvy and good instincts. He was riding the desk – a dismal job, but light duty - while he nursed a bum knee from scope surgery.

"Ell – Tee, I've got this Korean guy in the lobby. I think you should hear his story. It's a little far out, but it might have something to do with those Asian only murders we got the Bolo on…"

Bolo, or Be-On-The-Lookout bulletin. It was an appropriate, if less than artful, name for a very simple but effective technique for sharing information inside the world of cop.

Barlow had listened to a bit of the story from Mr. Ahn, Kyong Sho, and had quickly buzzed him through the doors into the inner sanctum of the police station, and promptly parked him in a soft interview room. The room was considered soft in that it had decent furnishings and was used more for dealing with victims and witnesses rather than interrogating suspects and other unsavory types. Soft, but it still had a lock on the door.

Waiting patiently for his Lieutenant, Barlow stood outside the room with a copy of the subject Bolo in hand. When Black appeared, Barlow handed it to him and provided a thumbnail sketch of what he had learned. As he talked, he watched Black's face. He respected this man. He also appreciated having a Boss that was still a real cop - inside.

Every day, people walked into the police department. with wild-ass stories. Ahn could be just another kook. But Barlow had a feeling. He knew the guy's story was a little over the top, but he thought Black should be the one to make the call. As he concluded his briefing, he paused then pronounced solemnly. "This is either complete bullshit or it's so far above my pay grade… Come to think of it – it's probably above yours too, Lieutenant."

Lieutenant Black just nodded, sighed, took a breath, put on his best PR face and entered the room. Ahn paced the room in a clear state of agitation. Black performed social niceties and quickly got down to business. Mr. Ahn was a diminutive middle-aged Korean gentleman with a small pot belly, a serious face, and an enviable thick head of coal colored hair. His classic Asian moon shaped face wore round wire rim eyeglasses. Right off, Black noticed the eyes. Ahn's dark eyes burned with intelligence and sincerity. His English was passable, his tone professorial. His story was fascinating.

Black glanced at his watch, excused himself and stepped out into the hallway. He couldn't believe that more than an hour had passed since he commenced his interview with Ahn. The guy's story was amazing, to say the least – credible, but amazing. Black had a decision to make – and fast. He mulled it over as he walked the short distance back to the Watch Commanders office. This Ahn guy – if he was on the level – was copping out to being a fugitive from North Korea, illegally entered into the U.S., fearful that someone was going to kill him - as others had been killed, because he was a scientist, one of a group of scientists, who had been working on a super secret project inside North Korea, who for reasons of conscience had defected, and had come to America hoping to cripple the North Korean project and...

His head hurt. He chastised himself for drinking that third cup of coffee. He opened the desk drawer and rummaged around for the clear plastic, large economy size bottle if generic aspirin. He found it. The bottle was battle scared and nearly opaque with powder residue from constant shaking. Black shook out a couple of tablets. He tossed them back with a swallow of cold coffee – cup number four, he thought. This was going to be a long night.

The directory in front of him was open to Federal Offices. He had telephone numbers for the State Department, Immigration and Naturalization and the F.B.I. He considered his options. His gut told him that Ahn was being forthright. Black had been in the business long enough to have developed pretty good instincts. He'd also had enough time in grade to have worked with lots of Feds, to have been burned by a few of them. Poor Mr. Ahn was simply looking for some protection. He knew that there was no way to keep the Feds out of a case like this - forever... This case clearly had Federal aspects – but – it also had local jurisdiction stamped all over it.

He considered making his first call to the locals. After all, the Bolo had come from some detective in – he glanced at the paper - the Sheriff's office. The name was Greer – not familiar. Okay, Detective Greer was looking at a string of murders - trying to find that common thread – he liked this guy already - all the victims were Asian. He re-read the Bolo sheet. Christ! All the victims were Korean – everyone one of them.

Black muttered softly as he dialed. "Piss on the Feds." He dialed the number labeled "cell phone". Greer picked up on the second ring.

"Greer – you don't know me – This is Pat Black from Buena Park Police. Listen, I've got something going down here – something I'm pretty sure you'll want to know about – like right now."

Chapter 28
Sea of Japan

They lay in the darkness, entombed within the metal coffin that mere seconds before had been the multi-million dollar submersible, Dewey. Stunned, Sells quickly returned to full consciousness, his senses returning one by one. He hurt in several places; but at least most of his critical parts appeared to be working. He was alive. He was also in total darkness.

Dewey had tumbled like a football. Finally, mercifully it had come to rest. In the seconds before, there had been something... He replayed the previous moments through his mind. They'd been latching onto the last piece of debris, the blue light special – he thought about the little joke he'd made to himself – then there was a flash, a deafening noise and a quick passing sensation of heat, and movement – violent movement.

He moved his head, flexed his hands and arms. Other than the splitting headache, he seemed to be in one piece. He moved a hand to the right side of his head. It felt wet and sticky just above his ear. He continued to take stock of their situation. He was still strapped to his operating platform. But, his orientation was wrong. His inner ear, that finely tuned instrument from which the sense of balance comes, told him he was supine, face-up, and at a slight angle, perhaps thirty degrees or so, feet upward. The proper orientation was the reverse. He should have been the other way around, face down, head slightly above his feet. The pilot, Sells, was in the lower position and the systems operator, in this case, Gomez, was stacked on the platform above Sells. Each had three circular view ports next to their heads. With illumination from the service pod lights, each had a birds eye view to the unseen ocean world of depth. Additionally, there were scores of color displays and system controls that covered the curved surface of the interior of the crew module. Nothing was working, not a single display blinked or flickered. There were sounds. But, the most immediate of those were two. One was the creaking of the pressure hull, and the other was a low moan coming from Gomez above or actually below him.

"Gomez – Charlie, you okay?"

The only reply was more moaning and groaning. At least he's alive, thought Sells. And so am I – that's something.

"Mr. Gomez! Charlie! Can you hear me?" Sells reached around with his right hand and pressed a tiny stud button on his dive watch. The watch was really a small computer married to a time piece. An LED illuminated the dial. The soft light allowed him to take a cursory pass over the craft's instrumentation. That effort only confirmed what he already knew. Nothing was working. He fumbled for the small pencil flashlight that he carried in the right thigh pocket of his jumpsuit. Groping, his fingers found the familiar form. He withdrew it and snapped the beam on. Brilliant white light knifed through the blackness.

He looked above him, which he deduced was really below him now, and could see Gomez's arms and legs moving slightly. Then he played the beam back across the critical gauges and instrumentation. "Talk to me Charlie! Come on – say something to me – anything!"

"Wha... Where..." The noise was coming from Gomez. The marginal response was punctuated with a long spasm of coughing.

"Okay – good – at least I know you're still kicking." Lieutenant Phil Sells was the consummate professional. He knew how to be cool and deliberate in a crisis. A graduate of Annapolis, he'd ranked academically a whopping number two in his class. He was a natural athlete and kept himself in superb physical condition. Despite all, at this moment, he was scared to the very core of his soul. He knew, perhaps better than anyone else, just how much danger he and Gomez were facing.

Sells held two Doctorates, one in robotic engineering and another in oceanography. When the opportunity came along to join GTI/U.S. Government project, the Glomar project, as it had been called, he jumped. He was a perfect fit. He'd trained with the submersible development team in Seattle for almost two years, before being posted to the Glomar for the covert mission arrangement with GTI. He knew more about these submersible systems than any other human being alive.

Realizing the gravity of their situation, his thoughts darkened. This was turning out to be one of those days where there was not much more to do other than to kiss your ass good bye.

He quickly shook himself out of the mental funk and found what he'd been groping for. It was a small covered circuit breaker panel on the port side of his console. It was intended for use in a drastic emergency – a predicament such as this – one where the crew capsule separated from the operations platform. Sells deduced that that separation had already occurred. He lifted the cover and flicked the switch. Instantly, a small amount of current was fed from the battery system on-board the crew capsule to the air scrubber and emergency lighting systems. Pinpoints of soft light illuminated the cabin and a welcome puff of air was felt on his face. That task accomplished, he turned his attention back to Gomez. "Charlie – you with me here? Can you talk to me?"

"Mmfftt..." Accompanied by a little more arm and leg movement was the only reply from Gomez

"Okay – look – we've had some kind of problem – big problem - and the crew module has separated. We appear to be stuck on the bottom – upside down is my guess." As he worked at the controls, he continually spoke. Although Gomez was making occasional noises, there wasn't any coherent response coming out of him. Sells continued, "We don't have maneuvering and the communication links are toast... Actually, I'm really surprised we haven't imploded!"

Just then there was a tearing sound. The pressure hull groaned and then there was movement – upward movement. It felt like the capsule had lifted from the sea floor and started to right itself owing to its bottom ballast. Sells was certain they were moving, but he had no instrumentation through which to confirm. But, it felt like the capsule was moving. The depth measurement sensors were all attached to the operations platform which currently lay in a junk pile on the sea floor. Same for the Doppler scanner, its sensor had also been torn away. They were literally blind. Sells knew they were moving. He just sensed it in his bones. And the floor of the capsule was now down where it should be. He unbuckled his harness and pushed himself up toward Gomez.

Halfway up his nose bumped into the environmental systems panel. His vision scanned over the array of controls and displays. It hit his consciousness memory like a brilliant flash. The hull pressure monitor – amidst all the sophistication, all of the state-of-the-art technology aboard Dewey, there was a plain old fashioned Bourdon tube pressure sensor. It tapped the small air space between Dewey's outer pressure hull and the inner hull. Originally, the sensor was used for fine tuning during the construction and outfitting phases in the life of the submersible. It was never intended to be an operations device.

It was in an oddball location, not exactly easy to see from his station. Sells knew exactly how it worked - that minute changes in pressure between the hulls were measured with a simple air column and translated to digital readout, which, like ninety percent of the on-board electronics weren't working. But – there was a mechanical backup – a dial. He found it! He angled his head to stare at the small needle indicator, and its position relative to the tiny green luminescent numbers. He stared at that needle. He willed it to move. After what seemed like an eternity, the needle, which had been locked squarely over the digit 7, moved a couple of nano-fragments toward the 6. Sells blinked and tried to keep his vision and the small penlight locked on the dial. An agonizing lifetime was crammed into that succeeding minute. The needle moved again – this time it passed the 6 and headed squarely to the 5!

Excitement surged inside him. They were going up – slow as hell – and he knew they had more than a mile to go, but the capsule was actually heading for the surface!

Sells contained his elation for a moment and refocused on Gomez. He found him still strapped to his platform. He was semi-conscious, still mumbling and moving about, but he was only marginally responsive. Charlie had also taken a nasty hit to his head. There was a large scalp laceration and considerable bleeding.

Sells found the first aid kit and ripped open a couple of compresses. He applied direct pressure. After a while he unbuckled Gomez and rolled him onto his back. He brought several wraps of the bandage ties under his chin and around his forehead. Satisfied that he had done what he could to stanch the bleeding, he tied off the ends in repeated granny knots. Gomez started to come to again. His eyes flickered and he started mumbling – though not much made sense. Sells peeled back Charlie's eyelids and flashed his penlight across both pupils. One side was considerably larger than the other.

He grabbed Gomez's chin and yelled directly to his face. "Gomez! You with me?"

"Uhh – huhh…"

"We flipped over… And, it looks like you took a pretty good bang on the head." He figured that Gomez had sustained one hell of a concussion. He decided to put Gomez into a flotation vest. He uncased two, and wrestled with Charlie, finally securing him into the bright orange life jacket. It was no easy task, given the lack of moving around space in the crew capsule.

That task done, he belted Charlie back on his platform. Then, he went back down to take another look at the Bourdon tube indicator. The numbers were still getting smaller. Satisfied that they were continuing, however slow, their upward journey, he tried some quick calculations in his head. He was trying to estimate just how long it would take to reach the surface. He figured it would take a while... So he moved to the communications console and tried vainly to get something to work.

삼 질식시킴

He fooled with the communications systems for nearly thirty minutes. Finally, he gave up. He checked on Gomez and found him unconscious. He was breathing, but now he was completely unresponsive. Sells moved back down to his platform and the little Bourdon tube depth gauge. The numbers clicked over at a snail's pace, but they were getting smaller, which meant they were still going up. He patted the digital readout like one would a loyal dog, and thought about the complex emergency surfacing systems that were actually working! Nominal operation, the techies would say in that flat emotionless speech known only to engineers. Sells was elated. Something had badly damaged his prized deep water submersible, but its safety systems were working. Dewey was taking them to the surface!

삼 질식시킴

Dubord checked his watch. "Carter - talk to me. How're we doing on our rendezvous?"

Carter's fingers flew over his keyboard. We want to surface in about six minutes, Sir. We're getting close."

"Any indication of Dewey yet?"

Everyone just shook their heads.

"And where's the Han-Sung?"

Skipper, she's at five hundred feet and circling about four point three miles - bearing one six five."

"Good. Okay, Carter – your best quess - where's Dewey?"

Carter looked up from his console. "She's gotta be somewhere close, Skipper. I don't think you want me to go active...?"

Dubord just shook his head.

Sullivan was standing right behind Dubord. The Commander turned to him. "Okay, this is where it really gets dicey. In a few minutes we're going to surface. We'll look around and hope Mr. Carter's calculations are correct..." He flashed a glance a Carter who though seemingly immersed in his job, heard every word and flashed a thumb up. "If everything goes well, we'll spot the capsule, go right to it and get our men."

Sullivan nodded. "And if everything doesn't go well?"

Dubord just looked at the big man. He said nothing.

Carter's voice pierced the silent moment. "Sir, that corvette, Yang-Tou is heading back toward us. She sounds like turns for about ten knots... and heading more or less right toward us – bearing two nine five.

"How far...?"

Carter's response came before he finished the question. "She's approximately three point five miles and closing!"

"Copy that."

"And Skipper – we are well above the last layer. When we start rescue ops..."

"I know, Carter. Everyone's gonna hear us." Dubord finished his statement with a quarter turn towards Sullivan.

"Would this be part of everything not going well?" Sullivan asked.

Dubord considered that for a moment. "Now... the trick is to go get our men without starting a shooting war or some kind of international incident. Remember... we don't exist." He turned away from Sullivan barking orders. "Prepare to surface the boat. Standby rescue team. Helm, take us to video scope depth!"

The sleek craft cleanly broke the surface with its video scope tube. Instantly a satellite seeker locked on a U.S. communications bird in low orbit and flashed status traffic to the Glomar. The mother ship had already ceased her bogus operations and was steadily steaming west to rendezvous with Huey. The sub's forward display panels lit up with colorful surface views in all directions.

The crewman at the main sensor station reported. "Sir, the sea surface is running about five feet and long.... And there's no active radar or sonar at the moment. The surface contact and the kilo are still closing and... Skipper, I don't have a bearing on that twin screw trawler."

Dubord was glued to the video displays. He spoke over his shoulder to Sullivan. "The seas are relatively calm... that part's good... The bad part is if we don't spot something soon, we've got no choice but to search with active sonar. That basically rings the bell for our friends out there."

Sir, the corvette has just started active radar – UHF. He doesn't have us yet."

"Yeah, but he will - when we surface - Carter?"

"Thirteen seconds sir. Dewey should break surface in... ten, nine, eight..." Carter continued the countdown aloud. "Three, two one! Anytime now..." It almost sounded like a prayer.

Eyes were glued to the screens. There was nothing... nothing but water... for three hundred and sixty degrees around them, nothing but water, horizon and rust red twilight sky.

Chapter 29
Buena Park, California

Ichiro glanced at his watch. It was just a few minutes after midnight when he snapped off his headlights and quietly rolled his car into his pre-selected parking spot around the corner from Ahn's house. The night offered only a sliver of moon; and it had already dropped over the horizon. What light there was came from a carpet of stars, and the occasional streetlamp interspersed within the thick foliage from the old pepper and jacaranda trees that lined the quiet street. He reached up and popped the plastic lens off the car's interior light. With a finger, he pried out the bulb. He removed the key and dropped it at the edge of the floor mat – out of sight but quickly accessible.

He looked around and saw no one. Quietly, he opened the door, slipped out and moved quickly into the shadows. Attired in a black nylon windbreaker and black trousers, he was virtually invisible. He vaulted onto a cinder block wall and with cat-like grace, walked the slender top ledge until he was behind his victim's home. Quickly, he scanned the adjacent yards – no people – no pets – the approach was perfect. He dropped silently to the ground and concealed himself behind a large bush.

He stayed hidden for several minutes. When he was satisfied that his presence was not known, he withdrew the camera-like device he had used earlier. With a soft whirring sound, the device powered on. He pressed the buttons and carefully watched the display. In the darkness, the tiny screen cast a pale glow over his face. The device was not reading Ahn's transponder! "Shit!" The Korean language version of the common expletive slipped from his mouth. He closed the device. Still in a crouch, he pondered his options. This meant that either Ahn was not there or that his transponder had stopped working – or perhaps something was blocking the signal. Ichiro decided to enter the home.

The rear of the modest home had a sliding door with an aluminum frame and a line of small wooden casement windows. He moved to the closest one, peering inside. He moved quietly along the line of windows until he had examined them all. Two of the windows were closed and latched. The third was open about three inches. He moved to the sliding door. The drapes were drawn open and he could easily look into the dim interior of the home. He saw a table and chairs, part of a kitchen, and old sofa and TV. But he didn't see a living soul. He grasped the handle and lifted the slider a fraction of an inch from its track. The upward movement was enough to clear the latch. He carefully slid the glass door open about a foot. There was a slight metallic scrape as the door moved. He flattened his body to the outer wall and froze. He listened. He stayed in place nearly a full minute ensuring that there was no reaction to the sound of the sliding door.

He quickly moved along the back of the house, returning to the open window. Silently, he stripped off the screen and discarded it. With the heel of one hand he pushed up on the frame; the window easily and silently opened wide. He performed a quick look inside. The room was small and dark. There was a bed, an open closet and one folding chair. He saw no one. He backed his head out and scanned the yard one more time. Then, like a quick dark snake, he was over the sill and inside.

삼 질식시킴

"Skipper, there it is!" Carter could not conceal the excitement in his voice. On the port display screen, the crew capsule bobbed in the growing swells.

Dubord's voice rang through the control room. "Okay, people – let's do this right - and fast! Rescue team?"

"Standing by, Sir." The disembodied voice was tinny in their earpieces.

"Surface the boat – commence recovery operations!"

Ballast tanks blew and Huey surged above the surface of the darkening waters. She was quickly brought alongside the capsule. Four crewman attired in black wetsuits with rubber gripping shoes emerged from the sail hatch and clipped safety tether lines to recessed cleats on the deck.   Three of them spread out on the aft deck with securing lines and tools. The fourth, the team leader Jones, remained in the elevated sail, and barked a series of maneuvering orders via a small radio to the helmsman. With thrusters and using the following current, they quickly moved the boat to a position where they could capture the bobbing crew capsule.

Light was fading and the wind whipped at the surface. The submersible capsule banged alongside Huey with its hatch more or less on top. One of the crewmen jumped onto the capsule and quickly secured a line. A second line was thrown over. It was rigged and knotted around the hatch protrusion in an attempt to stabilize the pitching and bobbing. Two large socket wrenches were passed over and the men immediately went to work removing the oversized locking nuts that would allow the pressure sealed hatch to open.

Inside the control room, tensions were running high. Carter's voice had gone up at least a full octave.

"Skipper – we are lit up like a Christmas tree here. They've made us with a whole lotta surface radars and now we're getting pinged from the Kilo. The ominous ringing from the active sonar pulsed through the Huey's hull. The deadly sounds underscored the severity of their situation. Everyone, including their rider, Sullivan, understood how weapons ranging sonar worked. Carter continued. "Okay – now we are being hailed on marine VHF – speaking to us in – I think - Korean and fractured English, no less – They're calling 'to the un-identified submarine'!"

Sweat beads formed tiny rivulets and rolled down Dubord's face. "Copy that, Mr. Carter. Maintain radio silence and..." He spoke into his headset. "Rescue - how we doing up there?"

Jones strained voice came back immediately. "Capsule is righted and lashed – we're working on the last of the hatch bolts now."

"Roger that – fast as you can, Jonesy. Soon as you get our guys out, cut the capsule loose – hatch open!"

"Confirm – hatch open?"

"Roger. Let her flood.

There was a half beat pause before Jones responded. "Aye, Skipper. We'll scuttle her."

Dubord scanned the control room. He briefly locked eyes with Sullivan. "Carter!"

"Sir?"

"Dial your active sonar up to full blast. Give them two pings thirty seconds apart!"

Carter's eyes widened. "Aye, aye, Skipper." Carters hand flipped open the red cover guard over the ranging sonar controls. His finger hovered over the button. He glanced at Dubord. The Commander nodded. Carter's finger hit the button. The loud pulse rang through the water like someone had struck a giant bell with a hammer.

Sullivan's face begged the question, but he said nothing.

Dubord answered anyway. "I'm just trying to give them something else to think about." The second sonar pulse rang out. "If they think we are ranging them for a weapons solution – maybe we can buy a couple extra minutes."

"But... I thought you... You don't have any weapons," said Sullivan.

Dubord flashed a look. "We don't – but they don't know that." He spoke back into his headset, "Rescue, talk to me!"

Outside, under the darkening sky, the sea was growing taller and more fierce with each passing minute. Hundreds of miles away, a Pacific storm was growing, radiating bands of angry swells and current. The crew capsule banged around violently against the black sides of Huey. The submersible's hatch was now open and one of the rescue crewmen was hanging from his waist, his upper torso upside down inside the capsule.

Moments later, a limp form clad in an orange life vest and dark blue jumpsuit was hauled through the hatch. The unconscious form was half-way outside when the crewman turned to grab a tie line to secure the unconscious Gomez. It was just at that moment that the big wave hit!

삼 질식시킴

Ichiro, now inside the house, crept in silence near the door of the bedroom. He was spiked with adrenalin. His heart pounded in his ears obscuring his usually perfect hearing. Silently and stealthily he moved from room to room. In less than a minute he had covered the entire house. The place was empty. He considered waiting - to see if Ahn would return. His rational side warned him that he should not stay for long.

His mental exercise was interrupted by the sound of a car stopping in front of the house. Quickly, he moved to a front window. Peeking around the blinds he saw the distinct image of a black and white police car. Two uniformed men with flashlights were exiting the car. Casually, as if they were on some kind of routine business they strolled toward the house!

With cat-like speed he sprinted across the small house and slipped his body sideways through the narrow opening of the sliding glass door. Without making even a hint of sound, he disappeared into the darkness.

삼 질식시킴

The giant swell lifted the submersible crew capsule and flung it away from the submarine. The securing line on the hatch popped off, the other line held but the bulbous craft tipped and slid away, yo-yo fashion, from the submarine. As the capsule tipped, then righted itself, the open hatch was briefly submerged. Hundreds of gallons of water deluged the interior of the tiny craft. As soon as the capsule righted, Sells came charging out of the hatchway and immediately grabbed on to the remaining securing line.

Inside the submarine, Dubord was playing a deadly and dicey game of chicken with the approaching ships. The broken English audio track from the VHF radio was repeating, " – sovereign water of the Peoples Democratic Republic – cease all activity - stand by to be boarded."

"Comm - give me a patch to whatever channel they've been calling us on." Dubord's mind raced while he tried to figure out what he was going to say.

"You're on, Skipper…" The radio man pointed a finger at him and silently mouthed the word, "now"!

Dubord cleared his throat. "Uh, this is the research vessel…" He mumbled something unintelligible. "We are engaged in legitimate oceanography exploration within international waters. We are presently having difficulty with our equipment – however - we do not – repeat – do not require assistance." He ended by drawing a flat hand across his neck – the signal to cut off the transmission.

The radio man nodded as he switched off the transmission.

Outside, the situation was going from bad to real bad. Dewey's crew capsule bucked, kicked and strained against the lines. The two crewmen who were on top tried desperately to hang on. A thunderous wave washed one right off the capsule. He landed in the churning ocean right between the sub and the submersible. Held in place by his tether line, he could do nothing to get out of the danger zone between the hulls of the two gyrating sea machines. When the next swell smashed the two craft together, both of his legs were crushed.

The second crewman, Martinez, straddled one of the lashing lines with one arm, and had the other gripped around Gomez's midsection. He struggled to hang on.

The wave that trapped and crushed the other crewman plucked Gomez's limp form right out of Martinez' grasp and simply washed him overboard. Gomez's body vanished into the black water.

삼 질식시킴

Jones straining voice crackled in the headsets of the control room personnel. "Captain…" His breath was heaving as he spoke. "Rescue team has secured - they are aboard - the main hatch is closed and locked – cleared to dive!"

Dubord wasted no time. Helm – crash Dive! All ahead Flank – as deep and as fast as she'll take it!" The front end of the ship dipped at such a radical angle that everything that wasn't tied down, slid away. The crew instinctively grappled for anything above, alongside and below them to maintain their positions. Sullivan landed on his back and slid across the control room floor, his inertia being stopped only by a forward bulkhead.

Carter held up a hand. The other pressed his headset tight to his ear. "Skipper! Torpedo in the water!" It's the Kilo – he's fired on us!"

"Range?"

"Fifty-five hundred and closing. The fish has gone active, and it has acquired us!"

"Great – just what we needed."

"A second torpedo now, Skipper. Same range and bearing!"

"Got it – two fish and active!" Sullivan didn't know if Dubord's next pronouncement was for the crew or himself. "Its okay people - settle down – it's not like we don't know what to do here."

Sullivan struggled back to his feet. The deck was still pitched downward at better than a forty-five degree downslope.

Dubord watched the depth indicator. "Helm – on my mark I want a hard ninety degree turn to starboard… And keep your speed at flank! Carter - that first layer – it still about twelve fifty?"

"It is, Sir. About a hundred feet thick… and the two fish are probable type 53's… and they are moving with us - tracking us dead on…"

"Roger that."

Dubord's eyes were glued to the depth readout. At twelve hundred seventy feet he barked out. "Helm, make your turn now – mark!"

The floor of the boat surged up to everyone's left side as the small sub cork-screwed into a radical turn.

"Coming to new course zero six zero, Sir." The helm operator announced coolly. "There's your tight ninety, Sir."

"Very good! Where're the fish now, Carter?"

Carter turned grinning. "Both passing over us now, Skipper. Both above the layer!" He waved a hand over his head.

Sullivan saw a hint of smile flash across Dubord's face. "Great job, folks! Now, let's get the hell out of here!"

Just as activities in the submarine control room started to settle down, Lt. Jones, the rescue team leader, approached Dubord. His face was ashen. He stood in front of Dubord, his black wet suit dripping. "Sir – we need to talk."

Dubord eyed the younger officer. "How bad?"

Eyes mostly downcast, Jones responded. "Bad, Sir. We lost one and two are injured. Jefferson's hurt bad. Both legs broken, I think…" His voice cracked.

"Who'd we…?"

"Mr. Gomez, Sir."

Sullivan approached, looming over the other two men. He listened intently, blue eyes burning into the young officer.

Jones continued. "We got him out of the capsule - he was unconscious. Before we could get a line on him, a big swell hit and…" Jones looked Dubord square in the eyes – "Ripped him right out of Martinez arms before they could get a line on him. The water was – it just blew him right off the deck. He went right under – vest and all… I'm sorry…"

Chapter 30
Sea of Japan

Back aboard Glomar Explorer Sullivan fumed. He sat with others in Captain Marshall's ward room. Present were Dubord, Sells, Jones and a few others. They had just finished a debriefing session on the mission and were currently on a secure satellite link with COMSUBPAC and some high ranking weenie who was supposed to be with the State Department, but Sullivan guessed was probably CIA. Also on the conference call – but not saying much - was Doug McClure.

The sing-song voice playing through the speaker-phone – owing mostly to the digital scrambler - was the guy from State talking. "So, the bottom line is – in spite of the tragic loss of Mr. Gomez – who is – ah - was - a trusted patriot and valuable asset to our operations, we simply can not afford to start another international incident over this event. At this time, the United States military is just stretched too thin. We are up to our knees in the Middle East and - we know it's just a matter of time before China heats up the kettle over Taiwan. This administration would like nothing more than to deal with the North Korea problem – but the timing is – shall we say – inappropriate…"

"Inappropriate – my ass!" Sullivan could not contain himself further. "We're not talking about creating an 'incident'. We're just talking about sending a few planes and boats back to the area to conduct a simple search and rescue operation - in international waters, for Christ sake! I don't think this is too much to ask for the guy who made all this covert ops stuff possible for you folks - under the GTI banner!"

"Excuse me." The phrase resonated through the small meeting room. It was the disembodied voice of the government man. "Just who is it that is speaking now?

"The name's Sullivan – Michael Sullivan!" Mike barked back into the speakerphone.

Captain Marshall leaned over and placed a hand on Sullivan's forearm. He spoke. "Mr. Sullivan is Mr. Gomez's friend and associate. He had accompanied Mr. Gomez, and was present on the Huey when the accident occurred.

There was a slight pause. "Ah, yes. Mr. Sullivan... I am certain that the Navy professionals there can explain to you the foolhardiness of any such attempted operations – given that – the jurisdiction of the waters is in dispute and – that any such operation would, at best, recover only a body."

삼 질식시킴

Sullivan collected a few items and slammed them into his duffle. Captain Marshall had agreed to helicopter him back to Sapporo as soon as the shipped passed within aeronautical range. The cabin wall phone chimed. Mike grabbed it. "Yeah?"

"Mr. Sullivan?" It was the voice of the ship's radio operator. "I've got a sat-call for you from a Doug McClure..."

"Put it through," he barked. Realizing he probably sounded like an ass, he added, "Please."

There was a click, followed by tones and a short burst of static. Then McClure's voice came through, from the other side of the world, with eerie clarity. "Mike – I know your bent, I..."

"Bent doesn't begin to describe it... You were sure a lotta friggin' help in there – Jeez, Doug!"

"I'm sorry, it's just..."

"That a good bureaucrat knows when – he knows when to keep his mouth shut to protect his ass –right?"

"Well – no... I mean – yeah. You're right. But on the other hand, I can't do any of us any good if I get my balls trimmed..."

"Doug. This is Charlie we lost here. I can't believe that this is happening. Since when is the U.S. Government afraid to mount a simple search and rescue op to try and find one of its own? Especially, when it's someone as important as Charlie Gomez!"

"Mike, I..."

"Have you talked to the Vice-President yet? What's he got to say about this?"

"Yes, just a few minutes ago. Unfortunately, he's also carping the company line here. 'It's a covert op – there has to be deniability.' No one wants to go in there and risk starting another shooting incident or provide the opportunity for another Pueblo-type ship seizure."

"That's bull and you know it."

"...And everyone here seems to be taking the position that he got swallowed up in the swells and most likely drowned or..."

Doug, I've known Gomez for..." He paused for a breath. "Look, the point is, I don't know anyone who can take care of themselves better in open water than Gomez. Christ, if he got lost or abandoned, he'd just swim to shore, I've known him to swim from Newport to Catalina – and that's over thirty miles!"

There was a moment of silence. Finally, McClure spoke again. "Right – so – what do you really want me to do?"

삼 질식시킴

There were two loud raps on the cabin door, which opened before Sullivan could utter a sound. Sells, head swathed in a white bandage and Jones, the rescue team leader stepped inside. Mike considered them.

Sells spoke first. "Look, Mr. Sullivan. I know you and Gomez were tight, and we really didn't get a chance to talk much..."

"What do you guys need? I've gotta plane to catch." He said flatly.

Sells continued. "I got to know Charlie pretty good myself. We spent a lot of time together - in the DSRV Simulation-Trainer, then all over again, doing the real thing."

"Yeah?"

"My point is – that I want you to know exactly what I know – it's important."

Mike stopped his packing and listened. "Okay."

"First, he did take a bad hit to the head – at least a concussion, maybe worse. He'd lost a lot of blood. Second, he was – like – semi-conscious when we pushed him up out of that hatch, groaning and moving a little on his own. And the flotation vest – I guarantee it would not have just come off him. I put it on him myself – the right way - crotch straps and all."

Jones jumped in. "And we didn't just abandon the search when Mr. Gomez got washed over. We were outside for an additional twelve minutes – with at least one of us in a high position – looking down on the swells the entire time. It's true that we never saw him surface – but those were some pretty heavy seas. He could have just surfaced behind a swell – somewhere where we just could not have seen him."

Sullivan considered the two Navy men for a moment. Finally, he spoke. "Look, guys – I know how bad you feel," His words were uttered more to hasten their session than anything else. "I feel like crap, myself... I also know that you guys did everything you possibly could."

Jones was looking down at the floor. He nodded.

"Jones, you were up to your butt in alligators – I know that - and it's apparent to me that you and your men did a damn fine piece of work – to accomplish the recovery that you did." Sullivan's eyes flashed toward Sells.

The cabin inter-phone buzzed. Sullivan reached over and plucked the handset out of the cradle. He listened, twice said yes and hung up. Turning back to the men, he looked at them squarely. "Sure, I'm pissed. Charlie Gomez was – is - probably my best friend on this earth. If he's dead, I'll mourn his loss. If he's still alive – I'm going to find him."

삼 질식시킴

The helicopter from the Glomar Explorer touched down on the tarmac under cold leaden skies at Sapporo Okadama Airport. Fortunately, the pilot was able to set Sullivan within a healthy jogging distance to the private hangers where they had left the GTI Leer. Finding the hanger and the company aircraft was not a problem. He bluffed his way through two layers of security with his Sheriff's Credentials and an Ominous GTI identification card that Charlie had thoughtfully provided him. He keyed the door switch, and the main cabin door swung open. He stepped inside and tossed his duffle into the rear. Moving to the cockpit, he sat in the left seat and found the pre-flight check list. After a few minutes of clicking switches and checking this and that, he went back outside to walk the perimeter of the gleaming aircraft.

Dark thoughts clouded his head. He was bone tired. But the Leer Jet was his fastest ticket home. He'd have to drive it back himself. He was qualified, but just barely. He decided, somewhat recklessly, that strong coffee and the auto-pilot would get him through. He methodically moved around the plane completing his pre-flight inspection.

Satisfied that the aircraft was ready, he climbed back inside. Before take off, he had to make a telephone call. It was one call he dearly dreaded, but he knew he had to.

He checked his watch and quickly calculated the time zone difference to the West Coast. He found the portable sat-phone and walked back outside. He had to move completely away from the metal hanger for best reception. Standing in the clear, he checked the signal indicator. It glowed green. He dialed the country code and the unlisted number for the home phone of Fernando Gomez, the CEO of the vast GTI Empire and doting uncle to Charlie. After several rings, a matronly Latina voice heavy with sleep answered. He took in a deep breath and began his story.

Chapter 31
Santa Ana, California

Sullivan knocked on the frame of the open office door. It was 6:30 in the morning and Lieutenant Blair was seated at his desk. Hot coffee steamed at his right, half glasses perched on his nose and a six inch stack of reports waited to be devoured on his left. Mike spoke. "Lieutenant – got a minute?"

Blair looked up over the spectacles, the edges of his mouth hinting at a smile. "Ah, Sergeant Sullivan - the prodigal son returns – and a bit early, too. I thought you were taking a couple of weeks?"

"Yeah, well - about that." Sullivan stepped inside, reached behind him and shut the door. He slumped down into the chair. "Charlie Gomez is dead – or at least we think he's dead."

All traces of mirth were extinguished from Blair's face.

"Jeez, Mike, I'm sorry. What...?"

Sullivan spent the next few minutes giving his lieutenant a sanitized version of the events in the Sea of Japan. Of course, as the story went, he and Charlie had been on a GTI research ship, "visiting", when the accident occurred. He concluded with a pronouncement that he still had things to take care of and would have to be off work for a while longer.

"So – how much more time do you need? Things have started to pick up in the past few days." Blair hefted the stack of reports on his desk.

"I've got to do a few things, here - make a few calls – and talk to a few folks. Then, I'll just finish up my two weeks – if that's all right?"

"Of course, Mike... Whatever you want. Anything you want me to do?" He added.

Sullivan just shook his head. Slowly, he rose up out of the chair. His hand landed on the doorknob when Blair spoke up. "Do me a favor. Before you go, could you check in with Greer. He's been chomping at the bit to talk to you. It's about those Korean Murders."

"Okay."

Sullivan went directly to his cubicle, cleared a spot in the clutter atop his desk and started making calls.

An hour went by. People drifted in preparing for the days work. Mollie, the division secretary, strode by, stopped with a jerk and backed up to Sullivan's cubicle. Mike was just hanging up the phone. She radiated her smile of greeting and approval. "Hi Sailor! Aren't you supposed to be on vacation somewhere?"

He smiled back. "I am. I'm really not here – just an apparition, you see?" He swiveled his chair and extended his hands.

"Yeah, I see an apparition that hasn't showered or shaved for a while." She wrinkled up her nose.

Mike rubbed a hand over his stubbly chin. "Been kinda busy – just got off a plane."

She nodded and walked off. Sullivan's cell phone buzzed. He pulled it from his pocket and looked at the Caller-ID. It said "unregistered" and displayed fourteen digits. It wasn't a number he recognized. He flipped it open.

"Mr. Sullivan?"

"Yes…"

"It's Bill Dubord."

There was a long silence. Mike's mind churned for a moment. "Yes, Commander – what's…"

"I've got some information – it's important. Can you find someplace with a Codex?" The term was slang for a U.S. Government-only secure digital telephone.

Sullivan thought for moment. "Yeah, I can. Might take me while."

"Make it as quick as you can and call me back at this number." Dubord read off a series of numbers then clicked off. Mike scribbled them out on a pad. He thought it might be a satellite phone number. Then it dawned on him that it was probably a Codex aboard the Glomar. He stared at his cell phone display for a long moment. It was as if he was trying to divine some piece of information from the little communications device. He hadn't expected to hear from the Glomar's First Officer again. There was excitement in Dubord's voice – and more – a tinge of urgency. *I'm tired and getting punchy*. He thought. He flipped the phone cover closed.

Mollie appeared and placed a steaming white mug of black coffee on his desk. "Here, you look like you could use this. And before you leave, talk to…"

"I know – I know. Talk to Greer." He said turning back to his phone with a wave. Mollie toddled off. "And thanks for the coffee!" He said to her backside, as she disappeared.

Mike had several more calls to make. He skipped them all and went straight to Stretch. He dialed the number. One ring and the phone was answered by a sultry female voice, kind of a husky Marilyn Monroe with a little something else thrown in. She announced the number dialed and said, "How" – with extra emphasis on the 'how' - "may I help you?"

"Hi - Mike Sullivan calling for Stretch."

"May I tell him what this is about?"

"It's personal…"

"Of course, Mr. Sullivan." The sexy voice oozed. "Mr. Stretch, hasn't come into the office as yet. May I have him call you?"

"Listen, this is very important. I need you to locate him and connect me right away. Can you do that?"

"I'm sorry Mr. Sullivan. Mr. Stretch is unavailable at the moment. I will see that he gets your message as soon as possible. Thank you for calling, and have a nice…"

"Wait!" Mike's head buzzed. He just remembered. There was a security code that Stretch had given him. It was like a password phrase, it sounded like some kind of gobbledygook. Stretch told him to use it anytime he needed to talk with him immediately. He tried to remember the phrase. It came from an old fifties sci-fi movie. Patricia Neal had to say the phrase precisely to the giant robot or else – something bad would happen. What was that phrase…?

"Yes, Mr. Sullivan – was there a further message?"

"I'm supposed to tell you – something – a phrase – Latin or something like that. I'm supposed to use it to tell you - or rather to convince you to contact Stretch immediately…"

"Yes."

"Oh damn – what was that…" He searched his memory, desperately trying to pull up the recollection of the phrase.

"Yes."

"It's – ah – something like – klattor – klatoo…"

"Yes."

"Can't you help me out here? This is really important!"

"Yes."

Suddenly, recollection blossomed. In a wink, the phrase suddenly appeared in his mind. "I've got it." He nearly yelled into the phone.

"Yes."

Carefully, he pronounced each syllable. "Klaatu barada nikto". He waited. After what seemed like five minutes, he realized he was holding his breath.

There was a long pause and the sultry feminine voice said, "Mr. Sullivan, please hold. I will connect you to Mr. Stretch, immediately."

삼 질식시킴

Exactly nineteen minutes later, with three blown stop lights, six right-of-way violations and sufficient speed to clearly establish reckless driving, Sullivan stood next to Stretch in his subterranean lab of his commercial building in Newport Beach. Stretch was barefoot, wearing faded levis and a wrinkled black tee shirt that declared "Jerry Garcia Lives" across the back. His case of bed-head hair was severe.

"Guess I rolled you outta the sack – Sorry." Sullivan said.

Stretch was sitting in front of a work bench with a pile of circuitry on top. Connected to it was a telephone handset that looked suspiciously like one that had been stolen from a pay phone. "You could've at least brought donuts." He mumbled.

"Sorry – no time."

"I work better with donuts."

"Sure you weren't a cop in another life?"

"Absolutely – I know what I was…"

"And that would be…?"

"You'll laugh."

"I won't laugh."

"Okay – I was a nun."

Mike decided to change the subject. He said, "You sure this thing will work?"

Stretch just glared at him. He said nothing.

"Sorry."

"It's okay. I told you that you'd laugh."

"I didn't laugh."

"By the way, have you talk to Greer yet?"

"God – even you too? I'm gone a few days and Greer has mobilized everyone I know. That guy should be promoted."

"It's about those murders, the ones with the things in their mouths."

"Yeah, yeah – just as soon as I get back." His exasperation was plain.

"Okay. We're ready to dial. Give me the number."

Mike laid a yellow sticky note on the bench. Stretch punched the numbers into a keypad. Light emitting diodes blinked and clicking sounds came out of the earpiece.

"Go ahead – pick it up." He said referring to the handset. "It'll work just like any other Codex you've ever used."

Sullivan hefted the handset to his ear. He listened to the familiar sounds of the digital algorithm synchronizer. He thought, *Damn, this thing just might work.*

Mike knew that secure phones sometimes took a minute or more to sync up. He covered the mouthpiece and spoke to Stretch, who was now at the other end of the room, trying to coax the flow of coffee from the brewer. "So where do you keep her?"

"Keep who?"

"I mean - the incredibly sexy broad who answers your phone."

Stretch was still facing away from Mike, working the coffee machine. A broad smile illuminated his face. "Oh, you mean Minnie." It was a statement of fact rather than a question.

"I guess – I never caught her name. I didn't think it was Suzanne's voice."

Stretch was grinning from ear to ear now.

"Anyhow…" Mike continued. "I'd say she's a little over the top, but very sexy – efficient, but sexy."

"Minnie, huh. You'd like to meet Minnie?"

"Yeah, I'm just curious. I'd like to see if she looks like how her voice sounds."

"Just, how does she sound to you, Mike?"

"Pretty good, actually."

"Well here she is!" Stretch moved over to a computer terminal and typed on a black keyboard. Finishing, he spun the display panel around so Sullivan could see the screen. "Minnie - Say hello to Mr. Sullivan."

"Hellooo, Mister Sullivan." The velvet voice filled the room. Stretch tapped a couple more keys and the volume lowered. "It's a pleasure to meet you."

Mike was looking at a color cartoon figure of a voluptuous redhead in white strapless gown. The image was animation – incredibly lifelike, but animation none the less.

"You mean – I was talking to a – an answering machine?"

"Really, Sullivan, you don't have to be insulting."

"No kidding – you mean - the gal I was talking to is really a - a..."

"What she is – is one of the world's most sophisticated computers. That's what I mean."

"Excuse me, Boss." It was Minnie's voice again. "Could you please give me video feed? I would like to know if Mr. Sullivan looks as handsome as his voice sounds."

Incredulous, Sullivan figured that Stretch was pulling his leg. Before the scene could play out further, Dubord's voice came on the line. "Sullivan – you there?"

"Yes, Commander – I'm here."

"Sorry for all the cloak and dagger stuff. What we've got is hot, and we can't compromise our sources."

"Yeah, okay – I understand."

"Right then... We think Mr. Gomez is alive – we believe he was fished out by the North Korean Trawler – the twin screw job that was in the theatre..." He let that one hang for a moment. "And we've got hi-res pictures of him swimming in westerly direction just before they picked him up."

Excitement surged through Sullivan. Goose flesh sprouted on his neck and arms. "How the hell – I thought you guys said the NRO told you they didn't have any satellites over the area at that time. Where did – how did you...?"

"Suffice to say, the old man wasn't about to have us back out without even trying to find him. He just couldn't talk about what he was doing. He pulled in some favors – some favors of potential career ending size."

"Tell me."

"It seems that the aircraft carrier Kitty Hawk was on patrol in the East China Sea - and Marshall went to school with the Kitty Hawk's Skipper. Bottom line, they were close enough to divert one of their E-2C Hawkeye birds a few hundred miles north for a weather check, and they came back with a big score."

"Damn, I think I owe you guys an apology."

"Mike, listen." That was the first time Dubord had ever referred to him as anything other than, Mr. Sullivan. "It gets better. The Hawkeye was able to cruise in the area long enough to catch not only the trawler recovering Gomez, but they tracked and photographed the boat all the way back to a harbor at Chyongjin. She put in there and took somebody kicking and screaming off the boat who looks a lot like Charlie."

"Jesus – you guys are good."

"Can you take fax pictures over this connection?"

Mike looked at Stretch, who head was bobbing up and down. "Yes, we can."

Minutes later a series of black and white photos were laid out. The resolution was incredible. There was no doubt it was Charlie Gomez, bandaged head and all. It even looked like he was fighting mad when they pulled him out of the water. Sullivan scanned all the pictures and returned to the phone. "So what's the plan?"

"Well, that's the bad part. We don't have one. We can't use the pictures to force diplomatic pressure. Officially, we don't exist. As much as we all want to just go in there and get him, we just don't have those kinds of resources."

"Yeah." Sullivan's voice was flat.

"I was kind of hoping you might have some ideas."

Mike didn't hesitate. His face set taut and the blue eyes flared with the gleam of plan. His voice was quiet and even. He gripped the phone tight. "As a matter of fact, I do have some ideas."

Dubord went quiet; he listened.

"First, understand, that I, quite frankly, don't give a damn about protocol or proper procedure. Secondly, I disagree that we don't have recourse or the resources. Hell, I bet between you and me, we can come up with all the resources we need."

An uncomfortable moment of silence passed between them.

"Will you help me?" Sullivan asked.

"Absolutely!"

"Good. Let's go get him back!"

Chapter 32
Anaheim, California

It was not quite 2:00 AM when Ichiro parked the rental car in the side lot of HappyLand Hotel. He popped the door. As he slid out from behind the wheel, he heard a commotion coming from the exterior second floor balcony. His attention peaked when he realized the noise was coming from the area of his room. Quickly, he scanned the parking lot. He was looking for obvious signs of security, police or other persons of authority. Seeing none, he ran the short distance and vaulted the stairs. On the second floor landing he stopped cold, confronted with a small cluster of people standing outside the door to his room. There was a gray haired couple in robes and an overweight man in shorts and a tank top. Each craned their necks and wore the curious, almost prurient, look of those about to view a bloody accident scene.

Guests of the hotel, Ichiro surmised. He could plainly hear Jiro's voice coming through the walls. He was screaming in Korean. His incessant yelling sounded like hysterical nonsense, babbling sprinkled with cursing. The rant was punctuated by the crashing sounds, banging and the distinct cracks of furniture breaking.

Ichiro froze on the landing. Momentary indecision temporarily paralyzed him. He knew he had to do something – anything - and he had to do it quick. He had to stop this, and take control of the situation.

He silently cursed his brother. Jiro's imprudent actions had damaged their position – their mission was in jeopardy due to the previous events, now, with this, it may be seriously compromised. Fleeting seconds passed as his mind raced. He knew what he had to do. Putting on his best American friendly-guy smile and accent, he approached the small knot of serious faces that clustered outside the door. "I'm real sorry, folks. My pal in there, he just went off and had way too much to drink. I'm real sorry for the ruckus, folks. I truly am."

The grey haired woman clutched her robe at the neckline with one hand and with the other, wagged a pointed finger at Ichiro's face.

"You and your friend should be ashamed! Such behavior! Decent folks can't even get a night's sleep!" She had tight pink plastic curlers in her hair. The curlers jiggled as she spoke. The grey haired man, apparently her husband, stood next to her saying nothing. He just nodded.

The thought of instantly killing her – killing all three of them – briefly flitted through his mind.

Ichiro stepped to the front of the spectators, and now stood with his back to the hotel room door – room key in hand. Palms outstretched, he continued to lay it on thick. "I promise you, I will take care of the situation. There won't be anymore disturbance. Please, just go on back to your rooms. I promise you - I'll take care of everything…"

A stocky woman with tight curly short brown hair and an even tighter face appeared at the back of the group. "What's going on here?" She demanded in not-too-convincing display of assertiveness. She continued, not really knowing who to direct her comments to. "I'm the night manager - and whatever you people are doing up here has to stop – immediately! Or I'm calling the police!"

Ichiro saw that she was holding a walk-around phone. "Please – that's not necessary." His voice was dripping with honey-like sincerity. "My friend" – gesturing to the room behind him – "is just drunk out of his skull. I've just been out for while. I thought he was sleeping it off when I left. But, I guess he got roaring around again. I'm back now - I'll quiet him down – promise!"

Sensing the gaggle of spectators was breaking up, he turned and made a production sliding his key in the door lock, though he made no move to open the door.

Apparently satisfied, the crowd started to recede. Pink curlers whispered too loud as she and her man ambled off. "Whaddya bet - they're some of those – you know – sissy boys – and this is some kind of lover's spat?"

About ten feet away from Ichiro, the night manager lady stood firmly rooted. Mercifully, Jiro had quieted for the moment. Phone-in-hand lady spoke. "You've just gotta keep him quiet. I mean it! Just one more outburst, and I'll have to call the cops." She shook her wireless phone at him almost as if it was a weapon.

Ichiro literally oozed charm. "Oh, please… Now, don't do that. I can keep him quiet. Really, I can."

Just then, Jiro started screaming again, at the top of his lungs. He wailed as if he was enduring the seven agonies of torture. Then there was a loud slap and the sound of glass breaking.

She was just starting to buy into Ichiro's line, a hint of smile cracking at the edges of the tight mouth. When Jiro started in again, she shook her head. "That's it – I gotta do what I gotta do. I'm calling the police! She punched three numbers on her phone, held it to her head, turned and moved quickly away from Ichiro and the room.

He thought about going after her. But, knew he had only precious seconds. Jiro uttered a low wail. Ichiro flipped the latch and opened the door.

Chapter 33
Newport Beach, California

After leaving Stretch's place, Sullivan drove directly to his home in Newport. He punched the automatic garage door opener as soon as his Mustang pulled into range of the alley entrance to the 31st Street beach front home. The sectional door motored upward, and the Mustang eased inside. In seconds, he was out of the car and inside the house, not even bothering to close the outer door behind him.

Sullivan's beach house was a 20th Century relic amidst 21st Century multi-million dollar mansions. A simple cottage style bungalow, it featured the forties Craftsman style of architecture that was so prevalent in the early days of California. Originally, the tiny home had been built right at the edge of the white crystalline sand. The orientation was such that the front door and porch were actually facing the ocean. The Newport boardwalk, literally a wooden plank side walk, passed right in front of the cottage. In the mid-sixties, one of the previous owners added the attached garage and the City tore up the old boardwalk and replaced it with a ribbon of concrete.

First time visitors would eventually get around to asking the obvious question, often without a shred of delicacy. "How does a Sheriff's Detective Sergeant manage to pay for home like this?"

With a small smile, his answer was always the same. "Oh, it was just a little family money."

Sullivan's first priority was the telephone. He needed to arrange for money, equipment and transportation. Second, he needed a shower and a change of clothes.

Charlie's Uncle Fernando was his first call. He quickly promised everything Mike asked for, including a pilot and a fast aircraft. The senior Gomez handled it all. Mike marveled at the resilience of the old man. In spite of just having heard of the probable death of his nephew, scant hours before, he handled the news of Charlie's rescue by the North Koreans and probable detention quite well. The old man was clearly used to giving orders, and as much as told Sullivan the considerable resources of GTI were being placed at his disposal.

Mike finished his fourth telephone call. With the more crucial elements in motion, his thoughts were starting to focus on that shower. The sound of a car pulling up interrupted his thoughts. A car door slammed, and was followed, in seconds, by a sharp rap on the back door. Mike jerked it open. A surprised Greer stood at the threshold, hand poised to knock again.

"I heard you the first time." Sullivan barked as he moved away from the door and waved Greer inside.

"Sorry to barge in like this…"

"Yeah - I'm sure you are."

"No – really, I had to see you – have to talk to you – they told me you're taking off again for a few days."

"Look - I'm sorry – But, I'm kind of buried in this other thing – everybody told me you wanted to talk about the Asian murders…"

"Korean murders, Mike. You were right. All of the victims are Korean."

Sullivan's eyes widened momentarily in curiosity. The events at hand reasserted and he said. "I'm – well, frankly, this other thing is kind of – no, not kind of – it actually is, life and death – not mine – somebody else's. Understand?"

As he spoke, he pulled out a yellow chrome and Formica chair from the tiny kitchen set. He indicated for Greer to sit. Tim dutifully did so.

Sullivan opened the refrigerator and stared at the near empty shelves.

"Yeah, well – that's just it. This Korean murders case – it's taken on unbelievable dimensions. Things are happening and…"

"Want a beer?"

"What?"

"Beer – want a beer? I'm afraid that's about all I've got."

"Mike – its 9:30 in the morning."

"What? Oh, yeah – well, its 9:30 for you – I'm still somewhere on Chinese time, I think. He popped the caps on two bottles of Heineken, planted one in front of Greer, then sat down at the table across from him. Sullivan took a long pull from his bottle.

"Oh, what the hell." Greer picked his up and drained a third. He set the bottle down on the table and belched loudly. "Mmmm, that's actually not too bad this early in the morning."

Mike glanced at his watch. "Okay, here's the deal. You talk – I listen. But, I have to catch a plane in about two hours – you've gotta drive me to the airport. Deal?"

Greer lit up. He grinned, opened his battered portfolio case and started arranging papers on the tabletop. Invigorated, he looked over his case files and said, "Man, where do I start?"

Mike checked his watch again. "Let me save you some breath. I just left Stretch a little while ago. He gave me the short version on the dental-transponder devices. Fascinating stuff! What else you got?"

"You think that's fascinating? Wait till you hear the rest of it? You're going to think I've slipped a gear. And you know what? I wouldn't blame you in the least..."

"Okay, you've got my attention. Fill me in."

Greer told Sullivan of his sessions with Mr. Kim, briefly recapped each of the murders and then started in on the blind luck appearance of Mr. Ahn at Buena Park P.D. He told of Ahn's story of being a scientist working on secret military projects for the North Korean Government, of their discovery in 1954 of a crash landed craft of probable extra-terrestrial origin – not unlike the story of the Roswell incident of American history.

For a half hour, Greer plowed over the details of Ahn's story. He told of the North Korean's draconian efforts to keep their discovery secret, and how a select team of specialists had been recruited to examine the craft and to try to understand how it worked. Greer talked about Ahn's explanation that the project had spanned more than forty years and had consumed the lives of hundreds of workers, most of them killed or presumed killed by the oppressive North Korean leaders, in their zeal to keep their precious secret from the world.

He told of Ahn's description of their recent successes, the development of the Gravity Flux Amplifier, a device that harnessed the natural waves of gravity and converted them to a form of clean usable energy. He read the phrase carefully from his notes and showed Sullivan a group of rough sketches and schematics made by Ahn during the interview. He told of the North Korean attempts, with limited success, to construct a flying craft that was powered solely by the flux amplifier.

Sullivan sat quiet and listened. Greer's information was stunning. There was no other word to describe it. Mike didn't move a finger through the remainder Greer's dissertation. He just sat and listened.

Despite the fact that he was bone tired and jet-lagged beyond belief, he quietly catalogued the information and contrasted it with the facts he already knew. In his mind, he organized a list of questions for clarification but held them for the time being.

Sullivan displayed no emotion or hint of reaction. Inwardly, he could not believe the coincidence of life that had dropped these events in his lap. Events were taking place on both sides of the world, yet they were all connected. The connections were strange and terrifying, but they were absolute.

Greer continued, explaining Ahn's pronouncements as to how the North Koreans planned to use their secret gravity flux amplifier both as new power source and as a weapon. The flux amplifier tapped a virtually unlimited raw energy potential. It was the plan of the North Korean leaders to use this power to elevate their country to a position of military and economic super dominance. They believed that properly used their lock on the gravity flux amplifier would bring the end of dominance by the western world.

He moved into the part of the story where Ahn and a group of his coworkers had conspired to defect. Theirs was a position of conscience. They were not soldiers or politicians. Most of them, but not all, had been raised in the oppressive regime of the North. Some had been kidnapped, selected for their expertise and forced to work in a Gulag-like environment.

They, like many of the inhabitants of that tortured land, waited with finite patience for the end of the pseudo-communist regime to come. They waited for the failed grand experiment of social control to wither and be cast upon the dust bin of history, much in the manner of the former Soviet Union and the other eastern bloc communist countries. They longed for the re-unification of the two Koreas, reconciliation after generations of artificial division had been imposed upon families, cultures and traditions.

Ahn told of their attempts to flee, of limited successes, outright failures resulting in horrible punishment, including death. Finally, a number of them were able to escape, and by a variety of routes, come the United States. Ahn knew that some of his associates had made contact with U.S. officials and through them had gained assistance in the form of money, new identities, jobs and places to live.

Ahn, unlike many of the others, had chosen not to divulge his presence to the American Government. He said that he didn't trust them.

When it became apparent that North Korea had agents working in California, systematically killing each of the former members of the "Energy Project", Mr. Ahn chose to reveal himself.

Greer was coming to the end of his story. He pushed two pieces of paper across the table. Both were Xerox copies. One looked like a drawing of a coin or medallion with the figure of a dragon. It was about the size of a silver dollar. The other paper had four characters of Asian writing on it – Korean writing.

"What're these?" Sullivan asked.

Greer tapped the Korean writing first. "This is the name of their secret project written out in Ahn's hand. He told us that this was the codeword that identified their outfit and their work with the gravity thing."

Mike stared at the writing in silence. The paper was inscribed "활력계획"

Greer continued. "Ahn pronounced it for me. I asked him to write it out – in Korean - for me. I thought it might be useful."

Mike nodded and picked up the second paper, the one with the picture of the dragon. "And what about this?"

"This is something that was missed in the first two homicides scenes. It was there at both places, but nobody picked up on it as being of any evidential value." He looked at Sullivan with a sheepish face. "You know, a lot of Asian folks have oriental things, décor and artwork in their homes. It was one of the Fountain Valley guys that picked up on it while reviewing photos from some of the other city's crime scenes. He got us looking - and the damn thing shows up – in every murder scene so far."

Sullivan canted the drawing a bit, trying to make sense of it. "Found at each scene, eh?"

"Yes - always in the same form – on a small square of paper. It's called an intaglio wood carving print – black ink on kind of a tan coarse-like paper..."

"Rice paper?"

"Yeah. How'd you know?"

"Good guess – that's all."

"Well, anyhow, it's apparently some kind of oriental symbol. It's kind of fuzzy, but we think it is supposed to be some kind of dragon – perhaps with a lion's head on it? No one is certain. So far it's un-identified. The crime lab is trying to get a symbology make on it."

"Interesting, very interesting." Sullivan said.

Each copy is about two by two inches square, dropped somewhere inside each scene, not necessarily close to the bodies – one on a coffee table, another on a nightstand – places like that."

"What do you think it is, maybe a calling card, a trademark?"

"Don't have a clue."

Mike fingered the paper. "Your - Mr. Ahn see this?"

"Not yet."

Mike nodded.

"Look, Mike, I really need some help here. Since you've worked for the Feds – well, I figured you'd have some idea as to how I should proceed with this mess. I think that I'm in – or we're in – way over our heads on this deal..." His voiced trailed and he reached for the remainder of the now warm Heinekens.

"Who else knows about this? Sullivan asked.

Greer thought for a moment, examining the beer bottle label. He looked up, re-acquiring eye contact. "Actually, no one knows it all. You're the first one I've laid out the whole story to."

"It's important, Tim. I've got to know exactly, who knows what, about this."

"Sure. Well, Lt. Blair knows the basics, he knows about my contact with Ahn but I didn't tell him the UFO part – I was a little concerned that I'd be tossed out of his office."

Mike smiled and nodded.

"Then there's Mr. Kim, Stretch and Pat Black from Buena Park Police. They each know a piece but not any one knows the whole deal."

"Okay. Anybody else?"

Greer was thinking and shaking his head. "That's it. Wait – there's Mikami, the pathologist. He only knew about the dental devices, but not everything – not what they really are." Greer could practically see the wheels turning in Sullivan's head.

"Where is Ahn right now?"

A look of embarrassment crept across Greer's face. "He's staying at my sister's house in Irvine... I hope that's okay. I just couldn't think of anywhere else to safely park him for a while."

Sullivan grinned. "Good job, Tim! That's what I call showing some initiative!"

Greer didn't quite know how to take that one. He just smiled.

"Okay, first thing is – we get Ahn into a safe house with some serious protection." Sullivan grabbed the phone and dialed McClure. While the call was connecting, he turned back to Greer. "Whaddya know about government security protocol – compartmentalization – need to know, that sort of thing?"

"Not much – probably just what I've seen on TV and maybe some Homeland Security briefings for local cops... Why?"

Sullivan grinned again. "Governments are secretive by nature. It's some kind of an inbred protective mechanism that pencil-pushers developed to consolidate and hold on to their power. They compartmentalize their secrets by attaching layers of rules, classifications and enforcing strict need-to-know procedures. Sometimes it gets so convoluted that the left hand doesn't know what the right hand is doing – even when they should."

"Right – like the FBI and CIA not sharing info around the 9/11 incident." Greer injected.

"Correct – but think of it about twenty times worse. Sometimes it gets so bad – like where information gets buried so deep that it actually gets forgotten – people retire, pass away, files just disappear..."

"Yeah, but what does this have to do with...?"

"Because, I'm about to commit a major federal crime, disclosure of classified info. I'm going to share with you some things that I've just recently learned, information that just may directly be connected to your Korean murder cases."

Greer blinked.

Sullivan continued. "I'm already about neck-deep in this caper. I'm afraid I have to drag you in - right along with me!"

Chapter 34
Oahu, Hawaii

Sullivan approached the car rental customer service counter at Honolulu International Airport. The Hawaiian Air flight from John Wayne in Orange County had been smooth and uneventful. He even managed to get some much needed shuteye.

"Would you like to take the extra damage insurance, Mr. Sullivan?" The shapely clerk asked in her best professional persona. She did this while silently mouthing the word "no" in such a way that her supervisor, standing behind her, could not see what she was doing.

She had a vibrant red flower tucked over her right ear. Sullivan knew that this was bit of island lore that signified her availability. Mike picked up his drivers license and credit card, and thanked her with a warm smile. He declined the insurance. She winked, sending him off to the shuttle that would take him to his car.

Twenty minutes later, he'd worked his way through the metro traffic pattern to the top side of Oahu's largest city. He cruised northward on Hawaii Highway 2. It was a beautiful clear afternoon. The dense hustle of the city soon gave way to the green hills of Wahiawa. Soon after, the H-2 highway ended and merged into local 99. He continued north.

As he drove, he thought about where he was going, and the man he expected to see. He also thought about what was going to happen when he got there. It had been many years since they had last crossed paths. That encounter nearly resulted in death – for both of them. Sullivan wasn't quite certain as to how he would be received.

Acres of gentle rolling pineapple fields whizzed by on both sides of the highway. When he had nearly reached the North Shore, he took the turn off for Waialua and continued northwest. Mike recalled that this roadway ended just beyond the Coast Guard Station at Kaena Point, the most western spot on the island. Presently, he reached the point where the roadway narrowed so it was barely wide enough for one lane.

The ride to Kaena is a bit off the standard tourist trail. On the left, island vegetation cascades from the hillside and, in spots, nearly grows across the road. On the right is the constantly changing landscape of volcanic rock, sand and endless ocean. If you happen to be there during the right time of the year, you might see some of the tallest and longest surf in the world.

Homes in the area are few and far between. Squatters, students, economy travelers and surf bums sprinkle encampments along the strands. They come and go much like the South Pacific tides.

Sullivan drove until he spotted the landmarks. One was a rocky outcropping that hung partially over the roadway and another was the battered blue and white county sign that marked the property line for a small airfield. He wheeled the gray Ford sedan off the road and left it.

The late day sun hung an hour above the western horizon. Flame red plumes of cloud already clustered in promise of another spectacular Oahu sunset. He walked north through the trees in a direction generally toward the beach. After a few minutes, he found what he was looking for. The small wood frame cottage looked like a squat block sitting atop low stilts in the sandy soil. The framed windows were hinged at the top, and propped open on little sticks without benefit of screens. The high pitched roof was thatched, expertly tied and woven from dried palms. There was a broad porch covering the entire waterfront length of the cottage. The porch contained a mix of battered stuffed and wicker furniture. It also contained the front door.

He stepped on the porch and neared the door. He stopped, looked and listened. From some distance away – a place not inside the house – he could hear water running. There were three other huts that he could see along the strand. It appeared, at least at this house, that there was no one at home.

He stood quietly on the porch for a few more seconds. The front door stood invitingly open. He poked his head inside for a look. The bungalow was divided into three rooms. The largest was a living room - kitchen combination. The other two were a bedroom, with a rumbled king size bed, and the other was a large bathroom. He neither saw nor heard a soul.

Deciding to chance a more thorough look, he stepped inside. In one corner of the main room, there was a table filled with books and papers. He went there first and browsed through the material. Not finding anything of interest, he moved next into the kitchen. There, also, was nothing that captured his interest. He opened the refrigerator door. The ancient cold box was a Crosley, white with a chrome handle, probably from the fifties. For some reason, he liked things from that era. They just seemed to be simple and sturdy, perhaps from a time more ordered and less complicated.

The hinges of the old refrigerator door squeaked as he opened the box. Inside he saw cartons, milk, orange juice, five brown glass bottles of locally brewed beer and some cheese and fruit. He lifted the milk carton and sniffed. It was okay. He closed the door and turned. Intending to go through the bedroom next, he took two steps and paused.

An idea bloomed. He retraced his steps to the Crosley and opened the freezer compartment. There it was. He withdrew the frosty half-full liter bottle of Russian vodka. A smile spread across his face. In a whisper, he said, "Hello, Nikolai. How'ya been?"

He returned the vodka bottle to its chilly berth, and, on a whim, snatched one of the beers. He roamed around the main room pausing to view several photos on to the wall. The pictures all looked to be of local scenes and people. A number of the photos were of a beautiful Eurasian woman taken in various backgrounds. In some of the pictures, there was an older man. He tapped the bottle top against a face. "Bingo." He said softly.

Giving the bedroom nothing more than a cursory walk-through, he stepped back out onto the front porch. There, he selected the most comfortable chair, and settled down to watch the impending fireworks display on the western horizon. He opened and sipped at the beer. Glancing at the label, he chuckled. It said, "Maui Waui – Pale Ale". He settled in to watch the sun perform its blazing daily dive into the ocean.

A few minutes later, he again heard the sound of running water. Going to the edge of the porch, he looked around and figured out that the sound was coming from a spot about two hundred feet off to the right. There, attached to an outside wall of an outbuilding was a full blown shower, complete with hot and cold faucets. Luxuriating in the cascade of water was the delightfully naked form of a young woman. Sullivan leaned to better enjoy the view. She had nicely tanned skin – no suit lines – long black hair – longer still, shapely legs. All in all and even at the distance, it was quite a picture.

There was a battered pair of old binoculars atop one of the seat cushions, Bushnell 7 X 50's, with a brown leather strap. He picked them up. Reading the name on the glasses triggered warm thoughts about Audrey Bushnell. He rolled the focus knob until he had a clear picture. He abruptly stopped thinking about Audrey... The beauty in the shower was the same woman in the photos on the wall.

Nikolai, you dirty old dog, what are you doing with this gorgeous young monkey, way out here – why she's young enough to be your daughter, you old... Hell, maybe even your grand daughter! He mused. He continued to watch her through the glasses as she finished performing her ablutions, and then methodically turned off the shower valves. She picked up a large white towel and at first blotted her hair. Then she toweled off her chest and arms. When she went to work on her backside, Mike decided to put the binoculars down. The lenses were starting to fog.

Bringing nothing with her but the towel, she walked towards the cottage. She spotted Sullivan on the porch when she was about a hundred feet out. The only indication was a minuscule hesitation in her gait, as she ambled towards the little house. Mike continued to watch her approach. He thought, *"This chicky is a cool one, a very cool one.* The woman made no attempt to cover herself.

At about twenty feet away, she bent over, and performed a little maneuver that shook out her hair and flipped the gleaming black wet mass onto her back. Then, she draped the towel over her right shoulder and mounted the first step. Saying nothing, she stood in front of him with hands on hips. Her pose was defiance or a challenge. He sat quiet. She eyed Sullivan. Her left nipple stood at full attention; and there was a serious set to her mouth and face, that was offset, perhaps outright contradicted, by the mischievous twinkle in her eyes. He guessed her to be mid twenties, tops.

Mike slightly raised the beer bottle in a small gesture of salute.

She spoke. "Hey Brah! That my beer you be drinkin 'n my chair you be sittin'?" The tonal island lilt to her voice was as charming as it was faked.

"Could be – if you live here."

"Damn ri!" - the second word came out like rye – "I be leevin' here." She gracefully moved past him and went into the house. A pleasant flowery scent floated in her wake. From inside, her voice returned, diminished only in volume as she moved from room to room. "And I don't recall that I be knowin' yah, Brah."

Mike heard the sounds of drawers opening and closing. He sat still, listened, and said nothing more.

"So… Yah come stealin' - rapin' or jist visitin'?"

"I'm just visiting – and thanks for the beer – by the way."

"You're welcome, Brah. Say – yah gotta name?"

"Yeah, I gotta name."

"Yah gonna tell me, Brah - or do I gotta beat it outta yah?"

Mike had been looking out towards the surf line. Twilight was in full court press. A lone surfer, with a long board tucked under his arm, walked toward the house. He was still a good distance off.

The woman's voice picked up in volume as she softly padded back out onto the porch. "Actually, I won't beat yah, Brah – I jist shoot yah." Her last statement was punctuated by the distinct metallic clack sound of a revolver hammer being pulled back.

He slowly turned, eyeing the woman over his right shoulder. She'd slipped into a short flowered shift that clung perfectly to her very nice figure. She was a beauty. In the quickening twilight, he could easily see the multi-racial features flowing through her intelligent face. About five foot six, she had the classic Asian round face and jet black straight hair. But the dominant feature was her eyes. They were like large almonds, huge, nearly amber in color and ever so slightly uplifted at the outside edges. The nose was aquiline, a definite European influence. The combination gave her a mysterious, almost hypnotic look.

In her left hand, she held a small Smith & Wesson, blue steel, two inch. It looked like a Chief's model. Her right hand was connected to a hairbrush, with which she was making strong and repeated long strokes against her hair.

Sullivan looked back towards the beach. "That's not really necessary - you know."

"It is though. If I don't comb it out right now, it'll tangle - bad."

"I mean – the gun."

"I know what you mean, Brah."

"The name is Michael."

"Nice name – Michael."

"I'm here to see…" He didn't know what name to use. "The man that lives here… I've not come to hurt – anyone." He took another small pull from the beer.

"And I believe yah – Michael. I'm jist gonna hold thisa gun to make me feel good. Okay, Brah?"

"Yeah, it's just… That particular gun - is very unstable when you have it cocked like that. Slightest thing could make it – go off."

"Really. Yah mean it's not like in the movies? Can these things really go…" Blam! The concussion echoed out over the sand. "Off - like that?"

Chapter 35
Anaheim, California

Ichiro quickly closed the door and pressed his back to it. He flipped the deadbolt to the locked position, and took in the disarray of their hotel room. It looked as if someone had tossed in a grenade. The room was in shambles.

Jiro lay sprawled half across the bed, half on the floor. His right hand gripped the knife with the razor serrated blade that he had used to dispatch many of the traitors. It looked as if Jiro had gone into some kind of a hysterical frenzy. He was howling and crying. It did not appear that he was even aware of his brother's return.

Ichiro spoke to him in easy even tones. He knew he only had minutes before the police would arrive. "Easy, my brother..." He spoke in Korean. "I have returned now – everything is fine. Look! I have more medicine to ease your pain."

Ichiro stepped in behind his brother, and grabbed the wrist of the hand that held the knife. He easily removed the weapon and discarded it out of Jiro's reach. He pushed aside some of the clutter and pulled his brother's feverish body up on to the bed. Jiro whimpered. Ichiro held him for a few seconds, comforting him without speaking further.

Abruptly, Ichiro pulled his brother's upper torso into a near sitting position. From behind, he expertly grabbed Jiro's head and twisted it until he heard the cervical vertebrae snap. Ichiro held his brother still for a few more seconds.

For an instant, Jiro's consciousness climbed up out of the haze of infection that raged within his body. A brief moment of lucidity occurred. He blinked, his gaze went to his brother's face. The look was one of disbelief. His breathing rattled then stopped.

Ichiro felt the life slip away from his brother's body. He could not bear to look into the sightless staring eyes any longer. He laid Jiro back on the bed facing away from him. He looked around the room and found the large bottle of alcohol he had used to clean Jiro's gunshot wound. He splashed the flammable liquid over the bedcovers and onto his brother's body. He snatched a book of paper matches, complete with the smiley face logo of the HappyLand Hotel. He struck one and set the entire book afire. He dropped the small torch of yellow-orange fire onto the bed and set the room ablaze.

He moved quickly into the bathroom. There was a small sliding window just above the shower. The opening was barely big enough for a man. He stripped out the sliding window pane and screen. He wrapped a towel around his fist and beat out the remaining glass and metal frame. He managed to wiggle his body through the narrow opening and hung suspended by his fingertips.

The drop to the ground was at least fifteen feet. Fortunately there were shrubs and ground cover below. He released his grip, and fell, landing with a lung shuddering thud at the exact same moment that a police officer banged on the door to room 232. Ichiro recovered his breath and like a wisp of smoke, disappeared into the night.

Chapter 36
Oahu, Hawaii

When the gun fired, Sullivan froze. He knew she was playing with him. He just didn't have all the rules down for this game.

Despite the gunshot, the surfer arrived without haste. He leaned his long board against the building, and walked up onto the porch. He eyed Sullivan. The man was in his early sixties, about six foot, still in fairly good shape, well muscled with a slight belly. His skin had the wrinkled tone of old leather. It was the classic skin of an older person who had spent too much time under the rays. The face and grey eyes were intelligent, crinkled and well lined. The blond hair, still fairly full, was streaked with grey.

There was a long moment before recognition set in the steely eyes. Then he spoke. "Don't worry about her – I mean her handling a firearm. She's been an expert with a pistol since she was ten. I ought to know, I taught her - myself."

The man directed his next comment to the woman, "Vika, stop brushing your hair for a moment. I need you to watch this gentleman very closely - while I search him." The man's use of English was deliberate and text book perfect. But there was a curious almost un-identifiable accent. "And if he should do anything, at all, untoward – please shoot him, Dear. Shoot him in the head."

The woman put down the brush, and assumed a two handed Weaver stance with the revolver.

Abruptly he said to Sullivan, "Stand up." and motioned with his hand..

For a second, Mike thought about hanging on to the beer bottle, perhaps to use it as a weapon. He quickly discarded the notion, set the bottle down and stood up, hands up and out at shoulder level.

The blond man quickly and roughly spun Sullivan around, expertly frisked him, and then pushed him back down with one word, "Sit."

He'd emptied Mike's pockets. Among the debris was his wallet and police ID folder. He inventoried it all, paying particular attention to the driver's license and Sheriff's ID card and badge. Then, with a smirk on his face, he crossed his arms and stared at Sullivan.

When he spoke next, the language was Russian, perfect native elocution, perfect educated Russian. The dialect tended towards the Ukraine. "So, Pasha, this is quite a development – you showing up like this." He glanced at the open ID folder. "And what is this - you call yourself - these days – Mikhail? Misha - no?"

Sullivan's response was a bit slow. He hadn't had the occasion to wrap his mouth around the tongue of the Motherland in – how many years? Mike said, "Wasn't it you, Nikolai, who first taught me that a name was like an item of clothing - to be worn – used and discarded as the situation requires."

"Yes – this is probably true. But, I still like your old name better. Aleksandr – that was a good name, full of character... It denotes strength and power. This Mikhail – it is like a pussy cat. It sounds so..." He used the idiom for 'squeaky', but in Russian, it didn't sound right to Sullivan.

"Nikolai, like it or not, this is my name. This is who I am - now."

"Yes, of course... What about this police business? This is cover identity, yes? I never would dream, in a million years, that you - of all people - would cultivate an interest in joining the - Militia!" He spat the Russian word out that roughly translated to "Civil Police".

"Enough of this banter - I have business."

"You certainly do, Pasha – or maybe I should now call you, Misha. Yes, Misha. Tell me why your business should not begin with me having Viktoriya shoot you right now, and we bury your rotting carcass in the sand?"

"You always did have a thing for nicknames, didn't you Nikki?" Sullivan parried.

"And you always had a thing for the ladies – is this not true?"

"You don't seem to be doing too bad in that department for an old fart!" Sullivan cast a leering glance toward the girl.

The blond man's eyes widened a bit on that one. "Hold your tongue, Comrade. This is my daughter you desecrate. Her name is Viktoriya."

"Daughter!" Sullivan's surprise was real. "Nikolai, I had no idea... Truly, no idea!"

Nikolai switched back to English. "Viktoriya Irina – say hello to Mister..." He glanced again at the police ID. "Mister Detective

Michael Sullivan. He is an old..." Nikolai groped for the appropriate word. "He is a former associate of mine."

Viktoriya continued to hold the gun on Sullivan. Mike continued in Russian. "Irina – of course. Now I get it. She is beautiful, Nikki – beautiful, just like her mother."

An expression of wistfulness momentarily passed across Nikolai's face. "Yes, she is." He quickly recovered, swelling at the compliment.

Sullivan seized the moment. "Now, for God's sake, tell her to put the damn gun away so we can talk some business. I'm here to - sweeten your - retirement."

"Horse shit! You are here because you want something from me."

Mike eyed the man he had known so well, so many lifetimes before. If there were one man in the world who was capable of springing Gomez from wherever he was in North Korea, Sullivan now stood before him. Mike spoke. He was straightforward and earnest. "It's true. I want – no - I need your help."

"And perhaps you shall have it, Pasha. By the way, these days I like to be called Gordon." Nikolai gestured to his daughter, and she lowered the gun. "Do you like that name. I borrowed it from a bottle of gin."

Mike smiled.

"Perhaps we should speak in English. Vika's Russian is only fair, and I know you do not wish to be unnecessarily rude."

"Of course."

Nikolai fingered the two papers he had removed from Sullivan's pockets. They were the copies Greer had given him from the Korean murder case files. He unfolded and studied them both for a moment. "Let me guess. Whatever it is that you want – it has something to do with these." He waived the papers gently in one hand. "Vika dear, take a look at these." He handed both over to the woman who still held the gun, but now casually, upside down by the trigger guard.

She looked at the hand written sheet first. She looked up at her father and said, "Energy Project?"

Sullivan couldn't help but notice that all trace of island accent had departed from her voice.

Nikolai said, "Correct. Now what can you tell us about the picture?"

Light fading on the porch, she stepped back inside and examined the paper under better illumination. In less than a minute she returned and handed it back to Nikolai/Gordon. She addressed her father directly – ignoring the presence of Sullivan. "It is from the Chosun Dynasty. I believe it is called the Hang-Il insignia. It was a medallion signifying the power of the office of the last great dynasty of Korea, the line of Kings that ruled for nearly five hundred years. It ended with the occupation of Korea by Japan in 1910. I recall recently reading of the death of the last person in the blood line to the Chosun throne. The man died in obscurity somewhere in Japan."

Nikolai beamed. To Sullivan he said, "See what a great education can do for your children? Vika is a graduate of the University of Pyong Yang."

Properly impressed and groping for something to say he said, "Impressive – I see you received your mother's excellent mind as well as her good looks."

A strange look crept over her face. "You knew my mother?"

Sensing that he may be getting into dicey territory, Mike flashed a quick glance at Nikolai."

For a fraction of a second, the blond man looked a bit weary. He recovered quickly and smiled. "There is that – and many other things we need to discuss. Perhaps you would have supper with us – we could talk and then you could tell me what small service I could provide for the enormous amount of money you are about to give me."

For the first time since his arrival, Mike began to breathe a bit easier. He also believed that he'd come to the right man.

삼 질식시킴

Vika and Nikolai served up a delightful dinner of pan fried fish, salad and more of the local beer. Over the meal, Sullivan briefed his old friend on the covert mission that resulted in Charlie Gomez becoming a guest of the North Korean Navy. He omitted only the details about what they thought they might be recovering from the underwater crash site. But he told his old friend virtually everything else. Nikolai listened keenly.

Mike laid out Greer's theory connecting the murders in California and the events in Korea. He told of the defectors being forced to work on the "Energy Project" but omitted any inference to the suspected extra-terrestrial origin of the power source. Mike knew he would have to deal out most of his cards to get Nikolai to play. Information was the currency of his business – his former business. The only remaining issue was how much money Nikolai would extort for his services.

After dinner, Viktoriya again picked up the medallion paper. She studied it closely. After a while, she excused herself and went to the cluttered table in the living room. From somewhere she produced a laptop computer and got on-line. She worked the internet for a few minutes while the men talked. Finally, she returned to the table.

Nikolai interrupted their discussion. "Pardon me, Misha." Directing comment to his daughter, he said, "Okay, Vika – I know that look. What is it?"

She placed the paper back on the table, and tapped the image of the medallion. She had her scholarly voice on again. "I was generally right about the medallion. But, there was something that just kept bugging me. So I did a little research."

"And..."

"And, I was right. It is the medallion of the last Royal dynasty of Korea, the Chosun – but the name goes back even further – and the image itself – it has been changed a bit."

Nikolai said, "I don't understand. What does this have to do with Misha's problem?"

She looked over at Mike and smiled. "It may not mean anything. It may just be another obscure piece of the puzzle."

Both men waited and listened.

She continued. "The Chosun dynasty came into being in 1392 Common Era. It lasted until 1910, like I said before, that's when the Japanese invaded and colonized Korea. The dynasty name and the origins of the Chosun medallion or insignia actually go back much further. The founding royal dynasty of Korea was called Gojoseon. The pronunciation of the name is similar to Chosun."

Mike nodded. She continued. "All of that occurred around 2300 B.C. Anyway, the lion headed dragon emblem was adopted back then. Except, in your picture, the symbol has been flipped or inverted." She pointed to the image.

Sullivan said, "I don't get it. What do you mean? Is it upside down?"

"No, it's been inverted laterally. You see, in your copy, the body of the dragon curved off to the left of the center line. In the original, it curved off to the right. I saw a website picture just now. I would have printed it out, but we're out of paper." She flashed a look at Nikolai.

Sullivan's cell phone started ringing. He looked at the Caller-ID. The display read "GTI, Inc." and was followed by a series of numbers he didn't recognize. He held up a hand to Nikolai and Vika and punched the button.

The man's voice said. "Hello, Mr. Sullivan. This is Mateo…"

Recollection did not come instantly. "I'm sorry, who…?"

"It's Mateo, sir. The GTI pilot from…"

"The Guatemala run! Of course – Ferdie - how are you?"

"I'm great, sir, thanks – and I'm inbound, with the Gulf Stream. I should set down at HNL in about seventy-five minutes."

"Wonderful. Frankly, I didn't expect such a classy ride."

"Mr. Gomez said you needed speed, range and a good pilot. I hope I'll do."

"You will better than just do…" Mike thought for a moment. Ferdie, I'm up near Kaena Point. Know where that is? It'll take me a while to get back down to Honolulu – a couple of hours at least."

"Would you like me to divert - to come to you?"

"You can do that?"

"Roger. Stand by a moment."

In the absence of conversation, Mike could just barely make out the faint whine of the Gulf Stream jet engines. A few more seconds passed and Mateo's voice returned. "Mr. Sullivan – there's an airfield just east of the Coast Guard Station. It's a small one – about two thousand feet and uncontrolled – but the weather's good and I can easily put in there."

"Christ Mateo. That's, like, right around the corner from where I am. Talk about curb service."

"I'm here to take care of you, sir."

They spoke for a moment longer and Sullivan rang off. Returning his attention to his hosts, Mike said, "Sorry, that's my ride. Where were we?"

Vika picked up the thread of their conversation. "Chosun… You see, these were difficult times. Most people lived in a strange culture. Feudal Lords warred viciously over tiny plots of real estate. The people were kept in check through various primitive belief systems that included black magic and well organized bands of soldiers – cutthroats, really – that terrorized everyone into submission. These guys would do all the dirty work for the Kings. Well, this symbol, way back then, was the insignia for the…" A puzzled look captured her face. She looked at her father and uttered a phrase in Korean, "용병 군인".

Nikolai considered her statement. He said. "Yes, soldiers - mercenary soldiers?"

"Yes, kind of like Japanese Samurai, but without honor."

Sullivan piped up. "Kind of like Korean Mafia?"

Viktoriya laughed. She had the most delightful laugh. "Yes, very good – like Korean Mafia – the bad guys!"

"So…" Mike continued. "Maybe, whoever is doing the Korean killings in California is using this ancient symbol as a calling card – perhaps one with a little historical and psychological intimidation attached to it?"

"That is a good theory." Vika offered and the group lapsed into another quiet moment.

Nikolai spoke up. "Thank you, my dear. I am certain that Mr. Sullivan enjoyed that almost as much as me. Now would you take a short walk so I can speak to our guest in private?"

She nodded to her father, smiled at Sullivan and disappeared.

For a moment nothing was said. Sullivan broke the ice. "She is one smart kid."

"Yes, she is. But now you need to tell me what it is you have omitted. What earthly reason could the DPRK idiots have for running around inside the US killing people? You are holding back, Misha. If you want my help - and you are correct in assuming I am one of the few that can get you in and get your precious Charles Gomez out – well, its all or nothing…"

"I know - In for a penny, in for a pound. Is that how that goes?"

"Exactly. Now give."

Sullivan took in a long breath and let it out. He started in. "Remember the Roswell thing in 1947…"

Twenty minutes went by. Nikolai leaned back and let out a low whistle. "That's quite a story… How much money can you give me?"

Without hesitation, Sullivan answered. "I have authorization to pay you a hundred thousand in any form you request."

Nikolai laughed. He got up and walked to the old Crosley refrigerator. He came back with the vodka bottle and two small water glasses. "Five hundred thousand! Half now and half when we retrieve your precious friend, Mister Gomez." He poured a couple of inches of the semi-frozen liquor in each glass. The vodka eased out of the bottle, flowing like syrup. "Shall we drink to our agreement, Misha?"

Mike's face was set in stone. He glared at Nikolai for a long moment. Slowly he picked up his glass and clanked it against the other. "Deal."

Nikolai laughed again and tossed down the scalding drink. "You never were a good negotiator, Pasha-Misha. I know you need me – and you know I was going to get more money from you." His laughter continued.

Sullivan stood up. He tossed back his drink – savored the raw taste of the alcohol for a second and put the glass down. "You're right, Nikolai. I do need you. And you did beat me out of more money – but, I still got a good deal. I was ready to go to a million."

The color drained from Nikolai's tanned face. "A mill…"

"Come on, get your stuff. We've got a plane to catch."

Chapter 37
Santa Ana, California

The vibration feature on Greer's new cell phone was so vigorous, it nearly walked the device off the edge of his desk. Although he had the office phone tucked between shoulder and ear and was thoroughly engrossed in conversation, in true outfielder form, he reached out long with his right arm and captured the buzzing bundle of electronics just as it made its suicidal leap for the floor.

It was the inscrutable pathologist, Dr. Mikami on the line. "Good morning Detective. I have an interesting case this morning – a burn victim - from Anaheim. I think you will want to see this one."

Greer groaned. Not another dead body. He thought. He cleared his throat. "Doc – can't you just tell me about this one. Understand, I'm not complaining, but, for me, it's a little early in the day for a body."

"Too bad, Detective. You are a detective, are you not? This one has to been observed. Besides – it'll be good for you – builds character."

"Right – just what I need, more character. So what's the interesting part?"

"Remember the little dental device things that we discussed before - the ones that I was supposed to forget about? Well, we have another victim. Actually what I mean is we have another device in another victim."

"Another Korean murder? Where'd this one come from? I hadn't heard about any others since the Garden Grove case."

There was a slight hesitation. It was if Dr. Mikami was groping for the right words. "Maybe Asian – I can't readily tell as yet. But definitely murder – I think they just tried to cover it up with the fire."

"Christ – it's a bad one, huh?"

"Yes. This case would be what you police guys call a 'crispy critter'."

Greer felt his stomach turn and tasted bile in his throat. He sighed into the phone. "I'll be right over."

Minutes later, Greer stood next to the diminutive Dr. Mikami. They faced a white vinyl zippered bag lying atop one of the stainless steel examination tables. The form inside was small. Mikami handed Greer a mask. "You may want to put this on.' Mikami slid his own mask over his nose and mouth and waited while Greer fumbled with the strings to cover his face.

"Is it a child?" Asked Greer.

Mikami's hand went to the zipper. The dark eyes peeking over the mask considered the detective. "No. It's an adult." He thought about trying to prepare Greer for the shocking site of the body. "You see, fire is – devastating to the human body. The heat causes the muscle tissue to contract; often, much of the mass is consumed. What you end up with is often small – and never pretty. Ready?"

The closure silently slid open. Instantly, the pungent stink of burnt human flesh and fecal material filled the room. Greer stepped back.

The form Mikami uncased was shriveled to something about the size of a ten year old. The arms and legs were drawn into a fetal-like position against the torso. Chunks of burnt flesh fell away from what was left of the face and arms as Mikami manipulated the body out of the sack.

Greer turned away and gripped an adjacent vacant examination table. Waves of nausea rolled over him.

"Try to breath shallow and through your mouth, Detective." Mikami was kind enough to give Greer a moment to recover – actually several moments. The nausea subsided. Greer returned to Mikami's side. "You okay?"

Greer nodded. "What – what can you tell me?"

"This is an un-identified subject. The story is - he came out of a hotel fire in Anaheim. Anaheim P.D. originally sent him over as a straight casualty. The report was – that there was some drinking – some kind of disturbance – the usual stuff. When the patrol officers showed up, the room was fully involved in flame. I hear it was pretty bad – it spread to other rooms. They got all the people out and knocked down the fire. When they got inside the room where the fire started, they found this gentleman."

"Jesus…" Greer pressed the mask to his face and tried to look at the body. It was all he could do to focus, to suppress the constant gag reflex.

Mikami continued. "It looks to be arson. They found some traces of an accelerant – looks like it was dumped around the head and hands – probably to make identification difficult. We're pretty certain that he is Asian. Preliminary tests on the hair gave us that much. DNA will confirm it."

Greer nodded.

"There are several interesting things. First – he had a gunshot wound. It looks to be several days old." He steered Greer to a nearby X-ray light panel. He snapped it on and fluorescent light illuminated pictures of the torso on the table.

Greer could clearly see the shape of the slug. He could also see the familiar shape of the lingual retainer affixed to the bottom front teeth of the victim. At least in the x-ray images, the dental retainer looked identical to the others.

Still on the bullet. "It looks like it lodged in the posterior shoulder muscle mass near the cervical vertebrae. It looks pretty intact, too."

"So, it wasn't the fire that killed the guy?"

"Not even close. We've done a prelim study on some of the lung tissue. This guy didn't breathe any smoke – not a bit. Strange thing is - the gunshot wasn't the cause of death, either."

"Okay, I'll bite. What was?"

"Here. Look at the cervical vertebrae." He pointed a few centimeters above the image of the bullet. "See how these vertebrae are distended and out of alignment?"

Greer peered close at the image but really didn't have the faintest idea as to what he was looking at. "Yeah."

"This guy had his neck snapped. Death probably came pretty quick."

"Broken neck – Could it be from a fall?"

Mikami shook his head. "Probably not. This damage was done by hyper-rotation of the neck. In other words, somebody had to force the head to rotate well beyond the point where it is supposed to stop." Mikami rotated his own head from left to right, laterally. "This is the kind of thing that the movies like to portray as being easy to do. In reality, it takes a lot of strength and know-how to kill a person this way."

"What are you trying to tell me, Doc?"

Mikami's eyes twinkled in the harsh lab light. He considered the question for a moment before replying. Finally, he said. "Who ever killed this guy – they really knew what they were doing".

Chapter 38
Sea of Japan

Once again, the group was assembled around the conference table aboard the Glomar. A crewmember knocked and entered with a tray of steaming coffee and rolls. He set it down, and paused making eye contact and asking the silent question to the ranking man in the room, which happened to be Commander Dubord. Dubord nodded and the crewman discretely withdrew.

Present were Dubord, and ship's officers McMillan, Sells, Mike Sullivan and a disheveled looking Nikolai, who was attired in cut-offs, a flowered shirt and rubber flip-flops. Two additional middle aged men, also dressed in the ship's non-descript uniforms, were present. Both were unknown to Sullivan. One was Asian.

Moments later the door opened and Captain Marshall entered. He took the seat at the head of the table and started right in. "Mr. Sullivan." He nodded at Mike and cast a disdainful eye on the scruffy Nikolai.

Mike was certain the pause was his cue for an introduction. He cleared his throat and began. "Captain – gentlemen, this is Mister – ah – Gordon, Mister Nick Gordon. He's a former associate of mine – who just happens to have a great deal of knowledge and familiarity with the DPRK." Mike fell silent.

Most around the table simply nodded. Captain Marshall was eyeballing Nikolai like he was some kind of vermin within their midst. In his head Mike was preparing amplification to the introduction. Before he could begin, Marshall added. "Okay – let's not waste a lot of time. I understand you gentlemen" – he hung another long look on Nikolai – "have some kind of rescue plan you wish to discuss?"

Sullivan jumped right in. "Yes. I want you to help us rescue Gomez."

"And just how do you propose to do that, Mister Sullivan?"

"I want you to facilitate the insertion of a small team into North Korea. It will be me and Gordon." He added. "We're going to locate Gomez, spring him and get him out of there."

"Am I correct in assuming this is not a sanctioned mission?"

"Yes Sir, you are correct in your assumption that our government has taken the position that they don't want to start another international incident and have declined to help..." He decided to add the word – "directly." However, GTI is throwing everything they've got behind it."

"Yes, I've already received my coded telex message from the CEO..." He drummed his fingers on the table. "Look, Sullivan. Be reasonable here. You're asking me to endanger my ship and crew. And, if I understand the situation correctly, you don't even have a clue as to where Mr. Gomez may be held..."

"That's right, sir. As of this moment, we don't know - exactly. But we have some good intel and by the time we get on the ground, we hope to know, pretty much, right where to go." Sullivan was stretching the truth about as far as he could.

"For Christ sakes, man. It's been – what - eight days now. They could have him anywhere. What do you guy's plan to do, rent a car and just drive around the countryside while my people stand by in hostile waters waiting for your return?"

"That's exactly what we expect you to do." Nikolai's unsolicited statement delivered in that weird accent of his froze everyone at the table. Sullivan sensed the immediate need to recapture Captain Marshall's attention. Before he could speak Nikolai continued. "Of course you are concerned, Captain. I appreciate that, perhaps even more than you realize. But the fact remains that your job is relatively simple. You drop us off, then after a few days, if all goes well, you pick us up. We are the ones who will be in constant jeopardy."

Marshall's jaw started to tighten. In his world, he wasn't used to being challenged– not even a little bit. Before he could respond Nikolai's voice dropped to a softer notch. He continued. "Captain – my true name is not Gordon. I cannot tell you my name, but that doesn't matter. But, I will tell you a little about my background. For many years – nearly thirty – I lived in what you people call North Korea. I speak the Hangul language; I know their culture and customs. More importantly, I have a pretty good idea of where this Mr. Gomez may be held. North Korea is not the biggest place in world. Believe me when I tell you – if Mister Gomez is there, we will find him."

Marshall continued to drum his fingers on the table. It was clear that he was pondering his decision. He flashed a look at one of the un-identified crewman, the Asian. Marshall said nothing, he just pointed to Nikolai.

The Asian fellow leaned over and looked directly at Nikolai. He spoke in fluent, very native sounding Korean. "The Captain wishes to be further convinced that you truly possess the qualification for this endeavor."

Nikolai bowed from the neck demonstrating a token of respect for the man speaking. His response was in perfect Korean. "Of course. Who do I have the pleasure of speaking to?"

"My name is Kim, Il Jo. I am a Korean cultural specialist assigned to assist Captain Marshall."

"I see. How can I help you?"

"Tell me a little about yourself – your legend if you would, please – as if I was police or military and say - to confront you on the street."

"I would tell you that my name was – one of several and be able to back it up with authentic looking papers. If we were to meet in the far Northeast, perhaps I would tell you that I was the child of a Russian-Asian father from the seaport town of Khasan and a Korean mother from neighboring Sonbong – and that I worked between the two territories that make up the Nanjin-Sonbong trade zone dealing in consumer electronics – and perhaps you would like a complimentary portable TV or CD player?"

Kim laughed but stopped when he realized that everyone else at the table was staring at him. He directed his next remark, in English, and directly to the Captain. "He'd convince me. His dialect and diction is perfect. He's the real deal."

Marshall continued. "Okay – so you have a plan. And, you know a little bit about the country. Tell me, just how the hell are you two going to run around North Korea and not stick out like a sore thumb? Sullivan you must be at least six, five and that red hair! And you, Mister, ah, Gordon – at least you are smaller, but your hair and features…?"

Sullivan spoke up. "You are correct again, sir. And on that subject, would one these gentlemen your ship's Doctor?"

The sandy haired man next to Kim raised a hand. "Leversen - I'm the medical officer. Both of you look pretty healthy to me."

Nikolai grinned, looked at the Captain and then over to the Doctor. "Great! Doctor, we need a bit of your professional expertise... I want you to make my partner, here, look about a foot shorter and just a wee bit Oriental!"

삼 질식시킴

Nikolai stood in front of the small mirror whistling softly as he brushed his freshly blackened hair. He was dressed in a beige long sleeve shirt and brown cotton pants. He stood barefoot, but on the bunk, amid other items laid out were a pair of inexpensive canvas and rubber shoes. Each item of clothing, including the underwear, had been made in North Korea. There was a rap on the door. Nikolai said, "Come."

The door opened and Dubord stepped inside. "Wow, Mister Gordon. That's quite a transformation."

"Let us hope that it will be good enough to fool the fools."

"I wanted to tell you that we will be able to launch the sub within the hour."

"Excellent. Shall we go see how your good Doctor has done with my tall friend?"

Minutes later, in the ship's hospital, they stood alongside an exam table. Sullivan sat in his skivvies while Dr. Leversen poked around his scalp with latex covered hands. Sullivan's hair was also coal black, and his new Asian eyes were dark brown.

Nikolai just smiled. Dubord, on the other hand was thunder struck. "My God, how in the hell did you...?

"Like my work, do you, Commander?" Perhaps you'd like a brow lift and little tummy tuck, later on?"

"Doc, I gotta tell you, this is amazing." He stepped around Sullivan, viewing his face from different angles." How did you... I mean how did you get the eyes to look like that?"

"Actually, it was Mr. Gordon's idea. He's apparently had some experience at this sort of thing. He even supplied us with some of these." Leversen handed Dubord a fishing string-like device with tiny projections along the shaft. "Run your fingers along that and you'll feel the micro-barbs."

Dubord slid the string between thumb and forefinger.

"It's called a Barb String. It's been around for a while, used mostly for reconstructive and cosmetic work. You insert them under the skin to support tissue – that is to keep a constant pressure or tension on the skin and underlying muscle tissue."

"Interesting." Dubord continued to fondle the device.

"You can also use them for a quickie lift face if they're anchored properly." Leversen added.

The trio was examining Sullivan like he was a lab specimen. The doctor twisted Sullivan's head to one side and began to explain as if he were lecturing a class of students. "The procedure is fairly straightforward. We started by making an incision here, just above the ear, then we super-glue a tiny stainless steel anchor ring to the cranial bone. The ring acts as a tie off."

He turned Sullivan back to face them. "Rolling back the upper eyelid in the corner, here, we insert a piece of monofilament material under the lid and poke it under the facial skin bringing it out at the ear incision. Using that line, we feed the barb string. It glides smoothly in one direction, and when we reverse it, the tiny barbs dig in and put tension on the tissue."

"Then we tighten the line just enough to lift the eye edge to the right angle and tie it off. Viola – Irishman temporarily becomes Korean!"

Dubord shook his head. "Gotta hand it to you, Doc. That's absolutely amazing."

"Yeah, well, the hard part was angling for the proper tension so that the slant the eyes is about the same."

Sullivan was looking at himself in a hand mirror. "How long do you think it'll last?"

"Not long – few days – couple of weeks. Eventually, it'll relax, the muscles will adapt, I think. Hell, I don't really know, you guys. I'm an internist - and a fair surgeon – but definitely not a Beverly Hills M.D."

"What are you going to do about his height?" Dubord asked.

Sullivan spoke up. "What – are you disappointed that the Doc didn't take a few inches out of my legs?"

They all laughed.

Nikolai offered. "Actually, there are quite a few tall ones running around the north. It was the generations of Russian influence – teaching them all to be good little comrades – and the fathering of a few mixed background children. He'll be okay if he stoops a little and walks around with his knees bent a bit. He'll get used to it."

Chapter 39
Huntington Beach, California

Days passed. Once, he had made good his escape from the Anaheim hotel, Ichiro went about the business of re-establishing the operating foundation that he required to continue the mission. Only a small part of him mourned the death of his brother. The professional persona had taken over, and he coolly went about the business of damage control and re-grouping.

All traces of the identity he had been using were discarded. They had started out the mission prepared to use several names. Operational security demanded a safe place for storage of their identity documents. Rather than use something common yet difficult to use as a bank safety deposit box, they simply opened accounts at various commercial packaging and commercial shipping stores located in the greater Los Angeles area. It was a simple matter for Ichiro to appear at one of them, collect a box and have instant access to his new identity.

He now had all the material he needed, including a new driver's license, social security card and other miscellaneous personalized papers, including a ATM and credit cards, all perfectly valid with fat credit lines.

At a used car lot in Long Beach, he selected a plain Chevrolet and paid for it with cash. He outfitted himself with new clothes, lightened his hair a few shades, and started wearing a pair of rimless eyeglasses.

In his new name, he booked two weeks at a modest motel just off Beach Blvd. in an older section of Huntington Beach. The motel was one of those perfect places, not terribly discriminating, where many rooms were rented by the hour and cash was king.

Shortly after his departure from Anaheim, he had reported in via email. He had several methods of communication with his superiors. Email was, by far, the most convenient. A quick, thinly veiled message, and he was able to report all of the significant events, including the wounding and subsequent death of Jiro, his need to change locations and operational identity. For the time being, he had suspended his task to locate and eliminate the target, Ahn.

It was a bright morning, about 10:00 AM, when he walked in the small coffee internet cafe called Java Mainline on Main Street in Huntington Beach. Only a couple of blocks from the ocean, on this morning the usually busy shop was a bit thin on clientele.

Most of the patrons were young adults with sun streaked skin and hair. They lounged around in small groups sipping at their drinks and idly chatting. One read from a local weekly paper that focused mostly on surfing news. Another tinkered with a laptop.

He ordered a café latte and handed the girl behind the counter a twenty dollar bill. The girl was about sixteen. She sported short hair that was colored a bright shade of bright red that had never appeared in nature. On the right side of her neck, from ear to collarbone, was an intricate tattoo of a spider traversing a multicolored web. She handed him his five dollar cup of coffee and milk.

"Could I get a few minutes on one of your machines – gotta check my email." Ichiro asked flashing his perfect smile.

The coffee shop had three computers at small tables against the back wall. Each had rather small, flat panel displays. He sat at the one farthest from any other patron, and angled the display so that only he could see it. He typed in the URL for Yahoo mail and entered both user name and pass code. He had a series of email accounts that he used. Security dictated that this would be the last time to use this one. The page refreshed. There was one new message. He clicked it open.

To: 369travel691@yahoo.com
From:248mother680rain@hotmail.com
Subject: Sales report
We received your report and acknowledge your progress thus far. Problems are to be anticipated. You should re-double your efforts to close the remaining prospects. Thus far the sales campaign has been very successful. Some customers will be more challenging than others. Additional corporate resources may be used to close those clients considered most difficult.
Please add the following person to your active list of sales prospects and arrange for a presentation. We understand that he has expressed repeated interest in our products to area representatives.
96514 57862 11478 22458 39547 654 84578 14598 55247 36251 45987 97124 06953 15734 49217 65421 9125 44391 26276 95372
Best regards,
Roger

Ichiro produced a pen and copied the five digit coded number groups from the screen to a napkin. He folded the napkin carefully and put it in his pocket. He logged off the ISP and erased cookies and the browser's history. He even went so far as to power down the computer. Then he stood, scooped up his over priced coffee and walked out. He walked about a half block down from the shop, then turned west on a side street where he had parked his car. Finding it, he unlocked the door and slid inside. There was no one around. He decided to decode the message right there in the car. From the glove box he retrieved some blank paper.

He took a deep breath and closed his eyes. He controlled his breathing and tried to clear his mind. The technique he used was a method for which he had been extensively trained. It was a form of auto-hypnosis.

Ichiro's tradecraft was second to none. Top on his list of concerns was the constant need for tight operational security. To that end, nothing was left on paper that was not intended to be left. Most information that he carried on a job was stored inside his head.

Code papers and books were dangerous. They could be lost, captured and too often compromised by the enemy. The leaders had prepared Ichiro and Jiro well. Through auto-hypnosis, they could retrieve pages and pages of decoding matrixes that they had memorized. All that was necessary was to find the index string of numbers and access the material stored in his memory. Both brothers had been gifted in this area. Ichiro was always a bit better.

The index string was the first two digits of the third group. He glanced at the napkin. It popped out at him. "One-one". He closed his eyes and focused.

The loud rapping on the driver's side window jerked him back to reality. He popped his eyes open to see a woman in police uniform standing in the street along side his car. Parked slightly to the rear of his car and partially into the street was a small golf-cart size vehicle. It was emblazoned "Police Parking Control" and had a rotating orange flashing light on top. The woman held a large black plastic notebook – a parking ticket size notebook. "Mister, you're parked in a ten minute loading zone – I'm afraid I'll have to ask you to move it – or - I've gotta write you a ticket."

Putting on his best con face, Ichiro cranked the window down. Smiling he said, "Sorry. Guess I was just day dreaming. I'll move right away." He turned over the engine.

The lady cop bent down and looked and took a closer look at his face. She wore mirrored sun glasses. Ichiro could see the twin reflections of his own face staring back at him. She said, "Say – you okay?"

Ichiro smiled again. "Yeah – fine, thanks. Just a little preoccupied. I'll move it now."

She backed up a step. "Okay – have a nice day!"

Ichiro eased the Chevy away from the curb and drove off. He shook his head thinking about stupid Americans and their stupid sayings. Have a nice day. How asinine. He aimed his car back to the motel.

삼 질식시킴

Greer was just finishing his visit with Dr. Mikami and the burnt body from Anaheim. A tall man with graying hair approached them. He wore a plaid sports coat, loud tie and carried a dark leatherette notebook. Everything about the man, right down to his well worn crepe soled shoes screamed, "cop." He introduced himself.

"I'm Bruce Beauchamp from Anaheim P.D." Tim Greer was stripping off the latex gloves. They shook hands.

"I'm glad to meet you, Greer. Actually I was planning on looking you up, next. I understand you're the one looking at all the Asian murders?"

"Yes – Korean murders, actually. Unless you've got something I don't know about yet."

"Don't know – but maybe this might be another one for you."

Greer, wanting to get away from the stinking corpse on the table, steered Beauchamp into one of the tiny offices just off the examination room. They took some chairs.

"The scene is – as I'm sure you can appreciate – a complete mess. There's nothing like a good fire to screw up a good crime scene, right?"

"Truthfully, I've never had to deal with a fire scene. Got anything so far?"

"A few things, yes. Witnesses tell us there were two guys – that took the room..." He consulted his notes. "Four - five days ago, now, under what are certainly bogus names – they paid cash in advance. The two were variously described as male whites, late twenties to early thirties. One was supposed to be big and scary looking and the other, smaller, but also kind of weird looking."

"Weird looking?"

"Yeah. One of the wits described them both as possibly being of mixed ancestry – Asian and Caucasian."

"Interesting. What else you got?" Greer shifted in his chair. He was having difficulty getting the horrid smell of burnt human flesh out of his nostrils. The gag reflex was so strong he could barely track with the Detective was telling him.

Beauchamp continued. "An hour or so before the fire, one of them is in the room creating a hell of a donnybrook – yelling, screaming and breaking up furniture. Maybe some of the yelling is in a foreign language but otherwise – unidentified. After a while, the other one shows up outside the door, talks to some of the wits, including a night manager..." He flipped through his notes. "One Irene Comstock. This guy was doing his best to convince everybody that his friend was just drunk, and he was going to quiet him down. Comstock is the one that finally called it in, by the way. Anyhow, this guy goes in the room, a few minutes later, Patrol troops show up on the disturbance call, and the room is fully engulfed in fire. The door is locked from the inside, and the bathroom window and frame were smashed out. We think number two set the fire, and jumped out the window."

"Any physical evidence from inside the room?" Greer asked.

"Well, you know how fires go. We always get something, but it usually takes a while... We've got the body, of course. And the Doc's telling us about the bullet and the broken neck, we've got trace chemicals from an accelerant, possibly methyl alcohol, we've got some containers of medical supplies including some morphine, small prepared syrettes – the kind that are disposable – used for one injection and then tossed. Those might have been taken in a burglary from a Doctor's office in Santa Ana a few days ago. We're trying to connect those dots now, and let's see – what else..."

Beauchamp poured back through his notes, flipping the pages. "Oh, yeah. The hotel staff tells us that for the last couple of days, they haven't been admitted to the room for cleaning and linen. The big guy always stopped them every time. The hotel management staff was about to try and force the issue."

"So – what do you think, so far?"

"Well, putting two and two together – we figure the small guy, he either was shot when they checked in or got shot shortly thereafter. From the medical supplies and drugs – antibiotics also – it looks like they were trying to treat him on their own - rather than risk going to a hospital."

Greer had that funny buzz going in his head - the one that started up whenever he was on to something, whenever the pieces started to fall together. It was a good buzz. "So – what's next in your investigation?"

Beauchamp closed his notebook. "Mikami's going to give me the bullet and we'll do comparative work on that – although we don't actually have anything to compare it to."

Greer smiled. "Oh, yes you do. Get hold of Marty Blayloch at Garden Grove. They had one of the Korean murders, a father and daughter combo. Daughter fired a round and possibly plugged her assailant. Marty's got her gun – a .38 by the way – and some blood that didn't come from her or Daddy."

Beauchamp's eyes widened. "No kidding?" He grinned. "Damn, I love it when stuff comes together."

"Don't we all…" Greer was thinking. "We need Doc to squeeze enough blood and tissue out of the burn victim in there for us to work with. We'll need DNA comparison, not only to the Garden Grove crime scene unidentified splatters, but we'll also want to match it to what they scraped from under the female victims fingernails."

Beauchamp re-opened his notebook and was furiously scribbling notes.

"You know Bruce - I think we just might have our killer – or at least one of our killers – lying right in there on that table."

Chapter 40
Sea of Japan

The experimental submarine Huey cruised silently through black water. The boat moved at a depth of 1900 feet, a mere forty miles off the coast of the Democratic Peoples Republic. Their course was north westerly; their position, by most nautical standards, was well within international waters. By the rule of the paranoid government of the DPRK, they were violating sovereign space and subject to arrest, incarceration and probably much worse.

Three men huddled around the illuminated map table. They studied the chart display of the rocky coastline of the area around Chongjin, the seaport town where Charlie had last been seen. High altitude surveillance photos from the Navy spy plane had plainly showed a struggling Gomez, head swathed in bandages being dragged off the North Korean trawler.

Dubord led the discussion. Nikolai and Sullivan listened intently.

Dubord was talking. "I kind of favor this area to the north, just a little south of Pugo. There doesn't seem to be much along that stretch for several miles, just a lot of rocky coastline and a few villages."

"I agree." Nikolai chimed in. "Much further north, it gets too populated – and to the south – the closer you get to Chongjin – the same thing."

"Mr. Gordon, what do you know about surface patrols in this area?" He was still insisting that he be called Gordon. In his short time on board Huey, the crew had taken to referring to him as "Nick Gordon".

Nikolai looked up. "These North Korean boys take their coastline defense very seriously. Remember, they still think they are fighting a shooting war with the evil Americans, and that any minute the invasion forces will arrive – everywhere. These people have been brainwashed for generations. They really believe that Uncle Sam will attack them any day."

"Meaning…?"

"Meaning - we have to plan for surface patrols at least every hour and a string of on-shore watch stations – little rickety towers, as I recall – and possibly some crude underwater listening gadgets."

"I didn't realize they had any anti-sub technology."

"No offense, Commander, but there's probably a lot your Government doesn't know about these guys. That's the problem when you become too dependent on electronic intelligence. There's nothing quite as comforting as having a good man on the ground, sniffing around and calling home a couple times a week." Nikolai grinned obviously relishing the moment.

"The North Koreans have been playing around with building a listening system for years. Don't worry, it's nothing like the SOSUS system or even like the stuff the Soviets built... Understand, the little comrades aren't very good at much. They've been messing around with this stuff for over twenty years. Most of it still doesn't work worth a crap."

Sullivan was watching the interplay between the two. Nikolai's odd accent at times sounded Australian. Just when you thought you had it nailed, it would change and he'd sound European. Sullivan knew Dubord was trying to get a grip on just who and what Nikolai was.

"Still – perhaps maybe we should reconsider our ingress point." Dubord offered.

"No – it won't be necessary. Look, Commander, I've checked out the little water sled Mister Sullivan and I are going to be using. That is a sweet bit of engineering you've got there, by the way! Those little thrusters that just squirt water right through – Christ, with that quiet little machine, we could drive around these guys all day and night. They'd never even know we were there."

Dubord flashed a look at Sullivan. Mike took the cue. "Mister – ah - Gordon is here, because he is the guy. Nick has spent a good portion of his life living inside this country. I say we go with his judgment."

Dubord nodded.

Nikolai spoke up. "Commander, your ship will be fine – we'll be fine. Remember, most of this country is still using 1950's technology for just about everything. It's like the whole place is in some kind of time warp - like an Asian Cuba!" Nikolai laughed a little at his own little joke. "These are the same folks that spend every dime outfitting one of the largest conventional Armies in the world, but don't have sufficient resources to feed their population, let alone pursue anything else properly."

Sullivan thought it prudent to change the subject. "Okay, another reason to stick with this spot for our landing is, that Nick, Mister Gordon, here, seems to think that its likely that the North Koreans might be holding Gomez in a couple of places, one of which isn't too far from this Pugo." He fingered the coastal town on the map display.

Nikolai piped in. "Yeah, the spot we've selected is as good of a starting point as there is."

"Mister Gordon – if you don't mind me asking - we've agreed to lay off the coast for seven days to recover you folks. Just how do you plan to find this man within several thousand square miles of territory, and get back to the pickup point in that short time frame?"

Nikolai considered the Commander for a moment. Sullivan had already vouched for his ability. Nikolai considered his words carefully. "Commander, you are clearly expert in the command and operation of this magnificent ship…"

A hint of smile flitted across Dubord's face. "Boat - we call a submarine a boat."

"Yes, of course, boat. Well, I am the expert on North Korea. I have spent more years living in that country than many of you have been alive. Let's say - for the sake of discussion – that I know what I'm doing. If it is humanly possible, we will find Mister Charlie Gomez, snatch him and return to meet you at the rendezvous point in seven days! And if things don't work out – well, you can always fire me!" He ended with another little laugh.

Dubord and Sullivan got back to work. They went over communications, and discussed several what-if situations. Satisfied that they were about ready, Dubord suggested that they go aft for a final check out of their equipment before the drop off.

Carter stepped up and handed Dubord a folded paper. "Flash traffic, skipper, from Mom." Mom was the boat crew's nickname for the Glomar Explorer. Dubord took the paper, unfolded and scanned it quickly.

Carter was staring at Sullivan. Mike caught his eye. Carter looked embarrassed. He spoke. "Sorry, if I'm staring, Mr. Sullivan. I just can't get over how much you look like a goo…"

Sullivan cut him off. "The term is person of Asian descent."

"Yeah, sorry - Asian person - I meant. That's a hell of a job Doc did on you. Hell of a job!

Dubord was irritated. "Knock it off, Carter."

"Sorry, Sir." Quickly changing the subject he said. "Will there be any response to the…"

"Not right now. Thank you and go on back to your station. I need to think about this for a minute."

Carter stepped away. Sullivan spoke up. "What's up?"

"Looks like somebody back home might have figured out what we're up to out here. Marshall has been ordered to reposition the Glomar – basically to get us the hell out of these waters. He say's he can stall for three days to conclude operations. It means we have to move your recovery time up to…" He glanced at his watch. "Seventy two hours from now. Sorry, but it looks like you two are going to have to scramble."

삼 질식시킴

Sullivan and Nikolai stood in the pressurized aft equipment space. It was the same space that had previously held the deep submersible Dewey. In its place was a small but sleek underwater sled powered by electric fuel cells. The motive power was a series of steerable flow-jets, literally water squirting devices that quietly pushed the craft, like small jet engines, through the water. The craft had no markings, and like the submarine that carried the sled, it was painted a non-reflective slate color.

They were dressed in thin black dry suits. Next to them were two CCR 2000 rebreathers poised on donning racks. Two crewmen worked in the background preparing the underwater sled and other items of the team's equipment.

The two were traveling light. Mostly what they had were local clothing, a couple of maps, a small satellite phone, concealable weapons and a few other items mostly belonging to Nikolai. Everything had been encased in special waterproof bags, which were essentially economy size heavy duty plastic bags with space suit zippers.

Mike checked over the rebreather that he would be using. "Ever used one these before, Nikki?" He could tell from the look on Nikolai's face that mystery surrounded the device. "Here – check this out." He showed him how to back into the donning rack, strap on the back, the facemask and adjust breathing controls. "For now, just ignore all the gauges and controls. Everything is set correctly for our dive. The unit will adjust automatically as we change depth and so forth."

Nikolai, no stranger to scuba equipment, was clearly unfamiliar with the closed circuit breathing systems.

Sullivan continued. "We can talk underwater about a hundred fifty feet from one another. Our masks have been equipped with scrambled underwater communicators. If the comrades hear us, it will just sound like static.

Nikolai nodded, quickly taking it all in.

"A rebreather is a closed breathing device. It scrubs the carbon dioxide away and adds a touch of oxygen with each breath you take. It's quiet and radically extends your underwater time. Also there are no bubbles to give away your position. These puppies will allow us to stay under water for nearly eight hours."

Nikolai's eyes widened. "My God, I hope it doesn't take us that long to traverse four or five miles of water!"

"Of course not... We'll probably only be in the water an hour or so. The water sled can do nearly twenty knots flat out - unless, of course, we have other problems. In that case, we'd have a long swim to shore. Who knows? You might have to actually earn that half mil!"

Dubord"s voice came over the 1-MC, the sub's main intercom. "Prepare to launch the sled." Mike was still wearing his ship's com earpiece. Dubord's voice came through on a personal channel. "Mike – just wanted to say good luck. You know we'll stay here as long as we can."

"I know you will. We'll do our best to get back on time."

"Just a reminder, we'll float a satellite antenna every three hours, twelve, three, six and nine, just like we discussed. We'll give you a fifteen minute window every three hours. Please call home often."

"Got it – and thanks again."

"Don't mention it. Now go get our man."

"Aye-aye, Sir."

삼 질식시킴

At a navigational position that measures roughly five nautical miles from the North Korean coastline, the continental shelf abruptly falls off. It is a point where the coastal shallows literally drop off a cliff. The gentle downslope ran from the shoreline to the cliff's edge and the maximum depth over this range was about two hundred feet. Once over the edge it was like falling into the abyss. The bottom was literally thousands of feet away.

The super stealth submarine Huey rose silently along the cliff wall. In the depths the terrain was dead and barren. As the sleek craft rose slowly past the five hundred foot zone, a few forms of life began to appear. When the sub reached the cliff's edge, around two hundred feet depth, it was if they had landed on a new planet, a planet rich with life forms. The shallower the water, the more the marine ecosystem thrived. The dark ship hovered - suspended in silence - at a depth of one hundred fifty feet.

Sullivan and Nikolai were sitting astride the water sled. They were fully suited and breathing through the rebreather units. The voice of the diving officer rang in their earphones. "Okay, gents, we are going to flood the compartment now. Start equalizing your ears when you feel the water. We are going to take you pretty quick to four and a half atmospheres – that's about a hundred fifty feet – that's all. Holler if you can't keep up with equalizing. We don't want to start you guys out with blown ear drums."

Both Sullivan and Nikolai acknowledged. They started the somewhat difficult process of trying to blow air up their Eustachian tubes. In this case, the difficulty lay in the fact that they were wearing full face masks. Normally in a scuba diving situation, the diver can reach up and pinch off his nose as he exhales, thereby forcing a little air and slightly more air pressure into his inner ear. With a full face mask one cannot pinch, hence the equalization maneuver becomes a more difficult. Sullivan, an avid diver, with hundreds of hours of full face mask diving time, was doing fine. But, Nikolai had less than ten minutes instruction in pinch-less equalization. To be expected, he was having problems.

"Aiiieee!" Nikolai's plaintive cry was all Mike needed to hear.

"Dive officer!" Sullivan yelled. "Take us back up a bit! My partner can't equalize."

"Copy that, Mister Sullivan." The Pressure/Depth gauge on the wall in front of them had been going steadily down. It read "78" feet. The dial stopped on 79 then started to retreat.

When it read "30" feet, Nikolai exclaimed, "Yeah, that's better. Sorry, I haven't done this in a while."

Sullivan said, "Nikki, look – push the entire bottom of your mask up about a half inch." He demonstrated. "Feel that rubber block hit your nostrils? You can use that block to seal your nose, and blow out in short, sharp blasts of air. It'll work!"

Nikolai experimented and was soon giving the thumbs ups signal to Mike and the diving officer. The crewman's voice came over the intercom again. "Okay gents – let's try this again. Going down, down, down – thirty five, forty, forty-five... How you guys doing?"

Both divers flashed the okay signal, thumb and forefinger making a circle. The diving officer continued to take them down, only this time more slowly.

Presently, the compartment was pressurized to one hundred fifty feet. The diving officer waited until he was certain that both men were comfortable and functioning in all respects. Only then did he alert Commander Dubord.

Less than a minute later the command to launch came. The giant overhead doors swung open. Instantly, they were one with the surrounding ocean. Outside, on the surface, it was late afternoon. Sunlight still flooded the land. Underwater, everything was dark and mostly seen in monochromatic grays. Visibility extended to fifty feet, in spots.

The mechanical tethers were released and the craft floated upward. Sullivan goosed the throttle lever, effectively engaging forward motion as soon as their tiny craft cleared the submarine hull. He dialed up the illumination on the dash instruments and using the gyro-compass set a course for 270, due west and a gradual ascent to a depth of 75 feet. They were to make the run to the shore at a depth of 50 to 75 feet.

The eerie underwater gloom was pierced by two halogen headlamps. Where ever the light played, flashes of color would reflect back from the black and white world they traversed. Sullivan quickly figured out that the little craft could make speeds that would quickly overtake the headlamps limited range. He pulled the throttle lever back, and slowed to a more comfortable cruising speed.

Nikolai's voice broke the monotonous soft whooshing sound of the sled. "Everything is okay, Misha?"

"Just fine, Nikki. We're doing just fine." Mike did some quick calculations in his head. "I figure we've got a little more that one hour before we beach this thing. Maybe you could order us some cocktails and peanuts while we wile away the time".

Chapter 41
Offshore – DPRK

The underwater sled was equipped with high frequency sonar and infra-red sensing devices. Without any other reference points, Mike had been watching their progress on instruments. The most useful was a small computer display panel that collected data from all the on-board devices and fed the data into a map-like display that scrolled along before him. Mike could see a blip that represented their position, and another mark that was their intended destination. When he reckoned they were just a few hundred yards off shore, he slowed the craft to a crawl then eased it to the ocean floor. He managed to park the craft without stirring up much bottom silt. They needed some visibility. The depth meter showed 62 feet.

He twisted on the sled and looked at Nikolai. Reaching out, he pulled Nikolai's head to him until their masks touched. With the physical contact, they could speak to one another, the voice vibrations flowing right through the material of their masks. Mike wanted to minimize the use of their underwater communication units, which were essentially low-frequency radios. He spoke. "Time to take a look-see around."

Nikolai nodded, the edge of his mask squeaking on Sullivan's. He figured it out and held still. "Okay, I'll go." Nikolai reached down and grabbed a stainless steel clip attached to his seat. A nylon line reeled out. He clipped the line to his equipment, flashed an okay sign to Sullivan, and slowly swam upward toward the light.

The surface was calm, the swell almost non-existent. The time was late in the day, but not quite dark. The twilight was sufficient for a quick look around. Nikolai's head popped out of the water. He did a quick 360 degree turn and scanned the coastline and the horizon. He could see a couple of buildings, one of the watch towers off to the north a quarter mile or so. There were no boats. He spun around a few more times taking it all in. Satisfied that they could make landfall, he jerked on the cord three times in rapid succession.

Below on the sled, Sullivan felt the three jerk cord signal. He jerked three times for an acknowledgment, and then pressed a button that started the reeling in of Nikolai's tether line. The progress was intentionally slow, giving Nikolai time to equalize on the way back down. Within a minute or so he was back on the sled. They touched masks again.

"It looks great. We picked the perfect deserted spot." Nikolai gave Mike a quick briefing."

A minute later, Sullivan had the sled moving towards the shoreline. When they reached a point just outside the surf line, where the depth was about thirty five feet, the bottom was flat, sandy and pocked with rock piles, Mike, once again, stopped the sled. He flooded the ballast tanks and killed the main power. The sled was parked alongside a small reef. It was perfect cover. Nikolai and Mike unhooked, gathered their equipment bags and began their short swim to the shoreline.

삼 질식시킴

Two hours later, the two looked like any other Korean men of the area. Dressed in simple peasant clothes, they walked along the gravel roadway. Sullivan had on a round woven hat not dissimilar to the thousands of similar hats worn by the locals. Nikolai sported a battered and faded Red Sox cap.

They'd landed, as planned, within a small rocky cove. There, they stripped out of their dive equipment, gathered their essential items. They buried their remaining equipment in a shallow hole at the water line. It was a simple matter to use the sand and rocks to conceal most evidence of their presence. Each carried a map, and thick wads of the local currency, Won.

Sullivan, always preferring to travel light, carried the portable sat phone and a mini Glock 9 mm. pistol with a sound suppressor. Nikolai, on the other hand had pocketfuls of gadgets, including a portable GPS unit and a few other items he felt were required for their "field trip".

The night was moonless as they moved quickly and quietly along the roadway. Nikolai paused a moment to check the GPS unit. "We need to work our way south. Our first destination is Chongjin."

"How far?"

"Not far – it's about twenty-two kilometers. We'll need to check around there to see what we can pick up from the locals about

Charlie – we might get lucky, and have someone tell us where he's been taken."

"You're kidding, right? We're just gonna stroll into town and start asking people questions. Come on – what are we really going to do?"

Nikolai was looking at a folded map by starlight. "You'd be surprised, Misha. People here aren't much different than anywhere else. They love to gossip. Now look at this..." He pointed out several items on the map. "First we go to Chongjin. There we check around, see what we can find out. If that doesn't pan out, then maybe we go up toward Musan. That's up near the Chinese border. The comrades have a prison camp facility there and another one at Undok, a place here..." He fingered a spot northeast of their location. "My money is on the fact that they will keep him at either of those places. Both are close and easy. That's assuming, of course, they haven't as yet figured out who he really is and shipped him off to Pyong Yang."

"Now there's a comforting thought..."

The two resumed walking. Nikolai took out something small and dark and waved it around.

"That's the second time you done that. What is that thing?"

Nikolai brought the device closer. Mike inspected it under the soft starlight.

"A StarTac cell phone? It was the black plastic model so popular a few years back. You're kidding right? You're really looking for cell phone service – here!"

"Ah, Misha, when will you learn that we are living in the Twenty-first Century. Even backwater places like rural North Korea have some cell phone service – thanks mostly to the Americans."

"That can't be true, Nikki. This country has been embargoed for decades."

"Yes, it has been – embargoed, that is. But, you know Misha, the world economy works well despite the silly decisions made by political people. The Chinese and Japanese have some of the best cell phone systems in the world. Right?"

"Yes, they do." Sullivan agreed. "Especially the Japanese. They say cell phone service is better there than anywhere in the world, including the US."

"My point exactly. You guys sell to the Chinese, who in turn sell to the D.P.R.K. Yes Misha, it's true. A lot of the old analog cell phone equipment has ended up right here – and sometimes – around the towns and cities – it even works!"

"I get it. The old Motorola StarTac works..."

Nikolai nodded. "It works on everything, analog, digital, CDMA. It's really a great piece of technology. They should have never stopped making them."

"Yeah, well some idiot dreamed up the idea of putting cameras into phones. That's progress for you."

삼 질식시킴

Ichiro locked the door to his Huntington Beach motel room. The blinds were drawn. He sat down and faced the material laid out before him. There was the napkin with coded number groups, a blank sheet of paper and pen. He was reasonably certain he wouldn't be disturbed this time. He closed his eyes and breathed regular steady breaths. He relaxed and repeated the key phrases over and over in his mind. It took only seconds and he was ready. He visualized himself standing in a room with green chalkboards on all four walls. The boards were filled with five digit code groups. All he had to do was find the index string. He walked around the room casually eyeing the chalkboards as one might wander around a library browsing over the shelves of books. After reading over only a couple of the imaginary boards, he found it. The two digit index number, "one one!" It practically jumped out at him. He examined the number groups in that section. Of course, he knew them all by heart.

Ichiro's eyes snapped open. He picked up the pen and began writing out the groups. The entire process, took him several minutes. He didn't waver on a single digit. The numbers came pouring out of his memory like water from a tap. When he was finished, he set the pen down. On the paper in front of him were ten lines each containing five lines of number groups. Now all he had to do was synchronize the numbers with letters, and run out the decoding of his message. The process took a few minutes. He stared at the text.

NU TARGT – NM TIMOTHY GREER – POLICE DET – ORANGE COUNTY SHERIFF – HOM ADRS 16619 PENELOPE – TUSTIN - AUTO SILV MAZDA LIC 3ZXT187 – SUBJ HS INFO RE ENRGY PROJ – K

He went over the decode process several times to ensure he had not made a mistake. He had not. His work was perfect. He read the information over and over, committing it to memory - memory that was just as stable as his mastery of the code groups. When he was certain, he had it, he picked up the all the papers, the napkin, the code group matrix and the decoded message. He carried them into the bathroom and holding them over the commode, struck a match and burned each into black cinders. He dropped the residue into the bowl and flushed it away.

He went back into the room and sat on the bed. He stared at the wall and thought about everything. How interesting. Now they want me to kill a police officer, a detective police officer at that. Somehow, this man has learned too much about the energy project and perhaps about why Jiro and I are here.

He stopped abruptly. He was thinking of Jiro as if he were still in the present. He quickly chastised himself, and forced his thoughts to a more productive direction. I will have to learn as much as I can about this man, this, Timothy Greer. He savored the name. Up to this point, they had just been exterminating the traitorous vermin. This target would prove to be interesting. This was just what Ichiro needed to perk him up. This was the perfect challenge.

He got up off the bed, grabbed his car keys and headed out. He needed to find internet access once again. He had some information gathering to do.

Chapter 42
Chongjin, DPRK

Sullivan and Nikolai walked south along the road slowly inching their way to Chongjin. According to Nikolai's GPS and his interpretation of the map, they had about eighteen more kilometers to go. For more than an hour they walked and talked. Nikolai often made reference to his service for the Soviets. It was that affiliation that had originally brought him to the D.P.R.K. That had been many years ago and Nikolai had been very young back then, both in years and ideology.

Sullivan assumed that at some point in his career, Nikolai had turned and become a double agent, in the employ of Uncle Sam and the Soviets for quite a few years. Nikolai had enjoyed a long career for a spy. He was a resourceful and crafty man. He was also greedy.

Mike reminded himself that money was the foundation of the espionage business. He could hardly quibble with Nikolai over allegiances. The Soviets didn't exactly pay well. He knew all about that - first hand.

Twice, pickup trucks rumbled past them along the road. Both times Nikolai motioned for them to step off the roadway and conceal themselves in the shadows. The first truck was a battered old mini containing a lone man with a precariously high pile of cardboard boxes tied to the bed. The truck passed; they resumed their walk.

About twenty minutes later, motor noises were heard coming from the north. Nikolai signaled for Sullivan to stop. The vehicle was louder, this one a diesel. Once again, they stepped into the concealment of the shadows. This vehicle was also a truck, dark, old and square shaped, with a canvas draped cargo box. It had the sound and overall appearance of military.

"Army?" Sullivan whispered as it rolled by.

Nikolai held a single finger to his lips. Mike got the idea. Nikolai waited until the truck was well past them, and had continued on to the south. "They are probably just local representatives of the People's Worker Peasant Militia."

They emerged from their hiding place and resumed walking. Nikolai continued. "Did you know that almost everyone in this country's population is forced into some kind of military training?"

"I'd heard that, somewhere."

"Even the women and children from tender age on up..."

"Really?"

"Yes, the Dear Leaders have taken their paranoia of the West, and shaped it into a national obsession. The whole thing is run by the Ministry of Defense. The KPA - the Korean People's Army - is the revolutionary armed wing of the Worker's Party. It consists of over a million troops. Then they have the Reserve Training Unit. That one consists of almost two million folks including men from age seventeen to forty-five and unmarried women from seventeen to thirty. The entire reserve corps has mandatory training forty days out of each year."

"Amazing."

"Yes, it is. And there's more. Older men, ages forty-five to sixty, must belong to the Worker-Peasant Militia. They created categories for men from ages seventeen to forty-five and unmarried women from seventeen to thirty who are not otherwise carrying a gun in some other outfit. There are over four million of them, and they get to train thirty days of each year."

"Mandatory?"

"Very mandatory." They were huffing a bit as the pitch of the roadway climbed over a small hill. "For these folks, it's go to training or be shot! It's a very effective incentive." As they reached the hilltop, Nikolai pulled out his StarTac cell phone and flicked it on. He waved it around, checking for signal strength. "And there is more! They also have the Young Red Guards. These are the kids from thirteen to sixteen. These kids have mandatory four hour drill sessions each Saturday."

"Let me guess – the Young Red Guards are probably co-ed, right?"

"Correct – both boys and girls must belong to the Guards."

They reached the hilltop. Nikolai held up a hand indicating for them to stop. "Ahh – look, two bars!" He canted the display enabling Sullivan to see the readout. He punched in some numbers.

"And people worried about the Nazi's and their National Socialist movement..." Sullivan commented while Nikolai held the phone to his ear.

The call connected. He launched into a stream of Korean. The cell phone discussion went back and forth. It lasted about a minute. Nikolai concluded the conversation and flipped the cover closed. He was smiling.

"What?"

"That was our ride. I don't know about you, old man, but I'm getting tired of all this damn walking."

삼 질식시킴

Another hour passed. The starlit heavens had shifted to the point where a sliver of moon had eased its way into the eastern sky. Sullivan and Nikolai continued their trek. A car clattered in the distance. It came from the direction of Chongjin. Automatically, they stepped off the road and slipped into the shadows hidden from view by scrub pines.

The truck lumbered closer. It was an old and weathered. There were a few cardboard boxes tied down in the open bed. As it came closer, Mike noticed that the left headlamp would occasionally flicker on and off. It usually happened in synchronization with the truck's passage over the ruts and potholes.

As the truck closed with their position, Mike could see that there was only one person in the cab, wearing a baseball cap. As it passed by them, Nikolai produced a small pen light and flashed it directly into the rear window. Catching the light signal, the driver hit the brakes and the little truck, a Toyota, slid to a gravelly stop.

Nikolai stepped out and approached the driver.

A familiar feminine voice came from inside. "Yo baseo, Poppa!"

Sullivan almost had a heart attack. Seated behind the wheel, was none other than Viktoriya, "You boys likee a ride with pretty Korean girl?"

Nikolai fired back in Korean. "Vika, stop it! Speak only Hang-gul in the open."

Viktoriya immediately switched to Korean. "I am so sorry, Father. I will not forget."

Sullivan was stunned. He looked at Nikolai. "What is this?"

Nikolai, stood in the roadway, hand on hip. "Why this – is my daughter – I believe you two have already met. And this – it is our ride!" He motioned for Mike to get in and opened the driver's side door. "Scoot over, Sweetheart, Poppa will drive now."

삼 질식시킴

The three squeezed across the bench seat of the tiny truck. Nikolai put the little truck in gear and they started back down the road, the direction from which Viktoriya had just come.

She sat in the middle between the men. She couldn't stop staring at Sullivan's new face. The truck was so tight, especially for him, he had to remove his hat. "Does it hurt?" She finally asked while gently touching the skin above his left eye.

"It's fine." His answer was brusque. Sullivan had been on low simmer since their pickup on the roadway. Finally, he spoke. "Nikki – this is bullshit - having your daughter involved!"

"Quite the contrary. Observe - you and I had to sneak into the country. Viktoriya, on the other hand, simply walked in. This is a benefit of her status as a citizen in good standing of the DPRK. Besides, she's been doing this kind of work since she was a little girl. Right Vika?"

"Yes, Poppa." She smiled at her father and stuck her tongue out at Sullivan's frown.

"Still, I think this is a bad idea. This whole situation will probably get messy. She could get killed."

"Misha, believe me when I tell you that little Vika, here, can take care of herself." The biggest problem we have is you. And, if you will excuse me for saying so, despite your clever disguise, you stick out - like a turd in a punch bowl."

Sullivan shut up and went back to low simmer.

"Well you sort of look a – little bit Asian…" Viktoriya added trying to ease the conversation.

"Think so?"

"Actually no - you are the strangest looking Korean man I've ever seen." She laughed.

"Thanks – I'm just trying to fit in."

"You'll probably need to cut off about two feet of your legs – even then you're going to stand out like…"

Nikolai cut in. "Excuse me, but we need to talk some business here. Vika, what have you got for us, so far?"

"Well, the day they took the American sailor off the boat, he was taken first to the military precinct."

Nikolai cut in. "That would be like the police office or station."

"Shortly after that, he was driven to the local hospital for treatment. Apparently the medical people wanted to keep him for a while, the KPA vetoed that. Oh, by the way, he's in the custody of the local KPA boys, in case I didn't mention that."

"You didn't – but, we assumed as much. Do we know where he is, now?"

"Not precisely, but we have an idea. It's…"

"Wait!" Nikolai held up a hand to silence Vika. "We need to make a point - for Mr. Sullivan's benefit. Is it Undok or Musan?"

"Very good, Poppa. It is Musan. How did you know?"

"Elementary, my dear. Elementary. By the way. How much did that information cost you?"

Viktoriya's response was to hike up her dress so she could dig into the pockets of the jeans she wore underneath. She was wearing the traditional beige cotton peasant garb for a woman. Sullivan knew it was called a "Hanbok" consisting of a straight skirt and a bolero-like jacket. She had her hair pulled back in a tight braid and wore no makeup. Sullivan marveled at the realization that she did fit in – perfectly.

She pulled out a wad of money and thumbed through it. "That information cost me about two hours, fifteen hundred Won, and the promise of some hot sex in the future."

Nikolai looked at his daughter. One eyebrow arched.

"I would have gotten more, Poppa, but I needed some time to buy this truck, get some supplies and take care of girl things…"

Nikolai nodded and refocused his attention to the road.

"By the way, you guys need some local money? There's a plastic bag of it under the seat. Also some bottled water and some sticky rice balls." She looked at Sullivan. "Sorry, about the rice balls. It was all I could get." Then back to Nikolai. "And here is your ID, Poppa." She handed him a laminated official looking card with a grainy photograph of Nikolai's face, dark hair and all. He looked it over and pocketed it.

"Thank you my dear. You are a good girl."

"Just doing what you pay me for, Poppa." They rode in silence for a few minutes. She spoke up again. "Of course, we could cook up some ID for Mr. Sullivan if we had some time."

"Unfortunately, time is the one thing we have precious little of." Sullivan responded.

Nikolai chimed in. "Just remember, if we get stopped, let Vika and I do all the talking. Just stoop a lot and look dumb. The story that we will be telling is" – he thought a moment – "that you have something wrong with your throat and can't speak – yeah, let's make it cancer or something real bad like that."

Viktoriya nodded.

"Say, what's in the boxes in the back of the truck – that's a nice touch, by the way."

"Thanks. It's just some ceramics, plates, dishes rice bowls – stuff like that. Oh - and two boxes of soccer balls."

"Why soccer balls?" Sullivan asked.

She'd had to throw a leg over Sullivan to pull off the under-the-dress-to-the-jeans maneuver. He couldn't help but notice her delightful fragrance – the same scent he'd first caught on the porch of their bungalow – and her Reebok sneakers.

"Gifts, bribes, donations – whatever you want to call it. They love that sport around here – crazy about it."

"I see - so, what's the plan?" Sullivan asked.

Nikolai was quiet for a moment. "I'd say – now that we don't have to waste any more time in Chongjin - we drive through the night and try and make Musan. It's only about a hundred kilometers – but pretty rough roads and hilly terrain. We'll be lucky to get there by sunlight. Once there, we'll just have to play it by ear."

The group lapsed into silence for a while. The little truck continued its methodical progress over the road. They were nearing the town of Chongjin. The twinkle of town lights illuminated the horizon.

Viktoriya spoke up. "Say, have you guys heard about the earthquakes they've been having up around Musan? I guess they've been having one every few days – some of them pretty severe"

Chapter 43
Musan, DPRK

The room had a heavy metal door and no windows. They kept it locked, and opened it only when someone came in with food or to check on his injuries. His recollection of events was kind of spotty but he was pretty sure neither of those things had occurred very often during his stay. The place was like a giant cube about twelve feet square. Even the ceiling looked to be about that high.

Charlie lay on the low bunk. A single light bulb hung from a foot long piece of wire. It came right out of a hole in the center of the ceiling. The light was switched on for several hours each day, and then it was turned off. The cycle repeated. He was only able to guess at the number of hours on each side of the light cycle. They had taken everything away from him, including his watch. The garments that he wore were rough cotton pajamas, a kind of oatmeal color. In one corner of the room, there was a white plastic bucket with a lid. He knew he was supposed to use that container to relieve himself. He remembered being so shaky, he couldn't stand to walk to it the first time – so he crawled. It was either that or soil his clothes and bed.

His concept of time regarding the number of days he had been a guest at this facility was fuzzy. In more lucid moments he had finally decided that they were drugging him, but he didn't know how. The last couple of times anyone had come into the room, he had tried to engage them in conversation. Two times it was the same woman and once it was a man. Neither would respond to him. He finally decided that maybe these people didn't speak English.

He remembered the dive in the submersible, Dewey, and that something had happened, an explosion or something bad. He remembered his head hurt like hell; it still did, too.

He recalled being in the water and swimming, his eye on the setting sun. He remembered trying to swim like hell into the sun. He remembered that he was pulled out of the water and lay on the deck of a boat, a bunch of small Asian guys clustered around him jibber-jabbering. He didn't understand a word of it.

The light snapped on. It wakened him from a fairly deep sleep. The man was in his room. He pulled Charlie into a sitting position and slipped some woven sandals onto his feet. The man was not rough, but he wasn't exactly Florence Nightingale either. He said in halting English. "Up! You up, now!"

Charlie got the idea. He pushed himself up onto his feet. The room spun briefly, but he quickly stabilized. The man held him by the shoulders until he was reasonably certain Charlie would not fall. Now he was gently pushing Charlie towards the door. "Walk! You walk, now."

This guy needs to work on his vocabulary, thought Charlie.

Minutes later, he was seated in some kind of office. The walk had been brief, but it had felt good. They went down one long hallway, made a turn to the left and down another hallway before coming to this office on the right. This door was not metal, but wood. It had a number on the outside. It said, "105". His head was clearing. He still had a headache, but he classified this one as a dull pounder, at best. This was only a three aspirin headache, probably the lightest one he had had since he first woke up in this place.

Once in the office, he had been placed in a wooden chair and left alone. The chair was positioned in front of a table with another similar, but vacant chair. There was a window. It looked out over a courtyard of some type. He could see some vehicles and other buildings. The whole place had that retro-fifties and sixties military look. He was just trying to figure out if he was in jail or a hospital or both when the door opened. A man in uniform entered.

He was slender, Asian and dressed in an immaculate military uniform of some type. Charlie did not have a clue as to the uniform or its insignias, of which there were colorfully many. He did quickly understand that the man was some kind of official and full of himself.

The man stood, overlooking Charlie as if critically appraising him. Finally he spoke. "Good Morning, Mister Gomex." The man's English wasn't bad, but he pronounced Charlie's surname with an X, like in Tex-Mex.

"The name is Gomez – with a Z on the end – and good morning to you, Sir." Charlie had quickly decided that it wouldn't hurt for him to inject a small token of respect to the situation. "Mind telling me where I am – and how I got here?"

"Not at all..." Came the quick reply. You are in the Democratic People's Republic of Korea – I believe you Americans call this – North Korea." He hesitated a bit as if waiting for his pronouncement to settle in. Then, he moved to the other chair and sat down. He took out a package of some kind of strange cigarettes and fired one up – blowing a blue stream towards the ceiling. "You were rescued from the sea by the courageous Navy men of the Korean People's Army.

Charlie decided the guy must be some kind of officer. The glare of his spit-shine dress shoes looked like two black mirrors conveniently placed to look up some Jo-san's dress. He also decided he was going to blow some smoke of his own. "Excuse me – Colonel…"

"I am Senior Captain Rhee." The response was instant. Charlie figured he scored some points there.

"Tell me, Mister Gomezzzz …" The exaggerated emphasis on the Z was a bit much. "Why are you here, spying on the innocent people of our country? Don't you Americans have enough problems in the world, at this time?"

"Whoa – easy there, Captain…"

"Senior Captain Rhee."

"Of course – Senior Captain Rhee – I'm hardly a spy. I'm just a guy who works for a deep ocean mining company – I…"

"I would not lie further if I were you, Mister Charles Gomez. The consequences could be – severe. You see spying on the People's Democratic Republic is a capital offense. Do you understand? You could be executed."

"Okay…" Charlie's mind raced. "Listen, you guys are making a huge mistake! I'm not lying here. Yes, I'm Charlie Gomez. But, I ain't no spy. I'm just some poor working stiff who happened to be collecting underwater rock samples. I work for Marine Diving Technologies, out of Seattle." His statements had, at least a kernel of truth in them. MDT was a subsidiary of GTI. "We're just over here for a few weeks doing some marine survey work, and we had and accident and…"

"Yes, we know quite a bit about you already. You were cooperative enough to tell us a good deal when you were – ah – previously medicated."

"Well, good, then you know I'm telling you the truth. Now, when can I call my company and make arrangements to go home. I've got a wife and kids that must be worried sick." He hoped he wasn't laying it on too thick. By the way, I don't even know what day it is or how long I've been here."

"You have been here for some time. Your injuries were severe."

"What happened to me – I mean – how bad am I?"

"You sustained a concussion and other injuries. Our medical staff has taken excellent care of you. You will soon be well enough to stand trial for your crimes against the People's Republic."

"Look, Captain…"

"Senior Captain Rhee."

"Yes, of course, Senior Captain – with all due respect – can't we just call somebody here – so you guys can verify who I am and get me outta here. You gotta believe me. I'm not a spy. Hell, I've never even been in the service. Honest! I'm just a diving technician who…"

"We believe you are an American spy who was dropped off from an American submarine that was illegally operating in the territorial waters of the East Sea in violation of the sovereignty of the People's Democratic Republic…"

삼 질 식 시 킴

Some time later Charlie was taken back to his room and locked in. He lay back on the bed. He actually felt rejuvenated. He understood, or at least had an idea of the severity of his situation. But, he really enjoyed mentally sparring with that pinhead, Rhee. He wondered just how much, other than his name, he had told them while under sedation. This was one of those times when he was gratified to have a common Hispanic surname. He didn't think these guys had tumbled to his true identity. He wondered, though, if they had anybody bright enough to use the internet to look up Glomar and Marine Diving Technologies, and if they would make the connection to GTI. He drifted off to sleep wondering if his picture was still prominently displayed on the GTI website.

Chapter 44
Chongjin, DPRK

They drove towards the lights of Chongjin City. More than a mile out, Nikolai squirmed around and liberated his map and penlight. Handing the items to Viktoriya, he said. Find us a way to get around the main part of the city. We want to hook up to the main highway to the north – I don't know what number it is – it's the road that goes to Puryong.

She clicked on the light and poured over the map. "Not a lot of detail here, but I did pass through a 육군 역 earlier." She used a Korean phrase. "It was on this road, about a quarter mile outside the town."

For Sullivan's benefit, Nikolai translated. "What she said was 'Army checkpoint'."

"Was it permanent or mobile?" Nikolai asked.

"Mobile – just boys, really. They probably got bored and just decided to stop some cars. Mostly, they wanted to flirt with me."

"So – what happened?" Nikolai voice adopted a fatherly posture.

"I just told them I had the clap -: She replied with grin. "- And they let me pass."

Sullivan smiled. He liked this girl. She had spunk.

Moments later she said. "You know, I remember, from when I came the other way, I recall passing an intersecting road – it looked like it might cut off to the west or northwest. I guess that would be the right direction. It should be coming up soon - on our right. If it goes through, I betcha that it would connect to the Puryong road."

"Okay, speak up when you see it."

"Should be any time now."

They found the road and made the turn. The terrain looked much like outskirts of any populated area. They passed through a few settlements with clusters of huts constructed of mud and straw blocks, cinder blocks and scraps of metal and lumber. The predominant roofing materials were strips of corrugated metal and dull grey clay tiles. Over each grouping of rooftops, a permanent pall of wood and coal smoke drifted low in the air.

They saw very few other cars or trucks. The ones they did see were parked. They were about the only thing moving at the late hour. That fact made Sullivan a little nervous. If it bothered the other two, they said nothing.

The few buildings were interspersed with vacant fields, some farming, a few small orchards, some farm animals and rice paddies, lots of rice paddies. Other than the paddies, the terrain reminded Mike of parts of Mexico or other poor-as-church-mice countries he'd been in.

Presently they came to an intersection with a larger roadway. Nikolai stopped. Both he and Viktoriya scanned for road signs. There were none. Nikolai consulted his GPS unit.

"They're not real big on highway signs in these parts, are they?" Mike offered, more as a comment than a question.

"Oh, there are signs. You just have to know what to look for." Nikolai said as he steered the truck into a right turn and motored off to the north. "Sometimes it's going to be something as simple as paint writing on a rock – or sometimes at an intersection, there will be a cluster of signs on one pole or a tree – it's an economy thing." Within minutes they were headed into low hills and completely away from the civilization of the town."

Sullivan asked. "How's our gas?" He could see the needle of the gauge resting to the left of the "E".

Vika answered. I filled the tank before I left Chongjin. I don't think the gas gauge works. It should be about a fourteen gallon tank – and I'm not sure about the consumption of Hiroshi…"

"Hiroshi?"

"Hiroshi' – she answered matter-of-factly – "I always name my cars – don't you?"

He just shook his head.

"Well – in this case, my truck. I think it's good luck – sort of imparts a spirit to the car – it helps. You'll see."

Sullivan just nodded. He looked over at Nikolai. He was smiling.

"Anyway, the way its running and all, I think we can count on maybe 18 to 20 miles per gallon… The odometer is rigged for kilometers so you men can figure that one out…"

Nikolai spoke up. "I figure we'll have to get some fuel in Puryong or the next little town…" He glanced at the folded map. "That would be Komuson. After that, we are pretty much on our own."

"Anybody hungry?" Viktoriya reached under the seat, and pulled out a brown paper package wrapped with coarse twine. She dumped it on Sullivan's lap, and then dove back down, this time coming up with two small clear bottles of water.

The crest of a small hill loomed in front of them. As the ancient little truck crossed the peak, they were caught in the illumination of headlamps coming from the other direction. As the other vehicle passed by, they could see it was a military truck, OD green and box shaped with canvas over the bed.

"Shit! That's either Militia or KPA." Nikolai spit out the statement. After passing the Toyota, the army truck quickly braked to a full stop creating a large cloud of dust. The driver ground gears and turned his truck around in the roadway. Soon, the Army truck had closed with the Toyota and began to flash its headlights.

Nikolai spoke again. "Okay, I'm going to stop. Everyone be cool. Misha, be quiet like I told you."

Sullivan dumped the food package into Viktoriya's lap and quickly deployed his Glock. With his left hand he rummaged under his shirt and produced the silencer. He fitted it to the barrel just as Hiroshi, the truck, clattered to a stop.

Nikolai immediately got out and walked to the rear of the Toyota. He stopped there and waited. In the cab of the truck, he could see the forms of two men. The truck bore the markings of the Korean Army – the KPA. Both doors opened and the two uniformed men dismounted and approached. The driver stopped and stood near the left front fender of his truck. He was thin and young, probably not more than eighteen years old. He casually held a 7.62 mm AK assault rifle with the barrel pointed at Nikolai's feet. Nikolai thought the weapon was probably Chinese. It had the blond wood stock, so common to Chinese manufacture.

The second soldier, an older man, emerged from the passenger side, and approached Nikolai halfway between the vehicles. Nikolai bowed low and held his phony DPRK citizen identity card in both hands before him. This posture demonstrated maximum respect to the advancing soldier. As he stepped into the illumination of the headlamps, Nikolai could see the Corporal insignias on the older man's uniform.

The corporal spoke. "Citizen – you are on this roadway in violation of the civil curfew. You know this, of course. So show me your papers and tell me why you are driving at this late hour."

Nikolai bowed a second time, this time a bit deeper as the soldier reached out and gruffly took his ID. "I am so sorry, Sergeant. I am but a poor peddler who must have these goods in Hoeryong by morning."

"And who are these persons that accompany you?"

"The girl is my daughter, Hei, and man is Chong-Ho, he is my" – Nikolai took a deep breath and put on his saddest face – "most unfortunate nephew."

The soldier took the bait and asked. "What is wrong with your nephew?"

"Alas, it is a great sadness, he is mentally retarded." He let that one settle for a moment, and then added, "And now he suffers from cancer of the throat – he cannot speak."

The Corporal looked appropriately disgusted. "Enough of this, old man. Show me what goods you are transporting."

Nikolai bowed and moved to the cargo box. He methodically began to untie the ropes.

삼 질식시킴

Viktoriya and Sullivan stared straight ahead and listened to the conversation in Korean between Nikolai and the soldiers. She would whisper a bit of translation to Sullivan, then strain to listen more, again offering fragments of blow by blow of what they were saying, and then she would go back to listening. Abruptly she stopped. She glanced at Sullivan and whispered. "Act retarded!" She slid over and stepped out the open driver's door onto the roadway.

Sullivan had no idea what was happening. He desperately wanted to turn his head and view the proceedings, but common sense told him to stay frozen in the truck. Viktoriya, jabbering in the sing-song cadence of Korean, walked outside of the line of Sullivan's peripheral vision, towards the soldiers and her father. The next thing it sounded to Sullivan like everyone was talking at once. He transferred the Glock to his left hand and with the right cranked the truck window slowly to the fully open position.

The next thing to happen was that Vika stepped back into the frame of his vision, but now she was on the right side of the truck, at the edge of the roadway. He dared to slowly move his head an inch to the right so he could see her better. It looked as if she had lifted her skirt and had hunched down into a straddling position!

삼 질식시킴

Vika slid out of the truck and walked right up to her father and the two soldiers. She had a silly smile plastered across her face. The young soldier with the AK moved the muzzle towards her. She held up both hands, palms out, at chest level. As soon as Nikolai realized she was out of the truck, he turned and yelled at her. "Daughter, what are you doing? I told you to remain in the truck with Chong-Ho. Can you not see I am busy here with Comrade Sergeant of the Korean People's Army?"

She bowed repeatedly first to Corporal, whom her father had just promoted, and then to Nikolai and even tossed in a quick one to the kid with the rifle. "Forgive me, Father. I could not help myself. I have a pressing need to urinate – and quickly." She did a little dance with both hands at her crotch in order to emphasize the point she was making.

Nikolai just glared at her. The Corporal laughed and waved her away. With that she ran to an outcropping of rock and brush at the roadway edge. In the dim light, she made a production of lifting her skirt and crouching down in a straddling position. Once down, she dropped her left knee to the ground for stability and withdrew the pistol from a pocket. She was perfectly positioned for an accurate field of fire. She had a clear shot at the man with the rifle, and Nikolai could easily take out Comrade Sergeant, without a dangerous cross-fire. She waited.

Chapter 45
Chongjin, DPRK

Comrade Sergeant-Corporal rummaged through the cargo in the rear of Nikolai's truck. He grunted in a non-committal fashion over most of the goods. When he got to the soccer balls, he smiled in an approving manner. "Ah…"

Nikolai knew he'd hit pay dirt. "Perhaps Comrade Sergeant would accept a small gift – a token of apology - for having to deal with the likes of us this night?"

The soldier made no response. His eyes flicked up toward the truck's cab as if for some reason he'd suddenly decided to check out Sullivan. He moved around to the right and approached. Mike sensed him coming. He stared straight ahead.

The soldier stopped just behind the rear edge of the truck's door. He played the beam of his flashlight around Sullivan's head and the truck interior. Without warning he stepped forward and grabbed Sullivan's chin. He jerked his head to the right and flashed the beam of his light directly into Mike's face.

It took everything Sullivan had to control his reactions. He froze in place. He forced himself to stare straight ahead and do so in as blank and vacant manner as he could muster. When he felt the man's grip his chin forcing his face into the light, he let his mouth go slack and with his tongue pushed spittle through his teeth. The fluid flowed down his chin, directly onto the soldier's hand.

The Corporal released his face and exclaimed disgustedly. "Aiee, stupid moron!" He urgently wiped his wet hand on the shoulder of Mike's shirt. He quickly moved back to Nikolai and handed him his ID. "You will give us one box of the soccer balls and remove yourself from my patrol area – immediately!"

Nikolai handed the man a box and bowed deeply. "Yes, Comrade Sergeant – and thank you – thank you for your courtesy."

The soldiers quickly re-mounted their truck and drove away. After the KPA truck was some distance down the road, Viktoriya came strolling out of the brush, her pistol still in hand. Nikolai leaned on the bed of the truck with both arms, head down, rubbing his neck. "That was fun!" He finally said.

삼 질식시킴

The trio motored on for another fifty kilometers. Finally, Nikolai decided to take a little break. Finding a little stand of trees, he pulled the truck off the road and parked. They broke out the sticky rice balls and bottled water. There was also a paper package of pickled cabbage and turnip slices. None of it went to waste.

Over their meal, they talked. Sullivan wanted to critique their encounter with the soldiers. "We need to get our cover stories straight. If Vika had not overheard what you said to that gook about me being mentally retarded and told me – I would have had to kill the guy."

"I know, Misha. And I apologize for the sloppiness. I guess I'm getting rusty in my old age. I was really flying by the seat of my pants, back there."

"Yeah, well, I know we could have easily dropped those two – but the problem is, the more bodies we leave in our wake, the brighter color Korean homeland security cranks up to."

Nikolai laughed through a mouthful of rice at Sullivan's little joke.

"We could create such a ruckus that we'll end up starting world war three and never locate Charlie." Mike added.

"Relax, Misha. We'll do better. I'm really getting into the swing of things now."

"Details…" Mike said. "We have to know the details."

"I know. I just quickly made up a story and some names for you two - on the fly. Good ones too, I think. Chung-ho – that's you – by the way, you are my nephew."

"Yeah, I got that. What does Chung-ho mean anyway – tall, goofy guy?"

Viktoriya piped in. "It means righteous one. Very fitting, I'd say. And what is my name, Poppa?

"I think I called you, Hei."

"Oh, how nice – thank you." She looked at Sullivan. "It means sunshine goddess."

"Don't believe her, Misha. It means insolent daughter."

"Vika, that was quite a nice move you made back there – wanting to go pee and all. Smart girl."

"Thanks, Poppa. It also gave me a clean line of fire – just in case things went wrong. Also, you should know that my ID card has the name Soo."

"Details, folks – details." Mike decided to change the subject. "Vika, tell us what you heard about the earthquakes."

"I came in from the Russian Territories by ferry transport to Chongjin. In the couple of days I was there, it was all I heard about in the shops and marketplace. Apparently there has been a shaker, at least a small quake every day or so, usually at night. Some have been moderately severe, causing some building damage and a few injuries."

Nikolai shot a knowing look at Sullivan.

Vika continued. "One of the local merchants told me he thought the quakes may have something to do with the People's nuclear weapons research." She balled up a bite size portion of the white rice and popped it into her mouth. "Nuclear research is a big deal in this country. Despite their lack of a decent news media, word of mouth does get most stories around pretty quick. There's a bit of a sense of national pride that the tiny North Korea has the rest of the world quaking because they have a fledgling nuclear program." She took a healthy swig of water and handed the bottle to Sullivan. "Of course, another person - an old woman – told me she thought the quakes were clear evidence heralding the end of the world. And now we were all going to be punished for our sins. You guys ready for eternal damnation?"

Before anyone could formulate an answer, a low roaring sound crept over them. The ground lurched. The temblor began with a single violent snap then the shaking began. Vika had been sitting cross legged on the hood of the truck. She slid off. Mike and Nikolai were both standing when the quake hit and rode it out standing. The trees around them rustled like a giant gust of wind had come out of nowhere. The ground beneath them oscillated in waves. The entire process took less than a minute; then it was over.

Sullivan was the first to speak. "Christ - how did you arrange that?"

As quickly at the quake had come, it was gone.

Vika, who normally wore the stoic face of the Madonna was, at this moment, terrified. "Okay, you guys. This is just too damn scary. Just what is going on?"

"Relax, daughter, it is just an earthquake."

"I know that. What I don't know is why, and what's up with all the knowing looks between you two?"

Nikolai turned to Sullivan. "Perhaps we should tell Viktoriya about the 'Energy Project'?"

"Actually, Nikki, I'm a bit surprised you haven't told her already!"

삼 질식시킴

They drove on. Vika took the wheel which crammed Nikolai into the middle squeeze. As the kilometers flowed past, the men talked. They told her the story about the crash of the strange flying craft in the fifties, the recovery by the North and their long struggle to figure out how to make the gravity wave amplifier work. What they did not have to explain was the implication of such a tremendous source of power in the hands of the maniacs that ran the DPRK.

Viktoriya was quiet for a while – thinking it over. Finally she said, "You know, after all the years of hatred and fear of Uncle Sam, these poor backward people are going to finally have something to ram right down the throat of America."

Her father spoke up. "Your assessment is accurate – not particularly articulated well, but accurate. As you know, there's a lot of pent up hostility here – nurtured over generations of isolation from the mainstream of the world."

Sullivan listened, thought it over and finally offered, "I don't know, Nikki – Vika may have nailed it more succinctly than anyone else. If the North Koreans make this thing work, they'll be choking Uncle Sam for generations.

They rode in silence for while. Finally Vika spoke up. "You know, Poppa, there is a military facility in the area of Musan – right up against the Chinese border."

"Yes, dear. I know."

"Do you think…?"

"I think that anything is possible – quite anything."

Chapter 46
Santa Ana, California

Greer was getting antsy. Things were happening at warp speed on his Korean murders case. Actually, none of the murders were really his cases. They all belonged to the individual city police departments where the crimes had occurred. That's how jurisdiction worked. Because the Sheriff has county-wide jurisdiction, an absolute lock on forensic pathology, and best and biggest Crime laboratory under his control, their office was in a great position to provide coordination and assistance. In this case, it was Greer who had put most of the pieces together. That had put him in a unique position until Sullivan had made that call to his friend from the F.B.I. Then everything changed.

Now he was being hounded daily by Agents from both the L.A. and Orange County field offices. They had taken Ahn and put him into some kind of protective environment. Just what or where it was, he didn't know. They wouldn't tell him. He hoped the old man wasn't sitting in a jail cell somewhere. The immediate problem was that an F.B.I. Agent named Kirby, some kind of big shot, had called a meeting for this morning. Kirby was from the Los Angeles office. He had been sent to Orange County to pull together detectives from each of the cities where there the Korean murders were committed. He'd cleared it through Sheriff Hamilton, and was in fact using one of the Sheriff's Department conference rooms.

Greer's intercom rang. It was Lt. Blair. "Got a minute?"

"Yes sir."

"Good – come and see me – now."

A minute later Greer slid into a chair in Blair's office. "Close the door!"

Greer reached behind him and pushed the door closed. He said nothing.

"Know what's going to happen at this morning's meeting?" Blair pointed a yellow pencil at the electric wall clock. It read five til nine.

"We're going to serve coffee and donuts and the Feebies are going to tell us how to work our cases?"

"Don't be a smart ass."

"Sorry – I..."

"No – I'm sorry. You've been working your butt off on these murders. Hell, if it wasn't for your persistence, I don't think any of these other rocket scientists would have put these hits together..." Blair sort of drifted off in thought for a moment.

Greer cleared his throat and brushed some invisible something from the trouser cuff of his crossed leg. He spoke. "They're going to take the cases aren't they?"

Blair just nodded. "I just got off the horn with the old man." He referred to the Sheriff. "He just took the call from the Los Angeles Agent-In-Charge. It's sort of a courtesy thing between the higher-ups. He said that the Agents that will attend today's meeting will explain it all. He said they have to invoke National Security issues, and that will force the local cops out of the cases."

"That's bullshit!"

"I know."

"They can't do that. Where is the Federal offense? We have original jurisdiction over all homicide cases... Don't we?"

Blair sat motionless for a moment. "I don't blame you, Timmy. I think it's a buncha crap. So does the old man, if that makes you feel any better." He motioned to the clock and stood up. "We better get in there."

Greer stood, pushing back the chair. "Ell-Tee, it's really no sweat off our nuts. Hell, Irvine, Garden Grove, Fountain Valley and the rest are the ones that are really going to be pissed."

Blair just grunted.

"We get something going on a bunch of who-dun-its, and the Feds are coming in to scoop it all up!" Greer shook his head as they moved out of the office and headed down to the large conference room. He continued his dialogue. "The bastards... This ought to be interesting..."

"Yeah – maybe we ought to check our guests guns at the door."

삼 질식시킴

Special Agent Kirby turned out to be a short, perfectly groomed and coifed FBI Agent. He wore his requisite dark blue with faint pin stripe suit, black wingtips, white stiffly starched shirt and paisley tie. Greer and Blair took seats across from Kirby and his entourage of underlings. Blair convened the meeting and asked everyone, numbering twenty or so attendees, around the room to introduce themselves.

Greer took the time to evaluate SA Kirby. The man stood about five foot three in lifted shoes. About forty, he was thinning on top and wore his light colored hair in a Trump-like comb over. His face had that permanent pinched look that gave him a look of being in pain or bored. Greer could not decide which.

He watched the interaction between Kirby and his minions. It looked to Greer as if Kirby was a tyrant and the underlings were all properly buffaloed by him. Greer knew the signs. He had the misfortune to know and work with several Kirby-types over the years. Like this guy, he knew that many of this type suffered from a severe case of little man syndrome.

Marty Blayloch from Garden Grove was speaking. "We have a positive match on the slug taken from the body of the burnt guy from the Anaheim motel." Blayloch nodded to Beauchamp, who smiled and gestured for him to continue. "It matches to the gun found near our murder victim, Keiko Sung."

That was the first time Greer had heard that piece of information. He once again felt that tingling in the back of his neck. *Damn, things were really coming together.*

Blayloch continued. "It gets better. The egress blood spatters from our scene – same deal – those are DNA-matched from the Anaheim burn victim. And, tissue from that victim matches with the fingernail scrapings from our female victim. So, we now solidly have Anaheim's dead guy at our murder scene. We're convinced that makes him a killer – we think one of at least two."

There were a few fielded questions from investigators around the room. Beauchamp picked up where Blayloch left off. "Our burn victim is believed to be of mixed race, both Asian and Caucasian. In life, our boy – and we only have witness composites to work with – but we think he could have easily passed for a white guy. Presently, he is still an un-identified subject. We got usable fingerprints from subcutaneous layers – five fingers only – three from the left and two from the right hand. We've run what we have through all the systems and so far – no hits. He and the other guy – there's a flyer with copies of our composites and physicals going around the room – checked into the HappyLand Hotel, near Disneyland, a few days ago. We think number one might have sustained the gunshot wound within a day or so of check-in – and that fits with the Garden Grove murders - and that in subsequent days, number two was trying to treat number one for the wound. We found remnants of medical supplies and tied at least some of it to a burglary of a clinic in Santa Ana.

Beauchamp continued. "As I am sure you all know, we believe our victim was murdered and then the room was set afire with an accelerant." The detective went through a short version on the cause of death. "The room was locked – our guys had to break in – and we believe the second guy, his accomplice, slash killer, fled through the bathroom window that he busted out."

There were nods and murmuring sounds around the room.

"Although, as yet, we don't have a positive ID on our dead guy, the burn victim, we did come up with something interesting from the National DNA data bank. It seems that when they ran our victim through the system, they got a – well its not an actual hit – I guess they'd call it a semi-hit or maybe a partial hit."

Beauchamp grinned back at the quizzical faces around the table. "The story goes like this. About fifty years ago, there was a pilot shot down over North Korea that went MIA. His name was Griffin. Now, in the fifties, they didn't have DNA technology – Hell, maybe no one even knew what DNA was back in those days. But shortly before this pilot went missing, he donated some blood. When he didn't come back from his mission, I guess it was SOP on these Navy ships to take samples of the pilot's blood and save it for an eventual blood match – simple typing – it was the best thing they had in those days – to assist in body identification. Anyway – typical government tenacity – I guess someone had saved these samples for all these many years. So when the National DNA bank was started, the military samples – at least the ones that were MIA – were typed and put into the computer."

The room went stock-still silent. You could literally hear a pin drop.

Beauchamp continued his story. "Anyhow, the semi-hit comes back saying that the burn victim was a mitochondrial match. It was explained to me that this person could be a sibling or child of the Griffin sample in the national data base. Eliminating the obvious here, my bet would be that our unidentified subject is a direct descendant of the Navy flyer."

More discussion buzzed around the room. A minute or two passed. Blair pulled the group back together. "Okay, folks – if you would – I'd like Detective Tim Greer of our staff, to explain the facts that pull all the murders of the Korean victims – together. Tim…"

Greer opened his case folder and began. Earlier, Greer had talked to Blair, bringing him up to speed on all of the information taken from Ahn, including the extra-terrestrial energy source angle. Together, they decided how much information should be put on the table, today, agreeing it would be the short version, lest they sound like complete nuts to their colleagues.

Tim cleared his throat and began. "A number of weeks ago, we noticed a pattern of names emerging. We had a cluster of killings, all stabbing and blunt force murders in the County, all happening in the victim's homes during the hours of darkness. All of the victims had Korean surnames. So we started asking around and put out a couple of feelers and a BOLO soliciting more info. We picked up some scuttle-but from informants and some folks in the Korean community, but really had nothing conclusive until a Korean gentleman by the name of Ahn walked into Buena Park Police Department a few days ago and told his story. Buena Park called me in and I was able to interview Mr. Ahn."

Greer grabbed a quick look at the fidgeting Kirby. "He told us he was an illegal immigrant from North Korea, that he, and others, were scientists who had been working on…"

Kirby interrupted in a loud, nasally voice. "I'm sorry, Detective. But, I must direct you to stop speaking."

About twenty sets of unbelieving eyeballs locked on Kirby and his staff, most of which had their eyes looking towards the tabletop or the floor.

Special Agent Kirby continued. "At this juncture, I regret to inform all of you that under provisions of U.S Code One Thirty three, Title Seven, Section two-oh-two, and the secrecy provisions of Federal law, I declare this case – make that these cases – known as the" – everyone was watching Kirby. He was reading aloud from a document in front of him – "Korean murders cases to be classified under provisions of the National Security and Patriot Acts of Congress, and therefore shall become the exclusive jurisdiction of the Federal Bureau of Investigation. My staff is passing out copies of this document" – he waived the multi-page paper from which he was reading – "which is an order from the Justice Department. Each of you and your departments are hereby ordered to immediately cease all investigations, inquiries and or other work related to these cases. You are hereby ordered to immediately turn over all investigative reports, notes, photos files, papers and any other materials, relating to these cases that are in your possession or under your control. Members of my staff will now circulate among you and collect any data that you may have on your persons, today. Then, we shall make arrangements to go to your respective offices to collect the remaining materials. Additionally, each of you are hereby ordered and prohibited from discussing these cases further with any person except members of the FBI."

Kirby was nearing an end point of his Federal edict and looked around the room. Everyone glared at him. He continued. "I am obligated to inform you that should you fail to comply with this order - you can be prosecuted to the…"

Blair leaned over to Greer and whispered. "Can you frigging believe this? They're threatening to Martha Stewart us!"

Chapter 47
Komuson, DPRK

The sun was creeping into the east when Hiroshi, the truck, hit the dusty outskirts of Komuson.

Not much more than a village, it was home to a few hundred farmers, peasants and a few merchants. The terrain was hilly and like most of the Korean peninsula, the vegetation was sparse. From the approach, the travelers could see a good portion of the town. Along the main road, the settlement looked like a mud flow that may have oozed down from adjacent hillsides. The town's organization, if any, was a loose collection of huts and other constructions randomly dropped in place. A spider web maze of gravel roads and dirt alleys threaded between the buildings. Sullivan thought this would be a delightful place to get lost.

Nikolai found a place that advertised petrol for sale. From a hut, he stirred a skinny, ancient man with hair the color of snow. The slow moving senior was the keeper of the key to the pad-locked gas drum. He looked about ninety, and he had long flowing chin whiskers that matched the color of his hair.

Sullivan got out of the truck and stretched his legs. No stranger to poverty, Mike, none-the-less, was shocked as he looked around. There were several small children. All bore the signs of malnutrition, distended bellies, slender limbs and the characteristic vacant stare.

He was further amazed as he watched the old man, with bowed back and rickety legs, produce a heavy steel five gallon gas can. With an ancient hand crank pump, the old man methodically filled the can and then carried it to their truck. Carefully, he poured the contents into the fuel tank. The entire process took three round trips. Sullivan was certain the weight of the full gas can was close to the weight of the old man.

Viktoriya chattered something to Nikolai in Korean and disappeared. Mike last saw her dodging a scrawny tan dog that was terrorizing a small black pig. The pig was tethered with a short length of rope to a wooden stake and laid in the middle of the narrow dirt alley that served as the local thoroughfare. A trickle of foul water ran down the middle. The tiny stream split in two when it reached the pig and flowed around him. Sullivan could only imagine what interesting things the opaque liquid contained.

Nikolai peeled off some bills and handed them to the old man. He motioned for Sullivan to get back in the truck. Nikolai followed and turned over the engine.

In low tones, Sullivan said to Nikolai. "Where did Vika get off to?"

"You know – women – she had some shopping to do."

Nikolai pulled ahead a couple hundred feet and slowed.

Mike asked. "Just how bad is the food problem in these parts?"

Nikolai looked at his old friend and blinked. He was thoughtful. His vision, just for a moment, seemed to drift away, peering into an unseen place. Finally, he spoke. "It is bad, Misha. So bad that in places small children often disappear, especially the females. They're not valued as much as the males in this culture. For years there have been rumors about cannibalism. I can tell you that I have personally seen suspicious chunks of meat in peasant markets, meat that was probably human."

Any appetite that Mike had was quickly erased. "I thought the international community was pouring food aid into this country…"

"You are right. And, they have been for years – even those terrible Americans. In fact they send in more food and other aid than many of the others. The problem is the arcane system here. The food and fuel goes to the governing elite first, then to the military – and God knows they have enough layers of military. Anything left over – and that is usually guaranteed to be nothing – would only then end up with the peasants.

Viktoriya appeared from somewhere ahead and waved. Nikolai pulled up next to her. He opened the door and got out. She slid into the middle seat. He got back in and they motored off.

She carried two wrapped paper parcels. Mike asked. "What did you buy?"

"A little more food - I'm afraid it's nothing fancy – just some more cabbage and rice. This is really a very poor place."

"I noticed – and thanks – I love cabbage and rice."

"Any news, my dear?"

"Yes, Poppa. There is definitely something going on up north. Everyone is talking about the quakes. Some people are openly talking about the Military project…"

"I hope you were not too pointed in your questions. You know that about every third person around here is a spy."

She looked at Nikolai as if to say, am I an imbecile? But all she really said was, "Poppa - please. I was raised here, remember?"

"I remember – remember all too well."

"I spoke to three separate shopkeepers. Each time I started the conversation by saying something about last night's earthquake. That's all I had to say. The floodgates open and everybody wanted to talk about it."

"Sorry, Vika. You know what you are doing…"

"Some of the gossip has come from the soldiers who are working up at the Musan research facility. Occasionally, some come down to this little burg - for what – I'm not sure. But, they have a few drinks and talk too much. Many of the townsfolk think there will eventually be some kind of atomic accident around here. That's what the general consensus is. Everyone thinks that Musan is where the government is building its nuclear weapons."

Sullivan chimed in. "Any idea what the layout is going to be like – I mean like – what's located where and so forth?"

She shook her head. "Maybe, when we get closer, I can ask around and dig up some more. But asking those kinds of questions this far away – well, that would really throw up some red flags." She looked at her father. "Right, Poppa?"

Nikolai nodded. He was pensive, obviously thinking. "We are going to Musan because they have a prison there, a prison where they keep political prisoners as well as others. Musan itself is a little village or town, smaller than Komuson, I think."

"You know this place, Nikolai? You've been there before?"

"Once – a long time ago – over twenty years back… It's in the hills, or low mountains, which ever you'd like to call them, and it is close to the Chinese border." He smiled. "You've got to appreciate how these people think. Since they are in a constant state of readiness for the impending US invasion, it stands to reason that they'd keep their biggest secrets close to the border of their mean big brother. It makes it easy to call in help if things get bad."

Sullivan nodded. "Once upon a time, I read an intelligence report that described how the North Koreans had drilled into the side of a mountain to create caverns – caverns that amounted to a hardened installation for some of their pet projects."

"That is precisely correct. I have seen some of those installations - two, to be exact. Both were on the western side of the country. Come to think of it, they were virtual carbon copies of each other, at that. Since these people don't have a lot of imagination, it's probably safe to assume that the Musan facility has been built much in the same fashion."

"Why hardened though?" Viktoriya asked. "Do they really expect someone to bomb them?"

"They absolutely do." Nikolai had found the road that led to the northwest, out of Komuson, and through the hills towards Musan and the Border. He got the truck heading that way, back out into the country. He refolded his map and continued to talk. "Many in the DPRK hierarchy have believed for years that the US will eventually attack and probably will use their nuclear arsenal to finally settle the Korean situation."

The truck lurched over a series of pot holes. Nikolai continued. "They take events like the Americans going into Afghanistan and Iraq as tangible proof of their concerns. They think it's just a matter of time."

"All that paranoia, when the reality of Western strategy is to simply wait for the antiquated Communist system to self destruct on its own." Sullivan shook his head..

"The masses don't know that. And the governing class doesn't believe that. So naturally, if the US or anyone else was to hit them hard, they would want to have their most precious secrets and weapons in a safe location. And that means way up here."

삼 질식시킴

Sullivan had been watching the terrain since they left Komusan. He said. "Nikolai, how's about pulling over somewhere along here? It looks like there's no one around, and I want to do a check in with Dubord." He tapped his watch.

Nikolai nodded and pulled the truck off the roadway. For the moment, there was no one else around and nothing to block the signal. Sullivan got out and walked away from the truck. He found some rocks and crouched down. Keying up the Satellite phone, he verified that he had a good signal and punched in the numbers. While he waited for the connection, he checked his watch. It read nine o'clock straight up.

Minutes later, and with a tight face, Sullivan returned to the Toyota. He got in and closed the door. "Let's go."

Vika had taken the driving position. Nikolai was crammed into the middle.

Nikolai asked. "Did you get through?"

"You bet. It worked like a charm – first time, too. I talked to Dubord."

"And how's everything? They enjoying their little sail or, ah, float... Just what do they call that?"

Sullivan ignored that. "Bad news, I'm afraid."

"What?"

"Sounds like the Washington bureaucrats got to Marshall. The Captain has ordered Dubord to return to the Glomar – and right now. They want Huey out of these waters immediately. I guess Dubord and Marshall had a pretty good row on the horn over the issue of leaving us behind."

"They should... I mean that's crazy. What the hell are we supposed to...?"

Sullivan cut him off. "Dubord is being threatened with being fired from his GTI position, being returned to his regular Naval Commission status and then being disciplined by the Navy."

"What about our seventy-two meager hours?"

"Gone."

"Our extraction plan...?"

"Time for us to figure out plan B."

"Any good news?"

"Yeah, the weather forecast is for clear and sunny – no rain."

Chapter 48
Washington, D.C.

The dark sedan with Maryland license plates approached the south entrance to the Watergate underground parking structure. The car was a new Crown Victoria, the large non-descript four door that Ford manufactured only for government services. As the vehicle slowed, the driver reached down and slid a radio microphone out of its holder. The mike handset was equipped with a tone pad. He punched in a series of numbers and the steel gate ahead of the car obediently rose. The sedan slid into the underground. The driver brought the mike to his lips and spoke softly. "Twenty-three alpha arriving."

The terse reply was audible only in the driver's earpiece. The voice said, "Roger two-three-alpha." The transmission was digital and scrambled. To anyone who might have been eavesdropping, the signal would have sounded like two short bursts of water squirting through a garden hose.

The car stopped next to the elevator. A tall distinguished man of about seventy years emerged from the rear seat and pressed the call button. He was well known around the beltway, for that matter, he was a familiar face to a good portion of the world. He was often mentioned by media talking heads. They would use words and phrases such as patrician, aristocratic and elder statesmen. Near election time, his name was often mentioned, usually in the context of and with phrases like "White House" and "Presidential timber".

The doors opened and the tall man stepped inside. Rather than push any of the buttons for floors L through 22, he produced a shiny metal key and inserted it into the elevator control panel. The doors closed and the elevator went down – way down.

At a depth that would be considered nearly ten stories underground, he emerged into subterranean world known only to a select group.

While many people knew of the extensive system of tunnels and chambers constructed under the nation's Capital, the part he entered was classified, its very existence known only to a privileged few.

The Cold War provided the perfect justification to spend tax dollars on the D.C. underground world for elected officials, whose lives were considered more important than the rest of us, or at least necessary to insure continuity of government.

What started out as a system of bomb proof shelters and the tunnel system to service them, became a city beneath the city. Small electric vehicles whizzed about around the clock transporting documents, delivering Senators, Congressmen and other officials from point to point. The subterranean system completely eliminated the need to subject one's self to the traffic clogged and often smog filled streets above ground. The Washington elite had even found justification to install some services underground such as barber shops, convenience stores, and coffee shops within their private labyrinth.

Over time, the tunnel system grew and grew. It had been a simple matter to dig deeper and deeper, to create more layers that would be used by a select and knowledgeable few to facilitate their many activities that required absolute security, privacy and insulation from the constantly prying electronic eyes and ears of the media, intelligence services and the like. Tonight's meeting was one of those special occasions where the attendees needed insulation.

A black man waited next to a small electric cart.

"Good evening, Henry. Tonight, I'll just walk if you don't mind."

"Of course, sir."

The distance to the conference room was less than a hundred yards. Despite the fact that the tall man had lived more than seven decades, he was in excellent shape and enjoyed the brisk walk. He took off through the well lit tunnel. Henry, in the cart, followed at a discrete distance.

Minutes later the tall man emerged into another large chamber. He approached a doorway and spoke to another man. "Good evening, Senator."

"Mister Secretary." Was the reply, accompanied with a nod and a cordial smile.

"Is everyone here?"

"Everyone, except the Vice-President."

The two men entered the room, and took their places.

There were many familiar faces around the circular conference table, including elected and appointed officials, CEOs from several

Fortune 500 companies, and top men from every major oil company in the United States and Europe.

There were also several men who were not so easily recognizable. They were, none-the-less, some of the most powerful - and some might say - brutal men in the world. These were people who were used to shaping world events, men who held the economic power to control world commodities and make, often, arbitrary decisions that affected the lives of millions.

War, famine, pestilence – these were the cannon fodder of the power elite that assembled this night far beneath the Watergate.

There was one additional common factor shared between the assembled. To a person, they were all white males. There was not a woman, nor a brown, black or Asian face among the nearly thirty attendees.

The door opened and the Vice-President entered. As he took his seat, the large sound-proof door closed, and with a whoosh of air, sealed behind him.

The tall man, who was known to everyone in the room as Secretary of State, Cyrus Balthazar, spoke first. "Gentlemen – you all know why we are here. Events on the Korean Peninsula have reached – shall we say – a disturbing level. After fifty years, our little North Korean friends have finally managed to figure out how to operate their" – he paused to select the right word – "toy."

He paused for a moment looking at the faces around the room. "We believe that the catastrophic events of late, the Asian earthquakes, tidal waves and some unexplained large explosions are a direct result of their attempts to use a gravity wave amplifier."

"My Lord." The person speaking was the CEO of the British oil and gas monopoly. "Have they actually figured out how the thing works? That must make you chaps feel awfully good – given that you've had one of those things since – what – 1947?"

A bit of light laughter tittered around the table.

"You are - as always - absolutely correct, Basil." It was the Vice-President who responded. The room fell silent. "Our 'thing' as you put it, the craft, came from the Roswell crash in '47. The North Koreans got theirs in the early fifties. For those of you that may not know. The Korean peninsula has been a popular place for UFO sightings. During the war, in 1952, we had a couple of close sightings with some of our F-86 Sabre jets. In one of those instances two of our best pilots chased one of these things for nearly a half hour. Another case involved a large disc shaped craft that hovered very low over an infantry company near the Chosun Reservoir. The craft hung in the air right over the field of battle for nearly an hour. The reports said both sides took shots at it. Many of the eyewitnesses said that the craft appeared to be wobbly or unstable. When it left, it flew off deep into North Korean territory and disappeared. The historical assumption has been that the craft most likely went down. We believe that this is the craft the North Koreans salvaged and have been working on all these years."

Another voice spoke up. "If all this is true, why haven't the Chinese or the Russians taken the thing away from them?"

The Vice-President continued. "We think the Russians have their own extra-terrestrial craft to play with. They've had one for years. As to the Chinese, I have no idea."

Secretary Balthazar spoke. "Gentlemen, the bottom line here is, that for years, most of the countries of the western world have had their best people working in secret trying to reverse engineer the power and propulsion systems from these craft. The United States alone has spent billions on this effort. We've literally gone through a couple generations of scientists and today we're not much closer to understanding this technology than we were back in the fifties."

The Vice-President picked it up. "It's not like we've had any of these alien folks around long enough for them to tell us anything useful. I believe that we are the only country that actually plucked a living being from a crash site - and that creature died a few days later."

One of the men at the table produced a large cigar. He was listening and going through the manipulations of clipping the ends and lighting the smoke. His name was Simon Stuart and he was arguably one of the richest men in the world. Finishing with his cigar ignition process, he blew out a large cloud of blue smoke and began to speak. "And what we have found out about these craft and their power sources is enough to chill the heart of any oil man or economist that adheres to the belief that the world economy hinges directly on supply and demand of petrochemicals."

He made another cloud of smoke as the attention of the room shifted to him. "Look, the very reason we're all here, meeting in this overgrown gopher hole, is that all of us are scared shitless that somebody is going to come along and figure this puzzle out, before we do!"

All eyes in the room had turned to Stuart. "Think of it. Unlimited amounts of clean energy taken from the magnetic field of the earth. My God – just the thought - that the very gravity that holds my fat ass to this chair could be converted into a power source that would change the face of the world. A good deal of what we have today would change - transportation, power generation, most industry, and the entire economy of the world! I've said it before at these meetings and I will say it again. There is absolutely no way we can allow this discovery to get out – unless and until we can control it – absolutely."

Heads were nodding and the room's attention returned to Secretary Balthazar. "Thank you Mister Stuart. I think it is a safe bet that everyone in this room agrees with your assessment of the Gravity Flux Amplifier – Am I using the correct term for it?"

Simon Stuart nodded in agreement and waved away another blue cloud of carcinogens.

"So what remains now is to decide on a course of action. Exactly what do we intend to do about our little brown friends in North Korea?"

Hans Von Luebner, a German industrial magnate, was the next to speak. The staccato pitch and timber of his voice put strange emphasis on many of his words. "We have managed thus far to beat back waves of alternative fuels and technologies. We have delayed fuel cells, made hydrogen fuel unstable and expensive, we let our American cousins mix a little of that corn gas - how is it called – ethanol? Just enough to keep their farmers happy, yes? Electrics and hybrids are just now starting to come to market – but they are a joke… How should this one be any different? We should continue to use the carrot and stick."

A few heads nodded their agreement. "We make our financial offers to the North Koreans under the cover of the nuclear non-proliferation negotiations. If they continue with the idiotic position of refusal, we use military power."

The Vice-President was shaking his head while offering up a strange hint of smile. "Hans – there is nothing that many of us would like better than to take care of our little North Korean friend just like we did Saddam. But, I submit to you. The USA is doing most of the heavy lifting on the entire Middle East. We figure we've got at least another ten years of occupation before we can pacify that situation. And we haven't even gotten around to dealing with Iran yet.

Meanwhile we've got China growing out of itself... And then there's Russia... Most of us are writing hefty monthly checks to keep Boris afloat. I'm sorry, but it's just not the time for us to step in and take over another country!"

Secretary Balthazar asked. "What is the status of the energy module that was recovered by the GTI team in the Sea of Japan?"

"That device has been problematical." The Vice-President was speaking again. "Again, for those of you that may not know, the North Koreans managed to come up with a way to mount a gravity wave induction device into an old jet aircraft – a Mig, I think. The craft had several flights and during each one, the drain or interference it caused with the Earth's magnetic field was so severe, it caused major earthquakes and tidal waves. Finally, they crashed the thing; it went down in some deep water in the East Sea.

We knew they didn't have the means to recover anything in thousands of feet of water, so we mounted an operation with a covert marine exploration team. We did it under the GTI corporate banner. Our intention was to salvage what we could from the wreckage, so we could determine if they built a new gravity amplifier or just used the alien device, the one they've had in their possession all this time."

He shifted in his chair. "Well, not without problems, we got the module and sent it to our facility at Groom Lake. So far the damn thing has killed three scientists. We still haven't got it stabilized, but, we are pretty sure it's one the DPRK team made up themselves."

Heads bobbed and murmured as that piece of information settled.

"We also lost a man in the salvage operation. That man was none other than GTI's, Charles Gomez!"

A second round of murmuring buzzed the table.

"There have been reports that a body of a sailor, possibly an American, that could have been Gomez, was picked up by a North Korean ship. But, we don't have any more at this time." He lied.

"So what are we doing here?" Simon Stuart demanded.

Luebner spoke up. "If they know how to build them, I say we offer them money one more time – and if they continue to say no – then, we eliminate all their facilities. If nothing else, that will delay production of the devices for some time – especially if we all agree that none of us will help them rebuild."

"If we do this, we would have to make it look like it was coming from somewhere other than the US." The Vice-President said flatly.

Secretary Balthazar folded his arms and cradled his chin in thought. "Perhaps we could make it look like an internal accident – a problem - with their fledgling nuclear program."

Chapter 49
Musan, DPRK

They drove the entire day. The going was slow and rough. The road over the hills was old, rutted and, in spots, nearly washed out. Occasionally, they passed other trucks, cars and animal drawn carts plodding along in both directions. Thankfully, none of the traffic was military.

They watched for a place to buy more gasoline, but found none. One of the back tires blew. The spare was marginal at best. Finding an old rusty scissors jack, they quickly learned it was intended for some other kind of vehicle. They frittered away more than a hour to the process of tire changing.

By late afternoon, they had spent hours bouncing over set after set of butt-numbing ruts. Nikolai feared that their little truck was nearing the last of its fuel. Pressed to calculate an average speed for the days travel, Mike guessed they might have made a whopping twenty miles an hour.

Daylight was just beginning to fade, when the trio hit the outskirts of Musan. The town was situated in a valley. Approaching from the south, they climbed a rise that overlooked the bowl-like depression. Sullivan had been taking a turn at the wheel when Nikolai suggested, "Let's pull over here for a little re-con work. This looks like a good place to get a look around."

Mike steered Hiroshi, the truck, off the roadway and into a low stand of trees. Nikolai produced a small set of binoculars and they went through the brush and crawled out onto some boulders. The location afforded a perfect view of Musan and the valley around it. Nikolai folded his map to a blank spot of paper and with a fragment of pencil started making a sketch of the settlement below.

Mike looked through the binoculars and surveyed the scene.

Musan was a town that looked much like all the others they had traveled through. The construction of the buildings was the same and the layout ram-shackle. Musan was really not much more than a large village, but it did seem to have more electric lights than the other pockets of civilization they had visited. From their twilight vantage point, they could see a large well lit installation just west of the village. Everything about the appearance of the place said military and penal institution.

Mike handed the glasses back to Nikolai. "I think we just found the Musan county jail." He gestured to the installation just left of the town.

Nikolai gave Sullivan the paper and pencil. "Here – you be the recording secretary. I'll call out what I see - and you sketch."

Mike nodded. He flattened out the paper on a rock. "Ready when you are."

Nikolai had the glasses to his eyes. "First – let's get our orientation straight – that way is north." With his right hand, he pointed into the hills. Focusing on the military installation, he said. "I see a series of cinder block buildings – all rectangular shaped - laid out in a big square. The outside dimensions are about three hundred feet on a side. The width of the buildings is all the same – probably in the vicinity of thirty feet or so."

Sullivan was making a sketch as well as taking notes.

"I'd say the buildings are tall – maybe twenty feet to the ridgeline of the roof. The drop to the outside edges of the roof – same for the front and the back - is about five feet. That would make the outside walls about fifteen foot high. It's, maybe tall ceiling, single story, with a little attic space, perhaps. Got that?"

Sullivan was sketching. "Yeah, it's either that or two stories for very short people…"

Viktoriya approached. "Poppa, I should go get some gas and check things out - before the sun sets completely."

Nikolai lowered the glasses and glanced at his watch. "Yes, okay. Wait." He pulled out his StarTac cell phone. He flicked it on and waited while it searched for a service carrier. "Damn - nothing. Well, it's too much to hope for a little phone service this far north, I suppose. Vika, set your cell phone for simplex."

From under her clothing, she pulled out an identical black StarTac phone. She flipped it open and paged through the menus pressing buttons. "Got it." She clicked a button on the side. "Can you hear me?"

Her voice echoed through Nikolai's phone just like a regular two-way radio. "Perfect. Just remember, that around buildings, this kind of operation is only good for a couple of blocks – or a little farther if one of us is up on a hill - like we are now."

Viktoriya looked exasperated, but her tone was respectful. "Yes, Poppa, I know."

He nodded. "Fine - go! And try to find us a decent place to stay – and something good to eat."

She opened the truck door and withdrew the remnants of their food and water. With a smile and a wave she was back behind the wheel. "Be back soon." The little motor spun over and the truck named Hiroshi moved back onto the roadway and trundled its way down the hill.

Nikolai went back to his observations. "Inside the square of building is an open court – looks like hard packed dirt – couple of KPA trucks parked inside. Hmm, I don't see a truck-size access on this side of the building."

He handed Sullivan the glasses. Mike peered through and saw only pedestrian doors and a few windows. He also saw the two guard towers that topped out at about thirty feet above grade. The two towers were oriented diagonally and placed at the corners of a double span of chain link fence that surrounded the compound. There was about one hundred feet between the fence line and outer edge of the buildings. The fences looked to be about ten feet high and were topped with coiled razor wire. Every fifty feet or so there was a wooden pole with an incandescent floodlight. Power lines were strung between the poles and at one point snaked over a connection to the building. Sullivan handed the glasses back to Nikolai and filled in more details on his drawing.

삼 질식시킴

Several hours passed. They had finished off the remaining food and were swapping sips from the last water bottle. It was a fair night – cool but not cold. A quarter moon had cleared the eastern horizon about two hours following the onset of darkness. It rode its way across the brilliant star field above, providing decent illumination for their night adjusted eyes. Below them they watched the night activities of the town of Musan and the Military installation next door. Lights twinkled through the smoky haze that came from hundreds of coal fires and kerosene lamps in the valley below them.

They sat on the rocky outcropping, concealed from the road and talked. First, they dissected what they could see of Musan and the KPA installation. They agreed that if serious research was being done, any place around there, it probably wasn't happening at the installation they were watching. The activity level was too low and there weren't enough personnel or equipment. Also they couldn't see an airfield anywhere around them. They agreed that any big time project, nuclear research or otherwise, certainly would require an airfield.

As conversations go, theirs hop scotched from subject to subject. During a lull, Nikolai put the question to Sullivan. "Are you going to tell me the story, Misha, of how and why you came to be the Michael Sullivan, the policeman of California?"

Mike lounged back on his rock, arms folded behind his head. He watched the magnificent celestial progression of light twinkle above them. He was quiet for a long moment – pondering his response.

He thought about his life, the things he had done, the few people he had ever cared about. His thoughts drifted warmly to her – Claire. But, recognizing that this was not the time, he stopped himself. Instead, he went fast forward in the timeline of his memory. His mind drifted over to Charlie and his raucous family - and then it flitted to Audrey and finally settled on the remaining precious few people in his life that had ever meant anything to him. Finally he spoke. "Tell you what, Nikki. Let's make a deal. We've both got about a twenty year gap going on here. You tell me all about what happened to you – tell me about whatever it is that happened here - with Irina" – he spoke the name of Viktoriya's mother softly and with respect – "I'm just dying to know how you, the loyal Soviet citizen, ended up pensioned out in Oahu by Uncle Sam… You tell me yours and I'll tell you mine."

"Fair enough, Misha. We will probably both die anyway" – he laughed – "trying to arrange this insanity of rescuing your friend and then going – God knows where…"

"Nikolai, I've always known you to be a capable and resilient man. I'm quite sure you had a backup plan hatching in that head of yours long before we got the bad news from Dubord."

"I only wish it were true, Misha. I think this time - we may be in for – how is it you Americans say – a very sucky time?"

Mike laughed. "You're right – this is probably really gonna suck!"

Just then, Nikolai's cell phone buzzed. He flipped it open, listened and chattered a bit of Korean. The entire conversation lasted for less than a minute. He switched off and looked at Sullivan.

"Perhaps we shall continue our little talk for another time. Vika is just coming back now."

"How did she do?"

"As always, perfect. She's got it together for us. She returns now, to collect us."

"That's quite a girl you've got there, Nikki. She's brave and smart."

"Yes, she is those things. She is also foolish with the immortal thoughts of youth. She now lives in the world you and I used to inhabit. Remember, Misha. Remember when we were young and invincible?"

Minutes later, the little truck motored its way up the hill. Fifty feet from their spot, she killed the lights and pulled off the roadway.

삼 질식시킴

It wasn't exactly a Holiday Inn. For that matter, it really wasn't a hotel. It was the North Korean version of a roadhouse, this one operated by a family named Byung. It was a simple place for travelers to stop – and for a few Won, take some refreshment and spend the night. It also doubled as a brothel.

Viktoriya had obtained more fuel, had the blown tire replaced with one that looked equally as bad, but did hold air. She had restocked the truck with traveling food, paper wrapped rice balls, bits of cooked this and that and several plastic bottles of drinking water. She drove them back into town.

The place she had engaged was on the eastern edge of Musan, the opposite side of town from the "Korean Peoples Army Barracks". This was the literal translation of the name that the townspeople used to describe the military installation.

Musan was much like any other Korean Village. There was a collection of hovels, open air markets and peddlers of every conceivable form of goods. People milled about all hours, day and night. There were bars, tea rooms and social entertainments for those that had the time and money. A big part of the Musan economy was the Won that came from KPA regulars assigned to the installation next door. It was that group of unknowing fools who were to become the next information targets for the amazing skills of the daughter of Nikolai and Irina.

Arriving at the roadhouse, Nikolai cautioned Sullivan to go into his mentally retarded persona as the need arose. He also told him that, for appearances and security, he and Vika would speak only in Korean. Whenever it was necessary for them to speak English, they should do so only in whispers, and then in the center of whatever room they were in, preferably with doors and windows closed. The name of the game was to make it short and to the point.

Mike acknowledged his instructions just as they arrived at Byung's roadhouse. The front of the place blended with everything around it. There were no signs or other obvious markings. If you didn't know it was there, one would pass right by it.

The place was a jumble of rooms and make shift structures that looked to have been tossed together. In the front there were two large rooms set up for eating, drinking and socializing. Attached to the main rooms were a kitchen and a cluster of small spaces for the proprietor's family. Working toward the back, there were two rows of tiny rooms off a wide hallway. The small rooms were more like closets, windowless, each no more than eight by six feet. The minuscule spaces were nothing more than sleeping and sex cubicles, each with a straw mat bed and a thin sliding privacy door made of wood and paper.

They parked the truck in the rear, near a group of carts and bicycles. Theirs was the only motor vehicle in sight. Once inside, Vika led them to their room, situated in the rear, and it had a window, with a view that overlooked the truck parking space.

Their room was large by Korean standards, about twelve by twelve feet. It contained four sleeping mats, a small table and two chairs. A single light bulb fixture hung from the low ceiling. Once inside, Sullivan uncurled from his stooped walking position. Standing fully upright, his head cleared the ceiling by mere inches.

Nikolai closed the door and set the only form of security, an inside wire hook latch.

Mike whispered. "At least it'll be easy to change the light bulb."

Nikolai immediately shushed him to be quiet. He fired off a string of Korean. Vika responded in kind, bowed slightly and left the room. When she'd cleared the door, Nikolai re-closed it and replaced the hook latch. He then moved around and began to examine the room. He made a listening motion at his ear. Mike got it. He was checking the room for electronic bugs. Sullivan helped.

Twenty minutes later, Viktoriya returned with a tray. She had hot tea, chunks of dark bread and some kind of foul smelling spicy vegetable soup. Mike was gratified to see there was no meat.

She placed the tray on the table and rattled off some more Korean to her father. She moved to one corner of the room, looked back at Sullivan for a coy moment and then quickly stripped down to her not-too-stylish, North Korean cotton panties. She glanced back at Sullivan and then the panties went. Standing naked, she rummaged through a small duffle. She removed a black thong, a hot pink shortie blouse and a makeup bag. She dressed quickly and went to work on her hair and painted her face. When she was finished, the results were spectacular. She wore the face of a Kabuki dancer, was bra less and the short blouse left a steaming three inch gap of tummy exposed to the top of her tight jeans. She slipped on her Reeboks and tossed a small black purse over her shoulder.

Nikolai looked his daughter over. A mixture of approval and disapproval washed across his weathered face. They exchanged a bit more Korean and then she approached Mike.

She gestured for him to lean down to her face. He felt her warm moist breath in his ear as she whispered, "Time for me to go to work. You boys behave now." Then she planted a kiss on his cheek and blew out the door. It was a few moments before Mike could look Nikolai in the eye.

Chapter 50
Musan, DPRK

The distinct whump-whump-whump sound came out of the east. The familiar noise alerted both Sullivan and Nikolai at the same time. They looked at each other. Within seconds, the combined racket from the turbine engines and the giant rotor blades clawing through the air had reached the deafening stage. Sullivan went to the window and Nikolai to the door. Mike craned his neck but was unable to see the huge aircraft. The sound was so intense it nearly blotted out thought. Nikolai stepped out the door and melted into the darkness.

The bone shattering vibrations from the low flying aircraft penetrated everything. The rickety buildings shook, plaster fell from the walls. Mike thought that his dental fillings might pop loose. The pilot had to be flying a mere fifty feet over the rooftops.

The aircraft passed over. Nikolai returned. As he closed and re-latched the door, the fading helicopter engine sound changed in pitch and then increased speed. After a few moments, the engine sounds abruptly stopped.

Both men moved to the center of the room. Mike whispered. "Did you see it? It sounded like it just flared and..."

"It landed – yes - and very close – any ideas as to where?"

"Mike nodded. "It can only be..."

"Yes... There's your answer, Misha. The quad between the buildings, it is a helicopter port!"

"What kind was it? Did you see it.?" His voice was tinged with excitement but his words were barely a whisper.

"I only got a quick look at the underside. I am pretty certain it was a Mi-25 Combat ship – dual rocket pods, nose guns..."

"Russian!"

"Of course, Misha, fine Russian craftsmanship. Curious though..."

"What?"

"That's a very expensive aircraft for the Korean Peoples Army. They could barely afford to buy one, let alone maintain it for flight."

"Maybe they have a Rabbi."

"Maybe they have more than one." Nikolai answered with wink.

삼 질식시킴

The male attendant unlocked the door and entered his room. Gomez sat on his bed staring at the opposing wall. The man, as always, said nothing. He approached and examined Charlie's head dressing. He apparently decided to remove it and went about the task. The bandaging had been done in circular wraps, mummy style. It took a few moments to unwind and remove the gauze pads. The attendant took the soiled dressings and left the room.

Absent a mirror, Charlie gently probed his head with fingers. His hair had been buzzed off. At the top of his head and slightly to the back he felt two jagged paths of stitching that came together in a point. From touch he deduced that the blow to his head had lacerated his scalp in a triangular fashion, probably peeling back a flap of skin. Someone had done an earnest job of stitching him back together. The wound was a little tender, but dry.

The attendant returned. Catching Charlie probing his head, he of little words spoke. "No touch. No touch – eene-fection!" He pronounced the last word with some difficulty.

Charlie understood and dropped his hand. He remained seated, expecting a new head dressing. The attendant spoke again. "You come – now."

The attendant took Charlie by the arm and led him out into the hallway. After their short walk, they ended up at the same room he'd visited earlier, the one with the numbers "105" on the outer door. The attendant directed him to sit in the same chair as before. The attendant turned and left, firmly closing the door behind him. Charlie sat for a few moments. Nothing happened. He was facing the same window as last time. It looked out into the interior yard. He sat forward for a better look. Curiosity got the better of him and he stood and walked to the window. The courtyard was huge, at least a couple of hundred feet square – maybe more. There was a large double door opening on the opposing side of the yard. The opening was sealed by a king size set of double doors, big enough to drive a semi through. The door fabrication appeared to be reinforced steel and it looked like the doors were designed to slide laterally on a raised track to open and close. This time there were no vehicles in the open courtyard. Charlie looked over the expanse. There was something strange, something funny about the ground. It was brown dirt, the same brown dirt that he had seen everywhere else in this God forsaken land, but here, outside in this courtyard it appeared segmented or grooved in almost a symmetrical pattern.

From behind him he heard the door open and the familiar voice of Officer Smiley. "Mister Gomesss..." This time, the idiot, Senior Captain Rhee made his name sound like "go-mess".

Inwardly, he just shook his head. Outwardly he turned and smiled.

"You will take your seat and do not move further unless you are instructed to do so. Do you understand?"

Charlie moved over to his assigned chair and sat. "Absolutely, I understand you perfectly. You know, uh, Captain, your English is very good. You ever been to the States?"

I will ask the questions, Mister Gomesss." The impeccable Senior Captain Rhee went to the window, surveyed the yard and then lowered a curtain. You will answer my questions. Are we understood?"

"We are understood. Shoot!"

"Captain Rhee looked perplexed. "What did you say?'

"I said, shoot – go ahead – ask away – anything at all."

"Ah, yes – a colloquial expression – very quaint."

Captain Rhee carried a brown paper parcel wrapped in dark twine. He placed the bundle on the table and took his seat. He went through the ministrations of lighting a cigarette. Today it was a hard pack of Marlboros. The thought went through Charlie's mind that perhaps it was payday for the KPA.

Rhee pushed the package closer to Gomez. "Open this." He commanded. Charlie dutifully stood up and pulled on the twine bow. The parcel opened. It contained the clothing that Charlie had been wearing at the time of his rescue from the water. It was apparent that the articles had been laundered. "Oh, my clothes - thank you, thank you. I gotta tell you I am getting a bit tired of these outfits." Charlie plucked at his cotton pajamas.

"Return to your chair." Once Charlie was reseated, Rhee continued. "I am not returning... These items are" – he was searching for the correct word – "evidences" – Rhee's eyebrows arched up – "of your crimes against the peaceful people of Korea."

"Senior Captain Rhee – Charlie feigned both sincerity and disappointment. I thought we had that all cleared up. I told you before, you are mistaken..."

"Yes, your previous lies. Mister Go-mess, these clothes are" – again he paused as if searching for the word – "suspicious. They tell me the story of your lies and fabrications. Observe..." He fingered the items. There was the dark blue one-piece, coverall suit, a white tee shirt, white boxer shorts, multicolored argyle knit socks and an old battered pair of Nikes.

Gomez got serious. "Look – Captain, I don't quite understand what's going on here. I've already told you what we were doing and how I got here and..."

Rhee cut him off. "Silence! These articles of clothing are typical of those worn by a U.S. Navy submarine crewman."

Gomez thought that officer tight-ass was right about one thing. The blue coverall was the one garment that was standard issue on a sub.

Rhee's eyes narrowed to slits. "You are a crewman from an American Navy Submarine. It is senseless for you to lie further. Tell me now – tell me what your ship was doing spying in our territorial waters!" He stubbed out his smoke and immediately lit another.

Charlie thought that this guy's interview technique was really piss-poor. "Captain, please look at these clothes. They don't say anything about US, Navy, any government, or anything like that. Don't navy guys have their names stenciled on everything? The only thing my underwear says is "Calvin Klein". The jump suit is the kind we all wear on our ship – the marine survey and mining ship that I already told you about. Look – look at those shoes. Those aren't navy guy shoes. Hell, I bought those at South Coast Plaza - that's in California - Nordstroms – I think, about two years ago." Charlie was almost certain that he could see steam coming out of Rhee's ears. Maybe it was just the cigarette smoke.

The Senior Captain decided to change tactics. "The doctors tell us that you have sufficiently healed to be transferred to..." Again, he appeared to be groping for the correct words. "S tandard custody. Soon, you shall be transported to – another facility. They will not treat you as well as we have. Things will be difficult for you. If I were you, I would cooperate now. You should be telling me..." He leaned forward grinning, displaying a set of badly stained teeth. It was Rhee striving for sincerity. "Everything..."

Charlie thought that Rhee looked like a snake.

"You should tell me everything, absolutely everything that you know. I can help you. I have influence. But you must cooperate…"

Gomez dug in. "Look, Captain. I'm an American citizen. I appreciate that you guys pulled me out of the ocean, brought me here and have taken care of me. But, it's time for the games to end. I am a civilian. I am not now, nor have I ever been in the American military. I'm a mining technician. I work on a marine survey ship. I'm not a spy!"

Rhee sat back listening to Charlie's monologue and observed. He blew stinking streams of cigarette smoke across the room and said nothing.

"We could clear up this entire mess if you'd just let me make a couple of phone calls. Heck, I'll even reverse the charges!" Charlie lapsed into silence.

The two regarded each other for a full minute. Finally, Rhee again leaned forward slightly, and touched a hidden button. In seconds, three men dressed in KPA fatigue uniforms, men who were clearly not part of the medical staff, burst into the room. Gomez was instantly overpowered.

With heavy leather restraints, they buckled him, hands, legs and chest, to the chair. One of the men produced a glass hypodermic syringe filled with an amber fluid. Another man roughly gripped Charlie's head and bent it to the side. The needle plunged into his neck.

Seconds passed. They released his head. Instantly, the peripheral edges of his vision started to cloud. Rhee was speaking in that particularly irritating voice of his. "Yes, Mister Go-mess, we shall soon – clear things up – we shall make everything very clear…"

Chapter 51
Musan, DPRK

Morning twilight followed close on the heels of Viktoriya's return. She tapped lightly on the door. The men had taken turns napping. It was Sullivan's turn to be awake, sort of. He jumped up, startled at the noise, and let her in. She went directly to the table and fell into a chair. Mike realized she was exhausted. He leaned close to her head and whispered. "You okay?"

She smiled through her fatigue and motioned his head down. She brought her lips close to his ear and whispered. "Yeah, I'm fine, thanks - got lots to share, too. But first, I have to talk to my father."

Mike moved back and nodded. He went to the window and peered outside. Nikolai, now awake and upright, had moved into the second chair and sat with elbows on the table, rubbing his face. Satisfied that things around the truck were secure, Mike returned to the table and dropped to a sitting position on the floor. The dim morning light was just sufficient illumination for them to see.

Nikolai and Viktoriya conversed in Korean. Their tone was soft and confidential. It was frustrating for Sullivan, who dearly needed to know what was going on.

"Did you have any problems, my daughter?"

"None that I was unable to handle, father. The biggest problem was the overwhelming number of horny soldier-boys in this town. But I managed to maintain my chastity, barely. But enough of that, I need to tell you what I learned, and then try to get some sleep. I am exhausted! The big news - this is the place where they are holding the American, Gomez!"

Hearing that, Nikolai glanced at Sullivan, giving him a grin and the thumbs up sign.

Vika continued. "I talked to a woman... She works in the army compound, cleaning. Incidentally, the place is a prison in name only. She says they've just got a handful of prisoners in there, maybe ten bodies, at the most. The big news around town – honestly, these people have no sense of verbal security – the big news is the American prisoner they brought in the other day from Chongjin. She described to me how his head was bandaged and that he was put into the hospital part of the facility which is…"

Nikolai pushed their diagram across the table.

Vika picked up the paper, examined it and placed her finger at a point on the southwest side of the complex. "Right about here."

"Excellent. Not only do we know that our target is here, you also manage to narrow down the location. Excellent work, my daughter."

"Wait father, there is more, lots more."

Nikolai nodded. "You want something, tea or water?"

"No – thank you – I have been drinking tea all night. I may never drink any tea again." She continued. "I found out why there is no prostitute activity at this place. This and other houses are serviced by a traveling band of 'business girls'. They go from place to place, staying and working a couple of days at a time. Well, today they come here, to Byung's. This place will be filled with KPA for at least two days! We're gonna have to move."

"Perhaps… And then perhaps not. Please, continue." The wheels of planning were turning in Nikolai's head. "Wait. Did you see or hear the helicopter land last night?"

"Yes, there was one that flew over, shortly, after I went out. I didn't get a look at it, but it was loud, like military."

"Do you know were it went – where it landed?"

She shook her head. "I assumed it landed in the KPA base." She paused as if reflecting in thought. "Poppa, I was all over this village during the night. There is nowhere an aircraft could have landed. It must have gone into the army base."

"Yes, yes – go on. There is more?"

"Yes, on the earth tremor thing. I'm convinced that this is the research place, at least one of them. I got brave and at one point found myself on the western side of town within a stone's throw of the front gate of the compound. Right at the entrance, by the guard shack, there is a small white sign, written in Hangul. It says "Korean Peoples Army Musan Detention Facility. Under that in smaller characters, it says 'Energy Project'."

"You are certain of this?"

"Father, it was identical to the Hangul script on Sullivan's paper – identical! This is too much to be a coincidence. I think this must be the place."

"Can't be… For one there is not enough facility here for a big project, no airfield either." As the very words passed through his lips, Nikolai began to doubt them.

"Well, the townspeople call this place 'shaking earth town'. They have tremors nearly every day. Some days - two or three times."

"What else?"

"That's about it – That's the important stuff. I really need to sleep – at least for a couple of hours."

He nodded. She got up and stepped around the impatiently waiting Sullivan. She hesitated and bent to whisper to him. "Good news, Poppa will tell you." Patting his shoulder, she went over to one of the sleeping mats and dropped. Viktoriya went out, cold, the second she lay down her head.

Mike took a blanket and gently covered her. On his way back to the table he peeked out the window. There was still no one around. He sat down close to Nikolai, head to head and waited.

Nikolai spoke in whispers, raspy with morning voice. It took him several minutes to get it all out. Mike listened quietly. He knew Nikolai was making plans. Mike was making some of his own.

삼 질식시킴

Hours passed. Vika's eyes fluttered as she slowly climbed out of sleep. She was alone in the room. She lay on her back for a few minutes examining the cracked ceiling. She waited as her mind cleared to a fully wakeful state. Then she got up. She was still attired in her working girl costume. She glanced at her watch. It was mid-afternoon. She peeked out the window and saw that the truck was gone. Quickly, she stripped out of her clothing. From her bag, she took a loose fitting muslin garment – similar to a plain muumuu. She slipped the garment over her head. She took her pistol and put it under her dress, clamped between arm and ribcage. She went out to the benjo facility and attended to her needs, among which was transforming herself back into an innocent appearing peasant girl.

On the way back she ran into the wife of the proprietor, Byung. They exchanged the traditional Korean greetings and pleasantries. Mother Byung mentioned the fact that Vika's father had extended their stay for three more days and she hoped they would be comfortable and that their business was profitable. Vika was surprised, but displayed no inkling of it. In their discussion, Mother Byung apologized in advance for the anticipated heavy traffic expected at their place tonight. She left it at that. The woman did not elaborate and Vika did not press further.

A short time later, she was dressed in her traditional Korean dress, the Hanbok. Her duffle was packed. She was ready to roll. She was curious to know what Nikolai was cooking up. She decided to use the cell phone. Out came the StarTac and she was about to hit the send button when she heard the sound of the truck. She stashed the phone and went to the window. The truck pulled in with both men on board. Nikolai waved for her to come out. She grabbed her duffle.

Minutes later they were driving. Nikolai followed streets that took them generally in a northern direction through town. He talked. "Misha and I have cooked up a plan – at least half a plan – to finish things up and make a break for it."

Vika mentioned that she'd learned from Momma Byung that they were staying on.

"Not completely accurate. We now have alternate lodging. I decided we are going to keep the Byung place, at least for a while. I paid for a few more nights. It may prove to be useful. But for right now we're going to this other place we found this morning – Mister Sullivan and I have been quite busy, you see. It is a lodging place, as well, but without the 'business girls'." Nikolai inserted the Korean phrase for ladies-of-the-night. "We also got a nearby barn in which to park our truck. It could prove useful"

"So, we have a plan?" Vika asked.

Nikolai glanced at Sullivan with a smirk. "Yes, my daughter, we have a plan, of sorts. Unfortunately, it is one with a high probability of failure – one might even call it suicidal - but it is a plan."

"I can't wait." She said.

Sullivan tried to stretch his leg in the cramped confines of the truck. "I can't wait either, but first we need to find some food."

Vika nodded in agreement. "Absolutely, let's eat!"

Chapter 52
Musan, DPRK

They stopped at a small outdoor cookery. Vika came back to the truck holding two small brown paper packages. Tucked under an arm she also carried three brown glass bottles that looked suspiciously like beer.

With everyone back aboard, Nikolai steered the little truck through a few more zigzagging streets. Soon they ended up at a location on the north side of the settlement. He pointed to a ramshackle building with a small hand lettered sign in front. "There. That is our new place. I took it for three nights. I registered for my brother, there," – he looked at Mike – "and my daughter and me, same cover story. We are itinerant peddlers. Our room is in the back, number ten. Got it?"

"Got it. Number ten, G.I. She laughed at her little joke."

Sullivan asked. "I thought I was your retarded nephew?"

"You have just been promoted."

Vika asked. "What now?"

"Now, we go have a picnic." Nikolai followed a road that left the village and wound its way up into the northern hills. The road was mostly gravel and made up a series of switchbacks to wind its way steadily up. They found a good spot. There was some vegetation for cover, a rocky outcropping and the location was several hundred feet in elevation above the town. It was similar to the spot where they had stopped upon their arrival to Musan, but the view of the KPA complex was better. They were situated a little to the east, but they looked right down into base.

The sun was just starting to fade at the horizon. They sat on a rock and dug heartily into their meal.

After a few minutes, Mike offered, "I'm starting to get used to this diet of rice and what ever this is."

"Mostly pickled cabbage and - some other vegetables... You want to stay away from the meats around here." Viktoriya said.

"Yeah, your father already clued me in on that aspect of the economy."

"All the cabbage gives me gas - makes me sound like a damn fog horn." Nikolai took a long pull on his beer and belched loudly. "What do you think of this" – he read the label – "Comrade Worker's Beer?"

"No shit." Mike looked at the Korean writing on his bottle label. "That's what it really says?"

"Would I lie to you, Misha?

Vika laughed at the banter between the two. Then, a moment of seriousness crept in. "I find it fascinating – and even a little sad – that you two knew each other such a long time ago – even before I was born."

Mike nodded but said nothing. Nikolai offered, "Yes, Vika, it is true. Misha and I worked together right about the time that I met your mother. We had some" – his face darkened for a moment, as if a cloud had quickly passed over – "but that was a different time and long, long ago. I am certain that we are different men, today. Right, Misha?"

Sullivan met the older man's gaze. A silent moment hung between them. Mike raised his bottle. "To better times." They all clinked and drank.

Nikolai changed the subject. "Now, let us talk about what we may do tonight." He unfolded his diagram and spread it out before them.

They talked, argued and brainstormed for nearly two hours. The twinkle of small fires and electric lights below stood out in stark contrast to the dark backdrop of the moonless night. The view they had of the KPA compound was excellent.

Sullivan was examining the KPA base through the binoculars. He thought the symmetry of the design was interesting. First there was the double chain link fence line, with the corresponding line of floodlights. Inside that was the line of the buildings, arranged in a perfect quad. Inside the quad of buildings was the interior courtyard. Mike noticed for the first time that there was also a line of low level lights running around the inside of the courtyard. The lights emitted a soft green glow. Unlike the fence-line floodlights, these were installed low, probably attached to the building, too low to be seen anywhere but from inside or above. They formed a perfect square. He handed the glasses to Nikolai. "I think I know where the helo landed."

Nikolai peered through the glasses. "Yes – I see what you mean. It is a perfect landing pad for a chopper. But why did we not hear it take off, Misha? Those machines are so loud they could wake the dead."

"Maybe we slept through..."

Suddenly, Nikolai froze. He pressed the small binoculars to his face. Excitement caused his voice to quiver slightly. "My God – look – look at this!" The three of them stood transfixed as they watched the mystery of the missing aircraft unfold before them. A high pitched hum permeated the air. Coupled with the hum, there were machinery noises, grinding and the sound of heavy metal plates moving and clanking. Before them the center of the dirt floor of the courtyard dropped and in segments, started to retract. The three of them stood stock still, nearly immobilized with shock. They were witnessing the opening of gigantic doors – doors to a huge man-made subterranean cavern. Blue-white light poured forth from the chasm. The process of the doors opening took a full two minutes. The gigantic doors clanked loudly into a fully open position.

"I've never seen anything like this. This is amazing." That opening – it must be at least seventy-five meters square!" Nikolai exclaimed.

Vika pounded on Nikolai's shoulders. "Poppa – Poppa, give me the glasses, please! Let me take a look." Nikolai surrendered the binoculars. He turned to Sullivan with a grin. "I think – perhaps - the plan may have changed a bit. What do you think, Misha?"

Vika was offering the glasses to Sullivan when the ground lurched. There was a quick tremor, like a single shock wave. Vika, who had been perched on her knees on a large boulder rolled off into Sullivan. Both he and Nikolai were standing and rode it out. They watched, in fascination, as all the electric lighting below them, both in the town and on the KPA base flickered and then went out. A strange low hum filled the air. It was soft at first and then grew in intensity. Mike saw a flicker of something from the courtyard below. He brought the glasses to his eyes just in time to see something - it looked like an airplane with stubby wings - rising slowly through the portal.

The aircraft reached an altitude of about a hundred feet. It just hung in the air, silently hovering in a perfectly level configuration. Slowly it began to turn counter clockwise. The craft yawed about one hundred eighty degrees. It was now facing directly toward them, but at a lower elevation. Sullivan, Nikolai and Viktoriya were still looking down at it. It was at that point that Mike put it together. He recognized the craft. It was basically a Mig-19, radically modified, but still a Mig, none-the-less. The wings had been clipped to stubby projections. The tail and rudder assembly appeared stock, but the jet engine air intake had been closed off.

It was eerie. Other than the low hum, the craft made no discernable sound. It wobbled a bit and then slowly descended back into the cavern. A few moments after the craft had disappeared from view. The lights came back on. Mike looked at the other two. "Folks, I think we've just seen the fruits of the 'Energy Project', first hand."

They continued to watch the KPA compound. Once again, the air was filled with machinery noise. But this time the doors did not move. Slowly another object rose in the center of the portal. This time it was a helicopter riding on a flat platform. It was the Mi-25.

"Would you look at that? These bastards can't feed their own population but they've got an aircraft elevator in that multi-billon dollar complex that rivals what you would find on the U.S.S. Ronald Reagan." Nikolai handed the glasses to Sullivan.

Mike watched as the gigantic portal doors that covered the opening to the subterranean cavern reversed and closed to a position that mated perfectly with the platform the Russian helo perched upon. "And that answers the question of where the mysterious helicopter went."

The helicopter's engines were not running. No one could be seen, moving around the aircraft.

Mike turned to Nikolai. "Think we could do it?"

The older man smiled. "Beats the hell out of trying to drive out of here. There is one a little problem, though."

"Only one?"

"I can't fly a helicopter. Can you?"

Mike thought about it for a moment before he answered. He'd only had his hand on the controls of a helicopter once. And that time he'd crashed. On the other hand, Charlie Gomez could fly anything. But Mike had no idea what kind of shape Charlie was in. Finally, he responded with a confident tone. "Sure – I can fly it!"

"Good! Lets get to work." They boarded their truck and with lights off, so as not to attract undue attention, and bounced their way down the hill.

삼 질식시킴

They made their way back to their new "hotel". It was worse than Byung's place, but they required the privacy to finish their preparations. Viktoriya went inside and Nikolai backed the little truck into the barn. The two men unloaded the cartons of merchandise. With the bed of the truck empty, Nikolai decided to reload a couple of the boxes for appearance. He covered the bed with a dirty canvas, tied it with rope. Finishing, they went inside.

The first part of their plan involved the liberation of some KPA uniforms and hopefully an Army vehicle. For that element, they boarded the truck and went back to Byung's. They parked in their spot at the rear and slipped back into their room.

As anticipated, the activity level at Byung's had exploded with the arrival of the "business girls". With hair up, face scrubbed clean of makeup and attired in her floor length traditional costume, Vika eased the door to their room and slipped out to reconnoiter the festivities.

The tables of the two main rooms of the Roadhouse were filled with uniformed KPA men. Most were drinking beer and other foul spirits that Mister Byung offered. Some food was being served. At various tables men were loudly playing card games and something that looked like dominos. Quite a good deal of cash floated around the room.

Vika counted at least twelve "business girls" that had set up shop. Most were young, late teens at most. The girls would work the room, flirt, sit on a few laps, and recite over and over the classic line, "Buy me a drink, Soldier?" Of course, the drinks were a few ounces of weak tea and nothing more. This was the standard method that the proprietor used to extract his cut for the girl's services and the use of his premises. Through the night, Byung would tally up a tidy sum through the practice of the girls getting the soldiers to buy them "drinks".

Eventually, a girl would score a customer and escort him back to one of the tiny crib rooms. The average amount of time spent with a customer was about fifteen minutes.

She never saw a Momma-san or any other person of authority for the girl's. They seemed to be collecting their own fees. Vika noticed that one of the girls was a bit older, maybe a hard thirty. But, she too, was turning tricks as fast as she could.

Vika returned to their room and immediately went about transforming herself back into the sultry vixen.

Nikolai and Sullivan laid out their equipment on one of the sleeping mats. They had two rolls of duct tape, some cut lengths of rope and assorted other goodies.

Vika added her pistol and other items to the small pile. She decided to carry only her StarTac in the pocket of her jeans and some "girlie stuff" in a small purse.

Mike had his own assortment of goodies, including his weapon. He fitted the silencer to it and stowed the gun in his back waistband.

Fifteen minutes later, she was ready. Nikolai ran everyone through the game plan one last time. He hugged his daughter. "Ready, Vika?" She nodded. "Good, we'll be ready for you. Be careful."

"Wish me luck." She kissed Nikolai on the cheek and patted Sullivan on the shoulder as she slung the little purse over her arm, and sashayed through the door. Nikolai closed it to a thin crack and knelt down to watch.

Chapter 53
Washington D.C.

Secretary of State Balthazar sat at the antique oaken desk in the study of his Georgetown home. The telephone rang. He glanced up from the papers he was reviewing, and noted that the blinking light was his private, confidential line. He glanced over at the two hundred year old Ansonia timepiece faithfully ticking away on the adjacent wall. It was eleven thirty in the evening. As he reached for the receiver, he muttered to himself. "This cannot be good news."

He listened, spoke a few words and hung up. Fifteen minutes later there was a knock on his door. He was alone in the house. His wife of nearly forty years was spending the week at their home on Martha's Vineyard. Chester, his manservant, was away visiting his daughter in Philadelphia.

Balthazar rose and walked to the door. He peered through the peephole. Framed in the circular aperture was a tall man with cropped hair and dark suit. He had a grim face and a flesh colored radio earpiece. Balthazar opened the door.

The man nodded to the Secretary of State, and then spoke into his wrist. Another, similarly attired man opened the door to the waiting limousine. The familiar figure got out and walked the short distance to the front door. Balthazar closed the door behind his guest and they both went into the study. Balthazar gestured for the Vice-President to take a chair.

"Could I offer you a coffee, tea – a drink, perhaps?"

"Cut the crap, Cyrus. You know damn well I'll have some of that hundred year old scotch you hoard."

The Secretary poured two fingers of the rich whiskey into crystal glasses. He handed one to his friend and took the upholstered seat next to him. They clinked and sipped. Balthazar spoke. "And - to what do I owe the honor of this late night visit?"

The Vice President exhaled and closely examined the etching on the crystal tumbler. "Unfortunately, we believe that the time has come to take some – definitive action – on the problem we discussed at our last meeting."

"And – am I correct in assuming that you believe this action should – ah - mitigate the problem for the foreseeable future?"

"Correct. At least for the time being."

"And – we must be in a position to maintain deniability?"

"Absolutely – things must be arranged so that it appears to be their problem, their mistake or accident that causes the destruction of their facilities."

"I note that you use the plural. Are there more than a single location?"

"Unfortunately, yes. We believe there are two places where they are doing work on this project." From an inside coat pocket he withdrew a folded white paper. He handed it to Balthazar. "These are the coordinates for their main research facility. It's just outside a place called Musan. The second location is a few hundred miles to the west. Both of the places are dead bang on the Chinese border. Musan is the one we have to take out."

"You realize how this complicates things?"

"Yes."

"What about collateral damage?"

"Unfortunate."

"What happens if they are able to restart things at their other facility?"

"We cross that bridge…"

"Yes, yes – I get it. I'm just saying that it would really look bad if we pose the improbability that a mishap will occur in two places at once – kind of a double lightning strike – if you will."

"I know."

Balthazar put his glass down. He was pensive. "Have you considered the overall impact if we do nothing?"

"Meaning what?"

"If we do nothing… Look, analyze what you think is really going to happen. Do we really think this is going to be like a Saddam with nuclear ICBM's?"

The Vice-President tented his fingers in front of his mouth. He listened to his old friend.

"At least of few of us believe that this little monkey is more interested in maintaining his lifestyle filled with blond white girls and as much good booze, drugs and black hair dye that his aging body can possibly handle. The bottom line is that we don't think he really wants to rule the world… And if the North Koreans have figured out this gravity wave thing, then how long could it possibly be before we figure it out, as well – and everyone else for that matter?"

"Cyrus, I understand you, I truly do. I don't like this any more than you do. But the reality is that our world economy is based on petrochemicals. The introduction of this new energy source would be - make that - will be - a devastating impact on that economy."

Balthazar nodded and listened as the Vice President continued.

"As you know, I seldom agree with that pompous idiot Simon Stuart, but, he does have a point. If and when it comes, we have to control it. If we don't, there will be hell to pay." The Vice President paused for a few moments. He sipped at his whiskey. "There's more regarding the weapons aspect of this thing."

Balthazar looked up.

Our people are telling us that this machine, its power source – gravity or whatever it is – takes its power directly from the magnetic lines of the earth – taps right in."

"Yes, I've heard that as well."

"Well, the problem is, that the earthquake clusters, like that last Tsunami in Asia – we think it was caused by them tinkering with this gravity thing. Our people fear that the damn thing may have the power to literally rip the world apart. We can't let these idiots have that – potential. We absolutely can not!"

They were both quiet for a minute or so. Finally Secretary Balthazar spoke. "So – when do you propose for this to happen?"

"It should happen as quickly as you can arrange it." The Vice-President stood. Balthazar stood. The two men shook hands. "Thank you for the drink – and please give my best to Charlotte."

"You are welcome Mister Vice-President, and I will do that – and good night." Balthazar remained at his desk. Dark thoughts hung over him like a cloud. The Vice-President found his own way out.

Chapter 54
Musan, DPRK

A momentary hush seized the room as Viktoriya entered. She was so much more beautiful than any of the other business girls, it was no wonder. A few heartbeats of time passed, and the sound level quickly resumed to its full rowdy volume. Mr. Byung caught her eye and simply nodded.

Good, she thought. That was the sign she needed. Byung had assumed she was just another working girl, all the more for his till. She prayed she did not run into Mother Byung. That might be difficult.

She cruised around the edge of the room, aware that many pairs of eyes were undressing her, fondling her, bending her over and... Ugh, she decided not to think about that part.

She played her role to the hilt. Ignoring the cat-calls and other unsavory comments, she strutted slowly through the roomful of men. At a point, about one full circuit around the room, she found exactly what she was looking for, an officer! The bonus was that he was about the same height as her father, though just a bit more slender. She moved in, dumped a private off a close-by chair, and sat down next to the Lieutenant at a card table.

He glanced at her, smiled briefly and went back to his game. She said nothing. She simply sat close to him and aimed her considerable sexual radiation right at him, coy smile, alluring eyes, magnificent scent, and all.

After a few moments, the young Lieutenant began to visibly break out in a sweat. Vika sat calmly and waited for him to make a move. Byung appeared and placed a "drink" in front of Viktoriya. The Lieutenant could not get the money into Byung's hand fast enough. Vika ever so slightly tilted her head in tacit acknowledgement of thanks, but still said nothing.

Finally, the young man stood. He said to her, "Can we sit elsewhere?"

She nodded and stood. He picked up her glass and a brown glass bottle of "Comrade Worker Beer" and looking about, gestured for her to accompany him to a corner table that was unoccupied. As they sat, he said, "My name is Cho." It was his family name.

Vika replied, formally with a little bow. "My name is Kim, Hei." It was not the name on her ID card, but rather it was the name Nikolai had made up for her during the roadside encounter with the KPA soldiers. She knew that Hei meant grace. She liked the elegance of the name.

Lieutenant Cho smiled hungrily. She knew they would be taking a walk very soon.

삼 질식시킴

Sullivan and Nikolai waited in the darkened room. Through the slightly ajar door, Nikolai watched as the girls brought man after man to the cribs for a "short time".

Nikolai thought there must be at least a platoon of KPA regulars in Byung's place tonight. Business was good. He wished he knew just how many men were garrisoned at the Musan Facility. He liked to figure that their odds of success would increase if most of the troops were out on the town.

As an old soldier, Nikolai understood the importance of a little booze and regular pussy for the troops, fundamentals to the task of keeping the boys' morale intact. Especially, when they were assigned to some God forsaken spot such as Musan.

As he watched for Vika's return, he continued to think their plan through. Eventually, he realized the variables made little difference. What they really needed was some incredible luck if this mission was to succeed. Of course, he realized it was a crappy plan, bordering on downright reckless. But, he could foresee no other course for them to follow.

The relative quiet of their room was pierced by the sound of a truck motor and grinding gears, followed by vehicle door sounds and loud voices. The sound was coming from the rear. Sullivan moved to the window and peeked out. It was a KPA truck, similar to the one that had stopped them on the road to Musan, parked right behind their room, right next to their Toyota. Four soldiers were dismounting. It looked like two had come from the cab and two more were jumping down from the canvas shrouded truck bed.

The foursome chattered back and forth in Korean. Mike didn't understand what they were saying but they had all the appearances of four guys who already had quite a bit to drink. One was having difficulty standing and another was trying to steady himself on a fender of Hiroshi the truck, while urinating on the wheel and his boots.

Sullivan watched as two of the carousers walked around apparently heading for the front entrance of Byung's. The other two stayed by the truck, talking. Cigarettes were lit. Mike could see the men's faces as their matches flared. They were both just kids. He moved to Nikolai's position by the room door and whispered of his observations.

Nikolai nodded and backed away from the door. He stood up and whispered to Sullivan. "Here she comes – get ready."

Nikolai and Sullivan stood against the wall, flanking the front door. They heard Vika's voice and the sound of laughter as the couple approached. She pushed the door open and stepped inside, quickly moving to the middle of the room. She turned around, smiled and opened her arms to the young Lieutenant, who was eagerly charging inside, while working at the buttons of his tunic.

Sullivan stepped in behind the man. In one swift motion, he grabbed the officer in an arm lock choke hold. Sullivan was so much taller, the Lieutenant quickly was suspended several inches off the floor. Mike quickly applied a windpipe choke. The shocked Lieutenant was immediately silenced. The only noise that came forth was one quick, "Ugh". Nikolai stepped in and grabbed the man's flailing hands. Sullivan shifted his position enabling the application of forearm and bicep pressure against his carotids. The entire process took slightly more than a minute. The young man struggled but was no match for the taller and stronger Sullivan. His neck gripped in a vise-like hold, Mike felt the man's body go limp. He held the squeeze for another twenty seconds, and then allowed him to slip quietly to the floor.

Nikolai and Viktorija rapidly stripped Lieutenant Cho out of his clothing. Nikolai placed a sock in the soldier's mouth and duct taped it shut. He bound the man's ankles and wrists together with sturdy tape, both behind the back. He gave the tape a few wraps of tied rope, just for good measure.

When he was finished with the tie job, he removed a small disposable plastic syringe from his goodie bag. It was labeled, "Sodium Pentothal Solution". He gripped the plastic sheath with his teeth and pulled it off. He plunged the needle into the man's buttocks and injected the clear fluid. In a low voice, but still speaking Korean, he said, "Vika, check, and make sure this man can breathe through his nose. I don't want to kill him - just for being horny."

Ensuring that the Lieutenant was well on his way to dreamland and not death, Vika turned to her father. "He's fine. Okay, that's one down and two to go." She stood up and rearranged herself, preparing to return to the main room for the next victim.

Sullivan closed with her and whispered. "You might not have to go back." He motioned to the window. "Have a look."

Vika peered outside. The KPA truck and the two men were still there.

삼 질식시킴

Minutes later Viktoriya walked outside. The soldiers leaned against the front of the truck, talking, smoking and sharing hits from a large brown bottle. She strolled over. Their talk came to a halt.

The taller of the two men grinned, leered and elbowed his friend, excitedly. He said to Vika. "Hello, pretty woman. How about a nice blowjob?"

She ignored the vulgar remark. "You boys got a cigarette for me?"

The short one opened a box of foul smelling Chinese smokes and offered her one. Nodding her thanks, she took it. She brought the cigarette to within a couple of inches of her ruby red mouth. She made a major production out of running her tongue around her lips, over and over; wetting them and the several layers of lipstick she had just applied to a glistening shine. Then with her tongue, she rolled the unfiltered cigarette back and forth along her lips until it lodged in the corner.

Mouth gaping, the tall soldier stood before her with an unlit stick match held up. He blinked and swallowed hard as he watched Vika's antics with the smoke. Finally, his wits returned and he struck the match. Vika took his clammy hand in hers and drew the flame to the end of the white cylinder in her mouth. The tobacco flared and Vika blew a stream of smoke over the man's face.

Suddenly, from behind, both men were taken off their feet. Large hands clamped over their mouths, both were down and made instantly quiet. Nikolai slammed the pistol butt into the base of the skull of one. Mike dangled the taller one in a choke hold. In seconds, he too was down. Both were injected with the drug, and quickly stripped of their uniforms.

They trussed the bodies of the soldiers with duct tape and rope. They were tossed into to the rear of Hiroshi, the truck, and covered with the tarpaulin.

Vika and Nikolai stepped back into their room. He struggled into the Lieutenant's uniform. She collected their remaining things and checked on Cho. He was out cold. Nikolai handed Vika the uniform shirt, trousers and cap from one of the Privates. "Hurry, slip into these. You and Misha take the soldier's truck – you drive."

She nodded, hurriedly scrubbing off the dancehall girl makeup. She slipped the small soldier's uniform over her clothing, rolled her hair into a quick braid and tucked it under the cap. Then she stood before her father for inspection. "How do I look, Poppa?"

He checked her over. Except for the Reeboks, she would pass. "I'd try out their boots for a fit – other than that, you look perfect. How about me?"

She examined her father in the dull light. The transformation was amazing. He could easily pass for a Korean Army officer, despite the snugness of the uniform. Cho's holstered pistol was now on the leather belt around Nikolai's uniform. He handed the small revolver back to his daughter. "Here, tuck this out of sight."

They met Sullivan outside. Mike held up an AK-47 rifle. "Look what I found in the back of the truck – two of these guys – with magazines."

Nikolai grinned. "Good. Just in case. Now, let's go!"

With haste they mounted their trucks, Vika and Mike in the Army truck, Nikolai in the Toyota. They headed off into the night. Their first stop was a roadside ditch just outside of town. Cho and the two Privates were arranged, out of sight, in some tall weeds. "They'll be out for hours." Nikolai said.

They drove the short distance back to their other "hotel". There, inside the cover of the enclosed barn, they stashed the Toyota truck and finalized the plan for their approach to the base. Nikolai briefed them for last time, over their handmade diagram. "Okay – we go right in the front door, acting like we belong. The story is we are from the KPA base at Undok and we are under orders to pick up the American prisoner. Vika, you drive, I will ride on the right hand side, like King Tut – Misha, you must ride in the back – stay out of sight."

Mike nodded. He held the other soldier's cap. "I'm afraid this is all I've got that fits me."

Nikolai regarded him with a smile. "Then, Misha, It will have to do."

Chapter 55
Musan, DPRK

It was almost midnight when Viktoriya drove the KPA truck right up to the main gate of the compound. The lone sentry exited the small guard shack and approached the truck. Recognizing that the man on the right side of the truck was an officer, the sentry walked to that side and saluted smartly. Nikolai assumed his most superior military persona. He opened the door and got out. Ignoring the soldier who stood at attention, Nikolai stretched and groaned as if he had been on a long ride, then in an absentminded fashion, he casually returned the salute with a grazing touch to the brim of his recently acquired officer's cap. "We are just arrived from Undok," he announced in his perfect Korean.

The sentry was short. The top of his head came to right about Nikolai's collar line. "Damn it, stand at ease, Corporal, you look like you are about to choke." The sentry relaxed a bit. Nikolai continued. "We are under orders to transport a prisoner." Nikolai clutched and waved some papers in his right hand.

"Yes, Lieutenant. May I see your orders, please. I must..."

Nikolai interrupted the sentry, his feigned irritation growing. "Corporal..."

"Yes, Sir?

"Do you know what time it is? My men and I have been on the damn road for hours."

"Yes, Lieutenant – it is..."

"Do you know how bad the roads are between here and Undok? We are tired, hungry and I need to take a pee. Must you really inspect every fragment of paper we possess?"

The young gate sentry was flustered. "No, sir – I mean – yes, sir. Excuse me, sir." He saluted again and went back into the guard shack.

From the cargo bed, Sullivan watched the transaction between Nikolai and the gate guard. His silenced pistol pointed through a slit in the canvas. If the guard went for a phone or otherwise tried to communicate an alarm, Mike would have to take him out. Instead, the guard pulled a lever and the gate rolled open.

Nikolai quickly got in and Vika moved the truck. She drove to the spot on the quad where they believed the hospital wing was located. She parked the truck between the southwest guard tower and the outer door which bore a sign scripted in Korean, "임상". The sign said "Clinic".

For the moment, it appeared as if there were no other soldiers around. As he dismounted from the truck, Sullivan scanned the guard tower. He could see windows, but no interior lights. Mike thought, there could be no one in the tower, or there could be five guys taking a bead on us as... He let the thought go.

They gathered at the side of the truck. Sullivan was covered by a standard issue olive drab weather poncho he had found in the truck's cargo bed. He'd draped it over his head and pulled on the KPA hat. He had AK tucked under his arm. The short rifle was perfectly concealed.

Nikolai tried the door. It was locked. Quickly, he arranged Sullivan to stand between them and told him to slump down a bit. Satisfied, he knocked on the door loudly. Within a moment, it opened by a medical attendant, a woman. She looked at them quizzically. "Yes, what is it, Comrades?"

"This man is sick – he requires medical attention." Nikolai barked as he started through the door.

The woman stood aside to let them pass. As they moved in, she asked. "Why have you not come in through the main...?"

In a flash – Nikolai's pistol was pressed against the woman's throat. The cold steel jabbed hard against the soft flesh under her jaw. He placed his other hand over her mouth, and pressed her against the wall. He spoke. "Sister, if you do not wish to have your brains splattered all over this place, you will lead us to the scum sucking American prisoner - now!"

She nodded, eyes turning to wide ovals of fear. She motioned and said, "That way."

Quickly, they moved down the hallway, past doorway after doorway. The lights were set for low illumination. They passed an unattended nursing station and made a right turn, and stopped before a locked metal door. The woman said, "In there. Please, Comrade, do not kill me. He is in this room." She offered a ring of keys from her belt.

"Open it!"

She fumbled – found the correct key and unlocked the door. All four of them tumbled loudly through the door, closing it behind them. In the dim light, they found Charlie Gomez lying on the bed, snoring.

Mike went to Charlie and checked him over. He shook him repeatedly.

After a couple of moments, the eyes flickered, then opened. It took a few seconds for comprehension to settle in. Finally, he spoke. "I – I was wondering when you were gonna show up. Do you have any idea how much crap I've had to put up with in here?" Gomez's speech was thick and slow. It was apparent that he had been drugged.

"Do you even know how long I've been in here? And these goons – they're gonna put me on trial for – something - do you…"

Mike put his face next to Charlie's. His voice was a whisper but the tone was urgent. "Charlie – Charlie, shut up!" He pulled him up into a sitting position. He looked around the room and saw the sandals. To Viktoriya, who was just finishing gagging and duct taping the female attendant to a chair, he said, "Toss those sandals over here." He slipped them onto Gomez's feet. "Relax little, buddy. We're getting you out of here!"

Nikolai led the way. They moved out into the corridor and retraced their steps. As they moved along, Sullivan kept checking the rooms on the inside of the quad. He was searching for a window, or some opening to the interior courtyard. He was trying to see if the helicopter they had spotted earlier was still parked in place. Every room he went into had a blank wall. Finally they came to a door on the inside wall. It had a sign in Korean writing.. Mike pointed and asked. "What does this say?"

Nikolai shrugged his shoulders and translated. "It says, 'Field'." The door was locked.

Mike was trying to decide whether to use the AK to shoot up the locking mechanism when Viktoriya stepped in front of him. She held up a large key ring. "I borrowed these from Nurse Cratchett. I thought they might come in handy." The third key she tried clicked the lock over. Mike pulled the door open a few inches and everyone looked out into the courtyard. Not only was the Hind helicopter still on the pad, its running lights were on and the engines were turning at idle. Cockpit illumination showed the silhouette of a lone man with a flight helmet. He was in the right seat. No one else seemed to be around.

They looked at one another. Mike was the first to speak. "Can we possibly be this lucky?"

Charlie said. "Cool, a Hind – those guys waiting for us?"

Nikolai took the initiative. "Follow me." He squared up his uniform cap and took off walking purposely towards the aircraft. Vika and Mike followed with Charlie between them.

Nikolai got ahead of them and entered the aircraft. By the time the others caught up, Nikolai had the pilot by the neck and was pushing him out the door at gunpoint. Mike yelled to Nikolai. "Wait – we might need him."

"What the hell for? I thought you said you could fly this thing."

"Well, I - kind of exaggerated."

"You – what?"

"I sort of – stretched the truth…"

"This is a wonderful goddamned time to be telling me that…"

Charlie interrupted them. His drug induced fog was lifting. "Mike, I think I can drive this beast."

"You think, or you know? We don't exactly have a lot of time right now."

"I know – you'll just have to read - some of them Russian instruments for me."

"You're absolutely sure – You still look pretty loaded to me?"

Charlie turned and grabbed the material of Sullivan's poncho at chest level. "What's the worst that can happen? We might crash, right?"

"Okay, I'm convinced. It's your airplane, Captain. He grabbed Gomez and pushed him through the open cabin door. Vika followed and Sullivan scrambled aboard behind them. Charlie took the right seat, and Sullivan slid into the left. Gomez looked over the instruments and fixed a gaze on Sullivan. Mike could see the fire was coming back into Charlie's eyes. Gomez strapped himself in. With a little grin, he yelled over his shoulder. "Hang on, I'm taking her up!" He slipped the clutch and the five giant rotor blades started to spin. Within a few seconds the torque lock indicator glowed green. Charlie jammed the throttles forward and flexed his hand around the collector handle. He centered the stick, looked left and right and yelled at the top of his lungs, "Everybody ready?"

Nikolai stood outside the main cabin door alternating his head between the Korean pilot in his grip and the two maniacs in the cockpit. The deafening roar of the engines and the sudden tornado-like downdraft stirred clouds of dust into the air. Suddenly the pilot broke and ran away at breakneck speed. Nikolai jumped aboard just as Gomez twisted the collector control, and the giant rotors bit into the air.

The heavy Russian combat helo shuddered and lifted into the dark night air. The ship rose about twenty feet then the rear dipped dangerously low. The tail banged on the ground. Charlie was desperately trying to get the feel of the controls. He cranked the collector to its stops and pushed the stick forward.

Sullivan yelled. "Too much – we're gonna hit the building!"

"Got it – I think I got it!" Charlie yelled back and pressed hard on the right rudder pedal. The high powered Hind helicopter thundered and screamed. The giant craft rotated on a level axis. The nose came around one hundred eighty degrees and they started to move across the courtyard.

A group of men, each carrying AK rifles appeared at the end of the yard. The chopper was pointed right at them. Some of the soldiers knelt, others stood and aimed their weapons and fired. A dozen 7.56 mm slugs slammed into the fuselage. One round pierced the windshield and whizzed by Sullivan's head.

"Anytime would be good, Charlie! Rotate this thing!"

"I'm trying – I can't seem to get the RPMs up…"

Another volley of gunfire raked the airship. Sullivan ducked instinctively. His hand went to the joystick. The red cap read "автомат" Russian for "machine gun". Sullivan grinned. He flipped the red cap and pressed the auto-fire button. The front of the aircraft lit up in a blaze. Giant arcs of yellow-red flame sprayed across the courtyard. Several of the riflemen went down. The others scattered.

Just then the pitch of the engines abruptly changed frequency. The rotors dug into the air and the Hind rocketed into the sky. Within seconds, Gomez had climbed the aircraft to a thousand feet. He steered to the east, across the lights of Musan, and away from the KPA gunfire. Gomez yelled over his shoulder. "Okay - somebody gonna tell me which way to point this thing – right?" No one answered.

Sullivan was busy with the instruments. He was deciphering the Russian labels. First he turned off the running lights and made certain the radio transponder was silenced. Then he checked the fuel state and learned the Hind's gas tanks were nearly full. He was breathing a sigh of relief on that point when he realized that Charlie was rapping incessantly on his upper arm. Sullivan turned. "What?"

Charlie motioned to their rear. Mike swiveled his head around and saw Nikolai seated on the floor, his back and head resting on a rear bulkhead. Bright red frothy blood was bubbling out of his mouth. A crimson stain spread across the front of his KPA Lieutenant's tunic. Viktoriya knelt along side him. The grief stricken look on her face said it all.

Sullivan unbuckled and started to move to the rear. Gomez stopped him. "Which way do we go?"

Mike thought about it quickly. "Head east. Yeah, east and stay low – hug the terrain."

Charlie nodded and Mike moved to the rear.

He knelt next to the mortally wounded Nikolai. Mike gently probed and examined his friend's wounds. One of the AK rounds had pierced his chest on the right side, just above the nipple. He had a corresponding exit wound on his right rear shoulder. There was a frightening loss of blood and Mike also knew that Nikolai was bleeding internally. Sullivan knew instantly that Nikolai had a blown out lung and Lord only knew what else.

Vika took off her borrowed uniform shirt and ripped it into pieces. She was trying to apply direct pressure on both sides. Nikolai was trying to talk. Only gasping sounds and bloody bubbles came out.

Mike asked Viktoriya. "Do we still have the Duct tape?"

Tears were flowing down her cheeks. He knew she was incredibly brave, but right now she was having trouble keeping it together. Mike repeated the question.

She re-focused and nodded. Reaching into the goodie bag, she pulled out the silver tape. Mike wiped the blood from the entry and exit wounds and sealed them off with the tape. Instantly, Nikolai was able to breathe.

Vika rummaged through the bag. They had one remaining syringe of the Sodium Pentothal. Mike checked the load. It was a fifty cc. injection. He thought it might be too much for the weakened Nikolai. He uncased the needle.

Before he could administer the drug, Nikolai grabbed his wrist. "Wait, Misha, listen to me." His voice was weak and raspy. "The GPS..." He tugged at a pants pocket.

Sullivan found the portable GPS unit and put in into his bloodied hands. Nikolai fingered the buttons. He was selecting a waypoint. It was Nakhodka! Sullivan knew of the place. It was inside the Russian territories.

Nikolai put the GPS back into Mike's hands. "Go there" – he coughed up more blood – "the Russian - military - base."

Mike nodded.

Nikolai squeezed Sullivan's forearm. He said something. Mike couldn't make it out over the roar of the engines. He moved his head in closer. Nikolai spoke again. "It's up to you – it's all up to you – now." His head slumped over. Mike felt the older man's carotid pulse. It was thin, but at least, he was still living. They rolled him onto his side, wounded side down, so as to lessen the work of the remaining good lung.

Sullivan re-cased the needle, then gave it to Vika. "He won't need this right now. Maybe - give it to him later – when he wakes up." Then on second thought, he added, "Not the whole thing – only give him half." Sullivan doubted that Nikolai would ever wake again. He gave Vika a little shoulder pat and moved back to the cockpit.

Charlie was wearing a KPA aviator's flight helmet and fingering a paper aviation chart.

Mike handed him the bloody GPS unit. Charlie took it and pointed to a second helmet, gesturing for Mike to put it on. As he slipped the helmet, with full ear pads, over his head, the deafening engine roar was nearly erased. Through the intercom, he could hear Charlie's voice, flat and metallic, but clear. Charlie showed him some switches and Mike quickly figured it out. They were able to talk without screaming.

"So how is your friend?" Charlie asked.

"Bad – I don't think he's going to make it."

"Sorry – Say, who are these people, anyway?"

"Friends – I'll explain later. Right now, we've got to figure out where to take this thing. How you doing? You okay?"

Charlie flexed his fingers over the controls – "Yeah – good – I mean -I am really a hell of a lot better - now."

"You really do know how to fly this thing, don't you?

"Yeah, well – I sat co-pilot in a demo ride in Farnsworth a couple of years ago. Aren't you glad I've got a good memory?" He grinned. "So – where are we going?"

Mike tapped the GPS display. Charlie looked at it, and then corrected his heading. "So what's in – Nak-hod-ka... Holy shit! That's in Russia!"

Mike just nodded. "Can we make it?"

Charlie checked the Hind's instruments, the portable GPS and did some quick mental gymnastics. "I think we're in pretty good shape. We have nearly full gas tanks, and this ship can carry quite a load of personnel and cargo - and right now we're nearly empty. I think we can make it in a little more than an hour. The Hind should do better than three hundred kilometers per hour, and it looks like we've got a little tail wind – yeah, little more than an hour – but I'll have to go on up to altitude – we can't continue to hill-hop."

Mike was thinking. "Okay – still no sign of any company?"

"You mean of the type that might want to blow us out of the sky?"

Mike nodded.

Charlie shook his head. "So far, so good." Charlie paused for a moment. Then he said, "You know – flying into Russia might be a bit of a problem?"

"Yeah – no shit - in more ways than you know."

Chapter 56
Luzon, Philippines

Many years had passed since the United States had given up their military bases in the Philippines. A handful of the installations, especially the former Air Force bases had been converted to civilian use. One such place was the terminal for the Global Pan Asian Express. The company was young for an air shipping and freight service. GPA Express, as it was known, was only a few years old. But they had managed to nail down some of the most lucrative Asian contracts in the industry. GPA Express was a four letter word in the home offices of the likes of UPS and FedEx.

Ownership of the company was murky. If one were to search records, he would find a Swiss industrial conglomerate named as principal stockholder. The company flew an eclectic mix of aircraft, including twelve aging Boeing 727-200s. The company personnel were equally colorful. Pilots and ground crews came from many nations. A typical day at work at GPA Express often looked like a United Nations General Assembly meeting.

On this particular day, one of their venerable 727 trijets emerged from a maintenance hanger. In an obvious exception to their normal operating practice, that of being loaded in the open air cargo area, this jet had been loaded while still under the cover of the hangar building.

Captain Jan Van der Borg, a South African national, and co-pilot, Ted Halsey, a former Australian bush pilot, taxied their craft, with the radio call sign of "Global 306B" to end of runway 21B and went through their flight check list. Today's run would follow the same course that many of their previous flights had taken. Their first stop would be Shanghai. There, they would perform a thirty minute package touch and go. Once again airborne, they would head north across the Yellow Sea, cross the channel between the Wendeng Peninsula on the west and Paengdong, North Korea on the east. Like all international flights, the pilots would take special care to track away from the often volatile air space of North Korea. Cutting a wide margin, the GPA Express 727 would fly well around the air and borders of the DPRK and reenter Chinese territory, where they would turn slightly to the east and head for their third and final stop of the day, night, actually, because they would be arriving at the growing City of Changchun well after midnight. After a layover of a few hours, the crew would take off the next day and reverse their flight plan until they returned to Luzon.

What made this flight different in the minds of Van der Borg and Halsey was the fact that this was what they called, a payday flight.

Global Pan Asian Express had a select list of special clients. For these clients, GPA Express would occasionally pick up or deliver "special packages". Today's special contract would net the company millions of dollars. And, a major portion of that fee would go directly to the two pilots. Such was the business of contractors who handled the dirty work for governments that wished to be distanced from the horrific deeds they often felt inclined to mete out.

The Shanghai stop over went off as smooth as silk. Captain Van der Borg had his aircraft back in the air in a record thirty-three minutes from touch down. He turned over the controls to Halsey, and went aft to check on their special delivery package.

This 727 had originally been delivered by Boeing as a passenger ship. In that configuration, it was designed to have a tail door and retractable staircase. After too many years of service, and a few more years of Arizona desert mothball time, the aircraft was sold to GPA Express and re-fitted for cargo. The retractable staircase was removed, but the tail door remained.

Captain Van der Borg walked the length of the aircraft until he came to a long slender wooden crate that was secured to the deck, amidships and positioned directly in front of the tail door. From a storage locker, he produced a battery operated socket set and disassembled the crate. The top and sides were removed to reveal a sleek white and black air to ground cruise missile.

The near twenty foot device had been manufactured in a major European country. It was designated as a Mark XVB and was essentially a copy-cat version of the U.S. Air Force, AGM-86. The missile was powered by a turbofan jet engine. It was capable of traveling hundreds of miles at subsonic speeds. This one was self guided and smart insofar that it could fly, unassisted, over very complicated ground hugging routes that enabled it to evade radar detection. It was deadly accurate to within three meters. While it was capable of carrying a small nuclear warhead, today, this missile was configured for a powerful conventional warhead, a Bunker Buster.

Forty five minutes later, Van der Borg returned and took his seat in the cockpit. Halsey asked. "Everything ready?"

"Right as rain, Mate!" Van der Borg delighted in ribbing Halsey over his outback accent.

It was just past midnight when the GPA Express aircraft crossed to the west of Dandong, China at a cruising altitude of 31,000 feet. Dandong was the waypoint that set them well north of the DPRK. Van der Borg cruised another hundred miles or so then made a slight course correction to the east, just a few degrees, hardly enough to be noticed by a controller, if any were watching.

At the designated time, Halsey nodded to the boss and left the cockpit. He went to the rear of the plane and strapped himself into a personal safety harness which was tethered to the deck plates. He went to the missile and opened a compartment panel on the side. He punched an access and command code string into a keyboard and watched the display. Satisfied that he had activated the missile, he closed and secured the panel. Then he put on a backpack mounted personal oxygen bottle and checked the tail door release mechanism. He keyed a small radio. "Ready and standing by."

From the cockpit, Van der Borg acknowledged Halsey's message. He then switched to the aviation radio and dialed in the frequency of Changchun air traffic control. He glanced at his watch. Three minutes later he put the 727 into a steep dive and keyed the radio. "Changchun flight control – this is Global three zero six bravo. We have a situation, here – a loss of cabin pressure. We are on oxygen and making an emergency descent to ten thousand."

The crisp response was immediate and in near perfect English, the universal language of international aviation. "Global three zero six bravo, copy your situation. You are cleared to descend to 10,000. Do you wish to declare an emergency?"

"Uh, Global three oh six bravo, not as yet – it's a slow leak and my crew is working on it. We'll let you know."

Roger Global three zero six bravo. Be advised you have a mountain range at niner thousand in your flight path at one hundred twenty kilometers out – recommend you turn east fifteen degrees."

"Roger Changchun control and thank you."

Van der Berg leveled the 727 at 10,500 feet and switched to the small intercom radio. He keyed it and said "Now."

Halsey's reply was equally short. "Copy."

Halsey braced himself and opened the rear tail door. The pressure differential caused a quick tornado-like wind inside the airplane. Within seconds it subsided. Halsey quickly moved to the rear of the missile. He pulled a release pin and the missile rolled down a track and dropped into the night sky. Halsey worked his way back to the tail door and secured it.

Minutes later, Van der Borg informed Changchun control that they'd had a minor door seal problem - that it was holding pressure again - and they were returning to their assigned altitude.

The missile fell away from the aircraft in free-fall. At nine thousand feet the wings popped out and the guidance system began to search for the GPS satellites. Within another thousand feet of free-fall, the guidance lock occurred and the craft aimed for its first waypoint. At three thousand feet above the ground, its turbofan engine came to life. The sleek missile started to fly its own pre-programmed, circuitous route to Musan, North Korea.

Halsey returned to the cockpit. He slid into the right seat and looked at Van der Borg. "Well, there's another on-time delivery - courtesy of GPA Express."

Chapter 57
Musan, DPRK

Alarms were clanging throughout the KPA facility, both above and below ground. It took a few minutes for people to figure out what was happening. Clearly, an invasion by intruders and the theft of the Hind helicopter from inside a secure facility was not an anticipated event. The problem was further complicated by the early morning hour and the token number of personnel on duty.

Precious time was wasted while many ran around desperately trying to figure out what to do, whom to contact and what to tell them. One of the biggest problems was that everyone thought the intruders were Koreans. Were they spies? Did they come from the South? Were they part of the military uprising that everyone expected to happen, some day?

The ranking man on duty happened to be Senior Captain Rhee. Once he realized the enormity of the events that had just occurred on his watch. He felt ill. He waffled on making required notifications outside the base. He agonized over the events that he believed would most certainly end up with him being shot in the back of the head. Emotionally, he crumbled.

One of the Energy Project scientists – not a military man – suggested that their aircraft, the one with the gravity wave amplifier installed, could be used to follow and catch up with the intruders. Rhee jumped at the suggestion – any suggestion. In moments the segmented floor of the courtyard rumbled and clanked back into its fully open position. Blue-white fluorescent lighting from the subterranean lab poured forth into the night sky. Technicians hurriedly readied the modified Mig aircraft. Only one qualified pilot was found on the base. He was roused from sleep and prepped for flight.

Five nautical miles away, effortlessly flying over hills and valleys the cruise missile streaked across the black early morning sky. The onboard systems were performing flawlessly. The engine was strong. Infrared and radar enabled the craft to fly around and over any obstacle it encountered. The guidance system had long ago locked on to the coordinates of the Musan facility. The little machine was relentless. It cruised on and on focused only on its target. It took ninety seven seconds to close the remaining distance. One quarter mile away from its target, the missile nosed up and climbed to an altitude of one thousand feet. Then it arced over and dove straight into the yawning maw of the Musan subterranean Energy Project installation.

삼 질식시킴

Twenty nine nautical miles to the east and flying with the Hind helicopter throttles to their stops, Sullivan, Gomez, Viktoriya and the semi-conscious Nikolai saw the flash. The intensity of the light was almost unbelievable. The blue-white incandescence lit up the black sky and ground to midday levels of illumination. As quick as it came, it faded, and in seconds was gone.

"Jesus – was that what I think it was?" Charlie exclaimed. He was so excited he forgot to key the helmet intercom. Everyone heard him anyway.

Sullivan craned around trying to see what he could. The explosion was directly behind them, so the ship's airframe blocked most of the view.

Viktoriya yelled out at the top of her lungs. "Was that an atomic bomb?"

Sullivan keyed his helmet intercom. "If that was Nuclear, our asses are probably cooked. What's our distance from Musan?"

Charlie checked the GPS and said. "Maybe thirty miles and we are cruising at – make that - eight thousand feet."

"We are gonna feel a shock wave any time!" The words had barely passed his lips, when the pressure wave hit. Other than yawing the aircraft about fifteen degrees, it was not much worse than flying through severe turbulent air. Charlie quickly corrected.

When the aircraft angled, both Sullivan and Gomez got a glimpse of the orange-red mushroom cloud growing at the western horizon.

Gomez said, "Mutha a' God! You want me to bank around – so we can take a better look – since we're probably gonna to die anyway – or at least we're never gonna have any kids." He added.

Sullivan pulled out his portable satellite phone. "No, keep going. Whatever happened back there - well, there's nothing we can do about it." He started punching buttons. "I've gotta make some calls."

The first call was to Mateo. He was standing by with the Gulf Stream at Sapporo. Mike told him that he wanted him to fly directly to the military base at Nakhodka. There was a long pause, followed by some further discussion. Mike rang off. He keyed the intercom. "I've got Mateo waiting for us in Japan. I just told him to meet us at Nakhodka." He said matter of factly.

Gomez laughed. "And he told you to - pound sand – right?"

"Actually, he's looking forward to going to a Gulag. He said he's in."

"Amazing. That man's got cajones like basket balls. Remind me to get him a raise – if we ever get out of this."

Mike was back on the Satellite phone. He made several other calls, including one to Charlie's uncle and another to Doug McClure. His last call was a patch from McClure to an NSA monitoring center in Maryland. The duty officer was very surprised to be speaking to a man in a stolen Russian helicopter, fleeing from North Korea. When he finally switched off the Sat phone, he had the radio frequency for the Nakhodka Russian Military base air traffic controller.

Back on the intercom, he quickly briefed Charlie on what he was going to try. Then he reached over and dialed in the correct channel on the Hind's communication radio.

Sullivan keyed the transmit button and began his conversation in crisp Russian. The entire exchange took several minutes. Charlie watched his friend as the dialogue in Russian continued. He, of course, did not understand a word of it.

Mike was both animated and perplexed during the conversation. He repeated key phrases over and over. Finally, the conversation concluded. Sullivan slumped back in his seat.

Charlie spoke. "So, how did it go?'

Mike glared at his friend. "Russians can be the most pig-headed..." He stopped. "I don't know. I basically told them the truth."

"Which truth – or should I say - who's truth?" All of the drugs must have cleared out of his body, because Charlie was starting to look worried.

"I told them we were American agents" – Charlie's eyebrows went up – "That we had rescued a colleague from a KPA prison in

Musan, which apparently and coincidentally was blown sky high by a non-nuclear event shortly after our hasty departure."

"That was non-nuclear?"

"That's what Doug just told me. They already know all about it. And they already have confirmed that it was non-nuclear…"

"How do they do that?"

"I don't know!"

"So – what else?"

"The what else is - that we stole a KPA chopper to escape, that we have a Former KGB colonel and his daughter aboard - that the Colonel is shot in the chest and in desperate need of medical care – and – I guess that's about it. Oh, I also told them that they would get a call from some high ranking somebody in our Government who would vouch for us and let them know that this is all on the up and up."

"And they said?"

"That the minute that we enter Russian airspace, we would be blown out of the sky."

"Oh, goody. And, I thought we were going to have problems."

삼 질식시킴

The handsome young newscaster watched the red light atop the stage left camera flash on. He focused his well practiced gaze of sincerity and read from the teleprompter scrolling large white letters. "And this breaking news – Several Asian news agencies are reporting a huge explosion, occurring just about two hours ago, at a place called Musan, deep inside North Korea."

"Musan is described as a small farming village on the mountainous border between Korea and China. At first it was feared that the explosion, which produced a mushroom shaped cloud, might have been atomic in nature."

"The International Atomic Energy Agency has just issued a press release stating the explosive event inside the Democratic Peoples Republic of Korea was not - and we repeat – was not - nuclear in origin. The IAEA, which maintains nuclear monitoring stations around the world, was quick to issue their release. Their Acting Director was quoted as saying 'With world attention on North Korea regarding their nuclear experimentation and the world community's diplomatic efforts to negotiate a settlement to this problem'…"

Chapter 58
Over the Sea of Japan

Sullivan keyed the intercom. "I'm going back to check on the others."

Gomez glanced at him, nodded and quickly redirected his attention to the instruments. He said nothing.

Sullivan unbuckled and moved aft. The unconscious Nikolai lay on his side with his back against the rear bulkhead. Viktoriya sat with him, her back to the bulkhead, Nikolai's head rested in her lap. She watched as Sullivan approached. He silently questioned her with his gaze. Her response was equally silent, punctuated by a slow shake of the head. The look in her eyes said volumes.

Mike knelt down and checked Nikolai's vital signs. His pulse was weak, thready and his breathing was shallow and labored. Mike checked the duct tape seals on the wounds. Satisfied that they had done all they could, he leaned into Viktoriya's ear and spoke so as to be heard over the engine. "We're headed into Nakhodka - the airbase there – it's the closest place we can get him some help."

Vika stared wide-eyed at Sullivan. He started to stand. She grabbed him by the shirt and pulled him back down to eye level. "That's Russia! We can't go there!"

"I know." He gently wrapped his hand around hers, and began to pry her fingers away. "For that matter, neither can I." He said matter-of-factly. "Right now it's our only choice. We go there – or Nikolai dies."

Viktoriya nodded. "Maybe we'll all die." She released her grip on his shirt, but let her hand linger within his.

When Mike stood up, the helicopter's engine changed sound. It was like, it skipped a few beats. The huge helicopter lurched. The malfunction was more like a flutter, a wave-like pulsation interrupting the normally constant sound of the turbine engine. Mike grabbed an overhead handhold, and leaned around to look towards the cockpit. Gomez's hands danced over the controls. The engine sound returned to normal.

As he turned back towards Vika, Mike noticed the label on the overhead compartment next to the handhold he gripped. In stenciled Russian it said, "Жизнь Куртка". Sullivan recognized the words. He opened the compartment and rummaged around inside. He withdrew two life jackets. He handed them to Viktoriya. "Put these on, just in case."

She took them and nodded.

Sullivan pulled out two more of the flotation jackets and started forward. Once again, the Hind's engine fluttered. He didn't have to be looking at the airship's tachometer to know that the engine RPM dropped - dramatically. The aircraft faltered again and he stumbled. Grabbing anything for purchase, he regained his footing and worked his way back into the cockpit. He gripped the rear of Charlie's seat and yelled in his ear. "What's happening?"

Gomez hands furiously worked at the controls. He yelled back. "I don't know. We're loosing power for some reason!" Charlie tapped on the face of one of the instruments on the far left of his panel. "Tell me again, what's this gauge for? This is the one that keeps dropping out."

Sullivan craned his neck to read the Cyrillic label. The needle of the gauge hovered just above the zero mark. "It says 'Injector Pressure'. Does that make sense?"

Charlie thought about it for a second. The levity of his response was betrayed by the worried look on his face. "That either has to do with tire pressure or - the fuel system."

Sullivan moved to the co-pilot's seat and belted in. "What do you want me to do?"

"You could try prayer..." He said with a grin. Turning his head back to the windscreen he said. "Maybe she's got a bad load of gas – you know, water or something. I think it's definitely fuel related."

Mike nodded and got his headset back on. Rough air buffeted the aircraft.

"We may have another little problem."

Sullivan looked at Gomez. "Great."

"Seriously, look at this damn ceiling!"

Sullivan peered outside the cabin. The cloud layer was dropping fast. Charlie had been inching the aircraft lower and lower to stay under the clouds. The layer was gray-white, several thousand feet thick and blotted out all visibility. Gomez was scudding the helo, flying along in a thin clear pocket of air, between the water and the cloud cover above. Mike read the altimeter. The display showed one hundred sixty five meters. In his head, he quickly converted that to about five hundred feet.

Charlie continued. "Yeah, I think this baby's definitely got a fuel problem. It runs along fine for a while, then, it stutters. So far, it's recovered every time. But each time it burps, we loose some more altitude. Stack on top of that this ceiling... Pretty soon, we're gonna be dragging our belly gear in the surf."

"Copy that." Mike peered out at the sea surface below. The blackness of the night hid the vast expanse of cold dark swells eager to swallow the fragile airship.

Chapter 59
Tustin, California

Ichiro drove the grey Toyota through the alleyway of the Tustin Garden condominiums. In the past few days, he had purchased this second car, and tried to work surveillance on his new target.

He had learned a good deal about Greer and his daily routine. Ichiro had even managed to follow the man to his workplace in Santa Ana a couple of times. Moving through the morning commuter traffic was a challenge, but it afforded a perfect opportunity for cover. Maintaining a decent watch on the Greer home, on the other hand, proved to be, physically, quite difficult.

The small condos were stacked together like anthills made of wood and stucco. Developers had created exotic names for miniature homes of this type, many of which had been originally built during the sixties and seventies as apartments. The insane appreciation of real estate in the California market moved many of the old buildings into "conversion". The exterior of the buildings were cosmetically overhauled, the individual units were often gutted and refinished with new amenities and appliances. Then, they were sold for outrageous prices, mostly to young couples, just starting out, and to seniors interested in something smaller and more affordable.

The "Gardens" as the place had come to be called, was typical of the conversion projects that dotted Orange County.

The dwellings were clustered together, eight to a building. The buildings were arranged in square groups of four. In the middle of each square was a maze of overdone landscaping, pathways, a few discrete lights and perhaps a small water element such as a fountain or fish pond.

The layout of the buildings made watching difficult. Ichiro easily located the unit that Greer lived in. It was number 7 of building 24, an upstairs unit with a small balcony. He'd strolled the grounds a couple of times, but it was difficult to conduct any type of continuous surveillance without being obvious.

From the rear of the complex, he could see over the carport structure and view two small upstairs windows for number 7. He theorized that those were probably bedroom windows. About all he could tell from his quick drive-bys was whether or not lights were on in the home. The cars, on the other hand, were easier to deal with. There were no garages at the Tustin Gardens, only open carports. He knew that Greer drove a Honda. He already had the description and license number.

The first time he walked the grounds, he had seen a tall slender woman leaving Greer's condo. It was early morning and he saw her coming out the door, dressed nicely and carrying a large leather bag that could have been a combination purse/briefcase. From a distance, he watched as she firmly closed the door and locked it from the outside with a key from a large ring. At a discrete distance, he followed her as she walked to the carport.

From the same key ring, she unlocked and got into a grey Volkswagen Jetta. The Jetta was parked in the space right next to where Greer usually parked his Honda.

Ichiro figured the woman to be a girlfriend or wife. As the Jetta started to move, he was able to get to his car and follow. She drove a few miles to a tall office building in Irvine, just off the 405 freeway. She parked in an open lot marked "Employees Only", got out, locked the car and strolled into the building. He didn't lose sight of her until she entered the lobby.

Ichiro was no fool. He knew that this policeman, this Greer, would be a much more formidable prey than the cattle, he and his brother had previously dealt with. Greer probably carried a weapon of some type and might even be proficient in its use. On the other hand, he knew that most Americans, even American police officers, were soft and spineless. He believed that the vast majority of them feared violent confrontation, and, of course, abhorred killing. Ichiro was counting on that inexperience, and the hesitation that naturally went along with it, to be his ally. He would pick his time and place and make short work of this man, Greer. He would enjoy this job. He might even get the chance to kill the woman, as well. He relished that thought.

Chapter 60
Over the Sea of Japan

"How far out are we?" Mike asked.

"From Nakhodka?"

"Yeah."

Charlie squinted at the tiny display of the portable GPS unit. "About - two hundred forty miles, give or take a bit."

Mike just nodded.

Although it wasn't really raining, the mist was so thick that condensation streamed off the windscreen. Some of it blew inside via the bullet hole from the shot that hit Nikolai. Sullivan made several attempts to plug the hole, but nothing would stick. Currently, he had an oily rag jammed through the hole. The mass of material on the outside pounded and fluttered against the plexiglas, like a wounded bird.

"How's our airspeed?" Gomez asked. The dark cloud mass continued its steady descent to the ocean surface. In the last few minutes, Gomez had brought the helo down to a scant two hundred feet above the waves in order to continue visual flight. A growing headwind had slowed their progress and further strained their already tight fuel situation.

Sullivan checked the airspeed indicator, which was scaled in kilometers. He checked that against their small GPS unit and shook his head. "I think we're only making about one hundred miles per hour – and that's a maybe."

"I was afraid of that... Mike, we need to consider the possibility of..."

The engine sputtered. Wide eyed, Sullivan and Gomez looked at each other. The engine went through ten seconds of erratic oscillation before settling back down to a steady hum. They both resumed breathing.

"That we might have to ditch?"

"Something like that... Yeah."

"God, I hate the thought of going back into the water!" Charlie banged on the instrument board with the flat of his hand. "Why does it always have to be in the water? Why can't we get stranded in – say – the desert? Yeah, Death Valley or the Sahara!"

Sullivan reached for the controls for the second communication radio. He fingered the channel selector to the international emergency channel, 121.500 MHz. Unbuckling he said, Comm One is still on the channel for Nakhodka. Comm Two is on one-two-one-five. If you think we're going in, yell on both channels – and yell loud. I'm going aft."

Charlie nodded and Sullivan started to move to the rear cabin. The engine stuttered again. This time, the pitch of the engine revolutions instantly dropped to a low whine. The helo was struggling to maintain altitude.

Sullivan struggled his way back, hand over hand. He yelled at Viktoriya. "Hang on to something! I think we're going to crash!"

She didn't say a word. Face ashen, and eyes wide with fear, she simply nodded and wrapped her right arm around Nikolai's inert body. With her left, she pulled down a lashing strap from the bulkhead and wound it tightly around her forearm and wrist.

Sullivan frantically went through the compartments and storage cubby holes. He muttered to himself as he searched. "Is it asking too much to think that the damn Korean Peoples Army might have a life raft or an Emergency Locator Transmitter on their helo? Of course it is – we're just damn lucky to have found four lousy life jackets!" Just then his hand landed on a dusty faded yellow canvas rectangle. Korean writing was stenciled on the side of the suitcase sized package. He jerked it out and quickly examined it. It was old and had a rusty zipper that circled the outer edge. He pulled it out, onto the floor. "Vika!" He yelled at Viktoriya. "What does this say?" He pointed to the Korean writing.

She looked at it. A pained looked crossed her face. She yelled back at him. "It says 'water - water boat'!"

Mike tried to open it and the corroded zipper tab broke off in his hand.

The pitch of the helicopter engine changed once again. This time it whined, rattled loudly, then stopped!

Silence filled the cabin. Gomez turned his head and yelled at the top of his lungs. "Hang on! We're going down – this is it!"

Instantly, the blades of the Hind were released from the drag of the dead engine and began to auto rotate. The low altitude failed to provide a sufficient air cushion for a proper auto rotational descent.

Despite Gomez's best efforts, within seconds, the craft slammed hard into the water. In less than a minute, the helo pitched over on to its port side. A torrent of cold black water quickly engulfed the cabin.

When Gomez yelled his warning, Sullivan moved for the starboard door release and pulled. The air pressure literally blew open the right side cabin door, locking it into a fully open position. Sullivan was blown back by the rush of air and slammed his head into a bulkhead. Dazed, he dropped to the floor just as the air ship slammed into the water. The bottom of the helo crumpled and cold water cascaded inside.

When the helo tipped, the right side door opening was oriented to the top. The cold water kicked Sullivan's mind back to consciousness. He came up swimming strong, his survival instincts kicking into high gear. Mike was churning for the opening when he spotted Nikolai's body, fully submerged, floating in the cabin. Mike grabbed the inert Nikolai and pulled him up to the surface. He got their heads into the air. The water level was chest high and rising fast. Mike checked Nikolai's life jacket. Vika had it strapped on to her father properly, leg straps and all. Mike heaved and pushed Nikolai's limp form through the doorway and into the open ocean. Nikolai bobbed for a few seconds, then finally righted in a head up orientation. With no indication that he had regained consciousness, he simply floated away into the night.

Gulping deep breaths, Sullivan dove down and swam forward. He was headed for Gomez. When he got to the cockpit, he realized that Charlie was gone. The instrument and cabin lights were still glowing, providing a low level of illumination. Both seats were empty. He quickly turned, stroking and kicking his way aft. He was looking for Viktoriya. He reached the rear bulkhead where she and Nikolai had been. That spot was also empty.

Sullivan desperately needed air. He scanned around confirming, as best he could through the blurred water, that the helo interior was empty. White hot needles of carbon dioxide seared his lungs. Despite the twisting of the helicopter cabin, Mike's spatial orientation was still working. He still knew which way was up. He looked that way, and saw what he thought to be the outline of the doorway. He kicked toward it. Just as his head broke into the air, something banged him on the head. He spun around to see the floating yellow canvas case with the Korean writing. He gulped air and grabbed it.

The aircraft creaked and shifted. Mike knew he had only seconds to get clear of the airship. It was sinking fast and he knew the vortex would probably take down anything that was close by. Using the yellow boat case as a platform he pulled himself up as high as he could and yelled at the top of his lungs. "Gomez! Vika! Where are you?"

He waited – strained to listen – but heard nothing but wind, water, and the dying sounds of the broken Hind. He twisted and yelled out a second time. Still, there was no response. The nose of the helo sunk low and the tail rotor arced up out of the water. This was it! Mike knew he had only seconds to escape from the Russian made flyer; that in mere moments it would be a silent metal tomb, sinking to the depths of the East Sea. He vaulted through the hatchway and dragged the floating yellow boat case into the open sea.

Chapter 61
Santa Ana, California

It had been several days since the meeting with Special Agent Kirby, of the FBI. Like most cops, Greer had heard stories about FBI intervention in local criminal cases. To him, it was mostly scuttlebutt, not exactly the sort of thing that happened every day. But ever since the beginnings of the infamous war on terror, there had been more and more invocations of "national security" happening all around the country. Now it had happened to them, right in the heart of Orange County.

The reactions of the men and women, from the different police agencies, to Kirby's edict had been interesting, to say the least. Greer had not heard such loud and colorful expletives since he'd been a stone rookie busting up fights in biker bars. Testosterone had flowed liberally throughout the room as the assembled investigators properly reacted to the pirating of their murder cases.

A somewhat stunned and detached Greer heard a cacophony of comments like – "They can just go piss up a rope!" - "Over my dead frigging body!" – "Who do these Federal clowns think they are?" And these, of course, were some of the milder comments.

Right after the meeting broke, an apologetic, petite agent introduced herself. Special Agent Garcia followed Greer out into the hallway. "Mr. Greer, I'm sorry, but I've been assigned to follow you back to your office for your notes and reports that pertain to these cases." She smiled, uncomfortably.

He was about to give her a blast, when he caught Lt. Blair's piercing look. Blair held Greer's gaze for a moment. Tim got the unmistakable message. He gave Blair a nod.

Greer turned back to the diminutive FBI agent saying, "Right this way, Agent Garcia." Greer politely waved her towards his cubicle.

In the intervening days, Blair had commended Greer several times, patting him on the back for his excellent work on the Korean murder cases, but the message had clearly been for him to "get over it", and to move on to the pile of other cases waiting for some attention. Greer, being a good soldier, grumbled, but did as he was told.

As he reached for the stack of reports in his incoming box, he felt a touch on his shoulder. He looked up and saw Mollie blow by. As she passed, she dropped a manila envelope on the top of his pile. Over her shoulder she said "Special Delivery" then disappeared.

He picked up the envelope. It was hand addressed to him in neat block lettering, all capitals. The envelope bore a line of cancelled first class stamps with a Santa Ana postmark. There was no return address. He hefted it, held it up to the light and thought briefly about letter bombs. Dismissing that, he tore open the flap. Inside, he found an unlabeled CD-Rom disc in a plastic case and a folded piece of white paper penned in black ink in the same precise block letters. He read the short note:

Tim,
Before our cases were hi-jacked, we were doing some video image resolution work from the HappyLand Hotel CCTV tapes. These pictures came from our hard drive. The dark suits didn't quite get it all! Thought you'd like to have your very own picture of our second suspect.
Beauchamp
Ps. Burn this!

A smile spread across his face. He slipped the silver disc into his computer. The directory showed three JPEG files - pictures. He clicked them open. The images were black and white, images captured from an older model surveillance camera. The frames depicted a tall dark haired man who was walking. The background of the scene looked like a hotel corridor, light colored walls and rows of doors. Two of the images were blurred. The third image bore the stark grainy contrast of a picture that had been cropped and enhanced. The subject had apparently accommodated the camera by looking directly into the lens as he walked by.

Greer studied the face. He thought he saw a trace of Asian heritage. It wasn't much, but Greer deduced the man was probably Caucasian with just a drop of Oriental blood in the genetic woodpile. He mulled over the information Beauchamp had disclosed about the DNA of the American Pilot, the MIA, and wondered about the connection to the gunshot dead man they had found in the Anaheim hotel room. As far as he knew, that man was still unidentified. Or, if the Feds had the subject identified by now, they sure as hell weren't going to share.

Greer saw something else in the face. It was more of a vague impression or perhaps an intuitive interpretation. To Greer it looked like there was a purposeful cruelty to that face. Perhaps it was the eyes – maybe it was just the enhancement process – whatever it was, the look was chilling. Once again, Tim Greer felt that detective thing going off in his head. He leaned close, adjusted his glasses and peered at the image. Greer was convinced he was looking into the face of a cold-blooded killer.

He closed the file and removed the disc from his computer. On second thought, he put the disc back into the computer, reopened the pictures, and sent copies to the printer. He rummaged through his desk, finding a small memory stick. He plugged that into the computer, and transferred the contents of the CD-Rom disc to the memory stick.

He grabbed his folder and headed out. Near the door was a cluster of machines including a copy machine, laser printer, fax machine, and an industrial strength paper shredder. He stopped long enough to grab the pictures off the printer, then he dropped Beauchamp's envelope and CD disc into the shredder. The machine protested when it hit the plastic but did its job. Fine pieces of plastic and paper rained out of the ejection port.

As he unlocked his Honda, Greer's cell phone chirped. "Greer", he answered.

"Detective Greer..." It was a woman. There was a familiar quality to the voice, but he couldn't quite place it.

"Yes, this is Tim Greer. Who's this?"

There was a hesitation. "It's Jennifer Garcia." There was another pause. "We met the other day at your office – I'm with the FB..."

It clicked. "Ah, yes - Agent Garcia - of course, I remember you." Alarm bells were going off in his head as he fingered the computer memory stick in his pocket. "What can I do for you?"

"It might be a case of what I can do for you." She said, her voice dropping in tone just a bit. "Can you meet me somewhere for a couple of minutes of conversation?"

Greer's mind raced. "Sure, do I need to bring my attorney?"

Another hesitation – "Jesus, no. Look, Greer, I'm sort of sticking my neck way out here. I know we're not the most popular people with you guys right now, but I am trying to do something that needs to be done here – to help you."

"Sure, sorry, only kidding about the attorney." Like hell, he thought. "Where do you want to meet?

They agreed to meet at the Peace Officers Memorial, right behind the courthouse. Greer thought he was closer, which should put him there first. The FBI office was several blocks away.

He closed the door to his car, relocked it, and quick stepped the two short blocks to the Courthouse. When he vaulted the steps to the memorial, Garcia was there, alone and seated on a bench, seeming to read the list of names of police officers killed in the line of duty.

He sat down next to her, silently reminding himself to be very careful – that she was probably wearing a 'wire'. "Jennifer, is it? I thought all you guys had the same first name - Agent."

She bored holes into him with large brown eyes framed by a serious face. He hadn't had much of a chance to really appraise her during their first encounter. It had been brief. At the end of their meeting, she had accompanied him to his desk, asked him to collect up all his printed reports and handwritten notes on the case, took them, apologized and left.

He looked her over. She was small, barely five foot, and slender, pretty, but not a knockout. She was dressed in a conservative dark business suit, dark low heels and matching black handbag. She looked like any of a hundred attorneys that milled through the mall and the court building.

She spoke. "Look, Greer. I know you guys are pissed at us for yanking your cases – and you all hate our FBI guts because you think we don't share - but that's not what this is about."

The alarm bells in Greer's head really got loud. "Okay, uh – what would you like to talk about?"

"She shook her head. "Stop thinking that someone's trying to make a case on you and listen to me for a minute. Will you?"

"Of course."

She took a breath. "First, the ground rules." She turned on the bench seat and faced him directly. "Some of what I'm going to tell you is classified. That means, I'm in trouble for telling you; and you are in big trouble should you disclose this information to any third party. Got it?"

Greer nodded.

"So, none of this you got from me. Agreed?"

Greer nodded again.

"Ever hear of the intelligence project called Overlook?"

Greer actually had, but told her that he had not.

"Okay. Overlook is a classified program, but by now nearly everyone has some idea about its existence. In the wake of the 9/11 intelligence failures, Overlook was put in place. It's a massive computer data mining project that reads virtually all the email, instant messages, spam, file attachments, and other things that circulate on the internet. The program, kind of like a search engine, looks for keywords like 'bomb' or 'jihad' or any one of several thousand words and phrases that might disclose some terrorist plot or activity. With me - so far?"

Greer nodded again, wondering where all this was going.

"One of the things Overlook can do – and it's not well known outside of select law enforcement and intelligence circles – is this. It watches all the information systems that are connected to the internet and some that are not. This includes government systems, commercial, free, pay for service and just about any thing else you can think of. If somebody is collecting information on a given subject – say, like how to build an atomic bomb – it crawls the data and tries to identify the party who is doing the searching and collecting."

"Interesting, but how does it know who's using the computer? I mean, it doesn't give you personal identity, does it?"

"No – I mean, you are right. It does not. In most cases, all the system can do is trace inquiries back to an IP address. Once in a while we get lucky and can pin personal use on an individual – but that usually involves other corroborative processes."

"Got it." Greer was still trying to figure out where this was going."

She continued. "The system is generating so much information that, each week, or few days, a lot of it just gets tossed – to make room for the next batch coming and so on. The truth is that the FBI and other services get stacks of lists of 'possibles', but simply do not have the manpower to chase each and every lead down."

"Okay, I understand the information overload part – but why are you telling all this to me?"

"Because…" She looked at him squarely. "In the past few days, someone - we don't know who - has been putting together a package on you!"

Greer sat quiet for a moment. He was digesting the information and trying to foretell the implications of what she was telling him. "So, how do you know it's simply not my bank checking me out for a new mortgage or credit card application?"

Garcia smiled. "No… Look, Greer. This goes way beyond anything a credit application would trigger. Someone, out there, is literally scraping the bottom of the barrel for every bit of information on you - cars, financial, property records, DMV photo, school records, prior employment, medical records – you name it, they've tried, or they've already got it."

He studied her carefully. Everything about her demeanor told him she was being truthful and sincere. "How about another Federal Agency doing a work up on me because of my – he searched for the correct word – 'insight' on the Korean murders case?"

She shook her head. "No. I have a way of checking, even with heavy weights like the CIA. At the moment, I'm confident that there is no Federal, State or local agency making legitimate inquiries about you." A hint of fear momentarily clouded her face.

"You're really not supposed to be telling me any of this, are you?"

She shook her head and her voice softened. "My disclosure of this, to you, is a potential – career ender."

"Kirby?"

"He is" – she groped for the correct word - "a difficult supervisor."

"You mean he's an asshole."

She ignored his comment and continued. "There's more. Tim, you are the one that pulled this entire Korean murders"– she looked around them and returned her eyes to his – "energy project"- she'd purposefully used Ahn's code phrase – "case together". You've stepped on some major toes. It stands to reason that somebody out there might be pissed off to the extent that they'd like to hurt you."

"And Mr. Kirby told you, make that, ordered you, to keep your mouth shut about this…"

She just nodded.

"Okay then. I guess I own you a big one – seriously, thank you."

"You're welcome, but know this - some of the inquiry sources – their IP's, internet addresses – they trace back to…" She hesitated for an instant, and Greer watched in fascination as S.A. Garcia bit down on her bottom lip. "The IP's, they trace back to North Korea."

Chapter 62
Sea of Japan

Sullivan pushed the floating yellow case in front of him. He kicked furiously trying to put as much distance possible between him and the sinking helicopter. A few yards behind him, the twisted fuselage rolled and thrashed in the water.

The sounds of the aircraft sinking pierced the dark air. Sheet metal buckled and ripped; gurgling water filled the hollow spaces. Those sounds were punctuated by the hiss of gases and the metallic groan of rending metal spars and bulkheads. It was almost as if the Hind was alive and desperately struggling for a precious few more moments of life, before finally surrendering its mechanical soul to the murky depths.

With a death-grip on the case, Sullivan roller-coastered up and over six to eight foot swells. With all of his might, he desperately kicked and swam further and further away from the dying airship. When he thought he was a safe distance, he turned and hauled his heaving chest up onto the case. The rank taste of salt water and gasoline burned his throat and made him retch. He wanted to stop and take a quick breather, but knew he couldn't.

The water was cold but not freezing. He figured it to be in the middle fifties. He tried to figure out how long he could survive before the cold would leach the precious heat from his body. He knew that he – that they - had a while, but not a long while. Their chances would improve if they could get out of the water. Again, he thought about trying to open the yellow float case. He weighed that he might be slitting his own throat if whatever was inside the case was not buoyant. At least in its closed condition, the thing was floating and supporting his weight.

Mike watched in macabre fascination as the rotor tail of the airship hung a few feet above the surface of the water. It wagged back and forth, looking, he thought, almost like the hand of a drowning man, waving goodbye. Then without further fuss, it silently slipped away.

It was over. Except for the relentless swells, the sea surface was unbroken and quiet.

He cursed himself for not putting on that life jacket when he had the chance. But at least for the moment, whatever was inside this yellow case was keeping him on top of the water. He quickly dispensed with those thoughts and focused upon finding the others. He watched the intervals between the swells and waited to be carried to the next crest. When it came, he was ready. At the top of the swell, he quickly scanned around and called out at the top of his lungs. "Charlie! Nikolai – can you hear me?" Then the moment of wave crest was gone and his little float slid down into the trough, the low spot. He waited. At the next crest and the next, he repeated yelling out each of their names until he was hoarse and his voice cracked. He watched and listened, but heard nothing.

Time passed. Just how long, he wasn't certain. The dark was deepened by the cloud cover. Scant fragments of moonlight would occasionally filter through, offering a few precious moments of ability to see more than a few feet away. Sometimes, he could barely make out objects, even things that were close.

A little debris from the Hind floated around him. Twice he saw things that could have been a person, and he quickly left the floating case to swim over and check. The first time he returned to the float without a problem. The second time he chased down a piece of debris, he had to swim farther. He realized too late that he was down current from the float. Then the swells blocked his ability to see it. Panic nipped at the base of his brain as he spun circles in the water, again and again trying to reacquire a visual on the yellow float.

Finally, another swell carried him high and he spotted it about twenty five feet away. He tucked his head down and plunged through dark water, praying that he was headed in the right direction. He swam furiously until his fingers touched something rough. He grabbed on, then righted himself and cleared the seawater from his eyes. It was the rough canvas cover of the floating case. Elated, he grabbed the case and pulled it to his chest.

That was stupid. Stay with your float, you idiot. It's the only thing between you and drowning. After a few moments of self-chastisement, he heaved his upper body onto the float and hung on with all of his remaining strength.

More time passed. He called out again and again, but heard nothing in response. The yellow float case had folded canvas loop handles on two sides. He managed to slip his arms through to the elbows. This enabled him to prop his head and chest on the float and relax a bit.

He tried to take stock of the situation. So much time had passed, hours he thought. He was all but certain that the others were lost or drowned. Or if they had survived, they had drifted so far away, he would never find them.

A larger issue was, just how long could they survive in these waters? Not for long. He thought. Hypothermia or predators would take them. It became an academic question as to which would get them first. Sullivan's mind drifted...

Mike pulled himself back to reality. He performed the mental equivalent of slapping some sense into himself. He had to get a grip, figure out something. He lay still in the water, head resting on the float. The end of the broken zipper was only inches from his face. He thought about trying to open the float case. *What the hell. What do I really have to lose at this point? Not too much.* He mused. He slipped one arm out and began to inventory his pockets. He still had the satellite phone! A moment of hope surged through him. He keyed the controls. Damn, it was dead. He tried it over and over, but the water had obviously penetrated the case effectively ruining the electronics. The sat phone was toast. He held on to it for a few minutes. Finally, he flipped it into the water and watched it gurgle away. His pistol was gone, but he still had the silencer. He briefly thought that fact was amusing, and tossed that extra baggage item into the water. He still had his submariner's watch strapped to his wrist. He twisted it around in order to see the time. It read 4:30AM.

He continued rummaging. In one of his many pockets he found a small folding pen knife. Curious, he thought. He had forgotten about the small knife. He carefully extracted it and held it before his face. It had a pick tool. He changed position until he could use both hands. Carefully, he unfolded the pick tool; and used it to work at the zipper clasp. In a few seconds, he had the zipper moving. He slid it open about a foot and stopped. He slipped off the floating case, and began to tread water. He gripped the case with one hand and moved the rusty zipper along with the other. In a few moments, he had moved the zipper the entire circumference of the case. Water surged inside, yet the case and contents still floated.

First light began to color the eastern horizon. The pre-dawn sky offered a hint of light. Sullivan gingerly opened the canvas flap of the case and inventoried the contents. He wasn't certain as to exactly what it was, but it felt like rubber, canvas, plastic foam and... His hand felt a cold metal cylinder. It had to be. It just had to be - a gas inflator bottle – because it was securely attached to the thing in the case. Mike ran his fingers over the cylinder. One end was attached to what felt like rubberized canvas fabric. The other end felt like a valve gizmo with a ring on it. He slipped his index finger through the ring.

Funny, he thought. This feels just like the top of a hand grenade. He fingered the ring and jerked it away from the cylinder. Instinctively, he swam away, backing off from the case. At a distance of about four feet he waited, watched and treaded water. Nothing happened. He had just about decided the thing was a dud, or had long ago bled out.

Suddenly, the thing popped. The pop was cherry-bomb loud, just like a timed explosive device. Pieces of the case began to expand and unfold before his disbelieving eyes. Pale yellow floatation tubes inflated and formed the outline of the life raft! In less than a minute, there it was, a complete inflatable raft floating on the surface right in front of him. It looked to be about a three or four passenger model. Mike quickly closed the short distance, and hauled his body up and over the side.

He lay on the rubber coated canvas bottom of the raft. For a while, he didn't move. He just held perfectly still. The raft bobbed in the swells. An inch or two of water rolled around the canvas floor and lapped into his face. He coughed and sputtered, then heaved himself into a sitting position. He sat, dazed for a moment, not quite believing that he was actually out of the water.

The soft light was increasing, providing more and more visibility. The sea was flattening to calm, the swell now less than two feet. The cloud cover, which had practically been down on the sea surface when they crashed, was now rising.

From his slightly higher vantage point he could see farther. He scanned the horizon all around. There was nothing, no debris, no bodies, nothing but water in every direction. The only thing he saw was the zippered yellow canvas cover for the raft. It was floating just a few feet away. Mike reached out, grabbed it and hauled it aboard. He could see now why the boat case floated. Attached to the inside were two rectangles of foam-like plastic, each about two inches thick.

For several minutes, he called out again. He yelled out repeatedly in all four compass directions. There was nothing, no response, no sounds, not even a breeze. All he got for his effort was a sore throat.

He decided to examine the raft. It was more or less circular in fashion. It looked to have been made from mottled yellow-grey canvas that was coated with a rubber-like material. Overall, the pitiful thing looked to be at least fifty years old. The rusty inflator bottle was still attached to one of the three tubular air chambers. Stenciled to one side was the Russian word for "model" and a series of numbers. Sullivan knew that it was an absolute miracle that this thing had inflated and held pressure.

He knew that many emergency rafts were equipped with tools, signaling devices, even water and rations. Not overly optimistic, he searched around. He found a flap covered storage pouch, but it was empty. Count your blessings. He told himself over and over. That's when he heard it.

It was the one sound he really didn't need to hear, and it was getting louder. It was the sound of escaping air, precious air that was leaking from the raft! He moved from side to side trying to locate the leak. Finally he found it. The steady hiss of air was coming from the spot where the inflator bottle attached to the sidewall of the raft. He knelt before it and faced it close up. The steady stream blew cold against his face.

Mike knew that some boat inflators were designed to be used, then to be detached. Maybe this was one of them. Maybe he was supposed to remove the bottle. He put his fingers around the hardware. He could feel the air escaping. He forced himself to calm down, slow down and think it through. I don't want to force anything, lest make a bad situation even worse.

At the inflator bottle attachment point there were two knurled metal ring-like fittings. They were stacked atop each other. Mike noticed that the one closest to the air chamber was thicker. He was betting that one was a valve and the other, the one closest to the cylinder, was simply a threaded attachment.

Carefully, with cold cramped fingers, he went to work. The large fitting wouldn't budge. He tried it both ways. Again, he told himself to go slow and careful. He didn't want to break the damn thing off. He wiped his fingers as best he could and tried again. This time the ring turned. It moved clockwise more than one full revolution. Then it tightened and finally seized. It felt just like a valve closing. The hiss of air slowed, then stopped.

Sullivan sat back. The air chamber on that side was now soft and sagging. It had lost, perhaps, a third of its air in the time it took him to figure out and close the valve. The other two chambers appeared to be holding firm. Good. He thought. There must be some kind of check valves between the chambers. The inflator bottle hung down, gently swinging in the pitch of the swell. The movement was stressing the flimsy fabric around the valve attachment. He decided to try to remove the bottle.

Gripping the second, smaller of the rings he twisted it counter clockwise. At first, the ring resisted. His wet fingers slipped and denied him purchase. He wiped his fingers and tried over and over. Finally the rusty old ring moved. He unscrewed the connector and the bottle came free. No further air seemed to be escaping.

Mike slumped back against one of the firmer air chambers. The sun was now starting to peek over the horizon. Suddenly, he was exhausted. He lay back and closed his eyes. *Just for a few seconds*, he thought.

The heat baked his closed eyelids. He blinked his eyes slightly open, and was blinded by the direct sun. His lips were cracked and blistered. His throat felt like he'd swallowed a grapefruit sized cotton ball. He pushed himself into an upright sitting position. The inside of the raft was filled with water. The air chamber that had previously leaked was now empty and the fabric walls lay limp, flat in the water. Like a broken levee, the breached wall allowed the sea water to ebb and flow. Only the remaining two air chambers were keeping the raft afloat.

How long have I been asleep? Sullivan looked at the sun. It was almost directly overhead. He squinted at his watch. It read a few minutes after eleven. He realized he had been out for hours! He looked around. The glare of the overhead sun didn't help. He picked up the canvas boat cover and used it as a sunshade.

He surveyed the ocean all around him. He broke one of the foam plastic boards out of the boat cover and used it as a make-shift paddle. For three hundred and sixty degrees around him there was absolutely nothing but grey-blue water. He slumped back down in the boat. He desperately needed a drink. But he knew that ingesting sea water would only hasten his demise. He rolled onto an air chamber and scooped up some water. He sucked it into his mouth, swished it around and spat it out. It felt good, but tasted like shit. He lay there, staring at the water, when suddenly; something bumped the raft –

hard! He grabbed the sides and spun around to see the tall dark dorsal fin gliding through the water.

Panic alarms in his brain shot adrenalin throughout his body. His mind silently screamed the word – SHARK!

Chapter 63
Sea of Japan

The second time the Hind's engine burped, he knew. Charlie's stomach sunk. In that fraction of an instant, he knew that no matter what he did, the helo was not going to recover. Quickly, he released the rotor blades for auto rotation, checked his altitude and airspeed. They were only a couple hundred feet about the churning water.

Instinctively, he tightened his seat harness, and clamped down on the controls, straining to keep the plunging airship as close to level as he could. It was going to happen fast. He yelled over his shoulder at the others. "Hang on! We're going down – this is it!"

It took all of his strength to hold the sluggish controls as the vibrating Hind spun out of the night sky. He glanced at the GPS, and hit the radio transmit switch. He said, "Mayday – Mayday – Russian Hind Helicopter", and he recited the latitude – longitude numbers. The radio transmission was their only chance for rescue, and it was a one time deal. He had no idea if he was even heard.

The helicopter pan caked hard onto the surface of the black water. The shock of impact was bad, but less than what Charlie expected. The aircraft bounced and pitched on the sea surface. Within seconds water was gushing in and the helo started to roll.

Charlie punched out of his seat and grabbed the two life jackets Sullivan had dropped on the deck. He walked, waded and swam to the rear of the cabin grabbing a struggling Viktoriya along the way. He looped his right arm through both jackets, and with the same arm grabbed a wad of her upper clothing. With his feet and left arm he kicked and stroked and literally dragged her out of the sinking chopper. Within seconds they were clear of the doomed airship. Charlie swam furiously leading them both away from the ship.

As soon as Viktoriya's head was above the surface she began to yell at the top of her lungs. She cried out for Nikolai. Gomez pulled her with such fury that her head was soon again swamped. He didn't stop until they were fifty yards out from the sinking craft. He spun her around, righted her and started to put her into one of the flotation jackets. Only then, did he realize that she already had one on.

When he felt she was secure and stable, he backed off a bit and slipped his arms into one of the vests and fastened the straps. The other one he clutched to his chest.

He closed with her. She sputtered, spitting out a mouthful of seawater. "What – what about the others?"

"I don't know... Mike opened the cabin door - he must have gotten out."

"My – father?"

A swell crested and separated them by a few feet. Charlie paddled back over to her. "Don't know." He said to her gravely. She didn't answer. She just looked at him.

He leaned back and hollered out. "MIKE! SUL-LI-VAN!" He literally sang out the syllables of Sullivan in his rich tenor voice.

Vika took up the cue. She began yelling out. "Poppa – Nikolai!" Over and over they called out for the others. Then they would stop, listen and wait. They did this over and over. They never heard a reply.

Finally, Charlie stopped her. "We should try to conserve some energy."

Viktoriya nodded.

Charlie could see that she was exhausted. He removed a long tie strap from the spare jacket. With it, he fashioned a tether line, tying one end to her and the other to himself. He also tied off the spare jacket to the line. "There. This will keep us together, but allow us to keep our arms moving."

She offered him a bit of a weak smile. "I never did get a chance to say much to you. Things were happening – too fast, I guess." I know you are - Gomez – and you are the one..." She hesitated for a moment choking on seawater and maybe something else. She continued. "...Sullivan wanted to rescue."

Despite their situation, Charlie flashed Vika his pearly whites. "I know... And I want to thank you for helping to get me out of that place."

"You're welcome... For all the good it's going to do for us..." Her voice trailed. "What about Sullivan and my... Father?"

"I really don't know... Vika, is that your name?"

"Yes, Viktoriya. Vika is my – short name."

"Vika – it is then. Call me Charlie. That's my short name."

She smiled again. He thought she had a nice smile. Even half drowned, she had a great smile. "What about them, Charlie. You think they're dead?"

He knew he had to tell her something – anything. He briefly rolled it over in his mind. "Look, Vika. I don't know what to tell you about your Dad. Mike told me he was in pretty bad shape. Maybe he wouldn't have made it - even if we got him to some medical help. As for Sullivan, all I can tell you is that I've known that guy for years. I've seen him get into all kinds of jams and walk – or swim - his way out of it. If you're in trouble, there's no better guy to be sharing it with."

Vika just nodded.

Charlie continued knowing he was pouring it on pretty thick, that their chances were really about zero; but not wanting to completely dash her hopes. "If Mike got your Pop out - like I think he probably did - then they've both got a shot at making it." *At least as good as our slim chances of survival.* He thought.

Vika pulled herself close to Gomez. Fear shone in her eyes. She fumbled and found his hand, and with both arms clutched it tightly to her breast.

Chapter 64
Sea of Japan

The dorsal fin had circled and was now moving away from his raft! *If that's a shark, the thing has to be huge!* He watched wide-eyed, a combination of horror and relief flowing through him, as the creature swam in a straight line, away from the flimsy raft.

He tried to remember what a dorsal looked like on a Great White, but quickly dismissed that thought. He knew that these waters were full of predators, mostly Gray and Tiger sharks, not quite as large as the Great White, but every bit as mean and hungry. He looked around for something, anything he could use as a weapon... He had nothing – the tiny pocket knife, some pieces of canvas and foam plastic. He picked up the metal inflator bottle. Mike hefted it by the neck. It wasn't much of a club, but it was better than dying empty handed. He thought.

His blue eyes glinted with resolve in the high sunlight. Sullivan was no stranger to death. He'd seen too much of it and delivered it a few times in his checkered lifetime. He wasn't what one would call afraid. But he recoiled at the thought that his death would come in the form of violently prepared fish-food. He watched the surface.

The dark fin disappeared, but just prior, the monster had changed course, deviating from its formerly straight path, and slowly turned into a long lazy arc.

Frantic thoughts burnt holes through Sullivan's logic. If it comes back should I jump in the water and try to get away from the raft. Should I try to attack it? If I get a shot, where should I hit it?

The dark fin reappeared. The monster fish was tracking in a wide circle. Mike had heard the stories. Some sharks will bump their prey or at least make a first glancing pass - for a taste - before striking. Maybe he didn't like the taste of the raft. Maybe he'll just keep on going.

Mike struggled to get up on his knees as he realized the creature had come full about, and was now headed straight back toward him!

His attention was so tightly focused on the shark that he failed to notice that a second air chamber was rapidly losing air. At the creature's first pass, either its razor-like teeth or rough hide had punctured the air chamber. Sullivan was slipping lower and lower into the water. Now, he was nearly waist deep with one arm around the remaining air chamber, the other hand hefting his club, the puny air inflator bottle.

The shark was closing rapidly. He was picking up speed. Now, he was about fifty yards out, and aimed directly for the defiant Sullivan and his pitiful raft.

Twenty five yards out, Mike watched in horrific fascination as the creature dove. He tensed, waiting for the inevitable when... Suddenly, the sea in front of him roiled and exploded in fury. The twisting, writhing two toned body of the monster shark catapulted out of the water, arced over and slammed down on its back. It was a Great White and he was huge! He had to be at least twenty feet long.

The monster creature lay floating, on its side for a moment, quivering, mouth gnashing. Then it seemed to recover, righted itself in the water, and then quickly slipped beneath the surface.

Mike waited. A strange calm came over him. He knew this was it. He was convinced that at any second the bottom of his torso would be cut off by this man eater. All of his life, Sullivan had been a fighter. Every fiber of his being wanted to fight. But in that instant, he knew he was going to die. He was going to be fish food, and there was absolutely nothing he could do to change that fact. Then it happened.

The seas exploded again. He felt something slam into his underside, his legs and back. He was being lifted up and angled forward. The attitude of his body changed. He felt his body continue to be lifted upward for an inordinately long time.

His head rolled back and clunked onto something – something hard. He spread out his arms and felt – not the rough hide of a shark – it felt like cold metal and hard rubber decking! He was dead – right? This had to be a dream.

He squinted up at the glaring sun. Part of it was being blocked or shaded by something... He angled a hand up to shade his eyes. It was then he realized he was looking up at... The superstructure of a ship? No – it was a submarine! He was looking up at the sail of a sub!

Pulling himself into a sitting position, he looked around and realized he was lying, broken raft and all, on the fore deck of a surfaced submarine. Sheets of water cascaded and poured off the deck and everything around him. He heard the metallic sounds, electric motor whine, clanking and voices. A head peered over from above and looked down at him. The face belonged to Bill Dubord! Even upside down he recognized that grinning face.

"Mike! Just hold still – Don't move! We'll be on you in a second!"

삼 질식시킴

They sat in the cramped galley. In front of him was a mug of steaming hot coffee. Sullivan had been washed, poked and prodded and given dry clothes and deck shoes. He sported a brilliant assortment of cuts, abrasions and bruises - all minor injuries. The boat's medic had given him the green light, and now he sat in the mess. Mike had just finished the short version of what had happened, since he and Nikolai left the submarine a few days ago.

Commander Dubord sat across from him staring. "Jesus, Mike. You look like you've been through a meat grinder."

Sullivan's head and face was a mass of abrasions, cuts and lumps. The right eye was starting to turn crimson-purple. The subcutaneous sutures Dr. Leversen had so artfully used to set the Asian angle to his eyes had broken on the right side. He was sun burnt, lips were split and his face was lop-sided. But despite all, he was smiling.

Mike blew the steam off of his mug of coffee and took a hot slurp. "I still don't understand. I thought you guys had to pull out of this theatre - international relations and all. So how is it that you ended up back here? And, how the hell did you ever find me?"

Dubord waved him down. "Slow down, will you. A lot's been happening, since you were last aboard. Yeah, it's true, some major crap did hit the fan. And we were ordered out of the area. In fact, Glomar is steaming, right now, back to Pearl Harbor."

"And you and the boat crew..." Sullivan gestured around him. "You're what – on vacation?"

Dubord smiled and cocked his head. He was tall, lanky man, and had that typical toothy New England grin. "As far as anyone knows, Huey is still in its berth under the Glomar Explorer."

"Won't the cat be out of the bag when they arrive at Pearl?"

"Actually, they are…" Dubord glanced at his watch. "Going to be delayed with some mechanical problems – which should be happening about any time now."

Sullivan sat back and looked at the Commander. "I take it you're not doing this on your own."

"Let's just say its a little conspiracy of sorts – one that we've got to keep to ourselves – for everyone's sake."

"Captain Marshall?"

Dubord nodded.

"I knew I liked that old man." Mike said.

"It's like I told you before, he's old school."

"So, just how did you find me – and, what about the others?'

"Well, so far, you are the only known survivor." He paused to let that settle. "There's some kind of a search effort going on up there. There are a couple of small surface craft, Russian we think, that are cruising around. There's also one fixed wing and one helicopter that have passed over from time to time. We're listening to their radio chatter now. So far there's been nothing – I mean they've found nothing, as far as we know."

Mike stared at his cup. He was quiet.

Sensing the moment, Dubord added. "I'm sorry."

Sullivan nodded. Dubord continued his story. "After all the BS about ordering us out of this area, we did go back and re-berth with Glomar - made a bit of a production out of it for show. Then, just about the time Marshall ordered the Glomar to make way, we slipped back out and returned. We figured that we could put a few more days on station waiting around for you guys before we would be forced to make the speed run to rendezvous with Glomar - before they made Pearl."

Mike nodded.

"We had no idea where you were or what was going on until you made the Satellite call to the other Mr. Gomez in the states. One of the things he did was to send us immediate encrypted flash traffic. That let us in on what you were doing. Then it was a matter of some good guess work, and a little luck to position the boat along your flight path."

"Yeah, but talk about finding a needle in the haystack."

"Dubord shook his head. "Not really. It was this." He reached across the table and tapped the watch on Mike's wrist. "Remember when you and Charlie came aboard and we gave you the watches and earpiece communicators? Well, part of what they do is allow us to track you, like a locator system aboard ship and also if we lost someone overboard."

"No kidding?" Mike looked over his now battered watch with renewed awe.

"It's not world-wide like Global Positioning. It's just a low power ultra high frequency thing. But, in open water it usually works over a hundred miles or so."

"Skipper?" It was crewman Carter that slipped into the small space. He nodded to Mike. "Mr. Sullivan, good to see you back." Then he returned his attention to Dubord. "Sir, we've been listening to the radio traffic between the two Russkie trawlers. It sounds like one of them just fished out two people in flotation vests – a man and a woman – both of them alive!"

Dubord sat back and bounced the flat of his hand off the table. "Well, all right! How sure are we on the translation and where are they now?"

"We're pretty certain. It's Boyd who's doing the translation. He's a grad of the Monterey Language School. He's worked at..."

"Yeah Carter, I know..."

"Anyway, Boyd says the ship is talking to the land station in the clear, with no regard for security. It just sounds like any other search and rescue operation. The base station asks questions and the guys on the boat answer. So far we've heard them talk about two people recovered, a man and a woman, both alive, no names or descriptions other than to say they are 'Americanskies'..."

"Did they say what they are doing with them?"

"Yes Sir. The base station ordered them to return to port, and they took off steaming at a course of 295."

"Where...?"

"Sir, I'd put my money on Vladivostok. That course will take them straight in."

Chapter 65
Orange County, California

Ichiro believed that the time was coming close. He was ready. Two weeks had passed since he first focused on the new assignment, the police officer, Timothy Greer of the Orange County Sheriff's Department. In that time, Ichiro had painstakingly collected every available scrap of information about the man. What he could not learn on his own was researched by his colleagues and forwarded to him by email. Several times, he had carefully watched and followed Greer and the woman he lived with.

Ichiro memorized the daily routines for both of them. Like most Americans, they were creatures of schedules and habits. The two were easy and predictable. He knew the daily routes they drove, to go to work and to return home, the times of day they generally came and went. He knew the stores they shopped in, and the local restaurants and movie theatres that they frequented. Ichiro mused that he probably knew more about Greer than any other living person.

Despite the difficulty of getting close to Greer's condo, he had patiently watched and photographed the place from several vantage points. He had committed to memory every detail of the Tustin Gardens condominium complex. He knew the physical layout, the points of ingress and egress. He had identified several places that afforded cover. Perhaps, most importantly, he was picking up on the routines of the residents, beginning to develop a feel for who belonged in the area, and when they came and went.

In his mind, he believed he had enough information. This target actually presented no more challenge than any other. His decision was to hit Greer while he was inside his home. He chose to do it mid-week, in the middle of the night. He would take them both. He chuckled at the thought. He would enjoy killing the policeman. He would really enjoy killing his woman.

He also had decided that the job would require a staging location. It would have to be a place close by and convenient. Ideally it would be a place where he could wait in safety and comfort, be concealed from view, and watch for the perfect time to pay his visit.

Ichiro believed he had figured out the perfect method to accommodate that need.

He knelt. Reaching into the cardboard box, he scooped up the tiny dog from the crumpled newspaper upon which it slept. The animal was a male, barely eight weeks old, with tufts of curly buff colored fur. Two days earlier he had obtained the creature from a boy who sat with a box of the puppies, in front of a supermarket. The boy held a hand lettered sign that said "free to good homes". Ichiro had offered to pay for the baby dog, but was politely refused. Instead he stood, listening with feigned compassion, as the lad told of his female cocker spaniel's indiscretion with an unknown stray mutt, which had resulted in the brood of questionably pedigreed animals. Ichiro promised to "give him a good home" and walked away thinking if things didn't work out, he could always make a meal out of it!

The puppy opened its sleepy eyes, stretched and yawned as the cold blooded killer held it up for close inspection. The puppy angled its mouth to the tip of Ichiro's index finger and began to suckle. Ichiro recoiled in disgust and with a plop, and whine of protest, dropped the tiny warm body back into the box. He stood up.

Today was Tuesday. Perhaps in one or two more days. He thought. Wednesday and Thursday were always excellent days for killing.

Chapter 66
Sea of Japan

A privilege of rank, Commander Dubord was the only person aboard the submarine Huey that had a private cabin. The space was small, not much more than a closet. There was a bunk, a tiny desk and in one corner, there was an efficiency lavatory-shower combination that defied logic, even for a small person's use. How the Commander managed to use the facility with his six foot plus frame was a mystery, a bona-fide article of ship's lore.

The knuckle rap on the cabin door interrupted the neat notations he penned in his personal log. "Come!" He said in a loud voice as he closed the journal, and turned to see Sullivan stoop and enter the tiny space. Now two giant men filled the small cabin.

"Sorry to disturb you, Commander."

It had been less than an hour, since Dubord had finished with Sullivan in the galley, and sent him off to get some much needed sleep.

"Not at all... Take a seat." He gestured toward the tightly made bunk.

"Thanks." Sullivan replied. He gingerly lowered his bulk onto the edge of the metal bed frame, wincing a bit as he sat down.

"I thought you were going to go get some shut-eye?"

"Yeah, well I went back to the medic and had him finish clipping the sutures that - asianized my face. What with the injuries and all, I was starting to look a tad like an oriental Frankenstein."

"I noticed." Dubord waited, interlacing his fingers and flexing his hands out. "Just come by to visit... Or did you have something on your mind?"

"Sorry, Sir. I know this is going to sound a little awkward... But, I want you to let me off the sub."

Dubord blinked and sat quiet for a moment.

Sullivan gazed at the Commander steadily. He watched as the naval officer's face displayed tell-tale signs that began with disbelief, and ranged across acknowledgement, curiosity and finally accommodation.

"You're sure?"

"Yes."

"You know we're running at flank speed right now, so we can catch up with the Glomar?"

"Yes Sir, I do."

"And, that any further delay will make us that much more tardy for our rendezvous?"

"Yes, I understand that."

Dubord turned and faced the LCD monitor attached to the bulkhead behind his desk. He touched the screen and the image changed to display a map of the East China Sea with written information scrolling across the top and bottom. Over Dubord's shoulder Sullivan could see what looked like the southern tip of Korea and a smattering of islands, possibly the western islands off of Kyushu, Japan. A blinking green cursor represented the southward progress of Huey. Dubord turned back to Sullivan. "You're going back." It wasn't a question as much as a statement of fact.

"Yes... I have to."

"You know, they're probably all safe – at least two of them." Dubord quickly corrected himself.

"I know. From the radio intercept it sounds like Gomez and the girl were recovered. At least we know their safe and on their way to Vladivostok."

"And the other guy, Mister Gordon?"

"That's not his real name."

"We all kind of figured that out..."

"It's Nikolai... He and I, we go back – way back."

Dubord just nodded. "Okay, assuming we can do this, it'll have to be a fast drop, a boat drop. We could give you a Zodiac and get you close to..." He consulted his map, fingered and tapped the display until one of the islands zoomed up. "Fukue Jima! There's an airport there."

Sullivan nodded.

"What else will you need?"

"I could use another satellite phone and some cash – as much as you can lay your hands on."

Chapter 67
Sea of Japan

They were safe – sort of. The surprised deck hands that pulled them from the grey churning sea in their drift nets were manning an aging Russian fishing trawler. Vika and Charlie literally spilled out of the nets and flopped onto the deck along side the cod and mackerel. The whoops and yells of the crewmen brought the giant electric davit to a slamming stop, and the boat's skipper, a crusty old fisherman named Antonov, running from his wheelhouse.

Charlie thought they all looked like stereotypical Russian peasants. Each had dark hair and eyes, coarse features and squat compact bodies. Several of the men sported a blending of Asiatic features which hinted at the mix of their ancestral bloodlines. They spoke an east Asian dialect of Russian sprinkled with bits and pieces of Chinese. One of the crewmen, suspecting that Vika might be Korean, tried a little of that language on her. She, wisely, chose not to respond, deciding to stick with what Russian she had.

Once aboard they were hustled into an interior cabin space that doubled as a sleeping, living and eating quarters. Two of the crewman stayed with them. The men talked back and forth as they helped the half frozen and water-logged pair out of their floatation jackets and wet clothes.

Hypothermia not withstanding, the crewmen were visibly much more gleeful about assisting Vika out of her clothes, than Gomez. She still wore the borrowed KPA uniform shirt and trousers over her blouse and blue jeans. Since the KPA shirt had no insignia, as far as anyone knew, she was just another young woman attired in green fatigues. The fishermen could care less about fashion. The two were wrapped in dry blankets and parked in old wooden chairs in front of a glowing kerosene stove.

One of the crewmen moved to the far end of the cabin where a make-shift galley had been installed. From a large burn-stained pot that was fastened to the stovetop with metal cables, he ladled out two steaming mugs of white fishy stew. Returning, he carefully placed each mug into their chalk-white fingers. Patiently, he made certain that each had both of their quaking hands firmly attached to the mugs before he let released his grip. Charlie and Vika sipped thankfully and hungrily at the spicy brew. Charlie thought it was the best damn thing he had ever tasted.

Minutes later, the boat's Captain, a swarthy man of sixty or so years burst into the quarters and assumed a position directly across from them. He was agitated and spoke in rapid Russian directing his comments to Gomez.

"Who are you God-damned people, and what have you done to piss off the Russian Navy? They are just now coming for us! If you are criminals, I would just as soon throw you back into the ocean!" He leaned in to Gomez's face to further emphasize his point. "I don't need this trouble!"

Gomez looked helplessly at Vika. "Any idea what he's saying?"

"Yes." She quickly translated the Captain's concerns. She finished by saying, "Let me try to explain things to him."

"Be my guest." Charlie extended a hand and sat back with a grin.

Vika spoke in Russian. "Captain. Please accept our sincere thanks to you and your men for saving us. We are American citizens. We were kidnapped and held as prisoners in North Korea. We escaped. We managed to steal an aircraft, and we were trying to fly to the Russian territories when we crashed into the ocean."

The Captain stood listening, his face a mask of skepticism. His arms crossed over his barrel chest and one grimy hand stroked continuously at a weeks worth of greasy beard on his face. "I know that much!" He roared. "The comrade Russian Navy Commander was kind enough to include a short description of your crimes in his radio instructions to us. He has ordered us to stand by while they come to our position to arrest you. The North Korean Navy bastards (he leaned and spat on the deck as if to emphasize his dislike for the North Koreans) are also out there looking for you. What the hell are you people – spies?"

A moment of fear rippled across Viktoriya's face. The Captain caught it and continued. "Understand me, Miss. I don't give a shit either way. We are just out here to make an honest living with the fish – and we don't want trouble from anybody, not our Comrade brothers - our Russian Navy friends – and especially not from those crazy North Korean Bastards."

Vika eyes never left the Captain's face. She quickly translated to Gomez who coached her reply. "Tell him we're not spies... Tell him we're just American tourists who made a wrong turn and..." Gomez held up his mug towards the dirty apron clad keeper of the galley who stood, arm on hip, watching the interrogation with amusement. "Maybe you could ask if we could get a little more of this delightful stuff."

Vika continued. "There were four of us on the aircraft – two more men. Has anyone else been rescued?"

"I don't know – I don't care!" The Captain replied.

One of the crewmen stuck his head into the cabin. "Captain, the Navy patrol boat is bearing down on us."

The Captain nodded his acknowledgement and turned back to Vika and Charlie. "I really don't care, Miss!" He said, letting out a long sigh. "Now, you can be someone else's problem!"

삼 질식시킴

Three days passed since Charlie and Vika had been pulled from the East Sea by the fishermen. Following their transfer to the Russian Navy patrol boat, they were taken to a military installation, with a medical facility, at Vladivostok. They were separated, each given examinations, clothing and locked in separate rooms. It wasn't quite jail, but it didn't appear as if they were free to simply take a walk to the nearest coffee shop on their own.

On the second day both were interviewed extensively and separately. They had no opportunity to collaborate with one another or to agree on a storyline for their captors. Gomez decided to go with a modified version of the truth. Vika, owing largely to her background, was forced to be a touch less truthful. The interrogations were soft. That is, they were not coerced in any manner. One might call the proceedings even cordial.

On the third day, at mid-morning, Vika, accompanied by a stern looking matron, was escorted to the interview room. Seated behind the lone table was the same man she had met with on the previous day. He was a short sallow looking man who had introduced himself as Arcady Filitov, an investigator with the rank of Major of the Russian Civil Militia or National Police. Also present, as was the case on the previous day, was another tall, dark haired man, who was not, introduced. Both of the men were attired in civilian clothes, inexpensive dark suits, white shirts and dark ties. The second man, as he had done the day before, simply sat in the back of the room and watched. He never spoke, nor was any reference made to him. He just sat, watched and listened.

"Good morning. Please be seated." Filitov gestured to the opposing chair. "Would you like some tea?" As he asked the question, he poured hot dark tea from a steaming Samovar into a clear glass teacup with a metallic filigree base. A suspicious Vika accepted the steaming cup and sipped at it lightly.

"Major Filitov, I appreciate your hospitality." Forcing a smile, Vika set her cup on the table top and continued in Russian. "I also appreciate that our presence here has caused you some difficulty. However, I am an American citizen, and I wish to contact my embassy." Vika's assessment of Filitov was that he was probably just a bureaucratic minion, stuck out here in the armpit of the former Soviet Union, not wanting to rock the boat, a man who's paramount concern was the covering of his own ass. Just typical, she thought, of the government minds that permeated the new Russian society.

In a manner that was clearly uncharacteristic for Russians, one that bordered almost on an apology, Filitov explained. "Yes, Miss… Our immediate problem is that we, that is, the Russian civil authorities, are having some difficulty deciding just what to do with you and…" He glanced at his notes. "Ah… Mister Charles Gomez. You will appreciate that your arrival here – the circumstances of which and the manner of which you came – is causing somewhat of a firestorm of conflicting interests."

Vika nodded.

"For the moment, I would like to set that matter aside. May we speak once again about your identity? You tell us that you are an American. That your name is Viktoriya Petrovla." His eyes bored into her. "Interestingly enough, you have a very Russian name, you speak our language like a native and… You are coming out of a communist country under questionable circumstances."

Vika nodded. "Yes, as I told you, my parents were Russian…"

For the first time since they had met, Filitov shifted to English, perfectly accented, fluent English. "You see, Viktoriya Petrovla, we have been able to confirm a good deal of information about your companion, Mister Gomez. He is – shall we say - very well known. He is also very wealthy and as you Americans say, very well connected."

Vika squirmed in her seat, her comfort level dropping a notch as she realized Filitov might be more sophisticated than the low level bureaucrat she had initially taken him for.

"In your case, we have learned very little. The American embassy tells us that they have no record of a U.S. passport issued under the name Viktoriya Petrovla." He sat back for a moment, pausing and stared at her. "There is also the small matter of the DPRK citizen's identity card found in your clothing, with the name..." He shuffled some papers in front of him. "Chung Mun Sook. The picture is – not very flattering - but it is a good likeness of you." The edges of his mouth formed a small smile.

Vika said nothing.

"And speaking of clothing, here is another interesting detail. Apparently, at the time of your rescue, Mr. Gomez was attired in a..." He paused as if searching for the correct words. "A cotton utility uniform – like – pajamas. These garments are typical of clothing worn by prisoners in the DPRK."

"Yes, as I told you yesterday, we were arrested by the North Koreans, but we..."

He cut her off. "The DPRK has tendered an official demand for the extradition of you and Mister Gomez. Their position is that you are criminals. You stole their helicopter, murdered members of the Korean Peoples Army, and are suspected of blowing up a military installation." He tapped his finger on the table. "Why, don't you simply tell me what is really going on here?"

삼 질식시킴

Some time later, after having concluded his session with Vika, Filitov prepared for another session with Gomez. He turned to his mostly quiet associate. "So Vassily, what do you think? Have we got us a real, honest-to-god CIA operative?"

"Have you considered that perhaps Miss Viktoriya Petrovla is an operative from our very own SVR." The tall man matter-of-factly used the new term to describe what had formerly been the KGB, the infamous Committee for State Security, whose pervasive operations had infiltrated every aspect of life, in the former Soviet Union's glory days.

"Hmm..." Filitov thought out loud. "Perhaps Miss Petrovla is Directorate S employee?" He referred to the department within the

KGB that was responsible for creating elaborate cover identities and legends for covert agents that were planted inside many countries, friends and foes alike, including North Korea and the United States.

The tall man nodded. "They would never tell us – the shits." His comment spoke to the long standing difficulties that existed between the KGB, now SVR, and the Militia. The KGB had such all encompassing powers that they routinely looked down their noses upon all others in Soviet government, including the National Police. To KGB, the Militia was lower than whale shit. The attitudes were mostly mutually held; and, despite political changes, they continued, well into the twenty-first century.

As the ranking Milita officer in Vladivostok, Filitov had caused reports of the "rescue" of Gomez and the woman to be transmitted to all the appropriate Russian agencies, including the Foreign Ministry and the SVR. Since the DPRK was making such a fuss, he'd already had several calls with the Foreign Ministry, but the intelligence types, the SVR, had been strangely quiet. He pondered his next course of action. "What I really wonder about, Vassily, is why we have not yet heard from our esteemed Comrades of the SVR?"

The tall man pondered Filitov's very good question. Despite the rebirth of the new Russia over fifteen years ago, there was still so much distrust between levels of government that it stifled anything close to cooperation. Sometimes the simplest forms of communication went unheeded. The tall man furrowed his brow in thought. "You don't want to call attention to this matter too early."

"No, of course not."

"Will you consider giving them back to the Koreans?"

Filitov just glared at him.

"I didn't think so…"

"Let's put our two guests together for awhile, and see what may come out of their association. I think we still have much to learn."

Chapter 68
Fukue Jima, Japan

Sullivan kept one hand on the tiller handle of the small outboard engine and in the other, he held a portable GPS. His destination was the western tip of the island of Fukue Jima.

The tiny inflatable boat climbed up and over the dark swells and purred steadily towards the island. At the point where the sub surfaced to launch Sullivan, the distance to land was a mere fifteen miles. *Piece of cake*. Mike thought.

Dressed in an assortment of borrowed clothing, and covered by a waterproof overall garment, he expertly piloted the black inflatable toward the natural harbor formed by the curved peninsula on the Southwestern side of the island.

Dubord had organized the launch about twenty minutes before sunrise, so as to lessen the possibility of attracting attention. From the sub's sail, the Commander waved at the receding form of Sullivan and the tiny boat framed by the dark outline of Fukue Jima. *That guy's got more balls than brains*. He thought as he dropped back inside and ordered his boat to submerge.

Early light illuminated the harbor as Sullivan rounded the western tip and entered the anchorage. It was much larger than he had imagined. He crossed the bay and headed for the edge of a collection of moored boats, mostly commercial fishing rigs and others that looked more like utility craft and less like pleasure boats.

He spotted a white cutter with the classic three diagonal blue stripes from the deck to the waterline. He knew that would be the local Japanese Coast Guard contingent. He steered a path away from the cutter and aimed for a series of short finger docks with clusters of small boats tied up. Amazingly, there were very few people about.

The little town that grew up the hillside from the harbor was called Tamanoura. In the early morning light, it looked sleepy, accented by a pale blue-grey haze that hung over the modest terraced homes and shops. Sullivan knew that Fukue Jima was very close to one of the most historical places on earth. Nagasaki, a scant sixty-five miles to the east, was the second place on earth where nuclear power had been used as a weapon of war.

His mind flitted to Central California, soberly recalling the small atomic bomb that had been detonated only a year before by those Islamic nutcases... Once again, Mike Sullivan found himself up to his eyeballs in international intrigue.

He shook himself out of his musings as his tiny boat approached one of the vacant docks. He slowed, then cut the motor, and let the little boat drift until it gently brushed the end of the dock. He jumped out, line in hand, and tied up to a cleat. He looked around. While there were a few souls about, it didn't look as if he was attracting much attention.

Slipping out of the overalls, he rolled them into a tight bundle. Tucking the bundle under his arm, he walked away, never to see the little boat again.

Briefly, he hoped that whoever ended up with the sturdy little inflatable would make good use of it. It bore no registration or traceable identity of any kind. Even the small Mercury outboard motor had no ID numbers – anywhere.

About two short blocks away from the harbor, he found a small park that was deserted at the early hour. He scanned the southern sky and saw no obstructions. Placing his garment bundle into a refuse can, he sat down on a park bench and flicked on the Satellite phone. The signal strength meter glowed green. He placed two calls. Both were short and consisted mostly of Sullivan giving specific directions to the two people he had called. Now he was ready to make his third call.

He dialed the Satellite phone number he had for Ferdinand Mateo, the GTI pilot. It was answered on the third ring.

"I'm glad to hear from you, Mister Sullivan. I was really starting to get worried."

"It's good to talk to you as well, Ferdie. You might say I was a little tied up. How are you doing – more importantly – where are you?"

"Well, as you directed, I'm here – in Nakhodka - at the Russian Air Force base – just like we discussed last time. I've been here, waiting."

"What's your status?" Mike crossed his fingers. "I mean – are you in trouble - are you being detained?"

Mateo laughed. "To tell you the truth, I really don't know. If this is house arrest, they're making me pretty comfortable."

"You're free to move around?"

"Well, yes and no. At first they got real testy about me coming in the way I did... They sent up two fighters to intercept me. When they finally realized that I really was an unarmed civilian airship, they let me land. Once on the ground, they went through me and my airplane pretty thoroughly. Then, they hustled me off to some building for interrogation, but about an hour into that – it all stopped. It was as if someone – you know - someone in authority had called them and told them to lay off."

Mike blew out a sigh of relief. "Good, I think somebody did – make that call for you, I mean."

"Well, hell, since then, they've been quite accommodating. They directed me to park the Gulf in a corner of their hanger complex where there's very little traffic, they offered me quarters nearby; but I told them I had to stay with my plane. They've re-fueled my ship and brought me food and stuff every day. They even sent some little guy out here to stamp a visa into my passport – and he gave me a paper - I have no idea what it says – it's written in Russian.

"Okay, it's probably some piece of paper that gives you permission to land there. Remember, Russians not only invented bureaucratic red tape, they've perfected it."

"You've got that right. These guys are worse than the DMV."

Sullivan couldn't help chuckling at that. "So - what is it you are supposed to be doing? I mean, what do they think you are there - for?"

"The story is still the same. I'm here to pick up Mister Charlie Gomez and return him to the States. Beyond that, I know nothing. I guess I'm just supposed to wait here indefinitely."

Mike's mind was racing ahead – making plans. "Okay. Good. Here comes the change in your plans. Right now, I'm on Fukue Jima. It's an island just west of Kyushu. Know it?"

"Not off hand, but if you give me and my trip computer a moment... Ah, yes, there it is. Christ, you know you're right on top of Nagasaki..."

"Yeah, I know. Listen. There's an airport on the east side of the island. Right now, I'm on the west side. I'm going to rustle up some transportation, and I want you to meet me there – at the airport – as soon as you can get over here. Got it?"

"Roger that, Mister Sullivan. Looks like about – six hundred forty four miles. I'll get there as soon as I can."

"Great. But before you take off, I need you to pick up a few things for me. Got any money?"

"Yes sir. I've got company credit cards and..."

"No – I mean cash. Got any cash money?"

"Yes sir. As I was saying, we always fly with a little stash on board. I believe..." His voice lowered a bit in volume. "I think I've got twenty thousand or so in US dollars and few thousand more in Euros."

"Great. Okay, here's what I need..."

Chapter 69
Vladivostok, Russia

The matron opened the door to Viktoriya's room. In Russian, she said. "You will please come with me – now."

Vika silently rose to follow. As she passed by the woman she thought about how the woman had framed her directions. She actually said please?

She assumed she was going back for another interview session, and was surprised when, a short distance down the hallway, they stopped by a door. It looked like the door to a room, similar to the one in which she was being detained. Major Filitov appeared at her elbow. Smiling at Vika, he thanked and dismissed the matron. Saying nothing, he rapped on the door. Without waiting for a response, he unlatched and pushed it open. As she suspected, the room was identical to hers, decorated in middle fifties commie utilitarian. Charlie Gomez sat inside leafing through a well-worn year old edition of Time magazine. He jumped up, a combination of elation and curiosity on his face.

Flitov was putting on the dog. He was all smiles and as smooth as motor oil. He spoke in his perfectly accented English. "Good morning to both of you. We are close to getting this matter of your – unorthodox arrival - sorted out. I want to apologize for any discomfort you may have suffered, and want you to know that for the remainder of your time with us – we shall be making efforts to make you both more comfortable."

"Great." Charlie smiled back uncommitally. He waited for the other shoe to drop.

Filitov glanced from Charlie to Vika, checking her reaction.

Charlie picked it up. "Mr. Filitov, Do you suppose it would be possible for me to make some telephone calls, now? I'd like to contact the embassy and make arrangements for some transportation, that is, if we are about finished."

"Your embassy has already been notified as to your presence here. I understand they are sending someone over to speak with you."

"Good."

"We are preparing better accommodations for you – here within the compound. We have a – what you would call – an apartment for visitors. It is not a luxury hotel, but I hope you both will find it a bit nicer than the rooms here at the clinic." Filitov waved his hand around at the grim surroundings. "Shortly, someone will come and take you there. There is a telephone in the apartment and you are welcome to make all the calls that you require. Of course, you may want Miss Petrovla to assist you."

A momentary look of confusion flitted across Gomez's face. He quickly recovered and said, "Sure."

"With any language difficulties is what I meant." Filitov added.

"Of course."

While you are free to move about, I must ask that you stay within the confines of the compound - at least until we conclude our inquiries and settle this outrageous claim from the Democratic Peoples Republic of Korea about your alleged crimes."

Filitov nodded to both of them and moved toward the door. "It will be just a short while. I thought that perhaps you two would like to visit with one another." Opening the door he paused and turned back to them, a slight smile forming at the edges of his mouth. "By the way, there will be someone stationed outside your apartment. If you require anything, please ask that person." With that, he turned and walked out, closing the door behind him.

Vika quickly moved to the door. While she listened, she looked around. Charlie's room was just like hers right down to the metal framed furniture and lack of a window.

Gomez said in a whisper. "Who the hell is Miss Petrovla?"

"Shh!" Vika cautioned him. She pointed to the ceiling with both index fingers. Then she tapped her ears, and with thumb and forefingers made circles around her eyes.

Gomez said, "I get it – charades – okay – two words – ear rings – spectacles!"

Vika stood with her hands on her hips, her meaning unmistakable. She looked around the room and spotted the water basin. She motioned him to come to the sink near her. She turned on the water full blast. Heads close to the sink, they took turns whispering in each others ears.

"This room is probably bugged." She said.

"Really – yah think?"

Vika punched him in the shoulder. "I'm Petrovla, you clown." Viktoriya Petrovla, that's my name."

Charlie was massaging his shoulder. "Christ, you pack a pretty good punch for a girl. Is that your real name?"

"It is for now. Are you okay?"

"Fine – just anxious to get out of here. How about you? Did you finally dry out?"

"Yes, I'm well. But we are in danger. We've got to get out of here!" The urgency in her whispered voice was unmistakable.

"Say, what's with these guys? I thought we're supposed to be best buds now, with the Soviets."

"Russians – that's what they call themselves now. The Soviets have been gone since the early nineties."

"Yeah, them too. This Filitov character. Just who is he?"

"By title, he'd be about the main Militia man in this area – that would be police – like local police, except they use a national system here, its all like one big police force."

"Got it. Okay, wouldn't he have some jurisdictional problems with us showing up like we did? I mean – why aren't we dealing with their State Department or KGB?"

She looked at him with a look of exasperation. "Look – here it's called the Foreign Ministry and the KGB has also been gone since the nineties. Don't you rich guys ever read a newspaper?"

"Nah – waste of time. I've got people to do that for me." He radiated a ten kilowatt smile at her.

She just rolled her eyes in response.

He got serious. "Vika, you know, they just put us together, to get us to talk, and see what more they could find out." He pointed to the ceiling.

She nodded. Dropping to soft whisper, she said, "We need to figure out a way to get out of here. Now!"

Charlie started to open his mouth. There was a loud knock on the door. They turned abruptly and faced the door. Vika turned off the running water. Charlie sang out. "Come in."

The door opened. It was immediately filled with the unsmiling form of the chunky matron. This time she addressed them in stilted English. "You will please to come with me."

Vika and Charlie looked at one another and followed.

Chapter 70
Hong Kong, China

Like a white arrow, the Gulf Stream streaked smartly into the midday air from Fukue Jima. Minutes before, Mateo had talked with Sullivan via sat phone. Ringing off, he brought the Gulf Stream to a flawless landing on the private airfield. The one and only airport on Fukue Jima was not exactly overwhelmed with air traffic. There were no scheduled airline flights. A few charters, some cargo and the occasional private aircraft made up the twenty or so landings and takeoffs that occurred each day.

Sullivan stood, waiting near a hangar at the north end of the field. Mateo taxied the aircraft to a stop, set the brakes, and cut the engines back to idle. He unbuckled and moved to the fuselage door. It opened, and the electric staircase extended. Before the stairs hit the tarmac, Mateo returned to the cockpit and buckled back in.

Sullivan jumped aboard, hit the stairway retraction switch and closed the door. Mateo had the aircraft rolling for a takeoff position before Mike got settled into the right seat.

"Good to see you, Ferdie. You made record time." Sullivan said adjusting his headset and boom mike.

Mateo's eyes were following Sullivan's dyed black hair and facial injuries as he moved across the cockpit and settled into the copilot seat. "Nice to see you as well, Mister Sullivan. You look a little... ah..."

"Scary? Is that the word that comes to mind?" Mike said smiling.

"No, sir. Just... different." Changing the subject he said. "What's our destination?"

"Ferdie, you're too polite. I know I look like hell. You might say it's been kind of a rough week!"

Sullivan studied the older man who was the Chief Pilot for Gomez Transport International. Mike judged him to be about sixty. The short Hispanic man was fit and built solid as a rock. His head sprouted a full mane of iron-grey hair. The eyes were the interesting part, steely small and such a dark shade of brown, they were almost black.

Looking into Ferdinand Mateo's eyes Sullivan recognized considerably more than the GTI pilot he had met before. He saw things in that lined face that casual observers would overlook. Mateo was a man that had flown aircraft all of his life. A heavily decorated combat pilot, Mateo looked like the sort of fellow that had dealt out way more than his share of death and destruction. "We're going to Hong Kong." Sullivan said. "The Kowloon side – the old airport. We've got some shopping to do."

"I know it well." Mateo smiled as he reached for the controls of the trip computer. He punched in some data and turned back to Sullivan. "We'll be a little more than four hours at normal cruising speed. Is that good enough? I can burn us in a bit faster, if need be."

"Four hours will be perfect. Say - show me again - which of these controls patches my headset to the airplane's sat phone. As soon as we get airborne, I'm going to make a few calls and then, if you don't mind, I've got to get some shuteye."

삼 질식시킴

The shiny mane of long hair washed across her back. Crystal clear water lapped over them. She lay playfully face down in the shallow surf. The top of her bikini was gone and she sat upright, still averting her face, her hands covering her breasts. He reached for her. She moved away and laughed. She had the most delightful laugh. It started low and ranged over a full octave ending with a high staccato finish. He reached for her again – called out her name – "Claire." Slowly she stood up in the surf line, unfolding the long tan limbs. She turned to face him. A shower of diamond-like water drops cascaded from her hair. He looked into her face. A blur – perhaps caused by the water – fogging his vision. He rubbed his eyes and blinked. Her face cleared. It wasn't Claire! It was Audrey.

"Mister Sullivan..." Mateo's tinny voice over the cabin intercom shattered the moment and roused him from the unsettling dream.

Mike sat bolt upright. He checked his watch. They'd been in the air close to four hours.

Mateo's voice came again. "Sorry to wake you, Mister Sullivan. But you wanted to know when we were about twenty minutes out from landing."

Mike slipped out of the recliner and entered the cockpit. Yawning, he slid into the right seat and clipped on the headset.

"As you requested, I asked to be vectored into Kowloon, but the courteous Air Traffic Controller from the Peoples Republic has 'directed' us to land at HKG, that's Hong Kong International. That's their new airport on the west side – Lautau Island. No problem – I think – they probably just want to get their landing fees and exercise their customs prerogatives."

"Crap!" Mike glanced at his watch. "Now we'll burn up more time. The place I have to go is up the hill on the Kowloon side."

"Maybe because we're small and a private aircraft, they'll let us reposition after we go through their entry drills." Mateo offered.

"What's the landing fee to bring the Gulf Stream into a place like HKG?"

"It's usually about five hundred dollars, US." Mateo replied.

"Okay. Fold a grand into your passport and plane registration documents. If it looks like repositioning is a possibility, pose the question when we go through customs clearance."

Mateo glanced at Sullivan. "A little mordita. Good idea, it just might grease the skids." He used the Spanish word for "little bite", a commonly used slang term for a bribe.

"Did you get that digital camera?" Mike asked.

"Yes sir. Right in here." He tapped a black leather flight bag between the seats.

"Great. I'll need to take a couple of mug shots of you as soon as we land."

"Certainly… Make sure you get my good side." There was a lull in their conversation. Mateo seized the moment. "Excuse me, Mister Sullivan." His hesitant tone suggested he feared that he may be overstepping. "Can you tell me what – or rather – who – you are – I mean what name is on your passport – just so I'll know - when we land.?"

Mike chuckled. "Why Ferdie…" He held up the dark blue USA passport with the gold eagle embossed on the front. He flipped it open and flashed his photo, red hair and all. "It's me, Mike Sullivan. Who else on Earth would I be?"

Mateo simply smiled. "Very good, Sir. You'll excuse me now. I have to start my landing procedure."

삼 질식시킴

It was evening. It had taken the better part of two hours for Mateo and Sullivan to get through all of the bureaucracy associated with their entry into Hong Kong. When they were finally clear, Sullivan divvied up his list of errands between them. Mateo's request to move the Gulf to Kowloon had been politely denied.

No matter, thought Sullivan. He would get what they needed taken care of and hopefully, they would be back in the air before sunrise – late morning at max.

Mateo's tasks had more to do with the aircraft. He made arrangements to have the fuel tanks topped off, and filed a typical tourist flight plan that included stops in Bangkok and Singapore when they left Hong Kong.

From the airport, Sullivan took the new high speed train that followed the North Lautau highway, crossed the channel to the mainland and ended up in the New Territories.

His first destination was the tailor shop. One of his calls from the Gulf Stream had been placed to a tiny shop on the 9th floor of an old building in the Tai Po district. Years before, in what seemed like another lifetime, he had regularly purchased suits, shirts and other clothing items from the elderly couple that owned the shop. Although much time had passed, they remembered him and were pleased to rush some items, to make them from measurements they had on file.

Mike emerged from the changing room, slipping the suit coat up and over his head, almost like pulling on a sweater. He admired his new look. The suit was elegant, a dark blue wool serge with a fine, almost microscopic pinstripe running through the expensive fabric. The ensemble was set off by a perfect white linen shirt with roll collar and French cuffs.

He smiled. The look was a perfect Savile Row knock-off, right down to the accessories and shoes. A red and blue silk club tie knotted in a perfect Windsor knot completed the outfit.

The old man chuckled, his approval evident, as Mike checked out his reflection in the full-length mirror. Sullivan could easily pass for any one of a hundred well-to-do gentlemen who might be visiting Hong Kong, this time of year.

Mike thanked the old couple and paid them several thousand dollars for their trouble. As to the remaining items he bought from them, Mike asked that they be sent by immediate messenger to the Hong Kong Airport parcel service.

From there, he took a series of three taxi cabs, working his way steadily back to the foothills above Kowloon City. The taxi hopping was probably unnecessary, but old habits of the craft die hard. At about eight o'clock he walked into the bar of the King Lam Estate Hotel.

For fifty years, the small but elegant King Lam, from its position at the top of Taipei Road, had dominated the Hong Kong skyline. It was one of the better places, not well known to tourists, a place more preferred by discriminating locals. He was gratified to see that it had not changed much since the hand over of Hong Kong to the Chinese from the British.

As he strolled into the bar, he passed the private alcoves that windowed a majestic southern view into the evening sky. The barman appeared. Mike ordered a rare, single malt whiskey, neat, and turned away to gaze at the twinkling lights of Hong Kong Harbor below.

From the lofty perspective of the King Lam, Sullivan looked upon one of the most densely populated places on earth. Hong Kong was truly the merchandising capital of Asia. It was a shoppers Mecca. True to form, he was here shopping, as well. In his case, he was seeking items that would surely take him and Mateo further into harms way. He hoped not too far.

The bartender, a spectacled, slender graying Chinese man with an impeccable British accent, returned. He placed a heavy bottomed lead crystal glass half filled with clear amber fluid on a crisp white napkin. Mike hefted the glass, feeling the weight of it. He brought the liquid to his nose and let the aroma fill his nostrils. Slowly, he took a sip and momentarily closed his eyes as the warm liquor delightfully flowed over his palate. Commies or no commies, he thought. This scotch is absolutely wonderful!

He put the glass down on the bar. The bartender, his face a mask of indifference, stood directly in front of Mike, more or less at attention, waiting for his assessment.

Sullivan placed a crisp US one hundred dollar bill on the bar and gently pushed it towards the man. Sullivan looked at the bartender and said. "I'm looking for a friend, Oliver Hung. Perhaps, you could you tell me if he has been in this evening?"

The bartender's fingers flashed over the bill. The note simply disappeared. He leaned forward and spoke in conspiratorial tones. "And who may I say is asking for Mister Hung?"

Sullivan crossed his fingers and gave him an answer. It was a name from the old days. He watched as the barman moved to the other end and spoke quiet Chinese into an old black telephone instrument.

Within seconds, the barman returned. "Please be seated over there." He pointed to one of the vacant window alcoves. "Mr. Hung will see you presently."

Sullivan made a show of relaxing with his drink in an elegant upholstered leather chair that looked more like it belonged in an English gentlemen's club. In reality, he was thoroughly pumped up, adrenaline flowing, ready for anything.

Sullivan had no idea what the response would be to his "Oliver Hung" request. His comfortable seat afforded a view of the main entrance as well as another door, off to the side of the bar which he suspected went to private rooms – somewhere.

Sullivan was seeking a credential maker – a forger of official documents. They existed everywhere – but most of them produced crap. Many documents from the underworld appear to be official, but in the age of magnetic coding and instant electronic information, even the very best forgeries were garbage if they didn't tie to some electronic data base for verification.

Mike glanced at his watch. Fifteen minutes had passed since the barman's telephone call. He controlled his breathing and tried his best to appear nonchalant.

The arriving man was shaped like a doughy ball rolling along on stubby legs. He was Caucasian, short, grossly fat, mid-fifties or so, with thin wisps of mousy brown hair plastered across his mostly bald pate. He wore a wrinkled grey suit with an open collar dress shirt that had, once-upon-a-time, been white. His striped tie was knotted low and hung like two limp rags over his well rounded front. As he walked, he patted the perspiration on his face with a soiled handkerchief. Entering the lounge, he looked at the barman whose only response was to incline his head ever-so-slightly toward Sullivan, and nod almost imperceptibly.

The man approached. Sullivan stood, towering over him. Quietly, Sullivan said. "Mr. Hung, I presume?"

Chapter 71
Tustin, California

It was a few minutes after three in the afternoon as Ichiro walked the grounds of the Tustin Gardens Condos. As he moved between the buildings and the neatly landscaped common areas, he congratulated himself on the time of day he had chosen for this venture. It was afternoon, late enough that there was hardly anyone about, but not yet time for most working folks to come home. He was taking advantage of a perfectly placed activity lull that he had carefully observed in previous days.

Today, he sported a different look. It sprang from a combination of things, clothes, accessories and demeanor, all dimensions he knew to be critical for a disguise. Outfitted in a casual pair of worn sneakers, oversized blue jeans, a cheap dark windbreaker jacket, and toting a small backpack, he looked like any one of a thousand students or young working men. A few more subtleties helped to craft his new appearance. As he walked, he bent his knees and hunched over a bit. The overall effect was to reduce his imposing size. He wore a pair of silver rimmed circular eyeglasses which added an owlish hint of nerdy.

The effect was close to perfect. To the casual observer, Ichiro's appearance was so common that he was virtually guaranteed to be ignored by one and all.

As he moved along the walkways, he cradled the small puppy in the crook of his arm.

Stopping next to the front door of a first floor unit, Ichiro looked around. He was standing directly across the common area from Greer's place. Satisfied that no one was watching, he turned to face the door. He knew that this home was occupied by Mrs. Alma Parish, the elderly widow who spent most of her time tending to her potted flowers. Her passion was fuchsias. She had them everywhere.

Fuchsia laden pots guarded the front door. More lined and spilled out of the tiny fenced patio just outside her unit. Ichiro stole a quick glance over the fence. He turned back, amusement on his face. What he saw was an impenetrable mass of potted fuchsias, hundreds of

them. The plants virtually filling the entire postage stamp size patio.
The colorful plants were everywhere, hanging, on shelves, on low
tables and stands. Pink fuchsias covered the entire surface of the small
concrete slab.

He noted that Greer's place, across the courtyard, had a similar
patio. But in their case, with the home being a second story unit, it
was an elevated balcony of similar size.

Still standing in the doorway, he listened for moment, and then
softly knocked on the door. He stood directly in front of the peephole,
smiling and holding the puppy up close to his face. He waited.

When she came to the door, the shadow of her head
momentarily blocked the backlighting from the peephole. Ichiro
caught the brief, but unmistakable shift in light. He continued to hold
up the puppy and grin. There was the sound of the deadbolt latch
unlocking and the door opened to a hesitant six inches.

Peering through was the white haired Alma Parish. She stood
barely five feet, was wearing a flowered print dress, a grey cardigan
sweater with white socks and light blue sneakers. In one hand she held
a wad of Kleenex tissues and in the other, a pair of plastic rimmed
eyeglasses. She squinted at Ichiro and the puppy and furiously
scoured at the lenses of the eyeglasses.

"Oh my, what have we here?" Said Mrs. Parish as she
threaded the glasses through the tight white curls over her ears and
strained for a clear look at her visitors.

"Hi - Mrs. Parish. Remember me ? I'm Ben Channing... I
live on the other side of the complex..." Ichiro waved an arm behind
him.

The glasses bounced up and down as she wrinkled her nose,
trying to force her powers of recall.

The blank look testified to her lack of recognition. He plunged
on. "Listen – I was just coming home and found this little guy
wandering around – obviously lost..."

"Ben... Ben – who - did you say?"

"It's me - Ben Channing? We're neighbors. We've talked
before – over at the..." He waited for her to fill something in. She
did.

"Over at the homeowners association meetings?" Mrs. Parish
offered.

"Yes, that's right - Ben."

"Oh... Yes, of course, Ben! How are you?"

"Fine... I'm Fine, thank you. I've just found this..." He hefted the puppy directly in her face.

"Oh my – what a darling little dog!" Mrs. Parish pushed the door wide open, and reached out to scratch some tan curls around the pup's ears.

"I found this little guy wandering around and I thought I would try and see if anyone knew..." Ichiro glanced around to make certain there was no one else in visual or hearing distance. Mrs. Parish, like many her age, had a tendency to speak too loud. "Who he might belong to."

Alma Parish splayed fingers across her open mouth, trying to recall. "I don't think I've ever seen..."

Ichiro interrupted her. "You know, Mrs. Parish, I really think this little fellow needs a drink. I've been walking around for quite a while now. He's acting awfully thirsty – keeps licking everything." On cue, the pup's pink tongue appeared. "You suppose you could give me a little water for him?"

Without hesitation she nodded, then reached out and took the tiny body from Ichiro's outstretched hands. She turned and walked deep into her condo leaving Ichiro standing by the now open door. He quietly stepped inside.

Glancing behind to ensure that there was no one else about, he softly closed the door. The door latch clicked and he spun the deadbolt lever. Turning, he was momentarily surprised by the condition of Mrs. Parish's home. He had never seen anything quite like it.

What he saw was clutter and junk everywhere. Never had he seen such a collection. It looked to him as if the old woman had saved every item that had come into her possession in her eighty some odd years of life. The small home was literally stacked, floor to ceiling, with all manner of stuff, including empty food containers, old mail, newspapers, cans, jars, bottles, old appliances, boxes, and hundreds of empty medicine containers.

Every flat surface, countertop, tabletop, cabinets and furniture tops and most of the floor were completely covered with litter and debris.

Recovering his wits, he followed the path of Alma Parish through the warrens of clutter. He headed toward the small kitchen and the sound of running water.

As he silently approached, she stood at the sink, her back to Ichiro. So engrossed, she was oblivious to everything except the pup and the tap water flowing into a small bowl. She clucked and cooed at the little dog. At first, she tried to get the tiny animal to drink while she held it against her chest. When that didn't work, she set the bowl onto the floor and bent slowly and laboriously to place the puppy onto the linoleum. The dog showed no interest in the water. He kept trying to wander off. Mrs. Parish repeatedly pulled the critter back and repositioned him in front of the bowl.

Ichiro closed with Mrs. Parish. The distraction of her clutter was almost unbelievable. He had to, repeatedly, force his focus back to the old lady. Narrow pathways, in most cases only a foot wide, like man-made canyons of debris, meandered through the few rooms.

He stood behind her. She had just placed the puppy on the kitchen floor. With arthritic slowness, she pulled herself to an upright position and placed her hand on her hips. "Lands sakes – I don't think this little fellow is gonna…"

Ichiro struck. He seized her from behind. He clamped his left hand over her nose and mouth. With the weight of his body, he pinned her against the kitchen counter. Alma Parish struggled pitifully and quietly. The strong hand smothered her. She was completely immobilized, unable to draw breath or utter the slightest sound. Ichiro brought his right hand up and dug his fingers into her throat. His hands were so strong, the span between thumb and fingers so big, he was able to flatten the soft tissue of her neck and clamp down on the cervical vertebrae.

A sneer formed on his lips. He took a short breath and held it. His eyes narrowed and looked straight ahead to some unseen place. With a vicious twist, he snapped her head to the left. The crack of neck bone sounded like the slap of a wood board on a table top. Ichiro, with fingers deep into her flesh, actually felt the vertebrae snap.

The sneer turned to a smile. Like milk spilling from a crushed carton, the life of Alma Parish gushed away. He held her limp body against the kitchen counter. A full minute passed; he finally exhaled. He released his grip and stepped back. Her body crumpled to the floor.

Chapter 72
Hong Kong, China

The Gulf Stream streaked across clear black sky. At 28,000 feet the forward view was a solid canvas of blue cobalt sprinkled with a billion stars.

Mateo and Sullivan left Hong Kong Airport at about four in the morning on their declared flight plan, enroute to Bangkok. Once in the air, and a couple hundred miles out bound, Mateo made the standard turn to the south to avoid flying over the restricted airspace of the Chinese Naval installation on Hainan Island. Clearing the giant island that bordered mainland China to the north and the Gulf of Tonkin to the west, the aircraft should have made a following turn back to the west to continue towards its declared destination.

Instead, Mateo switched off the aircraft's transponder and put it into a gentle descent. Anticipating someone to notice the deviation from their published flight plan, they monitored all of the standard aviation frequencies, prepared to deliver a bogus story about mechanical problems. Perhaps, not a surprise for this part of the world, the need never arose. It was as if no one saw them or no one cared. At a point, about two hundred miles south of Hainan, Mateo gently turned the jet back towards the eastern horizon. Slightly less than seven hundred miles ahead lay the Philippine Islands, their next destination.

Sullivan refolded the chart and studied it intently. "So you've been to this place - Aparri - before?"

Mateo glanced at Sullivan. The night lighting in the cabin cast an strange soft orange glow over is face. Despite the dampened lighting, Mike could clearly make out the twinkle in Mateo's eyes.

Grinning, he answered. "Many times, Mister Sullivan – in fact, more times than I can possibly remember." He was quiet for a moment, thinking - remembering. "During the Vietnam war, we had bases all over the Philippines - big ones, little ones, you name it. Aparri was one of the small ones, but strategically important because it was the northern most airfield in the P.I. Have you ever been to the Philippines, Mister Sullivan?"

"Yeah, but, a long time ago. It was just a quick trip – a stop really - in and out of Manila – didn't really see much."

"The northern part is mountainous and kind of cut off from the rest of the major population centers to the south. Aparri is this little coastal town, small population, some farming, fishing and the usual. Nice people, from what I recall. At any given time, there's a certain number of banditos and leftist guerillas operating in the mountains nearby, but I don't expect we'll have any problems for our quick stop over."

Mike watched the older man for few moments. "You're really enjoying this – aren't you?"

Mateo didn't answer right away. After a few seconds, he spoke. "Let me put it to you this way. It's kind of like being a highly trained, prize thoroughbred, the one that always wins, always runs circles around all the other horses. Then one day - right in your prime – you get parked in the barn and used only for the occasional Sunday afternoon ride. Know what I mean?"

Mike listened thoughtfully. "Yeah, I think I do."

"Don't get me wrong. I've got the world's greatest job. There's nothing I'd rather do than fly – and my affiliation with the Gomez family has been a godsend to me and my addiction to air speed and altitude." Mateo laughed. "Where else could an old fart like me get to fly his choice of modern aircraft? Then along comes you and Mister Charlie, and your – ah – activities of late…" His grin got a bit wider. "Well, for me, it's like getting the old horse back into the harness. If you get my drift?"

Mike leaned back in his seat for a moment. "Ferdie, I do get it. On so many levels – boy – do I know what you mean." Mike waved the navigation chart, changing the subject. "Now, just where is this Aparri place we're going? It sounds Italian."

Mateo laughed. "Here, take a look at this." His fingers danced over the touch screen of the navigation system. The color display zoomed and showed the outline of Luzon, with a grouping of islands to the north. "The islands are called the Babuyans. Aparri is right there, on the tip of the peninsula."

Mike looked at the blinking yellow spot on the map.

Mateo continued his travel log. "The airfield was a gift from the U.S. Navy during World War II. We overhauled it during the 60's and 70's. It's not as well maintained since they kicked the U.S. military out a few years back, but they've managed to keep it functional, with most services. Now-a-days, it's just mostly used for local traffic and some tourist operations."

Mike nodded.

Mateo touched the screen again and different information was displayed. "It looks like they're reporting 28 degrees - that's centigrade by the way - partly cloudy, 83 percent humidity with current winds 4 miles per hour from the east. Sounds like just another perfect morning in the Philippines!"

삼 질식시킴

They had been on the ground at Aparri for two hours. While Mateo dealt with fuel and other issues, Sullivan found a ladder and propped it where he could examine the aircraft's tail. Not that anyone cared, his activities looked just like standard aircraft maintenance work. What he was really doing was carefully applying vinyl decals to the tail and fuselage. The decals were made of a special high tensile material, and were affixed with an adhesive that would withstand the punishing air currents of five hundred mile per hour jet flight.

Mike carefully applied the first decal over the American flag on the Gulf Stream's vertical stabilizer. The red white and blue colors were nearly the same as the stars and stripes it covered up, but there were only three wide bands of color, for the flag of the Russian Federation.

Finishing, Mike stood along side the aircraft to admire his work.

Mateo emerged from the interior and came around to stand next to him. The both inspected their plane's new look. "I'm just finished inside. How're you doing?"

"Whaddaya think?" Sullivan asked with palms outstretched towards the tail.

Mateo nodded approvingly. "I think we look just like a Russian Gulf Stream Jet." His gaze moved up the fuselage and stopped at the open doorway. There, on the inside of the door panel, now visible with the door propped open, and gleaming in the sunlight, was the gold on crimson insignia. "Ah-hah! Nice touch!"

"Yeah, I thought you'd like that one. I wasn't sure where to put it – on the plane, I mean - but I figured people will see it when we get on and off the aircraft."

"And that is the insignia of…"

"That, my friend, is the coat of arms of the Russian Federation, the golden double headed eagle with wings outstretched on a red shield. It was their state symbol – from the fifteenth century through the Marxist revolution, I think. They recently revived it when they started calling themselves Russia once again."

"Really? Just how many years do you think we're going to get for all this?"

Sullivan smiled. He clapped Mateo on the shoulder. "Look at it this way, Ferdie. Either our little plan works or it doesn't. If it works, everyone's happy. If not, you and I might catch a bullet in the head or maybe we'll be chipping ice in Siberia."

They moved back into the aircraft. Mateo took the steps first. "That's one of the things I like about you, Mister Sullivan. It's your optimism."

Mike followed. "That's true. I'm very much a glass half full kinda guy. And don't you think it's time you stopped calling me 'Mister Sullivan'? I mean, you and me, we could be cell mates for the rest of time."

Mateo waited to respond until Mike cleared the doorway before retracting the staircase and closing the cabin door. "Why – under the circumstances – I suppose I should. Thank you, Mister Sullivan."

삼 질식시킴

Five and a half hours later they touched down at Sapporo Airport in Japan. The plan, from this point, was straightforward and simple. They prepared themselves - food, fuel and bathrooms. They checked the Gulf Stream and made certain the craft was ready for the next flight. On the flight up to Sapporo, they had taken turns at the controls, enabling both to catch a few winks during the near six hour flight from the Philippines. Both were sufficiently refreshed and keyed up and ready for the next round.

Before takeoff, the last thing they did was to change into the articles of clothing they had picked up in Hong Kong. Mateo's outfit was pure Russian Bureaucrat. The tailors had produced an ill fitting suit constructed of dingy fabric. His shirt, shoes and other accessories were old, worn and looked to be typical Russian. Mateo looked perfect for his part of the low level Russian civil servant.

Sullivan knew that for his role, he would have to exemplify the other end of the spectrum. He changed back into the elegant suit of Hong Kong clothes.

It was now early evening. Although Vladivostok was less than two hours flight time from Sapporo, the plan for departure included a northern flight towards the long slender island of Sakhalin. Mateo obtained radio clearance and taxied the Gulf Stream out for take off.

Once airborne and well clear of Sapporo controlled airspace, Mateo dropped the aircraft to three hundred feet above the water and streaked towards the Tartar Straight, a body of ocean that lay between Sakhalin and the eastern Russian mainland.

Sullivan fingered the controls on an electronic module that was connected to the instrument panel by a bundle of colored wires. The labels on the switches and indicators were in Cyrillic characters – Russian. "Are you certain you've got this thing installed the right way?"

Mateo glanced at him. "Well, I couldn't exactly give it a live power test. But, yes, it's ready to go and should do its thing."

"Let me know when your ready."

"Roger that." Mateo quickly scanned his instruments and checked their position on the navigation display. He pulled the yoke back and brought the jet to twelve thousand feet. Leveling off, he turned to Sullivan. "Ready, now."

Sullivan reached over and dialed a frequency into the communications radio. It was the channel for the Russian Air Force Eastern air control, the people who made the life and death decisions about who could and who could not fly within Russian air space. He flicked another switch, this one on the outboard electronics box. He checked the display. "We are on and transmitting Russian I.D."

Mateo nodded. "Now would be a good time to talk to them."

The tension in the cockpit almost made the air crackle. Mike leaned forward in his seat and keyed the radio transmitter. In perfect Russian he said. "Eastern military control, this is Gulf Stream CV107 inbound from Tokyo to Khabarovsk – we have a problem." He was doing his best to sound like a bored, or perhaps cool in the face of danger Russian Air Force pilot. He had no idea how he would come across.

After an interminable delay, the voice of the Russian air traffic controller responded. "Gulf Stream CV107 – repeat transmission."

Before Sullivan could respond, Mateo got his attention and pointed to another display. "We're being painted by their radar and the transponder is identifying us."

"I just hope the code we're using is the correct one."

Mateo muttered just before Sullivan started in on another voice transmission in Russian. "Hope the Ruskies read us as comrade diplomats and not KAL 008!"

Mike continued in Russian. "Eastern military control, this is Gulf Stream CV107. We are inbound from Tokyo to Khabarovsk – we have a mechanical problem and require landing clearance at Yuzhno-Sakalinsk."

There was another short delay. Finally the controller responded. "CV107 – we have you at 360. I have no information on your flight. Confirming - you are a Russian Federation Diplomatic Service flight?"

Sullivan quickly flashed a thumbs up sign to Mateo. His voice thick with feigned arrogance he keyed the radio. "That is correct. Now that you have our identification, please clear us for immediate landing."

"CV107 – you are cleared for approach and landing at Yuzhno. Turn to 017 and maintain altitude."

"CV107, acknowledged." Sullivan turned to Mateo and smiled.

"It sounds like they're actually buying this load of crap." Mateo said.

"It's a good ruse. It's a little too late for anybody to be calling around asking questions. Russians are hesitant to do that anyway. It's the result of generation after generation being pounded down – fearing to question authority."

"Guess we know the transponder box is working." Mateo patted the gizmo between their seats."

"So far, so good. Ready for round two?"

Mateo grinned and nodded. "Anytime, Mister Sullivan, anytime."

Mike keyed the radio. "Eastern military control, Gulf Stream CV107."

The controller acknowledged.

Sullivan continued. "Our ХОЗЯИН" - He used the Russian word for boss, indicating the senior official on board the aircraft. "– has directed us to proceed to Vladivostok for repairs."

"CV107 – acknowledged. Are you certain you can make that distance?"

Mike waited a few seconds before making his reply. He notched up the arrogance level for his response. "Eastern Control – I am the command pilot and yes, I believe we can safely make it to Vladivostok!"

"Yes, Sir." Replied the harried controller. "You are cleared to proceed. Contact on this frequency if you require further assistance."

"CV107 – understood."

Chapter 73
Vladivostok, Russia

Lieutenant Pavel Grovotny was the evening shift commander of the Federation Border Guards stationed at Vladivostok International Airport. Known in the aviation community as VVO, the airport was formerly known as Kievichi Aiport, named after Khutor Kievichi, a century's old phrase that loosely translates to "Kievichi's homestead or settlement". Lieutenant Grovotny, a Ukranian by birthright and rearing, didn't know the history of this frontier assignment place and most likely did not care. What he did care about was that whoever it was that just landed at the International Terminal at this late night hour must be some kind of big shot because his men were hollering to high heaven for his immediate presence.

Grovotny was not used to being summoned away from his television set and the bottle of vodka he discretely kept hidden in his desk. Well, he sighed as he buttoned up his uniform tunic, the unending reruns of soccer games and pathetic Russian soap operas would have to wait. He seldom had the occasion to exercise his official capacity, and whatever was going on would at least break the monotony of yet another boring twenty-four hour shift.

Grovotny swished some cold rank tea around his mouth. He spat it out and glanced at himself in the small mirror. He smoothed down his hair and breathed into his hand. Satisfied that he had not consumed that much vodka this night, he moved outside to his battered Air Force issue, an ancient Vaz Zhiguli sedan, and prayed that the old machine would start.

The starter motor made hesitant metal grinding sounds and finally coaxed the engine to life. He jammed the shifter into gear and drove the short distance from the Border Guard offices to the International Terminal.

Enroute, Grovotny gave himself a quick pep talk. He was Pavel Grovotny, full Lieutenant of the Border Troops of the Committee for State Security. Well, they really weren't called that any longer. That was the old name, when the KGB, still ran the show. He corrected his mental wanderings.

Lieutenant Grovotny had been posted into the KGB Border Guards in 1993, a time in history where the winds of change were already blowing hard against the struggling embers of communism. Perestroika and Glasnost were terms that rolled off the tongues of the meek and powerful alike. A short one year later, Comrade Chairman Gorbachev signed the decree that eliminated the KGB, forever.

The Border Guards had been relegated to the Army, their fortunes and once elite status had plummeted. Once feared by virtually everyone inside the Soviet Union, the KGB and its myriad Directorates has been fractured into dozens of new departments within the new Russian Federation Government. Grovotny himself had lost all opportunity for significant advancement. While he longed for the old days, he knew in his heart he was lucky to have a job that produced a meager paycheck each month. He could still hear his mother's words ringing in the recesses of his memory. "Count your blessings, Pavel. Learn to be a good Communist soldier. Your reward will come."

He stopped his truck near the Border Guards office and dismounted. He took a breath, straightened his tunic over ample belly and strode into the office. Inside he was greeted by a sweating and visibly shaken Corporal Rudinov. The twenty three year old enlisted man was the ranking member of the Border Guards assigned for the night shift at the International terminal. It was not an uncommon occurrence to use such an inexperienced person for such an assignment. There were no flights scheduled to arrive until mid-day tomorrow. Rudinov's duties involved mostly standing around and looking important.

Grovotny inquired as to the reason for his late night summons. The young and emotionally raw Rudinov was having difficulty getting the story out. The young soldier had a stuttering problem that was exacerbated by stress. Presently, he was in such a state that he could barely talk. It took a few minutes, but Grovotny finally got the story. There had been an unscheduled landing of a Federation Diplomatic Jet, vectored in from Sakhalin. The flight had all the official clearances, and landed with the declared intent of seeking mechanical repairs. Once on the ground, this official, believed to be an important Moscow man, was insisting that the ranking officer of the Guards be summoned immediately.

"Alright, alright, Rudinov. For God's sake, calm yourself down."

"Y-y-yes, Comrade Lieutenant." Rudinov used the prefix term of the old days. He wasn't supposed to, but he did so to mollify his Lieutenant, who he knew was still living in the glory age of the former Soviet Union.

"Yes, yes. What else did he say?"

"N-n-n-nothing Comrade Lieutenant – n-n-nothing. He just got off the plane and insisted that you be s-s-summoned immediately. He said he was on a diplomatic mission and that absolute secrecy was to be enforced."

"Diplomatic? Secrecy? Is that what you said – diplomatic?"

"Yes, Comrade Lieutenant, did I not mention? The man has Diplomatic credentials."

Grovotny felt his anal sphincter pucker as that piece of information was processed in his mind. He knew that many times high ranking intelligence types like SVR agents would travel with Diplomatic credentials. Perhaps this man was Foreign Intelligence Service.

"I see. What is this visitor's name?"

"I-I-I'm sorry Comrade Lieutenant. I do not k-k-know. He would not t-t-tell me."

Grovotny muttered under his breath. "Idiot." His mind was racing. No matter. If this was legitimate, whatever name was given would be bogus – just a cover name. "Corporal!"

"Yes, Comrade Lieutenant."

"Who else knows of this visitor? Who else has knowledge that the plane has arrived or has interacted with this Moscow man or his party?"

The young man stammered some more. "Why, no one, Comrade Lieutenant. I called only you – and did so immediately."

Grovotny grunted and nodded.

"And – and - I have only seen one other man come out of the airplane. He was dressed in a dark suit, but he looks mean and military. He stays with plane – ordered to stay with it – I think."

Probably Spetsnaz or KGB muscle, Grovotny thought to himself. He briefly wondered if they were here to whack someone or to otherwise make some poor soul disappear. He liked to use the American mafia terms such as "whack".

Licking his lips, he quickly decided that this may be his moment, his golden opportunity. He could demonstrate his worth by helping this Moscow man, and in turn maybe get the recognition that he needed to get out of this armpit of the Russian Motherland. He rubbed his hands together in anticipation.

"Rudinov!" He barked.

"Yes, Comrade Lieutenant!"

"You are ordered to tell no one about these visitors. Got it?"

"Yes, Comrade Lieutenant!"

"How many men are on duty with you at the terminal tonight?"

"Only me and one other - Private Chenkov."

"Okay. I want you and Chenkov to seal your lips about this entire event. I want one of you – no, make that both of you - to get down to that plane and stand by with the other man, the guard. Don't talk to him - the guard, I mean. Not Chenkov. Wait, if he asks - I mean the guard - tell him you are ordered to stand watch over their aircraft. Understood?"

Despite the confusion that wandered all over the young man's face his response was, "Yes, Comrade Lieutenant. I understand."

"Good! Now get to it! Wait. Before you go – show me where this Moscow man is."

Rudinov pointed at a set of double doors. "Through there, Comrade Lieutenant. He waits for you in the VIP Lounge."

Grovotny moved toward the doors. He stopped, turned back to the still vibrating Corporal Rudinov. "And one more thing."

"Yes, Comrade Lieutenant!"

"No one is to get near that aircraft. Especially no Army, Air Force or Militia pigs! Got it!"

"Yes, Comrade Lieutenant! I understand your orders."

"Good." Grovotny smoothed his hair one more time and swaggered through the doors.

삼 질식시킴

Sullivan glanced at his watch and shifted position in the upholstered chair that he occupied in the terminal waiting room. He surmised that he had been parked in some kind of a special room for visitors with some rank or position. At least thus far, the ruse seemed to be working. The Russians, for all their rhetoric about equality and leveling the playing field, still ran one of the most class conscious societies in the world.

The remainder of their flight to Vladivostok had been uneventful. Mike used his Russian, speaking two more times with

Eastern Control before they were cleared for landing at VVO. Once on the ground, they were directed to proceed to a tired looking terminal building. He had since learned that this was the International Terminal. Not exactly JFK.

He'd left Mateo standing outside the Gulf Stream, looking like some character out of a bad gangster movie. The nervous Corporal of the Border Guards that came to meet the plane, looked as if he were about to pee his pants when Mike flashed his bogus Russian Federation Diplomatic credentials. The kid, had literally, turned grey and could not conclude their conversation fast enough. Mike had pulled the old bluff about demanding to see the ranking man and from the commotion he was hearing from the adjacent room, something was about to happen.

Sullivan took a breath, composed himself and tried to look irritated and bored. He looked around the room. The furnishings were sparse but decent. There was a coffee and tea bar, although it was not in service at this time of night. There were a few paintings on the walls and some travel posters that celebrated the attributes of vacation travel to North Korea, Cuba and a few other garden spots of the Third World.

He looked at his watch again. It was still set on Hong Kong time. He'd lost track of time zones. He reckoned it was about two in the morning, or so.

The double doors banged open and a short man wearing the uniform of the Border guards with the rank of full Lieutenant swaggered in. Sullivan decided to remain in his seat.

The Lieutenant walked to a point directly in front of Sullivan and stood at attention. Mike wasn't certain. But he believed the guy might have ever so slightly clicked his heels together.

Sullivan said nothing. Instead, he simply sat and stared straight into the face of the paunchy officer who he judged to be about middle forties, with either a severe case of rosacia or at least a red alcoholic nose.

An uncomfortable several seconds went by. Finally the Lieutenant spoke, still standing at his position of attention. "Sir, I understand that you are a Federation Diplomatic Officer and that you require assistance. I am Senior Lieutenant Pavel Grovotny, at your service. May I be told to whom I have the pleasure of addressing, Sir?"

Chapter 74
Vladivostok, Russia

Sullivan continued to sit in the presence of the Lieutenant of the Border Guards. It was as if he intuitively understood that this gesture of rudeness might slightly advantage him in this deadly game. Russian mentality was predictable and often easy to manipulate.

He forced his face to a state of utter blankness – a poker face - and continued to apprise the man who stood before him. The accent was definitely western. So he knew this guy wasn't from around here.

Mike knew that he was playing a dangerous game, one in which there was a fine balance between sufficient Russian arrogance and overkill. This whole caper was a ballsy affair. If, by some stroke of luck, it was to work, he would have to find the right crack in the Russian armor and whittle away at it.

Sullivan noticed that this Lieutenant's uniform still bore the green piping of the former KGB. Maybe that was a good sign. He'd heard how everything had gone downhill since the great changes in this country. Maybe this guy was still living in the past, and just maybe, he would be the crack that Mike needed.

He was banking on a lot, his bogus cover, their forged identity papers, his assumption that Charlie and Viktoriya would be somewhere in the immediate area, and that he could find them before the charade wore thin. Sullivan was confident in his own capabilities. He was no stranger to flying on the edge. But, in this instance, he knew he was dancing on the very edge of a precipitous cliff, and the ground beneath his feet was unstable as hell.

Sullivan stood. He towered over the Lieutenant. He glared down upon him. "Lieutenant." Sullivan's voiced dripped with aristocratic arrogance. I am Mikhail Bukolov." From an inside coat pocket, he withdrew two crimson colored credential cases. One was a diplomatic passport with the bold double headed eagle insignia embossed in gold leaf. The passport gleamed in the stark white overhead lighting of the lounge. The second case bore the insignia and gilt edging of the credentials of the SVR, the Russian Foreign

Intelligence Service. Sullivan purposely offered the passport, but withheld the second case.

Grovotny's reaction was predictable. His eyes widened slightly and nostrils flared upon seeing the credential cases. He gingerly accepted the passport and respectfully opened it. He went through the motions of turning the pages, examining Sullivan's photograph and thumbing through visa stamps. The artfully forged pages documented that this traveler had traveled extensively throughout the entire world, just in the past few months. *This fellow must be a very important Moscow man, indeed.* Grovotny thought. Finishing his cursory examination, he closed the booklet.

Sullivan snapped back the passport, and along with the SVR credential case, made them disappear into his jacket pocket. "Lieutenant, I am sorry to have inconvenienced you from your pressing late night duties..."

"Not at all, Minister. I-I-I..." Grovotny used the highest ranking title he could think of as he addressed the Moscow man. "I am here to assist you in any manner that I can." Grovotny decided to take a chance. He leaned forward. Dropping the tone of his voice to a confidential level he said to the taller man. "I am former KGB myself. You have but to say the word, and I shall make it happen for you."

Sullivan smiled inwardly but maintained his stoic façade. "Lieutenant! While I expect your cooperation, you will not use that tone nor utter such nonsense to me. Do you understand?"

Properly rebuked, Grovotny went back to rigid attention and began to vibrate ever so slightly. "Yes, Minister. I am so sorry..."

Mike cut him off. "Lieutenant, you will address me simply as Bukolov."

"Yes, Sir, Mister – ah - Bukolov." He nodded profusely.

It was Sullivan's turn to lean in; to turn to that tone of confidentiality. "Listen to me and listen carefully. I do not have the luxury of time to explain things over and over to you."

Grovotny continued to nod and to vibrate.

Sullivan continued. "I am here on a most secret and delicate – ah - diplomatic purpose. A short time ago, a man and a woman were plucked out of the ocean and brought into Vladivostok. As a Senior Lieutenant of the Border Guards, I am certain that you know of this incident?"

"Yes... er, ah, no."

"Damn it, man, which is it? Yes or no?"

"Sir, I know of the matter, but only in a minor way. I read a briefing report to that effect. I..."

"Briefing report – wonderful! I suppose you frontier peasants gossip about everything in this great bastion of social democracy."

"No, Sir. Our briefing reports are classified – they are only for officials of the Guards, so as to keep all the key personnel apprised..."

"Yes, yes. I understand your petty rules and procedures." Mike further leaned into the man, mimicking Grovotny's earlier tone of personal confidence. "These people are, shall we say, very important assets?"

Grovotny nodded.

"And I need to speak with them immediately. Do you know where they are?"

"Yes, Minister, ah, Bukolov. I understand they were taken to the medical facility at Primorsky Government Center. The, ah, Militia has jurisdiction over..."

Sullivan was surprised to hear that the local cops had them, as opposed to SVR or even the Border Guards. That fact alone could present more problems. "Yes, yes. I know all this. I need you to take me to them immediately. Do you have a car?"

"Yes, I do, but..."

"Lieutenant Grovotny. Listen to me. No one, and I mean no one, is to know that we are here, that you are assisting us, or to know any aspect of this..." Mike used the Russian word for military mission. He hoped to plant a further hint of ominous goings-on in the mind of the officer.

Color was returning to Grovotny's face. Mike sensed he was setting the hook in this guy – solidly. So, he decided to raise the bet. "Lieutenant, am I correct in assuming that you are not exactly happy with your posting here at Vladivostok?"

Grovotny sensed both peril and an opening. He carefully considered his answer. "Sir, I am happy to serve where ever my talents can do the most good for Mother Russia. This is, however, not the best assignment for a Kommitat officer." He purposely used one of the old regime words. It was another attempt to identify and portray himself as a KGB insider.

Sullivan picked up on the unmistakable opening. He planted a hand on the officer's shoulder. "Lieutenant... I wish you to know two things. First, at this moment, you are in a unique position to perform a great service for the Rodina. Second, I am in a position to assist you, greatly, in matters that have to do with your career. Am I making myself clear?"

"Yes, Comrade Bukolov, very clear."

삼 질식시킴

The ride from the Airport to the Government Center medical facility took only ten minutes. During the ride, Sullivan learned that Grovotny was single, and that his last remaining parent, his mother, had recently passed away. He had a sister, an unmarried school teacher, who lived in Berdyansk.

Arriving at the center, they passed through the perimeter guards without fanfare. The official car and the uniformed Grovotny were simply waved through without challenge. Sullivan tried to act important and bored. Once inside the compound, Mike was gratified to see that Grovotny seemed to know his way around. They drove a few blocks and stopped alongside a flat gray building that looked depressingly like a hospital.

Sullivan followed the officious Grovotny as he strutted inside and spoke with the matronly duty clerk. She informed them that the "ocean survivors" had been transferred to the cottages earlier that day. The cottages, she helpfully explained, were a row of small apartments reserved for families and VIPs whose medical treatments required an extended stay.

She concluded by both giving directions to the cottages, and informing the pompous Grovotny that there was a Militia guard posted outside of the "ocean survivors" cottage.

As they move away from the clerk's desk, Sullivan watched worriedly as the woman lifted the telephone handset, and between furtive glances at her receding late night visitors, she spoke in hushed tones to the party on the other end of the line.

Chapter 75
Tustin, California

Ichiro worked for a few minutes to clear Mrs. Parish's piles of junk away from the front window. He arranged a chair, the interior lighting and the window blinds so he could watch outside without being observed by passersby. Across the way, on the opposing building, he could plainly see the stairs, the front door and the balcony to the policeman's condo. He checked his watch. It would be dark in about three more hours. He had plenty of time to kill.

A shuddering groan came from behind him. Startled, he went to investigate. Alma Parish's body lay on the floor where he had dropped it. *She looks dead enough.* He thought.

He nudged her head with his shoe. There was no reaction. Curiosity piqued, he knelt next to the body and peeled back an eyelid. There was no pupil reaction. He checked for a pulse. There was none.

He decided that the sound coming from the body must have been a death rattle. He'd experienced that sort of thing before, but never quite as loud. He grunted and stood up. Stepping over the body, he went to the kitchen sink and washed his hands. As much as he enjoyed killing, he was disgusted at the touch of a dead body.

While he lathered his hands, the tiny dog reappeared. Apparently he had wandered off, exploring the debris canyons and arroyos of the Parish home. The pup hesitated near the body and sniffed. Then, he sat down and rhythmically wagged his tail while watching Ichiro at the sink.

Wiping his hands on a kitchen towel, Ichiro's thoughts turned to food. It occurred to him that the puppy might be hungry, as well. He opened the lady's refrigerator and rummaged. He found nothing of interest in the cold box, but hit pay dirt in the freezer. From there he produced a frost covered prepackaged dinner. He smiled as he read the label - sliced roast beef, potato and mixed vegetables. There was also a red package of macaroni and cheese. He tossed both packages, unopened, into the microwave oven and spun the dial. While he waited for the food to warm, his eyes meandered over the small mountains of trash, stopping occasionally to further investigate and identify some object.

His exploratory gaze stopped on the kettle atop the stove. He thought about a nice cup of tea. Rummaging further, he found tea bags and soon heard the whistling hiss of boiling water.

His meal prepared, Ichiro carried everything to the chair he'd arranged by the window and settled down. The puppy happily followed behind him, his tail rotating like a tiny airplane propeller and his small mouth drooling at the scent of warm food.

Chapter 76
Vladivostok, Russia

The Militia guard sat at a small table next to the door of the cottage he was assigned to watch. The wooden door was dark green. The number three was artfully stenciled upon it in fresh white paint. The man yawned with boredom. He turned the yellowed page on the well worn paperback book that was occupying his mind. The wooden chair creaked as he shifted the angle of his body to better capture the weak yellow light glowing from the single bulb protruding from the wall above the door.

Finishing the page, he licked a finger and turned another. He glanced at his watch and sighed. His shift would not be over for three more hours. At least he wasn't cold and he had this book to read. As his eyes squinted to refocus on the dimly lit words, he vaguely heard the footfalls of men coming down the walkway towards the cottages.

Still some distance away, the walking stopped. There was the low mumbling of muted conversation. When that sound stopped, one man approached the guard's table. The militia man looked up from his book, and recognized the uniform of a Border Guards Lieutenant. He quickly placed the open book face down, and rose to stand at attention. The Border Guards officer stopped directly in front of his table.

Sullivan waited until his new found friend and ally, Senior Lieutenant Pavel Grovotny properly braced the Militia Private. Their plan was for Grovotny to distract and if possible, to move the guard away from his post while "Bukolov" conducted a short and private visit with the detainees. Their agreed upon story was that Grovotny and his associate were State Security men conducting a highly sensitive and compartmentalized investigation. They needed to interview the prisoners immediately, and that no one without proper clearance and the need to know was to interfere or to even know of the contact.

As bizarre as the story sounded, Mike knew that many Russians would buy into it, simply because of their lifetime of conditioning. This was another result of life inside a paranoid society. One seldom questioned authority, or at least the illusion of authority.

He watched from the shadows. Grovotny engaged the young man, then together, they walked a short distance away from the Militia man's post in front of the cottage door.

Mike waited a moment, then made his move. In several quick strides, he closed the distance to the doorway. He gripped the doorknob and twisted. It was unlocked. The door swung open and he stepped inside.

삼 질식시킴

Viktoriya and Charlie found the cottage to be, by any standard, sparse. It was roughly a square structure that was divided into two rooms. On one side there was a room with a lumpy double bed. In the bedroom, there was a basin and a toilet, oddly configured against one wall, where functionality clearly outweighed modesty. The other half of the cottage could have been called a parlor or perhaps living room. That room contained a table and three chairs, a dilapidated old brown sofa and a stone fireplace with a quantity of small cut firewood. In one corner of the living room, there was a small countertop, a water basin and an electric hot plate. A black bakelite telephone, with a huge rotary dial sat on one edge of the counter. The telephone looked as if it had come directly out of a 1930's movie set. It was heavy and scarred from decades of use. A cable, covered in brown fabric, snaked its way from the instrument and disappeared into a wall socket.

They tried to place calls several times. The first few times, Vika used her Russian and hung up after a few seconds, telling Charlie that the polite operator had informed her that "circuits for out of area calls" were temporarily not available. After a while, Charlie tried, in English. He got a female operator who spoke stilted but understandable English. She told him the same story. After a while, they just gave up.

While Charlie was trying to telephone the outside world, Viktoriya inspected the rooms. In a matter of minutes she found three crude, and not well-hidden, microphones. The eavesdropping devices were grey colored metal discs, each about the size of a quarter and peppered on one side with holes. Vika took Charlie by the hand and pointed out the location of each device.

Later, a tray of food arrived. They sat together at the table and enjoyed a modest but warm meal which consisted of vegetable and mystery meat soup, chunks of dark brown bread with butter and hot tea, heavily laced with brown sugar. As they ate, they chatted, mostly just small talk and nonsensical blather that they made up on the fly for their own entertainment and the hopeful confusion of those listening. Their banter included parodies of well known television couples including characters from the "Lucy" show, "All in the family" and "Roseanne".

After their meal, Gomez suggested that they try to go for a walk. Testing the waters, they stepped outside. Vika spoke to the uniformed guard in Russian. She told him they wanted to take a stroll. He said nothing, simply nodded and extended one hand as if to okay their passage. Charlie reached over and took Vika by the hand. She looked at him questioningly, but left her hand in his. They walked slowly and she thought about how good it felt, both to be walking and holding hands with this charming man.

Hand in hand they moved along the pathways that connected the buildings. The place was huge. Clusters of buildings and seemingly miles of meandering corridors snaked off in every direction. The medical clinic was merely a portion of the complex. Gomez couldn't help but notice, that as big as the place was, there seemed to be few people working in the rooms. As they moved through out the maze, their guard followed them but at a discrete distance. He left them alone, but never allowed them to venture out of his sight.

"Do you think it's safe to talk out here?" She asked."

"You mean, do I think they're eavesdropping on us out here? I think they'd like to, but from what I've seen of their technology, I'd say no." These guys are still living in the fifties." He smiled at her and squeezed her hand. "I think out here, you're good to tell me all of your deep dark secrets. So, just where would you like to start?"

She pulled her hand away. "Men! You are truly all alike." She folded her arms across her chest, as if hugging herself.

"Come on. We're all not that bad. We're just focused a little differently than you of the fair sex - that's all."

"Let's talk about our situation."

"Okay, if you insist."

She eyeballed him. His expression was one of skepticism. "Do you have any idea as to just how much jeopardy we're in here?"

"I believe you're about to tell me."

"Listen to me. I tried to tell you this before – about how much danger we – at least, I - am really in here. If these creeps figure out who I am, they're going to…"

"Punch your ticket?"

She stopped, looked at him soberly and blinked. "Why – yes - exactly."

"Mind telling me why?"

"Okay. Look, here's the short version. My father, the other man who was…" Her eyes misted as she talked of Nikolai.

"Yes, Nikolai. Mike told me a little about him."

"Yeah, they apparently knew each other in the old days. Anyway, my father was an intelligence operative, State Security – first KGB, then after the changes in Russia – he was in the SVR. He was posted in the DPRK, that's North Korea. That's where he met my mother, who was half Russian and half Chinese."

"Not Korean?"

"No, but I was mostly raised there – Korean, I mean. Went through their schools, of course, learned the language, their culture… Anyway, Poppa was an important and resourceful man. For years he was one of the ranking State Security men in North Korea. Back then, the Soviets had a big stake in maintaining their client states. My father played a fair size part in that game."

Gomez nodded. They continued their easy pace around the pathways.

"When the big changes came, a lot of people got hurt. Poppa saw it coming, and did what he had to do to protect us."

"You mean he started playing ball for the other team?"

She nodded. "That's exactly what he did. He already knew everyone in the business, the Americans, the British, the Japanese and Chinese. It was no great leap for him. He was always his own man. He knew the Soviet system was flawed, that it would eventually die a natural death. It was just a matter of time."

"Sounds like your Dad was quite a guy." Charlie injected.

"He was - thank you. He was also a natural fit to - playing both sides of the street. For years he used his position, his knowledge and ability to travel freely. He made deals with everybody. He made a lot of money. He created a comfortable retirement and security for our future. After my mother died…"

"What happened there? To your mother, I mean."

"Cancer. Ovarian cancer – fast and deadly – about ten years ago. Anyway, he decided that it was time to get out. And we did. We've been living in the States, Hawaii, actually, for all these many years. You see, Poppa likes to surf." The eyes clouded over again.

He took her hand back.

After a moment, Viktoriya recovered. She continued. "When Sullivan needed help getting you out of the North, he came to Poppa. I guess they hadn't had any contact for a long time - many years. I further got the impression that maybe they didn't exactly part on the best of terms."

"Meaning…?"

She stopped walking and looked at him seriously. "Meaning, Nikolai considered killing Mister Sullivan when he showed up, unannounced, at our home."

"But instead, both of you decided to go along for the ride – to what – just help out, for old time's sake?"

"That – and there was a lot of money."

"Ah!" He nodded his understanding.

"So now, here we are, in the one country, on this earth, where we really shouldn't be. And, as you've no doubt figured out, our status with these folks is somewhat sketchy."

"Yeah… Well, I think our hosts are having some difficulty figuring out if we are honored guests or criminal prisoners." Charlie noticed that they had walked full circle, and were once again approaching the cottages.

Vika stopped him and pulled him around to face her. She glanced back at their Militia escort who was still a sufficient distance away to ensure some privacy. "Look, Charlie. I know you're a big shot rich guy. But, hear me on this. See that guy back there in the green uniform? He's Russian Militia. There're like the secret police. They have the power to make people disappear from the face of the earth. These guys don't have any ACLU or other bleeding heart groups to lobby for their activities, or whatever. There should be no doubt in your mind. We are prisoners!"

삼 질식시킴

Evening turned to night. Although not terribly cold, Gomez stoked a small fire, and they sat and talked. Hours went by. Charlie did the lion's share of talking, telling her about his childhood, and the family business. He did so because he'd decided that discussion at that level was safe.

He wasn't afraid of disclosing secrets, and he wanted his captors to understand how much drag, at least financial power, he could muster. If Viktoriya was correct, and their captors were trying to figure out what to do with them, better to let these impoverished people know that, at least, one of their guests had a large bank book.

It was late. Charlie sat on the floor, his back to the old sofa. Vika lay on the couch, behind him, their heads close together. Their last words spoken had to do with who would sleep on the bed – he wanted her to – she insisted that he take it. It ended with sleep claiming both of them, in place.

Chapter 77
Vladivostok, Russia

Sullivan eased the door closed behind him. He scanned the room. In the dim light he could barely make out the outlines of furniture. He stood in place for the several seconds it took for his eyes to adjust. When he was able to see, he spotted the couch and Charlie and Viktoriya, asleep. He was practically standing right on top of them. He knelt and touched Gomez on the arm. Just then, they both roused from sleep.

Vika came awake quicker and with a start. "Oh... what...?"

Mike clamped a hand over her mouth. This served only to frighten her more. She let out a muffled cry. He clamped down harder and tried to get his mouth near her ear.

Charlie abruptly came to. Startled by the dark form hulking over him, he came up swinging. The three of them tumbled on to the floor in front of the sofa.

Mike's whispers were desperate. "Vika – It's me, Sullivan! Stop it!"

Charlie had rolled off to one side. All he could make out was this large man-like form grappling with Viktoriya's neck. He grabbed a piece of something and was rearing back to deliver a haymaker blow when he caught the distinctive voice. He stopped in mid swing.

Realization of what was happening settled over them like dust falling through still air. Vika, eyes wide as saucers, stopped struggling. Mike was finally able to relax his grip.

Charlie pushed himself up into a sitting position. He whispered, "Hell of an entrance, Sullivan." His breath was heaving. "Is this a rescue mission or are you here to kill us?"

Sullivan clapped his friend on the head and whispered back. "Nice to see you too, Slugger." He pointed a finger at the ceiling. "Can we talk in here?"

Charlie stood up, shaking his head to indicate no. He pulled Vika up off the floor and gestured for Sullivan to follow them into the other room.

As luck would have it, the sole microphone in the bedroom was on the wall farthest away from the lavatory basin. Mimicking the trick that Vika had used earlier, he first flushed the toilet and then turned on the water full blast. Heads close to the running water, they talked in low tones.

삼 질식시킴

A few minutes later, the front door of the cottage opened. Sullivan emerged. Lieutenant Grovotny and the Militia Man stood a few paces away from the door. Mike gestured for him to come over. Leaving the Militia Guard, Grovotny approached Sullivan. "Yes, Sir?"

Mike's eyes burned holes into Grovotny. He knew this was it. Now or never, this thing was going to work or it would completely unravel. Sullivan took a breath and spoke. "I've made a decision."

"Yes, Minister. What do you want me to do?"

"We shall do it together." Sullivan made a clear cut point of including Grovotny. "We are going to arrest these two, and take them back to Moscow, immediately!"

Grovotny swallowed. "We..."

Mike cut him off. "Yes. You and I." He paused to let that thought sink in. "Pavel Ivanovich..." Sullivan used the Russian patronymic indicating familiarity. "I am herewith enlisting your service. I require you to personally assist me by helping to arrest these two - and further - to help me take them back to Moscow."

Grovotny couldn't believe what he was hearing. Moscow! What incredible good luck! He made his decision in a split second. He leaned closer to Sullivan and stood on his tip toes. "And what shall we do with this Militia man, Minister?" His hand moved towards his holstered pistol.

Sullivan put his hand on Grovotny's arm and ever so slightly shook his head. "No. You are his superior. Order him to come with us. Use whatever devices you can concoct. I just don't want him to make any telephone calls until we are airborne. Understand!"

"Perfectly!"

"Good. You deal with him, I'll get the prisoners."

Sullivan watched as Grovotny walked back over to the Militia guard and engaged him in rapid conversation. Sensing that this part was going well, he turned to go back inside. As he passed by the guard's table, he glanced at the overturned book. It was a translation into Russian, Tom Clancy's, Cardinal of the Kremlin. He could not suppress the smile as he passed back through the cottage doorway.

Minutes later, Sullivan pushed Gomez and Viktoriya out of the cottage. From behind he told them, "Act as scared as you can." The two were tethered together with a pair of stainless steel handcuffs that had come from the Hong Kong shopping spree. Mike pushed them roughly and they approached Grovotny and the Militia guard.

The guard was protesting. "I don't know. This is highly irregular. I should call someone."

Grovotny was all over the policeman. "Fool, do you wish to spend the remainder of your days on guard duty, or worse. This is committee business!" The phrase was meant to imply KGB. It was a phrase to strike absolute fear into the minds and hearts of generations of Russians. "Your immediate job is to obey me and to assist us. When we get to my office you can call anyone you wish! Do you understand me?"

"Yes Lieutenant!"

Grovotny led the party back through the maze of hallways to the spot where he had parked the Zhiguli. The five adults fit well, but nearly overburdened the underpowered automobile. Grovotny drove, the Militia guard sat in the right front and Sullivan and the two prisoners rode in the rear.

Upon clearing the compound perimeter, Sullivan pulled out his portable satellite phone and punched up Mateo's number. It was answered on the fifth ring. Mike had a predicament. He wanted Mateo to know that they were enroute; that he wanted to fly immediately upon their arrival. If he spoke in Russian, he knew Mateo couldn't understand a word, if he used English, it might tip off the two in the front seat. He decided to go for fractured Spanish. Mateo answered.

"Hola. Volvemos a su casa. Queremos alimento en quince minutos."

Gomez flashed him a pained look. Mike was praying he'd gotten the phrases right, or at least close to correct. He was also praying that Ferdie knew how to speak Spanish. The long pause was broken with Mateo's rich voice. "Ten four good buddy. Dinner will be on the stove when y'all gets here."

Mike heaved a sigh of relief and clicked off. He smiled at Vika and handed her the handcuff key.

Grovotny expertly wheeled the battered car through the streets of Vladivostok, heading for the International Airport.

삼 질식시킴

The duty clerk at the medical clinic did not like the tone of the arrogant Border Guards Lieutenant Grovotny. She knew him – a little – had seen him around. He was an officious ass. Further, she really didn't like the looks of the big man that accompanied Grovotny. The very idea that they would demand to see patients in the middle of the night – and, to top it off, that damn Grovotny smelled to the heavens like cheap vodka! She thought about calling someone. The clinic administrator came to mind. She dismissed that one. He was a crabby old man during the daytime. She didn't like him then, and certainly did not wish to call him in the middle of the night.

On the other hand, she did like that Major Filitov. She'd had a bit of a crush on the Militia official for years. He was handsome and always treated her with courtesy and respect. The two "ocean survivors" seemed to be the property of the police, anyway. They had a Militia man with them around the clock. That's it. She'd call Filitov. It was a good excuse to hear his voice again.

삼 질식시킴

Filitov hung up the telephone and returned to his darkened bedroom. Lying back in bed, he stared at the ceiling. The call had thoroughly awakened him, but only caused Anna, his wife, to stir. He gently stroked her back until her breathing once again hit the slow steady rhythm of deep sleep.

Unable to fall back to sleep himself, he lit a cigarette and blew smoke at the ceiling. Why should he care? He thought. Why should he care that the Border Guards wanted to talk to the Americans. After all, he expected someone to respond, eventually, to his notifications. So what, if they chose to arrive in the middle of the night, that was their business.

Just what time was it, anyway? He picked up his wristwatch and took a glowing drag on the smoke to give him enough light to see the hands. It was almost five in the morning. He got out of bed and went into the kitchen. He drew some water, lit the gas burner and set the water to boil. He sat down at the tiny kitchen table and lit another cigarette. While he waited for the kettle to steam, he replayed in his mind the events of the medical clinic woman's call. What was her name? Katrina - Karina... Karina – yes, that was her. She was the one with the nice ass – face like a donkey – but she did have a shapely bottom.

He made a cup of tea, and went through two more cigarettes. Finally, he decided to telephone back to the clinic, to speak with his Militia guard on duty. Maybe he could shed some light as to what was going on. He found the number and was once again connected to the clerk, Karina.

"Yes, Major. I was the one who called you." She felt a flash of heat as she listened to his deep voice. "I'm so sorry to have wakened you, sir. I just thought I should let someone..."

"Please. No apology is necessary. Yes – yes, you did the correct thing. Listen please – would it be possible for you to allow me to speak with my guard at the American's cottage? There is no telephone at his table but I believe there is an extension close by..."

"I'm sorry Major. But, your man just left - with the others."

"He left? His voice got louder. Suddenly he was stern and authoritarian. "Did you just tell me that my man has left the clinic?"

"Yes, Major. He left a little while ago, with the Border Guards and the American prisoners."

"Filitov jumped up knocking over his tea. He was sputtering. Goddamn Border Guards, he thought. What right do they have to... "Karina!"

"Yes, Major, I'm still here."

"Do you know – who it was – from the Border Guards – who came there tonight?"

"Why, yes, Sir. It was that awful Lieutenant Grovotny and one other..."

"Grovotny - Pavel Grovotny!" He spat out the name. "That filthy swine!"

"Yes, Sir. It was Lieutenant Grovotny. And I will tell you, confidentially, he's not nearly as nice as you are, Major."

Karina, the duty clerk, was talking to a dead telephone line. Major Filitov had hung up.

Chapter 78
Vladivostok, Russia

Grovotny's Zhiguli careened around the last turn, and headed straight for the gated entrance of the airport. They had less than a quarter mile to go when the first Militia car pulled in behind the Zhiguli sedan. There were two men in the car. The driver honked his horn and flashed his lights repeatedly. Grovotny floored it and the wheezing Zhiguli leaped forward. Just then, a second Militia car pulled in behind them. This one had a flashing blue light. The three cars raced toward the entrance gate.

The Militia guard in the front seat craned around. Recognizing the cars and his colleagues within, he turned to Grovotny. "Those are Militia officers following us. We should pull over and..."

"Grovotny barked at the younger man. "No!"

"What do you mean, no? What is going on here?" His hand slid down toward his Makarov 9mm pistol.

Sullivan poked the cold butt end of the satellite phone into the base of the young man's skull. In crisp Russian he said. "He means no, Tovarich. We are not going to stop, and if you touch that pistol I will splatter your head all over the inside of the Lieutenant's car!"

The young man's hands came up high and Sullivan reached over and removed the pistol, handing it back to Gomez.

Vika said in clipped Russian. "Want these?" She offered the handcuffs.

Mike took the bracelets and snapped one onto the guard's right wrist. Then, pushing him forward in the seat, he pulled the man's hands together behind his back and ratcheted the other cuff tight.

Two men were stationed at the main airport gate. Both were alerted to the speeding cars hurtling toward them. They stood at either side of the entrance, with weapons at the ready. The tilt gate was down in a closed position. When the guard realized that the lead vehicle was Grovotny's Zhiguli, he scrambled to raise the gate.

Grovotny slowed, only enough to holler at his men. "Stop those Militia pigs!" He ordered. "Don't let them in!" He ground some gears and the Zhiguli moved out in a blue haze of smoke.

Just beyond the gate, Sullivan could see the International Terminal building, and the Gulf Stream parked on the tarmac. The plane's navigation lights were on and hot gases blurred the night air behind the engines. Mateo was ready.

Sullivan clapped Grovotny on the shoulder. "Can you go directly to the airplane?"

Grovotny said nothing. He just nodded as the old car careened around another building, shot thru a small opening in the chain link fence, and wobbled out on to the tarmac. Within seconds the Zhiguli slid to a stop in front of two very surprised sentries, Corporal Rudinov and Private Chenkov.

Everyone bailed out of the car. Gomez and Viktoriya ran for the aircraft. Sullivan pulled the Militia guard out of the right side door and dragged him around to Grovotny, who was speaking hurriedly with the two soldiers.

"Rudinov!" Barked Grovotny.

"Yes Lieutenant?"

"I am placing you in charge. You will secure this facility until my return. Understand?"

Sullivan pushed the handcuffed Militia guard to the asphalt. Grovotny continued without missing a beat. "And you men will take custody of this Militia pig and detain him until I order his release! Is that clear?"

Both men saluted. Rudinov spoke. "Y-y-yes, Comrade Lieutenant. P-p-perfectly clear.

Mike heard the jet engine's RPMs increase on the Gulf Stream. Mateo's hand circled in a hurry up sign in front of his illuminated face in the cockpit window. Mike leaned to Grovotny. "We have to go."

He turned to Sullivan. "Minister, you are really taking me?"

Mike looked the Russian square in the eye. "Yes, I need you."

Grovotny smiled broadly. "Well then, let's go!" They sprinted towards the waiting aircraft. Mike pushed the officer up the stairs ahead of him. As the man ducked to enter the doorway, Sullivan unsnapped Grovotny's holster and deftly withdrew the pistol. He tossed the Makarov to Vika who quickly trained it on the Russian officer. A look of incredulity washed over Grovotny's face.

Sullivan glanced into the cockpit, and saw that Gomez was strapped into the right seat. He punched the stairway retraction switch and closed the hatch. He yelled to Mateo. "Now, Ferdie! Let's do it!"

Mateo yelled back. "I'm going right for the runway and lifting off. Mister Sullivan, you, or somebody, has to get on the radio and tell these guys in Russian what we're doing! What are we doing, by the way?"

"Wait, I'll be right there!"

He turned back to the now ashen faced Lieutenant Grovotny who was flanked by Viktoriya in a perfect Weaver stance, the Makarov aimed directly at the Border Guardsman's chest. Sullivan quickly spun the stunned Lieutenant around. Mike quickly frisked him and pushed him down into a recliner seat.

As he belted him in, he quickly explained to the man in Russian. "Pavel Ivanovich, listen to me. Years ago, I also, was a KGB man, of sorts. For many reasons, too complicated to explain right now, my life changed, for the better." He carefully watched the expression as color returned to Grovotny's face. "I am about to offer you something that will change your life forever. Whether or not you choose to accept this gift – this is completely up to you." He waited for some acknowledgement. The aircraft was rolling, picking up speed.

Finally, Grovotny nodded. "You are not from Moscow – are you?"

Mike shook his head. "No, these days, I live in the America."

Grovotny nodded again.

Mike continued. "Back there, I could have easily killed you. But I decided not to. You helped me. Now, if you behave, I will help you. If you refuse, we will have to kill you."

The Lieutenant swallowed. He said nothing.

Mike continued. "Stay here, stay calm, do nothing. I'll be back in a few minutes."

Grovotny nodded again.

The Gulf Stream was now screaming down the runway. Sullivan could feel the craft start to rotate and climb. He moved toward the cockpit and said to Viktoriya. "He has no English, I think. If he moves, kill him."

Chapter 79
Santa Ana, California

It was a Wednesday morning when Sullivan returned. He walked through the Sheriff's Detective Bureau. As he moved through the building, a wake of turned heads and open mouths rippled behind him. His striking appearance was the object of concern, curiosity and some outright disgust. The dyed black hair now sported a half inch of bright red roots. His face was misshaped and battered from the surgeries, physical abuse and other near-death experiences of past days. From the neck up he sported no less than nine significant injuries, some with black stitches. All were at various stages of healing. And those were just the visible things.

He said little to placate the astonished looks as he cruised through the break room, filled a mug with coffee, went to his mailbox and unloaded a fistful of papers, then wound his way back around to his cubicle and desk. He stood there, eyeing the small mountain of paperwork that had accumulated in his absence. There wasn't even a clear spot of Formica on which to set his coffee and message slips. He sighed, moved the edge of the pile aside and put down his things. He slipped off his jacket and plopped wearily into his chair. "Welcome back, Mike." He muttered softly and started through the stack.

Mollie was the first to appear. Sitting with hand over open mouth, she just seemed to materialize in the extra chair alongside his desk. "My God, Michael." She finally said. "You've got to stop taking these – adventure vacations. You look like you've been hit by a Mack truck, for God's sake!"

He leaned back in his chair and smiled. It was that perfect grin that she appreciated so much. "You wouldn't believe me if I told you the God's truth."

"Well, I'm glad to see you at least didn't get your teeth knocked out." She clucked.

"It's nice to see you too, Mollie. I…"

"Yeah, yeah, no need to get mushy – Okay. Now, Blair needs to see you – and Greer – make sure you find him pronto, before he pees his pants – and that weird friend of yours with the funny name and the blocked caller ID – String, or…"

"Stretch?"

"Yeah, that's the one, he's called about a million times – absolutely has to talk to you, as well."

"Thanks, Mollie."

"You are so welcome." She reached over and patted him lightly on the hand. "And I'm not even going to ask you what you've been up to."

"Good."

"But Mike…"

"Yeah?"

"You've gotta fix that hair!"

삼 질식시킴

It was late afternoon when Greer peered over the grey fabric cubicle wall and spotted Sullivan. "Mike – I heard you were back!"

Sullivan looked up, displaying his modified face to full view.

"Ouch – did that hurt? I don't mean any specific part – I mean – like - just all of it – generally?"

Mike set his pen down on the now somewhat clear desktop and sat back in his chair.

"Actually, this is…" He gestured around his face. "Sort of a souvenir collection. It was pieced together over many fun-filled days of events."

Greer came around the wall and sat down. "Jesus, it must have been a hell of a vacation."

"Yeah… You're not the first one to make that observation."

"I'm really glad you're back. Have you heard what's been going on?"

"More or less. Blair filled me in on cases and office intrigue, including the Korean murders cases – and the part about our good friends from the F.B.I. taking over. What else don't I know?"

Greer looked pensive for a moment. "There's another little wrinkle to this case – one that I haven't advertised much."

"Oh? Meaning the old man doesn't know it all?" His reference was to the Bureau Commander, Lieutenant Blair.

Greer shook his head and looked at him sheepishly. "It's sort of a personal wrinkle."

"Do tell."

"Let's take a walk, Okay?"

"Great idea. I could use some air."

Mike grabbed his coat and they hit the stairs ending up on a bench in the Civic Center Plaza. They talked for another forty minutes. Greer covered the entire series of events surrounding the Korean murders in linear fashion. Both he and Sullivan knew that his narration included some information that Mike already had heard, but the technique helped Greer get the story told, without missing a detail.

Sullivan listened patiently, interrupting only a few times for a clarifying question. Greer came to the end with the telling of his clandestine meeting with Agent Garcia, and her disclosure that someone was collecting information on Timothy Greer.

Mike listened carefully and processed the volumes of information. He liked Greer. The guy was young, but savvy. And he was sharp in a bookish, owlish sort of way. He didn't get rattled, could handle a ton of details without mixing them up. Best of all, he had intuitive logic and a good moral compass. Overall, he was a good cop. "So, your conclusion is...?"

Greer picked up the thread. "That we have at least one more killer out there, that - this is probably what he looks like..." He waved the grainy surveillance camera still shot of Ichiro's face from the Anaheim hotel. "And this maniac may be the one who is building a package on yours truly."

"Because?"

"Because – he believes or has been told that I have connected too many dots in this case, and could be considered a threat to whomever it is that wants all these Korean people dead."

"So you believe you are definitely a target?"

"Yes. If not a right-now target, I think I'm definitely on his short list."

"And there's been no new Korean killings since..."

"Nothing since they found the burnt guy in the hotel in Anaheim."

Sullivan thought about it for moment. "Timmy, you know, you might have just gone right to the top of this guy's hit list."

"I know." Greer stared at the photo of Ichiro. "Comforting thought, isn't it?"

"Okay, what are we doing about it?

"What do you mean, we?"

"I mean, what steps have been taken to protect you and your wife from this maniac?"

"Well, I sent her out of state. She's off visiting her mother in the Midwest."

"What else?"

"Nothing else. No one knows about this – other than you – now."

Sullivan shook his head. "Timmy, you gotta be joshing me. You're still staying at home?"

"Yeah, that and sort of sleeping with one eye open." He laughed at his little joke. "I mean, I thought about going to a hotel or something, but this could go on forever."

"Great. Well, I know you must be comforted by the fact that our Federal friends are sparing no expense to find this guy."

"Do you think…?"

Mike just glared through him. Greer sensed the anger and went quiet.

Realizing that he was making the younger man uncomfortable, Sullivan said. "Sorry, it's this stupid turf war mentality and Federal bungling that really pisses me off.

Mike shifted subjects. "This clown is probably watching you, right now, just waiting to make his move. We should have everybody and every asset we could muster on this one. Forget the fact that he's killed – what – about a dozen people so far? Now he's after one of our own. And the official story is that we don't know about it – right?"

"You've got it. Technically, we're not even supposed to know about this guy. Hell, there should be flyers out with this picture on it, BOLOs telling the story of how we think he's going to try and kill a cop – the whole nine yards. Instead, I'm just staying up nights with my gun in my lap."

Mike rummaged through his pockets. "Gimme a pen, will yah?"

Greer popped a Papermate out of his pocket and handed it over.

Sullivan scribbled on the back of a business card. He gave it to Greer. "I want you to plan on bunking at my place for a while, at least until we get this sorted out. Here's the address, the alarm code and…" He pulled out a key ring and shook off a brass house key. "This is the key to the side door."

Greer took the key and held it. "I don't know what to say. Thank you."

"Don't thank me until you've heard my snoring. In the meantime, get your tail back into Blair's office and tell him everything – and I mean everything - the Garcia part and all – that you just told me."

"You sure about this, Mike? I mean, she really went out on a limb. I don't want to burn her."

"Blair won't compromise Garcia." Sullivan was quiet for a moment, as if formulating a thought. "Greer, you're going to learn that there are a few folks out there that can be trusted. Some of them even carry a badge. Blair is one of them."

"Okay. I got it. Then I'll run by my place and get some things…"

"Wait up. I don't want you to make a show of taking stuff out of your place. This guy might be running surveillance on you. In fact, we should plan on the fact that he is. We should also plan on the fact that he's not working alone. He's probably got help. Lots of help."

"What then."

Mike glanced at his watch. "It's getting late. After you're done with Blair, go back to your place and wait for me. I've got to go meet a guy – just a quick meet. After that, I want to see your house – get the layout – maybe we can set a trap for this clown."

It was Greer's turn to write out his address. He handed the paper to Sullivan. "It's the Tustin Gardens Condos. Do you know it?"

A curious look crawled across Sullivan's face. He snapped at the paper. "Yeah, as a matter of fact, I do. I've got a friend who lives there."

"No kidding. Small world."

Sullivan thought about it for a moment. "You really have no idea just how true that statement is."

Chapter 80
Newport Beach, California

Stretch's reaction to Sullivan's new look was about like every one else's. "Christ, man! What happened to you?"

"Long story, pal. Too long for me to tell you now. Another time."

Stretch held up two hands. "Hey man, I'm not one to pry. But if it involved kinky sex, I'm always ready to listen."

"Yeah... Now, what is so damn urgent that you couldn't tell me over the phone?"

"Not something to tell you, it's something to give you. I've built something for you guys. It's a little something that I think you can use."

Sullivan folded his arms across his chest and waited.

"That tall guy, Greer..." The comment, coming from a man who was big enough to play pro basketball, was interesting. "The one you sent to me a few weeks ago - with the dental transponder thingies..."

"Yeah. I understand you helped him out quite a bit. Thanks for handling that."

"Oh – not a problem. Happy to help and all that. Thing is – I started really thinking about it. This whole notion of an elaborate RFID, radio frequency identification system – you know – a system to keep track of people who are wearing the devices..."

"Yeah."

"Well, I'd gone to a lot of work to bone out those units."

"Bone out?"

Stretch looked perplexed. "Reverse engineer them, figure out frequencies, binary code algorithms, how they were powered and so on. Anyhow, I got to thinking. If we had a transceiver that was capable of searching for these things and interrogating them, then maybe we could find some more murder victims - you know - before they become victims."

He paused, obviously waiting for praise. Sullivan finally said. "Well, great. I think it's a great idea!"

"As did I. So, I got to work building a transmitter – receiver that would work within the parameters, so we could sort of sniff around in the general population – so to speak."

"So to speak. Go on."

"So, the first one I made was about the size of a shoebox. I put that one in my car and cruised around for a while. I actually got a couple of blips on it."

"Where were you when you got the blips?"

"Oh, Santa Ana, I found a couple, then one in Garden Grove and one day I was in Long beach, over by the Queen Mary and I got a good one."

"Uh-huh."

"So, I got to thinking, this thing isn't worth a damn if you can't triangulate."

"Sorry, you just lost me."

"Triangulate – uh - direction find!"

"Okay, got it. Go ahead."

"So I reworked some circuitry, set up an LCD display, with a GPS grid and so on..." Stretch was watching Sullivan's face. "I'm overloading you with details. Aren't I?"

"A little. I'm actually fascinated, but truthfully I'm also kind of rushed." He glanced at his watch. "I just got back and I have another thing... Maybe you could cut right to the juicy end – just this once."

"Sure, sure! Man, I get it – Sorry." Stretch scooped up a cell phone off the workbench and handed it to Sullivan. Mike looked it over. The phone was brand new, an LGU 9000 Series, with a gleaming spun satin stainless steel case and a large color display. It was a perfect example of the latest in cell phone miracles, a camera for stills and movie clips, streaming video and internet, text messaging and of course, world-wide cell phone calls.

"Nice. But I have a cell phone."

"No, you misunderstand. That one's gutted. I'm just using the case. What you are holding is my latest version of the RFID tracking device. Go ahead, turn it on." Stretch grinned like a proud father, describing how he gave birth.

Mike found the power switch and touched it. The screen illuminated with a GPS map of the city block of Newport Beach in which they stood. Through cracked lips, he let out a soft low whistle. "This is amazing!"

"Yeah, it's pretty sweet." Stretch was still grinning like a Cheshire cat. "The short version is this... This puppy will find one of those transponder devices within a good mile radius and lead you to within three feet of them, or him or her or whoever."

Sullivan smiled. "Stretch, you are an absolute wizard!"

"Yeah, well, shucks."

"Shucks? Seriously, do you have any idea just how valuable a tool this may be?"

"Well, I figured this case of Greer's was serious stuff; and I just wanted to help."

삼 질식시킴

Sullivan's Mustang jumped onto the 55 Freeway from Newport Blvd. It was getting dark and already he could see the ominous long snake of white and red lights ahead of him. He was thinking about getting off the freeway and trying Main Street or maybe Redhill Avenue when his cell phone buzzed. The caller ID said "Private". He flipped it on. "Yeah?"

There was a pause followed by a sigh, followed further by the familiar sultry voice that he had learned to identify on first syllable. She said, "After traveling fourteen thousand miles and being gone six weeks, I was hoping for a little more than 'yeah', big boy."

Sullivan broke out in a big grin. "Hey there, Gorgeous! Did I tell you yet, just how much I've missed you?"

"Better – but, still not perfect."

"Okay, I really missed you – bad – and I'm looking forward to proving it!"

"That rings the bell. You've almost redeemed yourself!"

"Good – at least I think it's good. Maybe I'd better ask... Is make-up sex better than you've-been-gone-too-long-and-I-really-missed-you sex?"

Her tone dropped a notch. "I really missed you too, Mike"

"So where are you? State-side, I hope?"

"I'm at John Wayne, about to hijack a cab."

Mike abruptly pulled the wheel to the right and down shifted, cutting off cars as he crossed three lanes of crawling freeway traffic and headed for the off-ramp. Horns blared and he dropped the cell phone that had been cradled on his shoulder. He uttered some choice expletives, retrieved the phone and merged with southbound traffic on

MacArthur, headed directly for Orange County Airport. He fumbled for the cell phone. "Audrey - you still there?"

"Right here. What are you doing – Kamikaze driving?"

"I'm right around the corner. I'll be in front of the terminal in five minutes!"

He could hear the excitement surge in her voice. "Oh, Mike! That's wonderful! What a stroke of luck!"

"Hang on, beautiful. I'll be right there."

"Well, I'd hoped to at least grab a quick shower before I saw you... Brace yourself, this is going be one of those what you see is what you get moments."

A vision of his own bizarre appearance flicked through his head. "Yeah, well, this is true in more ways than you can imagine."

"Why? You need a shower, too?"

"Let's just say, the guy you're about to see driving my Mustang is really-truly Mike Sullivan."

"Uh-oh. That bad, eh?"

"I'll let you decide. This is my first day back, too. I've been getting it all day, from everyone."

"Where did you go? Or more pointedly, what did you do?"

"It's a long story. See you in a minute." He rang off.

삼 질식시킴

It was nearly dark when Greer pulled up in his carport. Blair had listened to his story with a grave expression on his face. He'd given Greer a mild blast for not coming to him in the first place after his sit-down with Agent Garcia. He told Greer to go along with Sullivan's plan for now; and that he would muster some help and make additional plans to do whatever they could to counter the threat posed by this Korean killer, whoever he was.

Greer grabbed his folder in his left hand, and then checked his gun in the belt holster on his right hip. He looked around and got out. Locking the car, he walked the short distance from the carports to his condo. He saw only a few people on the grounds, and no one that caused any concern. He took the stairs two at a time. On the landing, he checked the door to ensure it was still locked. He looked up at the upper door jamb and saw that the thin strip of tape he placed spanning the door and jamb when he left this morning was still intact. Good, he assumed no one had been inside. He looked around again, keyed the door and went in.

Inside Mrs. Parish's condo, Ichiro watched the man's arrival. He had just finished his meal, and set the containers on the floor to the happy licking attention of the puppy, when he spotted the tall man coming across the walkway toward Greer's building. Sure enough, that was him. Ichiro glanced at the copy of the grainy black and white driver's license photo. The man was looking from side to side as he moved. Ichiro caught a full frontal view of his face as he passed by. There was no doubt. This was Greer. This was his target.

He watched as Greer climbed the stairs, keyed the door and went inside. He checked his watch. It was nearly six thirty. The woman would probably be home soon. He smiled to himself, smug in the satisfaction that all things were going perfectly. He settled back in the chair to wait.

삼 질식시킴

The Mustang pulled into the red zone and Mike jumped out. Audrey, being nearly as tall as he, got off a quick eye level glance at the strange new look of her man, then, wrapped herself around him.

Her reaction to Mike's face was fleeting curiosity. In the excitement of their first encounter in weeks, her desire to hug, kiss, and be held easily overpowered her concern for his strange appearance. After a steamy minute, and much to the amusement of travelers streaming in and out of the terminal, Sullivan finally pried her off. Holding her at arms length he said, "You know, Audrey, they don't allow long term making out in front of the terminal any more - terrorist threats and all…"

삼 질식시킴

During the drive from the airport, Sullivan gave Audrey the condensed version of the preceding weeks. It was the extremely edited version, and left out virtually all significant details. He found himself instantly torn between wanting to spend some time with her, and knowing that he had things, important things to do. As they wound their way across surface streets to Tustin he explained. "So this kid that I work with, Tim Greer, he's been working this series of murders where all of the victims are from Korea, all immigrants who at one time had something to do with a super secret project inside the DPRK."

"You mean their nuclear program?"

Sullivan knew he didn't have the time for a decent explanation. He decided to back-burner that one, as well. "Yeah, that and some other thing the North Koreans have been doing. Anyhow Greer puts it together, that we've got some kind of a hit squad, probably from the North, right here in Southern California, systematically knocking off these Korean folks, all of them scientists or technicians who fled."

"Those rotten bastards... It's not enough for them to treat their own people like crap. They've got to send their lackey's over here to kill them, and for what? Wanting to live a better life? The bastards." She watched out the window and shook her head. She'd had her hair pinned up when he first picked her up. After getting in the car, she'd let it down and shook it out.

In his head, Mike was already starting to get lost in those auburn tresses. "So anyway, it turns out that this kid, Greer, did such a good job, that whoever's good for the murders, has decided to kill him, too. At least that's our supposition from the intelligence that's come our way."

"No." Her reaction was disbelief.

"I'm afraid – Yes. And here's another interesting part, Greer and his wife live in the same condos that you do!"

삼 질식시킴

Sullivan knocked on the door. Tim yanked it open before Sullivan's knuckle landed for the second time.

"Hi Mike, come on in."

Sullivan stepped inside. Greer closed and bolted the door behind him. Mike looked around. "Nice place you've got here."

"Thanks. You know what they say. 'Condo Sweet Condo'."

"Yeah, I've heard that." Changing the subject he asked, "How did it go with Blair?"

"Okay. He jacked me up pretty thoroughly for keeping it all to myself... Like you said, he promised to protect Garcia. He also talked about some protective measures for me. I take it he wants to kick it around with you."

"Uh-huh." Mike's eyes were roving around the small apartment-like home.

"So, just what is it you want to do, here?"

With Greer following, Sullivan moved from room to room taking in the layout, the position of doors and windows. "Mostly, what I want is to get a feel for how your place is situated. You know - the layout and exposures." The tour completed, they stood in the small living room. "I see you have just the front door, the sliding glass door to the balcony and one window to the front looking out on – what do you call that – a courtyard?"

"Yeah, the developers called it a garden quadrangle. Cute, huh?"

"And the two windows to the rear, the kitchen and the second bedroom... That's it, right?"

"Right. What's the big interest in the place, here? I don't quite get it."

"Well, look at it from the bad guy's perspective. If I'm a killer, and I've been given the job of taking you out..." Sullivan felt a quick involuntary chill run up and down his spine. It was a gentle reminder from the old days. "I'm probably going to want to see where you live. You can count on the fact that these people have already done that – and possibly intend to hit you right at home, probably at night."

"Not put a bomb in my car..."

"Nah, too Hollywood."

"Or sniper me out when I'm driving to work?"

"That's a possibility, but easy is the best path. My money is on the option that they'd try to take you at home, just like all the other Korean hits."

"Nice."

"Yeah."

"So, what do we do?"

"Tonight, nothing. You go on over to my place and make yourself at home. Just make sure you're not followed."

"Right. Lately, I'm getting good at that - watching my mirrors."

"Good, a little paranoia doesn't hurt. I don't see how anybody can make the connection between us, at least for a while."

Greer nodded.

"I won't be long. I'm just going to visit my friend – it's a girlfriend, by the way, Audrey Bushnell. She's the one that lives here in your complex – on the other side."

Tim just nodded.

"Take a few things with you - nothing that looks like an overnight bag - just stuff a few things in your pockets. We don't want it to look like you're moving out. When your ready, get on over to my place. I'll be back over there in a while, and we'll talk some more." Mike looked around again. "I'm thinking we could set up a counter-operation right here, if not right here inside your place, then maybe in one of your neighbor's units. Maybe we can nail this guy without killing him. Wouldn't that be nice?"

"Yeah." Greer's thoughts were drifting. He was thinking that perhaps he should have become a librarian instead of a cop.

Sullivan started for the door. "Oh, I almost forgot. Take a look at this." He pulled out Stretch's RFID tracking device and handed it to Greer.

Tim looked it over. "Nice cell phone."

"It's a little gift from Stretch."

A puzzled look appeared on Greer's face. "I don't..."

"It's not a cell phone. Stretch ginned up a receiver tracking device that will locate people with those dental things that you kept finding. He seems to think that this gizmo may help us locate some folks before they become dead folks."

Greer hefted the cell phone case and smiled. "Shouldn't this Stretch guy be working for the CIA or somebody who can keep an eye on him?

"Yeah, that same idea has run through my head a couple of times, too."

Chapter 81
Tustin, California

First, the puppy licked at the remnants of Ichiro's meal, then he raucously chewed on the containers. He growled and shook them with his mouth, leaving baby teeth impressions in the plastic and pressed cardboard. The trace amounts of food did little to satisfy the miniature bundle of energy. He danced around Ichiro's feet yapping and bouncing his forepaws off the killer's ankles. Ichiro tried to quiet the little fellow several times without success. He'd pick up the pup and pet him for a while until he settled down. As soon as he was put back on the floor, he would go right back to dancing and making that irritating high pitch bark. "Yipe-yipe-yipe!"

The incessant racket was getting on Ichiro's nerves. He didn't want to leave his window to search out more food for the dog. He needed to maintain his watch to make certain that both Greer and his woman were inside the condo when he made his move.

The tiny dog started up again. "Yipe-yipe-yipe!" The limpid eyes were pleading; the tiny forepaws bounced off Ichiro's legs. "Yipe-yipe-yipe!" Ichiro finally reached down scooped up the little animal. He cradled the puppy in his arms, stroking and soothing the little fellow into a quiet state.

He held the pup up and looked into its face. For a brief moment the two were frozen in time, nose to nose in a contrast of pure innocence and consummate evil. Ichiro uttered a disgusted sound and squeezed the tiny neck until the cartilage within turned to the consistency of gelatin. He tossed the still warm bundle of pale fur onto one of Mrs. Parish's prized heaps of trash and went back to watching out the window.

삼 질식시킴

Greer collected a few articles and started to head out. On the kitchen bar countertop, he picked up his keys, folder and Stretch's RFID tracker. Curious, he flipped the case open and examined the device further. He pulled out a stool and sat, examining the controls.

He pressed the button marked "on-off", and watched in fascination as the device powered up. The large color LCD was about the size of one of those palm computers. A map grid appeared on the display. Tim adjusted his glasses and examined the screen more closely. It was a map grid of about one city block. It was centered right over the Tustin Gardens Condos!

Amazed, he fingered the controls and noted that he could zoom in and out on the display, adding or subtracting details. At first, he zoomed out and could see map lines and coordinates, the outlying streets and even a bold line that he recognized to be the 55 freeway. He toggled the zoom for tighter resolution and brought the image back down to where he could identify the outline of specific buildings in the complex, even his building! *This is really cool!* He thought.

He wasn't in a big rush, so he decided to stay a while longer and try to further figure out the controls. Under his breath, he muttered something about wishing for an instruction manual. But over the span of the next fifteen minutes of trial and error, he managed to divine out a good portion the operation.

There was a green pulsing spot on the screen. The green pulse fit perfectly with his location. The position of the green pulse even moved ever so slightly when he walked from room to room. He rightfully figured the green dot was the receiver's location.

He zoomed the display back out to where he had an outline picture of several of the buildings within the Tustin Gardens Condos. That's when he saw it.

There was an orange pulse at the bottom of the screen. The orange spot was positioned within the outline of the building across the quadrangle from his condo. Tim's brow furrowed as he tried to understand the implication of what he was seeing. *Is this an actual tracking hit? Or is it some kind of stray signal coming from something – maybe a television, Wi-Fi, microwave oven or...*

He played with the device for a few more minutes.

Finally, he decided that it was getting late. He clicked off the unit, and dropped it into his coat pocket. Collecting the remainder of his things, he headed for the door. It was completely dark when he stepped out on the landing and pulled his front door closed. He twisted the key in the deadbolt lock and started down the steps. When he got to the bottom of the stairs, curiosity once again gripped him and he took out the RFID tracker and snapped it on. The green dot showed that his position had moved appropriately, but the orange dot had now turned to a deeper color. It was nearly red.

Watching the display, he started across the quadrangle. As he approached the building across the way, the green dot moved closer to the pulsing red dot, which was now a brilliant crimson. Fascinated, Tim continued to watch the display and walk around. He finally stopped directly in front of the door to Mrs. Alma Parish's place.

Tim knew her to be the kind old soul that grew all the fuchsias. She lived in the first floor condos, situated almost directly across from Greer's. He stood there, rooted in the darkness, trying to understand what he was observing. His thoughts were all over the place. *Maybe the old gal has a pacemaker – that this receiver is catching – maybe there's some kind of a medical telemetry device in one of the apartments.*

삼 질식시킴

Ichiro sat upright his chair. A man was opening the door of Greer's condo. Now he was outside, standing on the landing and fumbling with something. Ichiro quickly turned to his backpack and removed a pair of night vision binoculars. He snapped them on and raised them to his eyes; he spun the focus ring until the subject's face came into clear view. The light amplified image was made up of a hundred tones of green light, but there was no doubt. This was Greer!

He watched, trying to figure out what the man was up to. He'd seen the other man with dark hair come and go some time ago. That man only stayed a short while, less than ten minutes. Now, he watched as Greer walked down the steps and stopped. He took something from his jacket. It looked like a cell phone, the image in the binoculars flared white-hot as Greer angled his phone so its illuminated screen was picked up by the night vision binoculars.

Damn it! He thought. Quickly, he moved the optical device away from his eyes and waited for his night vision to return.

What was Greer up to? It didn't look like he was making a call. He was just waving that thing around like a... Now he was walking again. *He was walking this way!*

Ichiro slipped further back into the shadows and watched. The man, he knew as Greer, approached the very building in which Ichiro was hiding. For a moment he stood right outside the door to Mrs. Parish's condo!

Ichiro pressed himself against the wall and slipped a single finger under the edge of the curtain. He moved it ever so slightly so he could maintain a visual on Greer. The man was just standing there, staring at the cell phone.

Ichiro slipped his knife from a hip pocket. The knife was one of his favorites, a Solmes locking blade knife. Crafted like a fine surgical instrument in England, Solmes knives were made of special high tensile stainless steel with black composite casings. The blade was razor sharp and serrated on the lower half. Locked open it was only eight inches long, but in the hands of an expert, it was a formidable weapon, perfect for stabbing and ripping tissue, tendon and cartilage. In the darkness, he flicked it open and held it by his right side. The Solmes knife was his favorite tool for intimate work. Such a waste, he thought. Each time he used one of these perfect knives, he had to dispose of it. It was such a pitiful waste.

Ichiro continued to watch as this fool, Greer, walked away to the left, still holding the phone in front of him like a... Now, he turned and was coming back this way. He momentarily lost sight of him. Ichiro moved quickly to the sliding door and peered through the glass. He was gone. That could only mean...

Quickly and silently he moved to the front door. He carefully placed his eye to the peep hole and there... There he was. Ichiro held his breath and peered through the eyepiece. There, only inches in front of him, stood his target, Greer. The man stood perfectly still. He was just staring at his cell phone!

삼 질식시킴

Greer was perplexed. Whatever was causing the tracking device to trigger was right here, inside Mrs. Parish's house or maybe the unit above hers. He thought about knocking on the door – but, it didn't look like she was home. The place was dark and quiet. So was the place above her condo. He tried to remember who it was that lived above Mrs. Parish. He was thinking it might be that homely school teacher with the snorty laugh, but he wasn't sure. Finally, he slipped out his real cell phone and walked a few steps away from Mrs. Parish's door. He punched in Sullivan's number.

It rang several times before Mike answered. "Yeah?"

"Mike? Sorry... It's me, Greer."

Sullivan left Greer's place and half walked, half sprinted over to Audrey's condo. Tustin Gardens was a big place, at least an eighth of a mile square. Her place was on the east side and Greer's was on the western edge. He'd left the Mustang parked closer to Greer's side, a decision he was questioning about the time he arrived, about half winded from his rapid trek to Audrey's door.

A hand written sticky pad note was stuck to the door. It read "Big boy, come in!" It was signed with a customized smiley face, the one with demure down turned eyes with long lashes and long hair. It was sort of her signature piece in their personal literature. He plucked it off the door and slipped his key into the lock.

Inside, he doffed his jacket, gun and cuffs and laid everything on the bar. Audrey's two battered traveling bags had been dumped on the tiny living room floor. A light jazz melody drifted the sultry tones of Diana Krull from the CD player. The bathroom door was open about a foot. Steam rolled out into the hallway. He could hear her humming in the shower.

Briefly, he thought about stripping down and joining her in the bath – but, thought better of it, believing he should give the poor girl a break. After all she'd just flown about half way around the world. He knew from recent experience what a mind numbing joy that could be!

Instead, he loosened his tie and went to the refrigerator. He found a nice bottle of chardonnay, a Kendall Jackson. He also found two pieces of moldy cheddar and a head of decomposing lettuce. He pitched the garbage and went in search of stemware. He found two goblets, a corkscrew and went to work on the bottle. Within seconds he had the cork in hand and was spilling the fruity nectar into the glasses. He swirled the wine in his glass and took a sip. It was perfect! The Jackson was crispy dry with just a hint of fruit. He carried both glasses toward the bathroom.

Chapter 82
Tustin, California

Ichiro watched through the peephole. The man, he knew as Greer, stood with his back to the door talking into a cell phone. He held another phone is his hand. What the...? He glanced at his watch. It was not quite eight o'clock. His first thought was that it was too early for him to take out Greer, the likelihood of someone stumbling by was great. There were too many people out at this early hour. But, then... What was this fool doing?

A couple of times, he thought that Greer might walk right into the old woman's house. Could they be friends? Is he concerned because her house is dark? Ichiro began to doubt his plan. Perhaps he had made a mistake by placing himself so close to Greer's home.

His mind racing, Ichiro decided in a flash to kill the man – right now. Like a stealthy cat, he quickly moved to the sliding glass door that opened to the patio. Slowly, with controlled motion and deliberate quiet, he unlatched and eased the door. The huge sheet of glass glided open without a sound. Peering through the doorway, he could see him. Greer stood not twenty feet away. His back was to Ichiro and he was still talking into the phone.

Ichiro slipped outside and stepped between the potted fuchsias. The damn things were everywhere. He crouched low, and then eased his head up just enough to look over the low fence. He rotated his head to scan around. They were alone. It was just Ichiro and Greer. And, it was time for Greer to die.

He gripped the Solmes in his right hand and vaulted the fence in one graceful leap.

삼 질식시킴

Sullivan quietly eased into the bathroom. He stood for a minute grinning as he admired the lithe figure through the opaque glass of the shower. He set one of the glasses on the sink and with a forefinger traced a message in the steamy mirror. It said. "Welcome home lover!"

He dropped the lid on the toilet seat and sat, back to the wall and feet elevated on the hamper. It wasn't exactly a chaise lounge, but it was a comfortable spot from which to watch the show. He sipped at the wine.

Audrey turned off the water and pushed open the door. A long arm emerged and groped for the white towel hanging nearby. The towel disappeared into the shower. Mike watched with amusement as she went through the ministrations of cursorily blotting the water from her hair and body. She wrapped the towel around herself and tucked it together at chest height. With great deliberation, like a stripper gliding out to the pole, she dramatically stepped out of the shower and stood on the tiles, hands on hips.

Without moving from his perch, Mike picked up the second glass and offered it to her. She slid over to him, took it and bent low to clamp her mouth over his. Their kiss was wet, delicious and long. Audrey had one hand filled with wineglass, the other arm around Mike's head and neck. The fire in both of them stoked to perilous levels; her towel came undone, dropping to the floor; Mike's cell phone jangled.

삼 질식시킴

Ichiro made one last look around, he knew this would have to go fast. Killing Greer would be no big deal. But, if he was confronted with others and had to take the time kill them, he could compromise his escape. He slipped two potted fuchsias from the ledge of the patio fence and placed them quietly on the ground. Then, Solmes knife in hand, he braced his body to vault the fence.

Greer was apologizing profusely to Sullivan for the interruption. "Mike, I'm sorry. I know this is a crappy time, but..."

"Well, you're right about the crappy timing, but now that we're talking, what's up?"

Greer quickly explained about the signal he'd found with the RFID tracking device. "And, I'm thinking that..." He was having some difficulty processing everything. "Maybe there is someone around here who is wearing one of those things – maybe it's another intended victim – maybe it's..."

Sullivan's mind instantly kicked into high gear. He abruptly stood up, nearly knocking Audrey on her fanny. He moved quickly to the bar and his weapon. "Tim! Listen to me! You've got to get out of there – immediately! Think it through - there's a good chance that our killer is wearing one of those transponders and he's there right now – staked out on you!"

Greer was talking over Sullivan. "And, I think we should check this out. I..." He could hear Sullivan's voice yelling at him. The loudness and the buildings made the cell phone signal crackle in his ear. "Whadya say? Mike..."

With his left hand on the fence and the knife in his right, Ichiro jumped, both legs swinging over like a ten-point gymnast. Further along the fence, another clay fuchsia pot jiggled from the flexing of the wood. It teetered and fell to the pavement below.

Greer heard the pot smash on the concrete walkway behind him. He spun around in time to see the flying form of a man about to land on him. In an instant he recognized the face. It was the same guy as in Anaheim's photo! The same cruel face, dark hair and eyes, the slight Eurasian look. As the man closed on him, it was if time slowed for Greer. In that fraction of a second, a strange detached clarity came to him. He understood everything!

He knew this was the man who was the killer of all those Korean victims. He understood that he had gotten too close to the truth, and now this monster wanted to kill him.

Knife blade flashing in the dim light, Ichiro's form flew through the air towards Greer. Like a hawk about to engulf its prey, Ichiro came down for the kill.

In a way, Greer thought, the scene was almost funny. It was strange, in that, you could do years of police work, and somehow firmly believe to the very core of your being, that something like this would never happen to you. The now hit him like a bolt of lightning exploding in his brain. He was here. This was real. This was his time.

Training finally kicked in. Greer released both cell phone and the RFID tracker, instantly emptying both hands. He dropped to a crouch and threw up his left arm to block the striking blow of the body descending over him. His right hand snapped back the flap of his jacket and wrapped around the grip of his Sig-Sauer P229.

The man was coming at him from the left side. When the impact hit him, he rolled to his right. The attacker's knife blade slashed across his left forearm. Tim was so stoked with adrenaline, that he felt no pain. The Sig was coming up in his right hand. He jerked off two fast shots and the .40 caliber weapon fell from his hand

and clattered onto the walkway. The crushing weight of his attacker pressed him face down into the concrete. Greer heard the man yell and felt the air burst from his lungs as they collided. Greer was on the bottom unable to breathe, a stinging sensation growing in his chest.

삼 질식시킴

Leaving a stunned Audrey behind, Sullivan dashed out the door and began running towards Greer's condo. He tried to keep the cell phone pressed to his ear. Tim wasn't responding. He was still a few hundred feet away when he heard the unmistakable sound of gunfire. He vaulted a row of hedges and flew across the grounds.

삼 질식시킴

It took all of his strength, but Greer reared up and managed to throw the man off of him. The attacker jumped back to his feet and stood, knife in hand, ready to re-engage. Greer, now on hands and knees moved toward his weapon. He glanced back quickly to see a sneer form on his attacker's mouth. Greer dove for the handgun and wrapped his fingers around the rubber grips. He rolled to his back coming up in a two handed firing position. Pain seared up his arm and across his shoulder. The attacker turned and ran to the west, disappearing into the darkness.

Greer heard voices. People appeared, some hollering. Someone yelled out, "Call the police!" Another said, "What the hell's going on out there?"

He struggled to his feet. That was when he realized there was blood streaming from his left arm. The first slash from the killer's blade had laid open his jacket sleeve and the flesh inside.

Sullivan appeared to his right. "Greer! Are you hit?"

Tim tried to take an assessment. He checked himself over. He was winded, was having difficulty getting his breath. His left arm throbbed like hell. The Sig still swung in his right hand. "I think - it's just my arm. I think - I'm okay!" His mind cleared. "Mike! It's him; it's the guy from the Anaheim surveillance photo. He just ran that way!" With his pistol, he pointed off towards the west, down the walkway. "We've got to get him."

"Whoa." Sullivan pressed Greer's gun arm down, aiming the weapon towards the pavement. Sirens screamed in the distance. "You're staying right here. Medics are on the way. I'll get this guy!"

Greer started to protest. A dizzying wave of nausea came over him. Logic prevailed over bravado and Greer sunk down into a sitting position on the walkway. A woman appeared from behind him and wrapped a towel around his bleeding arm. He slipped the Sig back into his holster and waved to Sullivan. "Okay, I'm staying here." He looked up and Sullivan was gone.

Chapter 83
Tustin, California

Ichiro ran. He darted in and out of the landscaped pathways, flashed by buildings, and soon emerged into the carport area. Quickly, he found the spot where he had stashed his grey Toyota. As he jerked open the door and bent to sit, pain seared at his left waistline. He put a hand to his side and it came up bloody. Damn!

He was so spiked; he didn't realize that he'd been injured. As he cranked the engine with his right hand, he gently probed his left hip. He winced as his fingers found a hole about an inch above the pelvis.

He backed up, and then slammed the little car into drive and stomped on the gas. The tires spun rubber against the asphalt and the Toyota shot forward.

At full steam, Sullivan came running from between the buildings. When he popped out into the car park area, he stumbled briefly as he dropped out of a full tilt run to a walking pace. Gun in hand, he looked around all directions. A white BMW was coming down the lane from the outside street. Mike eyeballed the driver as he passed. The man, a balding, older white guy, with saucer sized eyes, realized Sullivan was holding a firearm and stepped on it to hurry by.

Mike continued to look around, certain that the killer couldn't be that far ahead of him. Just beyond the BMW, a grey Toyota sedan backed out in a jerky manner. Mike could just make out the outline of the head of the driver. *That's him!* The driver jammed the little car into gear and peeled out. The car wobbled, straightened, and sped down the lane. Sullivan broke into a run. The guy in the grey Toyota was headed for the outside streets.

In a few more strides, Mike reached his Mustang. He jumped in, fired the engine and took out after the Toyota.

Ichiro drove like he did everything else, with relentless aggression. He snapped the small sedan back and forth, turning left here, a right there, passing slow or stopped cars on the right hand side. He recklessly blew right through stop signs and red lights. Traffic was heavy on the surface streets, but not so that he couldn't pick his way through the congested mess.

The pain in his left side flared. Gripping the steering wheel tight, he clenched his jaw and willed the pain into the background. It worked! His mind cleared and he relentlessly drove on.

He kept glancing at the mirrors, trying to figure out if he had a tail. At first he thought he was in the clear, but after a few blocks of near out of control travel, he spotted the red Mustang convertible that seemed to be matching him move for move. Shit! He floored the Toyota.

Coming off a side street that merged into Newport Ave, Ichiro pointed the Toyota south bound. He went less than a block before quickly turning into something called Tustin Heights Mall. He cruised left then popped another turn, which took him behind some buildings. He knew he had to dump the Toyota. He needed to acquire some new transportation, fast. He came out in front of an L shaped strip mall with a huge parking lot. The anchor store was a large grocery. There were lots of cars and people. He pulled into a white lined parking spot and popped the driver's door ajar.

When he flexed to get out of the car, the pain in his side flared. What had been a dull throb, now felt like a red hot poker of steel ramming into his gut. Controlling his breathing, he sucked it up, and got out of the Toyota. Looking down, he realized for the first time that he was loosing a lot of blood. A swath of bright crimson soaked down his left side and pants leg. He needed to get somewhere fast in order to stop the bleeding.

Ichiro looked around the lot. He didn't see the red Mustang, but he did see a woman. She was just a few parking spots away, loading groceries into the side door of a silver van. The woman was about forty, short with curly dark hair. She slid the van door closed and moved around to the driver's side. Ichiro started towards her.

The woman opened the door, got in, then methodically snapped the seatbelt around her. She started the engine, and adjusted the rear view mirror.

Ichiro rapped on her closed window. She turned to the noise, and looked at him blankly. Automatically, she hit the switch to lower the glass about half way. Smiling, she said, "Yes?"

Ichiro reached a hand inside, and opened the van door from within. He grabbed the woman by the arm and tried to pull her out of the car. She started screaming.

When she didn't move away off the seat, Ichiro realized that the seat belt was holding her in. The Solmes knife flashed in his hand. With a single stroke of the blade, he slashed the seat belt along with the woman's neck and chest. Bright red blood spurted and she screamed again, this time in agony. Ichiro ripped her from the van and flung her to the pavement.

He jumped into the driver's seat, and jammed the small van into reverse. Tires spun. Blue-white rubber smoke filled the air and the vehicle backed out. The stunned and bleeding woman lay on the asphalt, screaming over and over. She pushed her head and shoulders up. Yelling at the top of her lungs, she said. "My baby - my baby! Please don't take my baby!"

The van careened in reverse out of the parking spot, and smashed into another car. Ichiro jammed the van into forward and shot out of the lot. In seconds he was back out onto Newport Avenue.

삼 질식시킴

Sullivan raced to keep up. Traffic was thick and the Toyota had a lead on him. Ahead, he caught a glimpse of a grey sedan pulling into a shopping area. Hoping it was the right car, he floored the Mustang, then braked to jump the curb and follow into the crowded parking lot.

In moments, he realized that he'd lost the grey Toyota. The sheer number of cars, the clutter and people overwhelmed the senses. Mike was infuriated when he saw that at least half the cars in the lot looked just like the grey Toyota sedan. He slammed the steering wheel.

Recovering his composure, he drove on, continuing to cruise and search the lot. With his left hand he punched 911 on his cell phone. The cell system connected him to Highway Patrol dispatch. Sullivan identified himself and asked to be transferred to the Sheriff's Communications Center. A man's voice answered, and as quickly as he began to explain what was happening, he was handed off to a woman.

The female dispatcher knew about the Tustin Gardens incident. She said. "Okay, Sergeant Sullivan, Tustin Police and our units are on scene now at the Tustin Gardens Condos. We understand there's been an officer involved shooting and there is one man down. Medics are also on scene. Where are you, Sir, and what do you need?"

She was good, crisp, and all business. He liked that. Sullivan quickly explained his pursuit, told her that he'd just lost the suspect vehicle in the vicinity of the Tustin Heights Mall and gave a quick description of the suspect and his vehicle.

Just then, he heard screaming coming from behind him. He dropped the open cell phone on the seat and spun the Mustang around. There was a commotion coming from a few parking rows over. The Mustang's tires squealed and within seconds, Mike slid the car up to an excited group of people. Some were attending to a woman on the ground, she was screaming and bleeding. He jumped out of the Mustang, grabbing the person closest to him. It was a grey-faced, older man. Mike spun him around and held him by the shoulders. At a distance of inches, he yelled into the man's face. "I'm a police officer! Did you see which way he went - the guy who did this?"

The man nodded and stammered. "Yeah, b-b-big guy, d-d-dark hair. Took this lady's silver D-Dodge van and went that way." He pointed towards the Avenue.

Sullivan released him and jumped back into his car. As he peeled out, the cacophony of people yelling and screaming receded. His brain filtered out and locked on to one clear phrase. A woman's anguished scream, yelling out. "He's got my baby!"

The Mustang slowed at the curb. He hesitated; wrestling whether to go north or south on Newport Avenue. He opted for south, and sped off towards the freeway.

Mike was driving and feeling around the seat, trying to recover his cell phone, when he spotted the van. The maniac was running half on the bike lane and half on the sidewalk, trying to get around a crowd of cars stopped at a red light.

The sidewalk was wide and mostly clear. Sullivan dropped the Mustang into low gear and roared along the same sidewalk, in close pursuit.

Horns blared, tires squealed and people jumped out of the way, screaming and yelling at the crazies that were endangering them all. The silver van got clear of the intersection and rocketed down Newport Avenue. At San Juan, the van made a screeching left turn and sped quickly into the darkness of a residential area. Sullivan was wishing he had a Brody knob as he spun the steering wheel one way and then the other, rear tires sliding out of the turn. The Mustang corrected and over-corrected, then bounced off a parked car and caromed through the turn. The tail lights of the van were growing smaller and smaller when Sullivan finally straightened out and roared into the darkness.

The residential streets were convoluted, a modern mixture of cul-de-sacs and limited outlets. Ichiro tore around corners, got stuck and backed up into rear skid turns to reverse direction. Sullivan wheeled the Mustang around. It took all of his attention and driving skill just to stay with this maniac.

삼 질식시킴

Ichiro had no idea where he was. The red Mustang was back on his tail. He couldn't shake that guy! On top of everything else, there was this screaming kid, about a two year old, strapped into a child seat in the rear. From the moment he'd pulled the woman out of the car, the damn kid had been screaming at the top of his lungs. He desperately wanted to silence the child, but it was too far back to reach.

Ichiro forced himself to focus. He had to drive, he had to get away. The streets twisted and turned. At one point he actually drove right by the guy in the Mustang, only going the other direction. Then he drove by a school and there – finally - there was a bigger street! Now, maybe he could get out of here.

He turned the van onto the frontage street, El Camino Real. It ran along the north side of the Interstate 5 freeway. Finally, he'd found an area that wasn't completely gridlocked. He sped down El Camino Real hoping to find an on-ramp to the freeway and his escape!

삼 질식시킴

In the 1950's the State Highway Department made plans for what was to become the main north-south roadway in California. Part of the National Interstate Highway system, this would be a section of route number 5. Parcels of land were assembled, bought up, taken by eminent domain, or outright confiscation. The very spot, through which Ichiro and Sullivan now raced, had been, a half century before, farm and ranch lands.

Tiny settlements, worker's shacks, one room schools, occasional churches, with modest graveyards, dotted the countryside of what would later become the patchwork cities of Orange County.

When the settlements were cleared for the highway construction, the graveyards were not always moved. It was always a big and expensive deal to move the mortal remains of the dearly departed. Societal convention forced searches for living relatives, permission documents, legal wrangling, court appearances, and, of course, the grim task of exhumation and reburial. When such unpleasantness and expense could be avoided, it generally was. Such was the case, in the spot of land that Ichiro and Sullivan converged upon this night.

While Ichiro, in the stolen van, hurdled toward the Interstate 5 on-ramp for Tustin Ranch Road, neither he, nor Sullivan, had any idea that more than fifty years earlier, decisions were made that would affect them, this very night.

It was November of 1954. The farming settlement of Coopersville, population thirty-seven, had to be moved. The buildings were to be razed and the ground scraped clean for the new elevated highway. Over the years, twenty four souls had been placed in a small graveyard next to the tiny wood frame church at Coopersville.

A highway engineer proposed that they leave this grave site intact, because it would fit perfectly within the design area's scruff land. Scruff land was the term for real estate that was required to be around and under a structure like a traffic ramp. It was land that was required, but upon which nothing could ever be built. It was the perfect compromise. Everyone agreed. The highway department even paid to have a tasteful black wrought iron fence installed. It was the kind with little arrowheads atop each paling, like rows of slender sentries, standing honor guard over the graves of forgotten loved ones.

Chapter 84
Tustin, California

Sullivan was just one short block behind the van. He made the turn to east bound El Camino and accelerated.

Ahead, Ichiro found himself coming to the next major street, Tustin Ranch Road. As he slowed for the intersection, the blue Interstate sign loomed in front of him. It was like a beacon pointing to his freedom! Despite the burning pain in his side and the screaming kid, he smiled and cranked a hard right, zooming toward the freeway.

He wanted to go south. In order to do that he had to pass under the freeway and take the immediate right turn. The graceful on-ramp sloped up gently in clover leaf fashion. It carried cars upward twenty five feet, from the surface street, through a near 360 degree sweeping right turn to merge with the four lanes of southbound I-5.

Ichiro made the turn and headed up the ramp. Sullivan was now only five cars behind him. The line of traffic slowed as they marched up the one-lane traffic ramp in perfect single file. Two thirds the way up, traffic came to halt! At the front of the line, a bob-tailed truck had stalled. Two men emerged from the cab. The hood was raised, and they fretted over their still motor. The long line of cars on the on-ramp froze in place.

Horns blared; patience of commuters wore paper thin. Ichiro cursed, opened the van door, and got out. Biting back the pain, he haggardly sprinted up the line of cars, desperately looking for another prospect to carjack.

Sullivan saw the guy jump out of the van. He yanked the Mustang's parking brake and killed the engine. Leaping out, Glock in hand, he sprinted up the ramp, following the limping form of the killer. As he passed by the silver van, he glanced inside and noticed the toddler still in the child seat. The little guy was crying, clearly unhappy, but safe. Relieved, he poured on the coals, and ran after the killer.

Ichiro made it almost to the top of the ramp. He realized then that every car was blocked solid by the disabled truck. Even if he took a car, he couldn't get out. There was no escape - that way. He went to the edge of the ramp and peered over into the darkness below.

A man yelled from behind. Ichiro heard something like, "Police!"

Sullivan had the killer in his sights. He was only twenty yards ahead. He slowed to a walk, trained his Glock on the man and yelled. "Stop! Police!" As he closed the distance to the killer, the man crawled up onto the concrete railing. What was he doing? Was the nut going to jump?

Ichiro could not see much detail in the darkness below. He judged the distance to the ground to be twenty feet or so, an easy drop for him, especially if there was vegetation. The dark haired man from the Mustang, probably another policeman, was almost on him. The dark haired man held a gun. It was aimed at Ichiro's chest. He was yelling.

Sullivan slowed as he closed with the killer. The man was perched on the concrete rail, legs straddling like a horse rider. Sullivan stopped about ten feet from the killer. He could see that he was hurt. Blood soaked the left side of his clothes. Sullivan yelled. "It's over! You can't go anywhere! Hands up - and come down off that wall!"

Ichiro raised his hands. A strange look crossed his face. As he watched the man with the gun, recognition blossomed in his mind. This was the same man he'd seen at Greer's condo. He sneered. His lips curled into an ugly grin, he spat out the words. "Stupid American Police - I killed your friend, Greer! Another time, I will return and kill you, too!" With that, he suddenly threw his leg over and disappeared – dropping into the black void below.

Sullivan, about to squeeze off a shot, abruptly brought the gun muzzle up. He ran to the ledge and looked down.

Immediately following the man's leap, Sullivan heard a series of curious sounds. His mind was trying to process and sort out the sounds. The first was a thudding sound, followed by a muffled groan and a whoosh. The last sound he heard was odd, like a wet, tearing sound. He peered down into the darkness, but could only make out dim outlines below.

He turned and yelled to the assembling crowd. "Flashlight? Anybody got a flashlight?" Instantly someone handed him a large metal flashlight. He aimed the beam downward.

The light beam illuminated a scene below that few were prepared to see. Sullivan played the light over the ground; he sucked in his breath as his mind dealt with the grim visage. It was a scene that would forever be burned into his memory.

Twenty five feet below, atop the remnants of the Coopersville graveyard, Ichiro's neck had landed directly on the line of spiked arrowheads of the wrought iron fence. The freakish impact was such that his head had been torn completely away from his body.

Ichiro's impaled head hung on the arrowhead tips, palings jammed into the back of the neck, holding the head in a position where it looked straight back up to Sullivan and the freeway onlookers.

The decapitated body lay a few feet away, arms and legs still twitching, heart still pumping, a bright puddle spreading like red oil over the weedy soil.

Sullivan moved the light beam back to Ichiro's face. The final sparks of life were ebbing fast. The lips moved and the eyes glanced left and right, searching and blinking.

Sullivan yelled down. "I know you can hear me, you bastard! Let these be the last words you hear! Burn in hell, you rotten piece of shit! And you didn't kill Greer! He's fine! So - Die! You rotten bastard! Die!"

The lips stopped moving. The remaining light in the cruel eyes faded to opaque stillness. The people above watched in horrific fascination as the final embers of the life of Ichiro, the assassin, turned to ash.

삼 질식시킴

Sullivan was forced to spend over at hour at the freeway on-ramp scene. When he was finally released, he called the Sheriff's Communication Center and was told that Greer had been taken to UCI Medical Center. He aimed the Mustang for the City of Orange and punched through the logging of cell phone calls that he'd missed. There was one from Blair and one from Audrey.

He called her line first, got voice mail and left a message telling her that he was alright, and that he would call her later.

Next, he punched in Blair's number. It was ringing for the third time, when he slid the Mustang into "Police Only" parking at the hospital.

Blair answered. "Hullo." His tone was flat.

"El Tee, it's Mike. Where are you?"

"I'm at the hospital. Where're you?"

"Just pulling up now. How's Greer doing?"

"You better come inside." Blair directed him to the third floor surgical unit.

Minutes later a panting Sullivan found a somber faced Blair in the waiting room. Curiously, Audrey was with him.

Sullivan took in their stone quiet faces. "How bad?"

Blair's eyes flashed from Mike to Audrey and back to Mike. "Very Bad." He said.

"Christ! What happened? I thought he'd just taken a hit to the arm."

Blair took a breath.   "Apparently, when they grappled – probably when the suspect first jumped him, Tim rolled or something – anyway, he got stuck in the back, between the ribs. It was weird. The blade rotated, it cut like a trap-door flap of tissue and nicked his aorta. He was…"

"Goddamnit!" Sullivan shook his head, not believing what he was hearing. "He was fine when I got to him… Standing right there on two legs - talking to me!"

"I know." Blair's voice was hoarse and shaky. "The docs told us that this was a one in a million injury. He was bleeding out – the whole time - but it was all staying inside the body cavity, the tissue flap closed and the static pressure buildup kept…"

"Wait a minute! Are you telling me that he's…?"

Blair nodded. "That's right, Tim's dead. They tried every…"

Sullivan was stunned. He backed away and stared off into space. Blair was still talking but Mike wasn't hearing.

It was as if time slowed. After a while, he felt a hand slip under his arm. He looked up. It was Audrey. She hugged his arm. Tears welled up and splashed over her cheeks. She whispered softly. "I'm so sorry."

Epilogue one

It was late afternoon when Sullivan left his office. He'd purposely scooted out early because he had an appointment. Instead of heading to the parking lot, he walked across Flower Street and slipped in, by the back way, to the Orange County Court complex. In the plaza between the buildings was the Orange County Memorial for Peace Officer's killed in the line of duty.

He approached the marble and granite edifice that bore the engraved names. Two men in overalls were just finishing up their work. One collected and packed tools and folded tarpaulins, the other ran a small shop vacuum, cleaning debris, remnants from power etching the latest name to be memorialized in the stone.

Mike walked to the left side of the memorial and for the umpteenth time read the details of the 1912 killing of Undersheriff Robert Squires, the first county deputy to be killed on the job. The workmen, having completed their tasks, departed. Sullivan moved over to the place they'd just vacated. The first thing he noticed was the color contrast on the spot of marble they had worked on. The newly cut letters were more brilliant than the older, weathered carvings. He wondered how long it would take before weather and time would fade the newest name to blend in with the others.

He thought about Greer. Six weeks had passed since that night. Mike wondered how many other names would hit this cold wall of stone within his lifetime. Finally, he ran his fingers over the newly cut letters. The relief was deep, cool to the touch, the angles and edges sharply defined. Fine granite dust came away on his fingertips.

A voice from behind broke the moment. "Mike."

He turned to see his friend, Doug McClure, standing, respectfully, a few feet away.

"Hi Doug." Mike walked over and extended his hand. "Sorry, been here long?"

"A few minutes – not long – I didn't want to – intrude."

"Yeah." Sullivan was a little embarrassed. "Garcia show up?"

"Uh, not yet."

"Listen, Doug. Thanks for helping me out with that Grovotny fellow. I appreciate you getting him status and a job and all."

McClure just waved a hand. "Don't mention it. We always have a place for a reformed Boris. I hear he's an interesting guy - already picked up some considerable English."

"Good. He'll make a great American citizen, someday."

"Yeah, I believe that."

A slender, nice looking woman in business attire approached them. "Excuse me. Are one of you gentlemen, Sergeant Sullivan?"

Mike looked the woman over. They had only talked on the phone, so he had no idea what to expect. Overall, his first impression was good. She had that Fed look; but with her, it was under control. He liked her eyes. She had a set of those dark penetrating, smart eyes, the kind that tracked and stayed with you. She was pretty, but not a knockout. Her demeanor was cool, confident and professional.

"Yes. I'm Sullivan."

She offered her hand. It was small, but the grip was firm and sincere.

Mike turned to McClure. "This is former SAIC, now Deputy Director of Homeland Security, Doug McClure." To Doug he said, "Meet Special Agent Garcia." They shook hands.

Garcia, offering a respectful nod to McClure, said. "Sir, I really appreciate the opportunity…"

"No – Please. From what I've heard about you, I should be thanking you. As to the opportunity part, well, that's all up to you."

"Either way, Sir, I want you to know that I'm pretty thrilled - Both to be talking to you and for the opportunity to work with your unit."

"Fair enough, Garcia. I believe that if you end up coming with us, you're going to learn a few new tricks real fast. Including, that we sort of fly by the seats of our pants, and that there actually are a few of us in government that are serious about straightening out the crappy relationships between the agencies." He paused as if to let the comment sink in.

Garcia watched him; she didn't even blink.

"As it works out…" McClure continued. "One of our biggest jobs, in this Homeland Security assignment, is to try to get people to pull their oars in the same direction."

Smiling, she flashed a quick look at Sullivan, then quickly returned her attention to McClure. "That's exactly what I've heard, Sir. And, I want you to know that I'm your man."

McClure chuckled at her little joke. "Great. It sounds like you're going to be a good fit to our team!"

Sullivan grinned. "Well, it seems like you two are going to get along just dandy."

"Dandy?" McClure asked.

"Sorry. Old head injury – takes over from time to time."

Garcia spoke up, directing her question to Sullivan and pointing to the new name etched into the granite. "Did you know him well? Timothy Greer, I mean?"

Mike thought about it for a moment before he replied. "I think I knew him well enough to know that he would be pleased, quite pleased, to see what we've arranged between you guys."

"I only met him twice, but I – I liked him, too, Sir."

"Yeah, he was one of the good guys. Well, you two have things to talk about, and I've gotta go."

McClure spoke up. I was just going to take Garcia over to your little Mexican place on Main Street, what's it called?"

"Chicos?" Garcia interjected.

"See! I told you she was okay." Sullivan grinned.

"Won't you join us?" McClure asked.

"I'd love to have another good meal on Uncle Sam, Doug. But, I'm afraid - duty calls - in another direction. Really, I have to go."

삼 질식시킴

Sullivan took an easy pace walking to the employee parking lot and his cherished old Mustang. A few days before, Mike had picked up the vintage convertible from the body shop where restoration experts had erased most of the damage that had occurred during his reckless pursuit of the half-breed maniac. His insurance company and the County's Risk Manager had settled most of the liability dust from the damage Sullivan had inflicted while trying to stop the killer.

The car had been nicely repaired, restored to near perfect condition. The one frivolous impulse to which he had surrendered, was color. Tired of the fire engine red, he had them repaint the car to a classic bright metallic blue. The color was called Intense Blue. Given the way his life had been of late, Sullivan thought it was appropriate.

He slid the convertible top down and cruised out First Street towards the 55. Shades protecting his eyes and the wind whistling through his, once again, red hair, he headed out for Newport Beach.

Ahead, the dipping sun changed from fire orange to blood red. Finally, it silently exploded at the western horizon in a brief blast of end of day fireworks. Behind him, the advancing night sky quietly turned indigo and, at least for a while, peace reigned supreme in his little corner of the world.

His cell phone rang. Thoughts about ignoring the phone wandered across his mind. It kept ringing. He reluctantly checked the display. It was Gomez. He flipped it open. "Charlie! How's the fourteenth richest guy in world?"

There was a slight pause – it was as if Mike had momentarily knocked Charlie off the script. Finally he recovered. "The fourteenth is some oil Sheik in the Middle East - and with his money, I'm sure he's fine. Now, if you're inquiring about my well-being, I couldn't be better. I've just sunk about everything I personally own in a new investment – and I'm coming by to talk to you about it – next!"

"Uh-oh, does this mean I should hide my checkbook?"

"This one is gonna be so good…"

"Yeah - heard that one before."

"Seriously - you heading home now?

"I am."

"Good, don't make plans. You and me are going to dinner."

"Really! Okay, where are you taking me? Someplace exotic?"

There was another pause. "In Montebello, there's this little joint called Bill's Paradise…"

"You're so full of it…"

"Be by to pick you up in an hour!" Charlie clicked off.

Sullivan laughed, closed his phone and went back to his ride home.

삼 질식시킴

Forty-five minutes later, Charlie drove up in the alley behind Mike's house. He honked the horn. Sullivan, pulling his coat on, emerged from the garage, the sliding door beginning to drop as he passed under it. He looked over Charlie's wheels. "The old Ford Explorer! I thought you'd finally junked this thing."

"Yeah, I'll do that about the same time you give up the Mustang."

Mike opened the right door and started to slide in. He hesitated. The interior of the early SUV had a distinctly different look. The standard front seat belts were gone and in their place had been installed six point harnesses, similar to the type that NASCAR racers used. The rear seats had been removed. Straddling the vacant spot was a large plywood box that had been painted flat black and bolted to the floor.

Charlie waved him inside. "Come on. Get in. We're gonna be late."

Sullivan sat on the edge of the seat and tried to figure out the harness.

"Look - like this – slip your arms into it, like a coat – with the metal thing in the middle of your chest."

Mike slipped into the contraption and got it buckled up. That's when he noticed that some of the dashboard instrumentation had been changed. In the well between the front seats, more electronics had been installed. "What's going on with your car, Charlie? Is this some kind of weird science project?"

"Patience, lad. All will be revealed." Gomez slipped the car into drive and it moved ahead. Instead of the usual engine noise, there was only a soft whirring sound.

Sullivan was examining the instrumentation. "Seriously, Charlie, What the hell's going on with the Explorer? Did you convert it to an electric drive?"

"Something like that." Charlie grinned, obviously enjoying the moment. "You see, GTI's been working on alternative energy sources for some time. When the Glomar team recovered the... Remember the pulsing blue thing that wrecked our submersible? Well, that was a version of the Gravity Flux Amplifier. We, of course, had to turn it over to Uncle Sam, but not before our boys had a chance to analyze it pretty thoroughly!"

Charlie made the left onto Pacific Coast and headed towards Huntington Beach. The explorer smoothly accelerated to sixty in an eerie silence.

Mike was getting the drift as to where Charlie was going. "So your engineers got a head start on figuring this thing out?"

"For the entire time that the Glomar was steaming back to Pearl."

"To reverse engineer this power source and this is…"

"This – that is - the engine that's powering the Explorer right now - is a prototype – yes – it's a variation of the gravity amplifier."

Sullivan was impressed. "Amazing! And we're not going to blow up or cause an earthquake?"

"Not even close. Actually, it turns out to be a fairly straightforward and safe little engine – once you understand the physics and all that."

"And you do?"

"No way - but, I've got folks on the payroll that are way smarter than me. And they assure me that this baby is quite safe."

"Yeah?"

"Relax. I wouldn't be driving it around, if I thought it would hurt a fly." His voice dropped to a serious tone. "But, Mike. Think about it. These things, massed produced, will change the face of the world economy in a heartbeat!"

Charlie's eyes glinted in the reflected dashboard lights. Just north of the Santa Ana River outfall, he pulled off to the side of the road. This was an open, wetlands area. The State Beach lay to their left, a water treatment plant to their right.

"This is the investment you were talking about?"

"It is."

It took only seconds for Sullivan to realize the serious implications. "So, exactly how many oil corporations are putting out contracts on your ass?"

"Properly handled - I hope not too many. But your conclusion is correct and inescapable. Many people are pissed already – a lot of them are in our government - I might add. It's no secret. Many folks know that the days of reckoning - the last days of oil – so to speak - are now upon us."

"So… GTI is going to make a killing?"

"Yes and no. If you're asking, are we going to hog it? The answer is no. We're going to give it away, to anyone and everyone. Not only is this thing big enough for everybody to make a buck, but, by giving it away, we…"

"You minimize the possibility that one group or nation controls the technology and holds the world hostage." Mike suggested.

"That and inside of a generation, everything from locomotives to toasters will run on these things. They are the perfect answer. They're clean, renewable and non-polluting."

"So, where do I invest my hundred bucks?"

"Charlie glanced over at his friend and smiled. "Not to worry. I've already tossed in all your savings, at least all that I have Power of Attorney over, into the project. By this time next year, you'll be worth a bundle."

"Okay… Enough - already. Let's go get something to eat. I'm starving! Where are we really going?"

Charlie opened a console between the seats. He withdrew a lightweight headset and put it on. He flicked several switches and levers and read over his instruments. "I thought we'd eat at that little place in front of the Tuna Club in Avalon. You know the one with the outside seating?"

Sullivan looked at his friend quizzically. Charlie checked his mirrors and when he was satisfied that no cars were immediately on top of them, he pulled back the wheel and the Explorer silently rose into the air.

Sullivan gripped the dash as the Explorer's attitude teetered like a child's top losing its spin.

"Relax. That big box in the back seat, it's a gyro stabilizer thingie. I just forgot to turn it on." He flicked a switch and the car instantly became level and stable. "By the way," He tapped one of the electronic boxes. It was an Aviation transponder. "We are ID'ing as a Robinson helicopter, in case anyone cares." Charlie grinned and turned the wheel. The front of the Explorer rotated and the car rose to two thousand feet, and then silently glided out across the ocean channel towards the twinkling lights of Catalina Island.

Epilogue two

In the years that Sullivan had lived in the little beach house, he had learned to appreciate the days of spring, especially Saturdays. In the mid seventies for the past week, each morning brought early and glorious sunshine that quickly warmed the white sand, and there was none of that damn June gloom that plagued the Southern California coast for most of the summer.

These were perfect days for a morning jog or, like today, just lounging, watching the kids with their boards floating in the surf line, hoping for that next bigger and better wave to ride.

He slurped at the, hot strong brew, convinced that when he drank coffee like this, the heady aroma shot caffeine straight to his brain, probably from the vapors, alone.

Speaking of alone, he was that, once again. After several weeks of being at home, Audrey was off again. This time, she was traveling to Africa to work in one of those upstart nations, trying to contain the dreaded flow of raw nuclear materials. Once again, Audrey Bushnell, of the AEC, would be gone for months.

The sun's rays glinted diamond shafts of light off the white sand. In the distance, a slender kid walked down the beach carrying a long board. Mike noticed, because the favored weapon for the army of surf city was the short board. In the distance, he watched as the figure steadily trodded south. Abruptly, the walker made a turn; leaving the hard packed wet sand, he trekked across the dry sand heading, more or less, directly for Sullivan's house.

As the walker drew closer, Mike sat up. He thought. *This isn't a kid. It's a man, an older man.* Sullivan stood. *No! This can't be!*

Fifty feet away, the fellow stopped and propped the long board upright in the sand. Brushing off his hands, he trudged the final few steps and stood before the stunned and disbelieving Sullivan.

They stood, separated by only a few feet. The man, grey-blonde hair cut short, hands on slender hips, waited. He was fit, trim and he sported the scars of two freshly healed bullet wounds on his chest and back.

"Well, Pasha-Misha..." The familiar accent was unmistakable. "Aren't you going to offer your old friend a cup of coffee?"

Acknowledgements

Writing is mostly a solitary endeavor. We writers think nothing of devoting hundreds of hours, usually alone, sometimes with the dog, in the dark, in pajamas, squinting at a pale computer screen.

Often, at the oddest times, we are compelled to retreat from real life, repair to our writing rooms, and furiously wallow in a momentary glut of thought; ideas coming so fast one cannot possibly get them all down. Other times, we stare blankly at the walls, ceilings, and family pictures waiting for that lightning bolt of inspiration.

Most who write have a cadre of helpers behind them. They are the support team that, encourages, chastises, and, prods us onward. They are the ones that pull us back from the netherworlds in which we temporarily live with our made-up friends, like Sullivan and Gomez, and help us to keep a foot firmly planted in the real world.

More importantly, it is they that live the writing experience with us, hanging on, listening to our every idea, no matter how goofy, agonizing with us over every phrase, and arguing everything from elements of style to moral ambiguities.

To each of you that have so generously helped me along the way, I offer my heartfelt thanks. Particularly, I'd like to thank my advance readers, for it is you that truly help me to set the course of my stories.

Once again, I am especially indebted to Betty Moore, whose eagle eye, editorial skill and unabashed opinions help to keep me real.

Finally, I would be truly remiss if I failed to acknowledge the one person in my life that has made my dreams come true on all levels. It is her ears that first hear the ideas, her eyes to first read each page of copy. It is her collaborative skill that breathes real life into my characters. She hangs with me through every sentence and chapter, and patiently reviews the unending stream of rewrites. She graces me with her common sense, her intuitive, sometimes uncanny understanding of people and her unfailing wisdom of life. She is my muse, my best friend, my darling wife, Lynne. Thank you.

About the author

Bill spent three decades in city police work, in Orange County, California, doing every job from rookie to chief of police.

Along the way he spent time in narcotics, vice and homicide. A veteran of Army intelligence and a graduate of the F.B.I. National Academy, he draws from his experience and the life and death issues of our time to weave compelling tales of crime and adventure.

A California native, Bill is an avid scuba diver and boater. He lives with his wife, Lynne and pal Scrappy in the coastal mountains of Southern California.

Books by William DeNisi are available at all major booksellers and on-line. Email can be sent to bill@denisi.com.

Printed in the United States
92790LV00006B/1-30/A